"Please listen, Lynn! . . .

You must have seen that I admired you. I know what you are and I'm telling you, not as a Yankee to a foreign friend of the Rebs, but as man to woman, that you're superb. As man to woman I'm telling you that we've shared so much that, no matter what happens, you'll always be part of me, and whether you like it or not, I'll always be part of you."

She lowered her head and he saw in that brief moment that her cheeks glinted in the light. "Kirk, Kirk, I've tried so hard to hate you and now you've spoiled it all!" Her head pressed forward against his chest.

"Am I right, Lynn, that we're part of each other, in spite of everything?"

"Yes, Kirk, but there's something else. I do feel differently about you. But about the war I don't—I can't . . .

NIGHT MARCH
Bruce Lancaster

PINNACLE BOOKS   LOS ANGELES

NIGHT MARCH

Copyright © 1958 by Bruce Lancaster

A Pinnacle Books edition, published by special arrangement with Little Brown and Company in association with The Atlantic Monthly Press

ISBN: 0-52340-164-7

First printing, December 1977

Cover illustration by Bruce Minney

Printed in the United States of America

PINNACLE BOOKS, INC.
One Century Plaza
2029 Century Park East
Los Angeles, California 90067

For

Jessie, Southworth,
and Margaret Lancaster

from

their husband, brother,
and brother-in-law

FOREWORD

THE Kilpatrick-Dahlgren raid on Richmond, starting point of this story, became a *cause célèbre* almost before it was launched, in February 1864, and left in its wake questions which may never be answered positively. In sending our fictional characters on the expedition, I have relied on a great many participants' accounts, on the *Official Records* and on later reconstructions such as Bruce Catton's in *A Stillness at Appomattox* and Howard Swiggett's *Rebel Raider*. It is a matter of great regret to me that Virgil Carrington Jones's excellent study, *Eight Hours Before Richmond,* did not appear until this book was in its last galley stages.

Official reports differ widely in point of time, routes followed, numbers, details of action. No two firsthand stories can be expected to agree, since writers set down only what they saw. A Vermonter may record the destruction of railroad installations near Frederick's Hall Station, while a New Yorker's memories of identical hours may be confined to ripping up track in dense woods or guarding an unthreatened flank. Variations will also be found concerning weather, terrain, minutiae of march, camp, action and such items as who was where and when.

With such a spread of personal recollections from which to choose, I have felt free to guide my fictional people along those recorded paths that best suited the story. Kirk Stedman and his waif cavalry command are my own creation. So is Jake Pitler, whom I substituted for the actual captain of D Troop (or Company, as then designated) of that fine regiment, the 1st Maine Cavalry. The crossing of the James near Goochland Court House is fictional and directly concerns fictional people only. Since the true story of Dahlgren's James River guides and the circumstances attending the tragic hanging of the Negro can probably never be fully determined, I have based my own version on possibilities and conjectures made by actual members of the expedition.

The great mystery of the "forged orders" is not likely ever to be settled. Mr. Jones has built a carefully and honestly reasoned conclusion that they were genuine, that Dahlgren's intent actually was to burn Richmond and murder President Davis and others. I cannot accept this verdict. Such measures do not fit the known character of Colonel Ulric Dahlgren. Technically, the steps outlined in the alleged "orders" seem far beyond the strength of his command even to attempt. It may be added that while many participants wrote of the raid (and some were frankly hostile to Dahlgren), I have yet to read an account which contains the slightest hint of any objective beyond the freeing of Union prisoners. It seems to me that by using Mr. Jones's evidence, an equally strong, equally hypothetical case can be built to uphold the forgery claim. Pro or con, it all comes down to a matter of opinion.

The scenes in Libby Prison have been reconstructed from many accounts, out of which I have selected those phases of an everchanging picture that suited the story best. The escape was reasoned out from other breaks without relying on any one incident. So in the flight through the mountains (a general route followed by many) and its events, the course of no one escape party has been pinpointed. "Lieutenant Brewer" actually functioned in and about the military prison at Salisbury, North Carolina. The appearance of the Stockdales in the mountains was suggested to me by several civilian accounts, notably Mrs. Chesnut's, of back-country travel in war years.

In the closing scenes of this book, one may speculate indefinitely on what would have happened had General John Hood smashed through Franklin and on to Nashville, where General George Thomas was desperately collecting troops. Hood's supply and transportation troubles would have been over. Recruits would have flocked to him. The psychological effect on the North of his breakthrough would have been profound and the Confederacy would have been immeasurably heartened and strengthened. Where Hood would have gone, what he could have done once Nashville was in his hands can only be conjectured. He was a gallant, driving general and his next moves would certainly have had a very grim menace for the Union. But he was brought up violently at Franklin by that scratch force under Generals John Schofield and Jacob Cox, thus dooming his last, despairing lunge to Nashville before it was ever under way.

Speculation aside, that Indian-summer day of November 30, 1864, along the Harpeth River displayed the finest qualities of those citizen soldiers of both armies, battered and exhausted but always sustained by their conviction of the rightness of their respective causes.

B.L.

Beverly, Massachusetts

INDIANA

OHIO

WEST

Louisville

KENTUCKY

Cave City

CUMBERLAND   RIVER   Abingdon

T E N N E S S E E   E. TENN & GA. R.R.

HARPETH R.   Nashville   Knoxville

Franklin   Murfreesboro   LITTLE TENNESSEE R.

McMinnville   Route of Kirk and Jake
                                    from Virginia

Manchester   HIWASSEE R.
Pulaski   Tullahoma
                 Chattanooga

Decatur   TENNESSEE RIVER   Dalton   S.C.

ALABAMA   Atlanta

GEORGIA

SAM BRYANT

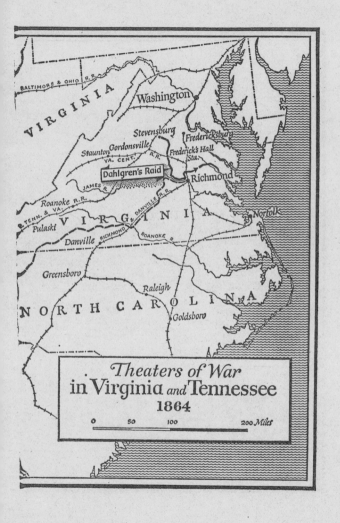

Theaters of War in Virginia and Tennessee
1864

0   50   100   200 Miles

NIGHT MARCH

1

The Secret Plan

Kirk Stedman waded through red Virginia mud and
across the threshold of Brandy Station, closing the battered door behind him against the thrust of the February wind. For an instant, raindrops clinging to his
eyebrows and lashes blurred his vision and he saw nothing but two opaque orange pools, one spreading from
the hanging lamp and one from the telegrapher's desk
in the corner. He swept a hand over his eyes and the
scene cleared. The civilian operator yawned over his instrument, boredly tapping out a message. Beyond him,
two company workmen spliced a muddy tangle of wires
with slow skill. The men glanced incuriously toward the
door and then went on with their tasks.

Kirk, boots squelching and drops pattering from his
old waterproof, moved under the hanging lamp, duck-
ing his head to avoid the heavy base, and pushed back
his sodden kepi. Light fell on his wet forehead, on his
wide-set dark eyes and storm-reddened cheeks, picked

1

out rain beads along his short black mustache. The operator glanced at him again, then called, "Afternoon, Cap! Didn't spot you, first off. Thought you were beyond the fords, chasing Rebs."

Kirk passed a tattered handkerchief over his square chin. "Last time out, they did the chasing. Any news on the down train, Phil?"

"It left Alexandria ten minutes behind and so far I got no signal from Catlett's, up the line. Likely it'll be twenty minutes slow, maybe more. Better wait in here. At least the roof's tight and we finally got the windows boarded up and oil for our lamps."

"Thanks. I may come in later and scatter more mud around." He straightened his kepi and pushed out through the door, the operator's "Any time, Cap, any time!" following him.

The mud was only about ankle deep close by the platformless station and Kirk worked his way along the side of the main building, trying to get out of the wind that swept fretfully across northern Virginia. But the wind followed him, driving mistlike spray ahead of it, falling like a clammy ghost hand across his face, worming down inside his collar, prying upwards under his vizor. Warped clapboards about him, ragged shingles above him bulged out drops of water, like overloaded sponges, to spat down on him.

He took off his kepi with the tarnished brass of crossed sabers and the initials D.C.I.T. on its slanting crown, shook a spatter of water from it, settled it on his short dark hair. Twenty minutes late, maybe half an hour. At least waiting in the rain and the slop was better than sitting in the airless chill of the station where Phil Cook would be sure to light up one of his fearful black stogies whose fumes made the lamps flicker and burn blue. And there was always a chance that the operator at Catlett's, an independent soul, might have airily neglected to pass on reports of the train's progress toward Brandy. Anyway, more than two years in the

Army of the Potomac had schooled him to wait with reasonable patience in far worse places and under worse conditions.

The wind blew harder, died, blew again, and with each shift the swirling milk-haze of rain closed in, lifted, closed, giving Kirk glimpses of ragged buildings off to the south, low ridges with desolate trees stark against the sky, then shutting off visibility until he could just make out the Indiana cavalry camp across the tracks. It was a cheerless settlement where clay or beef-barrel chimneys rose above sodden canvas roofs and plank walls. A few soldiers plashed miserably along the company streets, lifting their feet high to shake off mud clods. The ground about the station was worse. Broad puddles spotted the expanse of red mud like pools of stagnant blood. Traces of corduroying, solid enough until the recent thaw, showed at ragged intervals. Broken packing cases lay half submerged. An army wagon with a smashed axle slumped doleful and forgotten in a marshy field and near it a dead mule pointed four stiffened legs in protest to the clouds.

Kirk wrenched some boards loose from a packing case, tossed them onto the mud and stood on them. Soon they would sink into the slime and ooze, but for a few moments he would have the illusion of something dry and solid under his feet. He leaned forward, looking up the rails that stretched away, softly silver, in the wet gloom. But they lay empty and lifeless, gave out no distant swelling rumble, showed no orange pin-point of a headlight slowly growing.

Across the tracks, men shouted and a hut swayed, settled wearily as its clay foundations melted under the rain. He wondered about his own camp beyond Stevensburg to the southwest. If his huts collapsed, where could materials be found to repair the shelters for the twenty-six men who made up his cavalry command? A waif of the Army of the Potomac, the D.C.I.T.—the District of Columbia Independent Cavalry Troop—was

3

linked to nothing closer than General Alfred Pleasanton's Cavalry Corps Headquarters, an organization that rarely interested itself in the affairs of anything smaller than a brigade.

Footsteps squelched doggedly behind him and a hoarse voice hailed, "Hey there, Kirk! Didn't know you were expecting anyone on the down train!"

A thick-set, rather bowlegged captain waded toward him, a cavalry saber jutting from under a rubber poncho on which was stenciled J. C. PITLER, 1ST ME. CAV. "Hello, Jake. Had a telegram that the Ohio major I know in the Cavalry Bureau was coming down to see me. Unofficial."

Jake, whose ruddy cheeks were creased in a perpetual grin, raised reddish eyebrows. "About your troop?"

Kirk nodded somberly. "This is pretty near our last hope. No one else seems interested in us."

Jake worried out a knob of tobacco, gnawed off a corner. "Why, hell, that's good news. If your major's for you and no one else gives a damn, he can probably get that fool order killed. He won't have any opposition. I'd say you were sailing right into port. Isn't it about time for that train to show up?"

"It's late, but the operator'll shout if there's news of it."

Jake gave a short laugh. "Ever hear of an operator telling a uniform anything he didn't have to?"

"This one's Phil Cook. My boys and I found him in a clearing during Mine Run. His instrument was on a stump and he was sending just as if he was back in Pittsburgh or wherever he comes from. There was plenty of lead flying around, too. We snaked him out from under the feet of a parcel of Rebs and since then he's treated us almost like equals."

Jake hunched closer to the wall. "He know about your major?"

"Doubt it. Stuff like that isn't important enough to get around."

4

Jake spoke with his lips barely moving. "Maybe it's only the little things that get around. *One* mighty big one hasn't. At least not yet."

Kirk started, looked keenly at him. "You're sure?"

"I was at Cavalry Headquarters this noon. They're making out furlough papers for—well, let's put it that they're for men that *we* both know aren't going to be able to use them. Not right away."

Kirk mopped his face. "Damn this rain. I can't figure if I'm wiping my face with this handkerchief or the handkerchief with my face. Furloughs. I never knew HQ to keep a secret so long."

"I'll swear that only Meade, Pleasonton and Kilpatrick know about it. And us. Two twiddling little captains."

Kirk smiled wryly. "That's because we both happened to know something about Virginia real estate that little Judson Kilpatrick needed to know mighty bad. I guess you can count me out now unless Major Gray can fix things."

He broke off. Far down the tracks, hidden in misty rain swirls, a locomotive hooted. The station door popped open and Phil Cook's head thrust out. "Here she comes, Cap." Cook's head vanished and the door banged.

"So she's coming," said Pitler. "And, by God, here *they* come!"

The wet air was full of a grinding, churning sound. Out of the mists that swathed the camps, up the red mud-river of the Culpepper Road, loomed a column of white-topped ambulances and army wagons, all marked with the clover leaf of the II Corps. The six-mule teams labored on, their hoofs beating out a liquid plosh-plosh while the dripping wheels sent a hissing whine through the air. On the column came, a dozen vehicles in all, wheeled in a wide circle and drew up by the tracks. Some of them were decked with pine boughs and one wagon bore a long sign, lettered in red: II CORPS. WASH-INGTON'S BIRTHDAY BALL!

Rear curtains stirred and officers in water proofs spilled out over the tailboards. Kirk caught the glint of polished boots sinking into mud, the blur of a white collar half seen under a protecting muffler, white gloves and polished scabbards. Pitler crowed, "Hey! Look at the young Lochinvars! Shot in the tail with luck. Two minutes more and the train'd have been here and no one to meet it. Would I have liked to have seen *that!*"

The air was throbbing and the headlight's glow cut into the afternoon dimness while the broad-stacked locomotive rumbled and hissed. Kirk drew back against the wall. The locomotive was past him, slowing with every yard of track. Then he saw dingy, patch-windowed coaches, drenched platforms where men of the Military Railroads worked frantically at the hand brakes. He waded forward, calling, "I'm getting aboard, Jake. Keep shouting for a Major Gray in case I miss him."

Jake's hand checked him. "Not yet you're getting aboard, unless you hone to get trampled."

The nearest coach door creaked open and a plump, dark-haired girl in a red traveling dress stepped timidly out, an anxious-faced matron close behind her. The girl called, "Here we are and—" Her voice broke to a quaver as she stared at the mud below the car steps. "Oh, where's George? This *can't* be the right place!"

All up and down the five-car train, girls were calling, squealing with dismay, coming down a step or two, shrinking back. Pitler was alternately clucking and chuckling. "By damn, this is too bad. Couldn't someone at least have rigged a ramp, same as they do for mules? Just the same it's funny. Ever see a ma cat race a flock of kittens out a warm house and find it's pouring? Just like this."

The babel swelled. "I simply will *not* step into that!" . . . "Harry! There you are. Catch me. I'm going to jump!" . . . "*I* am Major Cranshawe's wife and I'll

6

thank you to see that something . . ." . . . "I don't care what you say, Aunt May. I *am* getting down here."

A wave of kepis and broad hats swept forward. Kirk saw girls, some delighted, some reluctant, settle into reaching arms. A fattish quartermaster captain splashed about excitedly, bawling, "Now, everyone just stay where they are. *I'll* tell you what to do." An ingenious soul led forward a detail of drivers who unfolded stretchers. A few adventurous girls were carried shoulder-high on the canvas frames, squealing and gasping at each lurching step.

The platforms were still jammed with skirts and bonnets. Some girls poised reluctantly on the upper steps while those behind swayed and clutched as others tried to force a way out of the stuffy cars. A slim, fair girl in soft blue gave a cry of alarm. Her little gum-booted feet shot from under her and she slid down the steps, exposing an embarrassing expanse of long, white-stockinged legs topped by blue garters. A cavalry cloak flared out, covered her and she was helped to her feet in a screen of uniforms and bonnets.

A wild-eyed lieutenant charged forward, spread a stretcher flat on the ground below some steps. Others whooped, began plopping down more stretchers. A surgeon dove into the melee, yelling, "Get those things out of the God-damn mud. We'll be toting wounded in 'em tonight."

Pitler shouted, "Wouldn't I love to hear the sweet nothings that'll be whispered in the ambulances! Look at that red-haired girl! She's mad enough to bite through a halter shank. And that major's catching hell from his wife." He broke into an unconvincing falsetto. "'And I'd like to know just what you were thinking, dragging me into all this. Making me go to a ball in an ambulance!' God, where'll they all stay? The ball's two days off. The hospitals are bulging with gals right now and you couldn't buy a room in Culpepper with a bucket of diamonds. Lucky this is the last trainload."

7

"See any men getting off?" asked Kirk, eyes darting from car to car.

"Listen, any man in his senses'd wait inside until the gals were shifted."

At last the platforms were empty and the locomotive hissed impatiently as the loaded vehicles began their slow roll from the tracks. Train crews were moving through the cars, slamming doors, shouting to each other. No heads showed against the blurred, cracked windows.

"Tough luck," said Jake. "Maybe you'll find a letter or a telegram when you get back to camp. Hell, this isn't the *only* day he could have come."

"The telegram said today." Kirk's mouth was dry and his shoulders sagged. Suddenly he straightened. "Someone's getting off the last car, rear platform." His voice cleared. "He's got crutches. Must be Gray. He's got a bad leg." A crutch jutted from the platform and a booted leg felt for the next step. Kirk ran forward, shouting, "Major Gray! Hold on! We'll look after you."

The crutch was abruptly tucked under an arm and a tall, slim man made his way, a step at a time, down from the platform.

Kirk's voice died in his throat. The man wore a very jaunty kepi cocked over one ear and a long cavalry saber dangled by his left leg. An orderly, standing just above him, watched anxiously, holding out another crutch. The slim man stepped carefully into the red mud, turned and took the second crutch. Then he looked up the length of the train, showing a very young, tanned face marked by a slim blond mustache and neat imperial.

Kirk stopped short. "God Almighty."

Jake panted, "What's the matter?"

Kirk said again, "God Almighty!" His voice dropped, hoarsened. "Don't you *know* him? Colonel Dahlgren, Ulric Dahlgren. Here, at Brandy Station. And *now*, of all times. Don't you see what that means?"

8

Jake Pitler went white. "His leg. He's got a wooden leg that works. It's jointed. Look at him step! God damn it, don't claw my arm like that! Sure, I know what it means." His eyes bulged. "It means the real big secret's out all over Washington. Every loafer in Willard's bar knows it. *He's* heard it *somewhere* and come hell-bending for a share."'

"All over Washington," said Kirk dully. "And—" his voice sank to a whisper—"and all over Richmond."

Pitler shook himself. "Nothing like a good kick in the guts to make you forget your troubles. Hell, maybe right now Bob Lee's sweating over his maps off there at Orange Court House, figuring the best spot to post a nice big reception committee."

The train began to slide down the track, heading for the siding from which it would start its return trip to Alexandria on the Potomac. The ambulances and wagons were moving away from Brandy Station in a reluctant column. Someone was plunking at a banjo under a white top and a ghost of song drifted out, feebly gay: "Shoo, fly, don't bother me."

"Going back to Steve'burg?" asked Pitler.

"No point in staying here," answered Kirk wearily. With Pitler at his elbow he squelched on through the mud, increasingly aware of how much he had counted on talking with Gray. And now, overshadowing that, were the highly disturbing implications of Dahlgren's appearance at Brandy Station, where Headquarters of the Cavalry Corps of the Army of the Potomac were established. He tried to turn his thoughts into less gloomy channels, but they only led to his own little command. The thaw and the rains had turned his horselines into horrible wallows that gulped down bricks and rocks and planks, leaving the mounts fetlock-deep and more in mud that would surely bring greasy-heel, scratches and malodorous thrush.

Pitler tugged at his arm. "Get your head up. We don't

9

know that the secret's out. We're just guessing. Dahlgren may be here for that damned ball."

Kirk shook his head. "Last time we heard of him, he was basking on his father's flagship off the Charleston forts. Look at that sunburn. Would any sane man leave an admiral's deck in South Carolina and come up into this muck unless he had *some* reason driving at him? He's not here just to have a lot of girls twitter over him. He could have had all he wanted of that just by going ashore to the base at Hilton. Head down there. You and I know about Dahlgren. This—thing is exactly what would appeal to him."

"With a wooden leg?" cried Pitler. "How could *he* get in on it? I agree it's funny he didn't stay with his old man, but anyone who's been made colonel before he was twenty-one is apt to do damn funny things. Or maybe the stump's bothering him and there's some special surgeon up here he wants to see. I can think of a million reasons to bring him up here without plumping for the first one we hit on."

"We were right—that first time."

"But how the hell will he travel? In a buggy?"

"He's got it figured somehow." He stopped short, red mud rising over his ankles.

Colonel Dahlgren was moving quite easily on crutches toward a shed, his orderly following. Dahlgren called and a cavalry officer emerged, saluted. Two orderlies led out a knot of saddled horses who tossed their heads and danced impatiently.

"Where's your buggy, Jake?" asked Kirk.

"It's somewhere. It's *got* to be."

As he spoke, a horse was led out to Dahlgren. The colonel slipped a foot into a hooded stirrup, gave a spring and swung a leg over the saddle. His orderly caught the mud-plastered boot, guided it carefully into the other stirrup.

"Well, God damn me for a tall green owl," breathed Jake as the colonel and his escort rode off toward the

10

south. "They must have spliced a new leg onto him. Hey—wait a minute! Did you have any tip he could ride?"

"Only something I saw in the Richmond *Examiner*. A few lines about their General John Hood. He got hit about the same time Dahlgren did, and had a worse amputation. The paper said Hood had been out riding with some Richmond girl."

"All right, all right! But the crowd we know about's not going riding with Richmond gals."

"Maybe not. Neither's Hood. Jeff Davis has booted out Joe Johnston and Hood's leaving for Georgia to take his place. He'll have to be in the saddle."

"Kirk, you're getting as stubborn as that mule in D Troop, the one who won't stop unless you use a whip and yell 'Giddyap' at him and who won't start until you commence taking off his harness and bringing him oats! Hood's commanding a whole army. Sure, maybe he can ride about a little, but he'd never be able to keep up with—a cavalry command. Neither would little Ulric."

Kirk forced a smile. "Go right on talking, Jake. Maybe you'll make me feel better. Where'd you leave your beast?"

"Tethered next yours in the long shed. I recognized your saddle blanket when I rode in. Let's get going. I got reports to make out when I get back to camp."

Kirk led out his hammer-headed blue roan and mounted. Jake pulled in beside him and the two started southwest down the Stevensburg road. The rain still swept down, but Kirk felt his depression easing a little. As always, the very presence of the Maine captain was comforting. He gave out a sense of solidity, of quiet confidence, that had a way of shrinking the fears and anxieties of others, a quality of which the rather matter-of-fact man was doubtless unaware. Kirk had sensed all this the first time that he had met Jake, back there by Fleetwood Hill just north of the tracks during the flaring cavalry combat of the preceding June. Jake,

11

riding on the flank of D Troop, 1st Maine, had called to him, "Looks like a lot of Rebs ahead. But I guess we look like a lot of Yanks to them. Want to come along and see who's right?"

That had been Kirk's first real introduction to the 1st Maine Cavalry. It was a fine outfit, top to bottom, but somehow Jake Pitler's D Troop stood out particularly in Kirk's mind. It had been recruited and officered largely from seaport towns and included shipowners, shipmasters, mates of all degrees as well as deck hands and cabin boys. Handicapped in almost all ranks by a colossal ignorance of war in general and of mounted war and horses in particular, it had been an object of ridicule in its early days, people said. The first drills had been conducted in nautical terms ("Lay aloft that horse and set a course two point nor'east by north!") that had reduced inspectors to apoplexy. But D Troop had also brought with it a high degree of intelligence, physical fitness and adaptability that had soon turned it into a crack command. It had even drawn high praise in a London paper from a British correspondent who was not inclined to look leniently on anything American.

And since Fleetwood Hill at Brandy Station there had been Aldie and Middleburg and Upperville and the long march to Gettysburg with Kirk's troop always on Jake Pitler's flank. You come to know a man pretty well, Kirk thought, boiling coffee with him on halts, riding with the two troops over unknown fields and roads by night, or toiling along, dismounted, toward buildings or woods that might or might not suddenly blaze with rifle fire.

And the two had discovered a still earlier association. The 1st Maine had ridden out in April of '63 in Stoneman's raid behind Lee's lines just before Chancellorsville. Kirk, then without a command, had gone with a New York unit as supernumerary officer. The two had not met, but each on that raid had noted and remembered certain things deep in the Confederacy. And what they had noted and remembered had, very recently, come to be of importance and had led to their inclusion in secret discussions at Cavalry Corps Headquarters and in the plans that came from those discussions.

Kirk started as Jake jabbed him gently in the ribs with a muddy riding crop. "Feeling better? You been kind of grinning to yourself. Sure, we'll fix up that major of yours and, hell, Dahlgren just came here to watch those gals tumble off the train."

Kirk laughed. "I said that maybe you were right." Then he added abruptly, "Glad you were along with me."

Jake masked his obvious pleasure in an aggrieved tone. "Oh, so you're glad I got drenched to the skin, plashing around the station with you when all the time I could have been cooking my knees in my hut?"

"You were soaked long before you left HQ and sneaked over to the tracks to see if you could leer at an ankle or two. Damn it, but the roads are empty. You'd never think we were right in the middle of an army. Not that I blame anyone for staying under cover when he can."

Jake looked to the right. "We got some company off there, coming across the fields by John Botts's house. Must be State-a-Mainers, hardy, like me."

Kirk turned in his saddle. The mists had lifted for a moment and he saw the four-columned house of the cantankerous Mr. Botts, who had consistently and loudly defied both his state and the Confederacy since the first days of secession. A file of horsemen was moving over a rolling field. "A brigadier's flag. Hell, that's little Judson himself, riding out ahead, talking to—"

Jake's jaws closed with a snap. "Yup," he said.

There was no need to name Judson Kilpatrick's companion. Tall and slim, Ulric Dahlgren bent from the saddle toward the wispy little brigadier. He was talking earnestly, his free hand moving in short, crisp gestures from time to time.

13

Jake moaned, "Sing me something, Kirk. Something lively like 'Tenting Tonight.' Set me chuckling about anything you can think of."

Kirk rallied himself with an effort. "Growling again, are you? Just because Dahlgren's trying to wheedle an invitation to the Washington's Birthday Ball from Judson?"

"That's just what I've been trying to think of," said Jake. "See, he's learned to do the polka. He wants an invitation to the ball and an introduction to the fat old gal who had that little firefly in green in tow."

Jake elaborated his theme while Kirk, silent again, rode on, smiling mechanically. His mind filled once more with disturbing thoughts. He could see furtive figures rowing by night south across the Potomac, being President's chief military adviser. Telegraph keys would would come to Braxton Bragg, the Confederate President's chief military adviser. Telegraph keys would begin clicking and aides in gray uniforms would go racing to Lee's headquarters off there at Orange Court House. Lee would send for Jeb Stuart, for Ewell and Ambrose Hill. "The intent of those people over there seems quite clear, gentlemen. I propose the following steps: You, General Stuart—"

Kirk started as Jake's crop touched his hand. "I'm turning off here, Kirk. Let me know if you find anything from Washington in your hut. Hell and holystones! If that damned major keeps elbowing you off, I'll take D Troop, go up to Pennsylvania Avenue and snake him down here myself."

2

The D.C.I.T.

The rain had stopped as Kirk rode past the camp of the 2nd New York and turned into his own street. Neatly spaced on either side of its forty-foot width, the huts of his troop still oozed water from their canvas roofs, but rude plank doors were opening and men were peering out, wrinkling their foreheads and squinting as though unable to believe that the rain was over, at least for the time being. Down the middle of the street two lines of horses, tethered head to head, were beginning to stir uneasily in anticipation of feeding time.

Kirk acknowledged a couple of salutes and leaned from his saddle, a keen eye on the hoofs. To his relief, all the horses seemed to be standing squarely, showing no outward sign of hoof ailments. More, the layers of brick and wood of the lines had not been swallowed up by the mud, and the straw that he had ordered laid down that morning still served as an adequate cushion. By the last mounts, Tom Latham, his first sergeant, came to attention. Kirk returned his salute. "Fine job on those standings, Sergeant. If they came through these last two days, they ought to do for a while."

"A freeze will help set them, sir. Wish I could find more brick, though."

"Know that burned house near Mountain Run? There's a brick path that runs down through an old garden to the water. I saw it this morning. Send a detail over and get what you want. Things been quiet here?"

"Too wet for anything else. Hay and oats kept dry under the tarps. Will you take stables, sir?"

"I've papers to look at, so you'll take it. No signs of foot trouble?"

"Only the scratches on Bill Dutton's mount, off hind foot."

"Good so far. I'll go over the whole lot with you after you've led out to water. We can't scamp grooming, but let's keep the boys out of the mud as much as we can." He swung down from his horse. "Have one of the stable guard look after Roquefort, will you?"

Latham surveyed the blue-gray greenish-mottled flanks. "Sir, that's a hell of a mount for a troop commander."

"If we had a colonel to raise a row at the remount depot, I might get a better one. But Roquefort'll do. He's faster than he looks and covers ground without heaving."

Kirk went slowly down the line, watching the men and their horses. The D.C.I.T., the *Ipse Dicit* to pun-prone Latinists of the Army of the Potomac, had had a bright beginning. Kirk's original unit, the Granite State Dragoons, a late '61 formation, had been frittered away, like most other cavalry commands, in picket duty, escort work, prisoner guard, convoying, serving under various local provost marshals. At Fredericksburg, in '62, it had been thrown, dismounted, in one of the last attacks against those Georgians behind the stone wall below

16

Marye's Heights. In a matter of minutes, the Granite State Dragoons had ceased to exist as a unit.

He could have gone home after that and joined some outfit then recruiting. He would almost certainly have gained a step. But rumor hinted at great things in the offing. The Union Cavalry was to be reorganized as a corps, instead of existing in scattered driblets. More, as a nucleus, a sort of *régiment d'élite* was to be formed, manned and officered from broken units like Kirk's, and other commands were to be combed for the cream of their personnel. They would be from all states in the Union and be known as the 1st District of Columbia Cavalry. General Joseph Hooker, then in command of the Army of the Potomac, was said to be interested in it, as was General George Stoneman, who would head the new corps. Even Secretary of War Stanton wa reported to have given it his icy approval.

Kirk, to his surprise, had been named captain of the first troop raised and, more, was told that a major's gold leaves would be his as soon as the regiment had been recruited more fully. Then Hooker lost command. Stoneman was relieved and the *régiment d'élite* dwindled to a single troop, drifting homeless about the Army, attached here, detailed there and at the very end of the list for supplies, equipment, horses, furloughs. The very thought of promotion was laughable. Since no recruits came in, the command shrank. Kirk's one lieutenant managed to secure a transfer and no replacement was forthcoming. So far he had been able to keep the lozenge in the angle of Latham's chevrons, but Headquarters was increasingly testy over the idea of a first sergeant for a troop of less than thirty men. Three line sergeants were allowed him, and three corporals.

Just the same, the D.C.I.T. was a good outfit. Colonel Smith of the 1st Maine Cavalry thought highly of it since the fight at Brandy Station in '63. It stood well in the eyes of the French Brigadier, Alfred Duffié, with his medals and crosses and exotic cigarettes. The present

17

brigade commander, young, wispy Judson Kilpatrick, gave it a high rating. But then, one never knew just what went on behind the pale eyes and pale Dundrearys of that New Jerseyman.

Kirk walked on to his clay-chimneyed hut at the head of the street and opened the ragged plank door. His orderly must have started the blaze in the fireplace just a few minutes before, as the interior was dank and smelled of wet horses and hay and mud and drying woolens and stale grease. He lit a candle, shucked his waterproof and kepi and sat down in a flour-barrel chair. Filling and lighting a short pipe, he unslung an oilcloth dispatch case from his shoulder and drew out some papers, frowning as he thought of his futile trip to Brandy Station.

His troubles had started back in December with a notice from the Cavalry Bureau. The D.C.I.T. was to be broken up, though no date had been set, and its enlisted personnel assigned to a labor regiment. Just that and no more. The bare facts were bad enough. The implications were profoundly shocking. A certain number of highly trained skilled cavalrymen would spend the rest of their enlistments, or the war, working as common laborers, their talents lost to the Army of the Potomac. All noncommissioned officers would revert to the rank of private and Kirk himself, having no command, would probably be retired.

Kirk had shut himself in his hut for two days, wrestling with his wave of hot anger at the stupidity and injustice of the plan. Then he had carefully drawn up a protest, pointing out that while the number of men involved was small, the Cavalry Corps in its present state could not spare even one trained trooper from its ranks. And the news of this dissolution would be known at once and would have a very bad effect on the morale of every cavalryman, for if a small unit could be so arbitrarily disposed of, so could a larger one.

He went on to sketch out the records of his men. Most

18

could easily qualify as corporals or sergeants. Some, like Latham, would make excellent junior officers or even troop commanders. But the future headed them for unskilled labor, with no rank. This point, too, would not be missed by men in other cavalry units.

His concern for his troop had led him much further, had engaged his intense belief in the absolutely vital role that cavalry could and should play, if victory were to be won. Shamefully misused in the early days of the war, the cavalry of the Army of the Potomac had been little short of laughable. Then, in early '63 it had been organized as a unit, like the infantry, as a striking force no longer tied down by convoy work or futile patrols or detailed as showy Headquarters escorts. Soon it was matching the best of the Southern cavalry, then surpassing it. But after Gettysburg, its successes had been forgotten and, not too slowly, it found its old, wasteful, useless role thrust back upon it.

Kirk leafed through the sheets of his carefully made copy and random sentences caught his eye. ". . . and now compelled to ride a sixty-mile circuit around the army while Lee's troopers, kept well to the rear, rest and recruit and keep their horses in condition, whereas ours are being worn out. When operations begin again, every advantage will be in the hands of the Southern cavalry. . . . to name merely a few, have not been assembled as regiments since the Mine Run campaign . . . regiments must be kept intact, organized into brigades and divisions, accustomed to work as such. . . . and similar panics can be attributed to the breaking up of major units into tiny, unrelated parts until every man, from colonel to trooper, is utterly lost when called upon to act with a larger body."

The report had drawn favorable comment from the bureau, but that was all. No one was interested in the immediate point, in championing the cause of so small a body as the D.C.I.T. against higher authority. Then an Ohio major, attached to the bureau, had written Kirk in

19

enthusiastic agreement. Something ought to be done and, in Major Gray's opinion, could be done. Major Gray, in fact, would give himself the pleasure of coming to Brandy to talk to Kirk as soon as possible. The telegram, setting the date, had followed and Kirk had gone to Brandy Station, brimming with hope that the D.C.I.T. might be saved. Kirk pushed back his chair. What the devil had kept Major Gray from coming?

The horses were being led back from water and the thick scrunch of their hoofs brought him quickly back to his troop. He stowed away his papers and rose. The end of the rain would probably mean a drop in temperature, so he discarded his waterproof and struggled into an infantry private's overcoat with captain's loops basted to its sleeves. His kepi had dried a little, but it still felt clammy as he drew it down over his dark hair and stepped outside.

The horses were all tethered to the long, gnawed pole that ran the length of the street and the troopers squatted by them, carefully scraping mud from hoof, pastern and fetlock with foot-long strips of shingle. Kirk walked slowly past the row of switching tails, his eyes on the hoofs. So far as he could see, not even the most slovenly of his men had tried to dodge the disagreeable task of scraping by furtively pouring water over the mud. Eight, ten months ago such trickery would have been the rule, not the exception.

He kept on, eyes roving from trooper to mount to trooper. The men seemed a little less listless, due, probably, to the rain's letting up. It was impossible to see the state of their boots, swathed in mud as they were, but their blue uniforms showed neat patches and cracked vizors had been mended, for the most part. The time that he had spent bargaining with a Pennsylvania sutler for a bag of sewing kits apparently had not been wasted. The horses, despite their shaggy winter coats, showed the results of his insistence on long hours of grooming, of his and Latham's endless struggles for hay and oats, for something to keep the hoofs as much as possible out of the mud in the erratic Virginia thaws. Long ago he had learned that carefully selecting a well-drained camp site was futile. Desirable ground that his command occupied was sure to be seen and coveted by a larger, senior unit, and the colonel of, say, the 1st Massachusetts Cavalry could always overrule the captain of the District of Columbia Independent Troop.

As Kirk rounded the end of the picket line, Latham saluted smartly. "Everything look all right, sir?"

"Fine. The boys have scraped enough. Tell Sergeant Creed to start feeding. Then a good half-hour grooming, fifteen minutes to a side."

There was no need for all this detail, this passing of commands. The troop would have gone ahead without a single order. But clinging to formality helped bolster Latham's authority over the twenty-six men—who should have been at least sixty. Kirk watched the feeding and the grooming, trying to size up the morale of the men. Fact and rumor ran a fantastic course in the army, but he was quite sure that no one of the D.C.I.T. had had any inkling of the troop's pending dissolution, of its absorption into an amorphous labor corps. Perhaps tomorrow or the next day would bring word from Gray. With a sigh, he left the picket line and made his way to his hut.

Footsteps squelched through the mud and Kirk turned to see the mail sergeant from brigade, big leather pouch over his shoulder. "Hello, Sergeant," he said. "What have you got for us?"

"Mostly home mail for the troop, sir. And this stuff from brigade and corps for you." He handed Kirk a half dozen envelopes.

"Thanks. Turn the men's mail over to Latham for distribution."

Kirk went into his hut, relit the candle and began to read the pronouncements of those authorities who sometimes designed to concern themselves with his command.

21

Usually that concern was negative, and this lot would probably follow the general pattern.

It did Furlough applications for five of his men were refused. Kirk shrugged. The furlough question was academic just now, as he and Jake Pitler knew, along with Pleasonton, Meade and Kilpatrick. He knew that many leaves had been granted to the Harris Light Cavalry as the Army still called his neighbors, the 2nd New York. There would be long faces among the New Yorkers when those furloughs were revoked, just a day or two at the most before the supposedly lucky holders should have set out for home. It would be hard on them, but secrecy was the essence of what was impending.

No mail from Newmarket, N. H., in his mother's neat script. In fact he had had no letter from his mother in over two weeks, but the last had been a fine, cheerful report. He had better ride over to Brandy Station and get Phil Cook to send her a telegram for him. He picked up the last envelope, a thick, bulky one, and looked at it in surprise. It was not Army mail, as he had thought, seeing no stamp on it. Now he noticed the frank of the Treasury Department on the upper right corner and opened the envelope quickly.

A half sheet of Treasury letter paper fell out and he read the few lines wonderingly. "My dear Kirk: Having heard a few remarks in Washington concerning your difficulties, I drafted the enclosed in the hope that it might be of some assistance to you. Make use of it and me in any way you may see fit. The Cavalry's usefulness seems to me beyond question. Yours faithfully, Winthrop Foster." Below was the stamp of the bureau of which Foster was chief.

"Well, I'll be damned!" he ejaculated. "I didn't think old Foster knew I was alive. I haven't seen him for years. What's he sending? Damned decent of him to want to help, just the same."

He unfolded the other sheets, the first of which was headed, "To Whom It May Concern," and ran his eye

22

quickly over them. Foster had written, ". . . have known both sides of his family all my life . . . prominent in founding of Colony and, later, State of New Hampshire. . . . Ensign Jared Kirk with Sir William Pepperrell at taking of Louisburg in 1745. . . . Captain Hezekiah Stedman killed at Saratoga while serving in Gen'l Glover's Brig., 1777. . . . Kirk is son of the late John Stark Stedman and Hannah Lucy Kirk . . . former active in extension of rural and urban schools; also in raising funds to care for indigent immigrant families. Prior to marriage, mother taught school in Concord, Pembroke, Hooksett; assistant to principal, Contoocook Female Academy. . . . J.S.S. died of malignant quinsy, brought on by overwork, 1855. . . . Hannah L.K.S. then resumed teaching Latin at Newmarket. . . . The son, Kirk S., subject of this letter, worked in local stores, in lumber camps, at Pennacook Mills, Manchester, to eke out family means; kept up schoolwork with mother's help; admitted to Dartmouth College, 1858; not only supported self, but remitted funds to mother; stood third in his class; left college prior to graduation to enlist in Granite State Dragoons; commissioned lieutenant, fall of 1861; captain, March 1862; since early 1863, Captain, District of Columbia Independent Troop; mentioned in dispatches at Brandy Station, Aldie, Gettysburg, Falling Waters. . . . This is the record of a man who would act only from the most honorable of motives and for the good of the service and of his country. I speak from personal knowledge of his life as a civilian. His life as a soldier speaks for itself. I have the honor to be, Sirs, your obedient servant, Winthrop Foster."

Kirk rose quickly, clattered wood into the fireplace. "Old Win Foster!" he muttered. "He didn't have to do that. I never thought he even liked me. Just a nod and a grunt when we met on the street at home. No way that I can see to use this, but—God, it helps just now."

He left the fire, flung open the door and drew in deep

breaths of the crisping air. Then he stood rigid. Colonel Ulric Dahlgren, orderly behind him, was riding slowly up the street, leaning from the saddle as though studying the condition of the horses and men. The last hope that the young colonel's arrival at Brandy Station might have been mere coincidence died in Kirk's mind. "He knows about the plan," he thought. "But how did he hear about it in Washington—and how many others have heard? At least he doesn't seem to have heard about the D.C.I.T. being broken up."

The plan, matured in the greatest secrecy, was on the surface a swift cavalry stroke against Richmond, whose defenses were known to be weak and manned largely by clerks and convalescents. It had been evolved in the brain of General Judson Kilpatrick, who had somehow managed to present it directly, over the heads of his superiors, to Secretary of War Stanton and then to the President himself. So Kilpatrick had returned to Brandy Station with his plan approved at the highest levels, much to the annoyance of Generals Meade and Pleasonton, who had not been consulted.

Two steps were involved. For the first, a heavy force of all arms would move west as though for a major attack against the Confederate left, which stroke Lee, from his headquarters at Orange Court House, would have to parry.

For the second, some thirty-five hundred sabers under Kilpatrick would sweep south by night, into the vacuum left by Lee's counter to the threat to his left, moving by back roads and through thinly settled country. Somewhere en route, a detachment would break off, cross the James River west of Richmond to the south bank. Then, while Kilpatrick's main force broke into the city from the north, thus absorbing the attention of the defenders, this detachment was to raid Belle Isle in the James, just south of Richmond, where there were thousands of Union prisoners, slackly guarded. The guards were to be overwhelmed, the prisoners freed and armed, so far as possible, from stores on the Isle, then rescued and rescuers would cross into the city and meet the main force. After that, the entire body, its mission accomplished, would fall back as swiftly as it had come, the released prisoners with it. It could follow its old route or, if necessary, swing southeast down the York Peninsula, where strong Union forces under General Benjamin Butler would meet it.

The plan, Kirk thought, was feasible *if* secrecy were maintained. So far as he knew, only the President, Stanton, Meade, Pleasonton and Kilpatrick were in on it. Just those five—and himself and Jake Pitler. And he and Jake had been brought in because they alone knew certain geographical details that were important. Even high-ranking officers who were to be intimately concerned were not to have the least hint until the last possible moment. There had been no trace of a leak in the Army, no speculation in the press.

Yet—here was Colonel Ulric Dahlgren, still convalescent from his amputation, but obviously knowing of the plan and demanding a share in it. Kirk was not concerned about Dahlgren's discretion. But if he had picked up enough in Washington to bring him to Brandy Station, others, with far different interests, might have heard what had come to him.

3

Reprieve

All through Sunday the rolling country to the north of the D.C.I.T. camp had been alive with thick blue columns and Kirk had kept his glasses trained on Sedgwick's VI Corps massing about Culpepper and beginning a slow lunge west. Now, in the hush of Sunday noon, there was more movement. White-topped wagons showed on low crests, vanished. Infantry formations showed in the gaps between brown hills, disappeared, were replaced by more blue files. Random winds brought a ghost of music, the blare of distant brass, the tomp-tomp-tomp of bass drums. By the broken swell of Pony Mountain, a few miles away, the fields were thick with troopers riding in long blue ribbons behind red and white guidons with George Custer's brigade flag opening bright to the wind beyond a clump of pines. Infantry and cavalry were beginning the feint to the west which was scheduled to precede Kilpatrick's dash south toward Richmond.

Standing at the head of the picket line, Kirk turned his attention to his own men. The sun was warm for late February and a light breeze kept the ground firm and dry. Normally, with routine duties over for a while, his troopers could be counted on to take advantage of every free second of an easy Sunday. They rolled up in blankets for that extra bit of sleep so treasured by seasoned soldiers. Or they wrote letters, squabbled over old newspapers, sunned themselves outside their huts and vanished into thin air at the least hint of an extra detail.

But today they stirred restlessly, their eyes always going to the fields by Pony Mountain. Although dismissed half an hour ago, several men fussed about their horses, whirling grooming kits, lifting hoofs to frown over shoes and nails. Others squatted by their huts, cleaning revolvers, squinting along the edges of sabers or crooning and muttering as they examined the undersides of saddles for leather cracks that could mean chafing and, very soon, a sore-backed useless horse.

The sun grew warmer, soothing, and the air was full of muted, peaceful sounds, the swish of horses' tails, the clop of shifting hoofs and the rhythmic chump-chump as the animals stretched their long necks down to the new-spread hay. If a few hens had been clucking and fussing about, Kirk could have fancied himself in a barnyard along the Piscataqua. George Bates, a lean, tireless Iowan, walked on past the horses, a saddle balanced on his hip. He paused by Kirk, looked off at the stir about Pony Mountain. "That got anything to do with us, Cap?" he asked.

Kirk smiled and shook his head. "Not that I know anything about."

Bates said, "No, guess not," and passed on, obviously not at all convinced.

It was all very puzzling. Despite Dahlgren's arrival and his continued presence, despite very plain indications that the secret move was common talk in Washington, it did not seem to have reached the Army of the Potomac. There had been hints of *something* afoot, of course, but everyone had apparently linked such rumors in with the move to Sedgwick and Custer, not going on in plain sight. And if further proof were needed, the furloughs issued to such outfits as the 2nd and 5th New York Cavalry, the 1st Vermont and the 6th Michigan still held valid. The lucky officers and men were counting on leaving next Tuesday. Lucky? Kirk wondered about the effect on morale when the truth became known.

Military music drifted in from the slopes of Pony Mountain and flashes of sun-touched brass against the brown fields told Kirk that Custer's beloved mounted band was playing his regiments onto the road. Such a move could only be headed toward the Confederate left flank and would swallow up little towns like Madison Court House and Stannardsville. Horses and men would splash through the upper reaches of the Rapidan, would water in Swift Run and Paddy Creek. Of course, the watchers at the Confederate signal station away off there on Clark's Mountain would pick up every troop, company and battery and send swift word on to Robert Lee at Orange Court House. "HEAVY YANKEE FORMATIONS MOVING TOWARD OUR LEFT!" And General Lee would certainly pay attention to that. "Damn it, he's *got* to!" thought Kirk. He watched his own men, still moving busily about, and the sense of sick depression that he had been fighting off since early morning swept back over him. He drew a deep breath, winced a little as paper crackled in his breast pocket.

Steady hoofs broke into his thoughts and he looked up to see Jake Pitler dismounting at the far end of the picket line, handing a cigar to the trooper who took his reins. Some of the tension left Kirk as the stocky captain strode up, grinning, past the switching tails. "Hello, Jake. All quiet with you?"

"You could hear an anchor drop. We're out of ear-

29

shot, aren't we? Yep, all quiet and it sure beats me. People had begun to wonder, but since yesterday they've spliced up all the rumors into what Sedgwick and Custer are up to. I came through the Harris Light, the 2nd New York, that is. The lucky furlough boys are all that one trooper sold his papers for a hundred dollars. *Caveat emptor.* We'll see some mighty glum faces when we do ride out past Harris and the others."

Kirk's jaws tightened. "When *you* ride out, you mean."

"Just me?" grunted Jake, puzzled.

Kirk pulled out a folded paper and handed it to him. Jake spread out the paper and his lower lip bulged as he read the telegram. "BEEN IMPOSSIBLE TO GET AWAY. NO HOPE FOR D.C.I.T AND A FEW OTHERS LIKE IT. YOU'LL BE GETTING DISBANDMENT ORDERS IN A FEW HOURS. SORRY I COULDN'T HELP. J. C. GRAY, MAJOR, USCAV."

Jake crumpled the sheet, then mechanically handed it back to Kirk. "God damn this! I'd been counting on your riding on my right flank, same as always. We've got to *do* something, get in touch with—"

"Nothing to do. God knows I've tried enough ways. What this means is that you've got to pick up the landmarks I was supposed to be looking for. Can you do it from the maps we've been over?"

"Sure, just the way you could pick up mine, if you had to. But, Jesus, this'll be the first time I've ridden out without you since—"

"Don't have to tell me. Now you better stay and have mess with me. I've got a quart of Monongahela whiskey to help it down. Then we'll go over my landmarks until you could spot 'em with your eyes shut."

Jake rode away after mess and Kirk waited somberly for the afternoon to slip past, bringing with it the fatal order of which Gray had spoken. As it crept on toward four o'clock, he jumped from his chair, unable to sit still longer, and stood in the door of his hut, waiting, with heavy apprehension sagging his shoulders.

30

At about half past four, his last waning hope died. A courier from Headquarters was turning into the street, riding directly toward him. The dreaded order had come, and with it, the death knell of the D.C.I.T. He signed for the envelope and then stood holding it in an unsteady hand as the rider trotted off. Suddenly Kirk set his chin, ripped open the envelope, bracing himself for the message inside. His hand shook even more and sweat stood out on his forehead. He drew a deep breath, shouted, "Sergeant Latham!"

The first sergeant shot out of the nearest hut. Kirk went on, still shouting. "Have Music sound 'Boots and Saddles'! And look—pick out the steadiest trooper we've got. Send him out to the main road and if any messenger sounds from HQ, have our man tell him that I've gone to Brandy Station, to Washington, anything. Just get rid of any messenger. Don't let one near me. Understand?"

"Right, sir," Latham shouted and the diminutive bugler in his yellow-frogged jacket sent a cascade of quick, stirring notes into the fading day. Troopers tumbled out of their huts or from among the horses, buttoning their jackets, tightening their belts or settling their kepis. Kirk caught an angry mutter as the troop formed in double line before him. "Hell of a time to snake us out! God damn near night!" . . . "Hell, are we supposed to catch up with Autie Custer and him with a four-hour start on us? Ain't a horse in the outfit that won't poop out."

Roll call was soon over and then men broke ranks, clumped sullenly off to the saddle racks. Latham faced Kirk. "We're going to follow after Custer, sir?"

"We'll find out," answered Kirk. "Now I want you to see for yourself that every man's got his five days' rations in his saddlebags, that no one skips the extra oat rations and that all canteens are filled. My gear's all ready and I've told Chivers to saddle up Roquefort for me."

Half an hour later, Kirk, astride the mottled Roque-

31

fort, surveyed the D.C.I.T. as it formed in column of fours. The troopers, suddenly gigantic in their light-blue caped overcoats, were settling themselves in their saddles, fussing with the tubular oat sacks strapped to their pommels on their ponchos and blankets on their cantles. Kirk caught a mutter: "For what we are about to receive, let's hope to Christ we can be thankful."

Kirk glanced up at the darkening sky. "Going to rain, sure as shooting fish," he muttered. "Can't we *ever* start out without getting baptized?" He caught Latham's eye, down at the end of the column, and raised his arm, calling, "Troop, atten-*tion!* Forward—ho! Column right—ho!" He gave the arm signals for each order, and befrogged little Music, riding behind him, blared out the bugle commands. Perhaps it was ridiculous to use the drillbook words, the arm signals and the bugle as though the troop were a brigade. The men would have answered just as accurately if he had said, "All right. Let's go. Head out of camp and hit for the Richardsville road." But Kirk was sure that such formality made them less aware of their waif status, let them know that they were an integral part of the Cavalry Corps of the Army of the Potomac, even if they amounted only to an understrength troop. He was equally sure that indifference on his part could easily change them into a slack, shiftless outfit of no use to themselves, the corps or the Army.

The troop was clear of the camp, heading over rough fields toward the Richardsville road. Above the sound of one hundred and eight hoofs chewing away at the Virginia soil, above the creak of saddles and the clink of scabbards, Kirk heard mutterings: "This'll take us plumb east. This won't take us to Custer! What the hell we going *east* for?" Someone growled, " 'Cause it's orders, that's why."

Orders! Kirk felt his chest tighten. Orders to join Kilpatrick! There was little chance now of the disbandment order overtaking the D.C.I.T.

The guidon, riding a few yards ahead of the troop, suddenly halted, swung his mount broadside and sat looking down a side road that was thick with the sound of hoofs and accouterments. Kirk threw up his hand, ready to signal "Halt!", when the guidon turned his horse ahead and resumed his steady progress. Abreast of the side road, Kirk saw that it was choked with waiting cavalrymen, a long string of guidons shimmering in the dying light. The nearest waiting trooper called over his shoulder, "Hey, Bob! It's only them Ipsie Dixies! Won't be long in passing." Kirk's men began to shout in recognition. "It's the old Harris Light! Hi, New York!" Lower tones rumbled speculatively. "Harris, huh? With us? Must mean real doin's. And I seen Cap Pitler out of the 1st Maine nosing around our camp this morning. Harris, Maine and us. Like the fight to Brandy all over again."

The byroad was left behind and the troop wound on through scrub growth, across a gurgling run and onto clear ground. "Don't remember woods off there, sir," said Sergeant Clancy at Kirk's elbow.

"Not woods." Kirk pointed. The light was failing fast, but the long, dark clumps that might have been young trees were revealed as heavy bodies of cavalry, motionless against the sky. The road slanted toward them and Kirk leaned forward in his saddle. To himself as much as to Clancy he said, "Color-bearers on gray horses.—3rd Indiana. Pants strapped under shoes—1st Vermont." One by one he identified them: "17th Penn., 5th New York, 18th Penn., 5th, 6th, 7th Michigan. Horse gunners. Ransom's battery. Who's—" He straightened, called over his shoulder, "Music! Sound attention!"

The four quick notes flared out just in time. On a mound to the left, two men were watching. One was small and spare, standing with a booted foot on a log, forearm across his knee. The other, tall and slim, stood erect, an orderly shouldering two crutches behind him. Kirk raised his saber in salute, but General Kilpatrick barely lifted one finger to the brim of his hat in acknowledgment. It was impossible to know if he were pleased or displeased with the D.C.I.T. His eyes stared pale as ever. No shade of expression passed over his deeply undercut lower lip and not a hair of the pale Dundrearys stirred. Beyond Kilpatrick, Colonel Dahlgren came to rigid attention, right hand snapping up to his vizor. Then the two were lost to sight.

There was more cavalry ahead and all at once derisive shouts sailed up: "It's them Ipsie Dixies! Hey, what kep' you?" Kirk's men set up a joyous yelping: "Hi, State-a-Maine! What kep' you?" The seemingly meaningless question dated back to the early days of the troop's association with the 1st Maine, marking an occasion when both units made a difficult and dangerous rendezvous well ahead of time. Since then it had become a sort of mutual recognition signal between the two, a jeering accusation of nonexistent tardiness invariably launched by whichever group sighted the other first.

A rider closed in beside Kirk and Jake was thumping his back, shouting, "What happened? Jesus, I'd plumb given you up for good! What happened?"

Kirk threw an arm about Jake's shoulder. "Happened? Nothing but an order from Kilpatrick to join him at once. That's all. And I've muddied my trail, so anyone from HQ with disbandment orders for us will be riding in circles trying to find me."

Jake whistled. "Hey, did you tell little Judson that the orders were on the way?"

"*Tell* him? Why the hell should I bother him with that stuff? He's got enough on his mind as it is."

"Just the same—" began Jake.

"You're acting sorry that I did come. You want all the glory?"

"Kind of counted on it. But since you insist on crowding in on me, better come and report to Kilpatrick and Dahlgren. Turn your troop over to Latham and tell him to find our adjutant. You'll tie in with us as usual."

Kirk had a few words with Latham and then swung Roquefort after Jake's bay. The latter called, "Swing left here. Little shelter with two lanterns slung from it. See the wagons beyond?"

"Only three wagons? We're sure traveling light."

"Look beyond 'em. Six ambulances. Little Judson may kill off his horses, but he sure sees to his men. I've picked out the second ambulance on the right, upper left stretcher."

"Glad to know where you'll be. I'll send you flowers."

"Sure. Sea strawberries trimmed with kelp. Here we are."

An orderly took their horses as they dismounted and the General looked up with a quick, birdlike motion. "The D.C.I.T.?" he said sharply. "Should have been here sooner." He glanced at Dahlgren, who was frowning over a map under a lantern. "You want to talk to Stedman, Colonel?" Kilpatrick's manner seemed a little detached, as though he were waiting for something to break up the interview.

Dahlgren looked up and the glow fell across his fine-drawn features. Kirk had never seen him at close range before and was struck not only by the extreme boyishness of his face, but also by an odd quality, almost a transparency. It was probably due in part to the light and part to the long convalescence that had followed his amputation. Whatever the cause, it produced an eerie effect. It occurred to Kirk that a man of the Middle Ages, confronted by the Colonel, might well mutter of a miracle, of a return from the grave—and then cross himself reverently.

Dahlgren held out a thin hand and Kirk was surprised by the strength of the grip. "Glad to have you with us. Mind looking at this map? I've asked Captain Pitler about these points marked in pencil. They're correct? Good. Now Pitler says that this point *here* is *your* observation, not his. How do you *know* the troops can pass here? All this happened quite a long time ago, you know."

Kirk studied the careful sketch. "I *know*, sir, because we were chasing some Rebs, just mounted militia, and that's where they went. We didn't follow, because we were chiefly concerned in getting back. To put it very bluntly, we were lost and didn't want to stay that way."

Dahlgren smoothed his blond goatee. "At least, all that makes it easier for us now." He turned to Kilpatrick. "Have you any questions, General?"

Kilpatrick's fingers drummed on the plank. "No. No. We had several conferences before you came up from Washington."

Dahlgren picked up his map. "You've been in on this from the start. But there's one detail that the General tells me you don't know. I'm commanding the detachment that'll break off and hit for the James crossings above Richmond. Some of us, and the main body, are going to distribute copies of the President's Proclamation of Amnesty; you know, the one that pardons all Rebs who'll return to their old allegiance. We've got thousands of them to drop along roads, in houses, schools, courthouses, taverns, everywhere. You and Pitler'll lead my detachment, and I'm not loading you down with any of that stuff. I thought you'd better know the reason in case you see other outfits racing off from the route. They'll be getting rid of copies. The President is most anxious that his message have the widest possible distribution."

"Only reason we got the plan through was agreeing to play postman," said Kilpatrick tersely.

Dahlgren went on. "That's all, then, gentlemen." He glanced at Kilpatrick. "Now—really, sir, I think I better get my command stirring. It'll take a little time to get four hundred fifty sabers onto the road."

The General slapped his hands on the table. "Headquarters! We've had no word from them yet and can't start till we do. The field telegraph's dead and no couriers have come in. If this keeps up, we'll see sunrise right here." He crouched over the plank, gripping its edge, staring hard beyond the lanterns where someone was calling. A frightened aide butted past Kirk, holding out an envelope. The General snatched at it, ripped it open. Then he gave a tight shout. "Got it! Listen—'The Major General commanding directs that you move at once.' " He flung his arms into the air. "Now! Get going! All of you!"

So the secret plan was about to be launched! Kirk felt a quick, cold tightening in his chest and glanced at Jake. The stocky man was chewing at the insides of his cheeks, eyes fixed on the lantern beyond Kilpatrick. Dahlgren rose easily. His orderly moved out of the shadows and the light turned the crutches he held out into curves of yellow gold. The Colonel took them, nodded pleasantly. "See you gentlemen at the rendezvous."

As Kirk and Jake mounted, Kirk said, "At least we don't have to play postman with that proclamation."

Jake, easy again, laughed. "We're too important for that. Cavaliers. Laughing, dashing, fast-eating. We're going to be the point for the whole detachment. The rest have got the papers, all right, though, those from the 2nd and 5th New York, 1st Vermont and 5th Michigan. You ought to see them. Their saddlebags are bulging like the sides of a moses boat. You know, Kirk, I've been thinking about a lot of things. Been a nice day today—up to now, I mean."

"Suppose I agree with you. What happens then?"

"Nice and sunny and clear. Now, there's a ridge back home, up to the north of Waldoboro. I've been up when the air was clean as a new tumbler and still you couldn't see the valley floor. Kind of a haze you don't notice till you get above it."

Kirk shaped a reply with a flippancy that he did not feel, then choked it back with a start. "Is the ridge about as high as Clark Mountain off yonder?"

"No, but close enough," said Jake. "Come on, let's trot."

Jake's thinking was only too clear to Kirk. A ground haze could have covered the flat lands below Clark, hiding from Lee's signal station the thousands that Sedgwick and Custer had led west, toward the Confederate left. Over his shoulder Jake called, "That's just one thing we'll find out later. Sure is getting dark. Lucky I'm part cat, on my great-grandfather's side. That's Michigan off there, 5th New York just beyond. We bear left here."

A fat raindrop spatted down on the back of Kirk's bridle hand; another struck against the nape of his neck. "Cross off one thing to find out, Jake. We've found it," he called. "It's going to be a wet march." A gust of wind rippled the skirt of his overcoat. "And a cold one."

4

Canadian Girl

The whole command, more than thirty-five hundred sabers strong, had slipped away into the night drizzle without a single bugle note, heading south and east. At the head of the D.C.I.T., Kirk felt solid walls of black rise on either side of the road as ragged woods closed in, felt fresher air and more rain when the world to the right and left of him lightened a little to tell him of open fields. Fifty yards ahead he could sometimes make out Sergeant Clancy and the half dozen troopers nosing their way along, closing in when the second growth was too thick, fanning out whenever open stretches gave them a chance. Beyond them, he knew, were the picked men in Confederate gray, moving with a casualness which they probably did not feel.

A sag-roofed cabin passed, a splintered oak, a trickle of a brook. He knew them all from bygone night forays and mentally ticked them off while the road stretched on, east and south, east and south, but with each turn veering a little more from the east and pointing a little more south.

He sat tense in the saddle, eyes and ears questioning woods and fields, impatient of the night and the rain that blurred his sight, of every creak of saddle leather and smack of hoof that dulled his hearing. He was sure that, so far, he had caught no sound other than the flow of the column, had seen no movement, no glint of light other than the stir of trees or the dull shimmer of water. No sound—but there had been another sound. There it was again. He checked his horse until a scout was beside him. "Listen, Chris. Hear it? It's been with us for the last half hour. Is it real?"

The night went dead save for the sound of the column. Then the three liquid bird notes trilled again. Chris Rowan, a lean, leathery man, bent his head, then nodded. "Sure enough whippoorwill, Cap."

"Damned early for them to be about. At least it would be at home."

Rowan volleyed tobacco juice into the night. "Maybe he's not got a calendar. But that's all that's wrong with him. I'll be taking a cast up ahead and see what the boys out beyond Clancy are doing." The scout trotted off and was soon lost to sight.

Kirk rode on, keeping Roquefort on a soft strip where hoofs fell almost noiseless, past Clancy and his detail. There were woods to the left now and the whippoorwill, lost and ghostly, sent its plaintive query into the night. Kirk shivered. "Damn that bird. Does he think he belongs to the D.C.I.T.?"

Something gave an evil, clicking sound ahead of him and he called softly, "Chris? Put down your gun. Where are the others?"

Several shapes materialized beyond Rowan, and Kirk halted. "I'm going ahead. If they're watching for us, they'll be jumpy and one man can draw fire as well as a dozen. If you hear any shots, hit back for the troop and then to the 1st Maine detachment."

40

The ground fell away in a long, gradual slope and soon he had the smell of a river in his nostrils. Leaning forward, he made out the dull ruffle of the river, of the Rapidan that had run red so often since '61. There was a clump of trees just visible at the right of the road as it dipped to the water's edge. Ely's Ford. He could have sketched the opposite bank from memory, so often had he sent his horse, with the D.C.I.T. close behind, through its shallows. There the road curved a little west, then swung south past a house always known as The Ellis Place, and thence still south through the hideous tangles toward a now ruined half mansion, half tavern called either Chancellor's house or Chancellorsville.

Slowly he rode down to the water's edge, dismounted. The far bank was part of a dead planet, for all the life it showed. The drizzle had let up and no longer hissed into the Rapidan. The wind blew from the south, shutting off the sound of the approach of Kilpatrick and Dahlgren. Just the river and the eager gulping of Roquefort as he plunged his muzzle into the Rapidan. From the trees to the right, the bird sent its song up again, over and over. Kirk mounted and rode back and forth in the near shallows, sheets of water splashing back with each step of his horse. The far bank was still silent.

Kirk fought against an impulse, yielded to it and drove Roquefort on across the ford. The Rapidan was low and the water just brushed the bottoms of his hooded stirrups. There was a final lurch, a scramble and he was on the south bank, seemingly alone in a dark world where the rain had begun to pelt again. There was a rustle of the river, the beat of the rain, the steady breathing of his mount, but beyond that there was silence.

The impulse still strong on him, he dismounted, tethered Roquefort to a thick sapling. Then he unbuckled his saber, fastened it to the saddle and started up the slope, his right hand folding back the flap of his holster.

The sound of the rain was enough to mask his footsteps, but the clank of the scabbard might have carried through it.

He was at the crest, looking south into hostile territory. Crouching, he made out the dark mass of the Ellis house against the darker sky and moved on inland. Fifty yards, one hundred—and he stopped. He felt the blood pounding in his ears, but the night gave back no sound, no stifled whinny, no mutterings, no clink of equipment, no stir of men. If an ambush had been set, it lay deeper inland. There was little chance of a sudden fusillade smashing down into the column as it wallowed helpless in the ford.

Back at the river, he mounted, refastened his saber and rode a few yards into the water. There were silvery splashes on the far side and he called, low-pitched, "Rowan? This is Stedman. All quiet. Send word back." Soon the ford boiled as the fours of his troop churned across and he closed in on Latham on the flank. "Take 'em right on. Keep your eyes peeled. I'll catch up." His men pushed ahead, the horses digging at the slippery bank.

There were more troopers in the water and Kirk checked a familiar, stocky figure. "Jake! I've been over the crest. I swear the place is empty. I could have heard a mouse trimming its whiskers. Any outfit big enough to bother us would have been *bound* to make some noise."

Jake beat the water out of his kepi against his knee, then crammed it back on his head. "Boy, you're just plain deep-fried in luck! Thanks for passing the word back. I sent it on to the 5th New York a bit behind us. Ready for some riding now? Whoever gets to Chancellorsville first waits for the other. Two scouts go on with you. Rowan and the rest are with me. Good luck, Kirk. See you at the rendezvous or in Libby Prison."

Kirk's troop was moving ahead steadily behind the scouts as he overtook it. He called to Latham, "Good work. Now take the rear and keep 'em closed up. No

42

straggling. Any man whose horse breaks down will have to look out for himself." The tireless whippoorwill took up its three notes again and Kirk shook his fist toward the sound. It no longer alarmed him, since the scouts, trained to recognize all noises of the night, had pronounced it unquestionably real, but its monotonous repetition added to the strain of the march.

By a broken wellhead, he took a dozen troopers on a slant across boggy fields, heading for a spot marked in his mind by past patrols. Later a hollow by a millpond was scoured and then a dark grove near the ruins of an icehouse. Dismounted in still another grove, he and Burton, his chief scout, pawed the ground until they found a discarded blanket, the charred wood of an old fire. Kirk fumed to Burton, a Minnesota woodsman, "Have the damned Rebs gone underground for the winter like a lot of chipmunks?"

"They ain't told me. Sure God they ain't here, though. You say you hit outposts here before?"

"Twice. I can't figure it. Nothing yet and we're way south of the river. Mount up. Find us that cart path you told me about and we'll prowl it."

The clearing where Burton thought a small bivouac or patrol might be found was empty and the night hung still as ever. Kirk jumped as a trooper burst into a fit of hollow coughing. Then he steadied himself. Just the same, a sudden pounding of hoofs, a rifle shot would be almost a relief, something like a welcome breaking of the endless tension. He dismounted his men at the far edge of the clearing and told them to check their cinches and bridles and make sure that their rolls were secure on their saddles. Reins over his arm, he stepped back and his foot slithered off something smooth and round. He put a hand down, drew it back quickly as his fingers slid over the eye sockets of a human skull. Beyond it, gleaming with an odd phosphorescence under the rain, curving ribs reached out. A trooper smothered an oath, another gave a skip and a jump, muttering.

43

There were bones everywhere. Kirk's mind jumped from the ghastly remains to their meaning. At least he and the scouts had not missed their way. The spot must be a fringe or corner of the Chancellorsville battleground.

He remounted his men, who wriggled and shivered as their soaked trousers met wet saddle leather, and signaled forward. The trees were thinning a little, then suddenly fell away and Kirk looked out onto open country, hummocky under the night sky. Off to his left rose a huge building with chimneys lifting above a tattered roof. "Chancellor house," said Burton at Kirk's side. "Orange Turnpike runs over yonder, smack-dab east of Fredericksburg. Hey—cavalry!" Burton crouched, then stood in his stirrups. "See 'em? On the pike off there, comin' from the west. I'll take a cast ahead. Come on if I whistle."

"And if you don't?"

"That's up to you. I'd skeedaddle, if it was me."

He rode off into the gloom while Kirk sat marveling at the scout's eyesight. He himself could hear the stir of mounted men, but his vision told him nothing. A keen whistle split the air, was answered from the pike. Kirk hesitated, then trotted forward, the troop following him.

Suddenly Burton, accompanied by another rider, moved toward him. Kirk stared, then dropped to the ground. "Made it, Jake! What did you find?"

Jake dismounted beside him. "Not a damn thing. Country's empty as a turkey run at Thanksgiving. Beat up some old camps, but there wasn't as much as a bacon rind in 'em. How about you?"

"The same. Better get going again." His men had halted behind him and were jeering at the Maine troopers, calling, "What kep' yuh? Been dawdling most an hour waiting for you."

Jake said, "Wait a minute. 5th New York, west of us, snapped up a picket and sent us word. North Carolina cavalry, dismounted. Weren't on the alert, not expecting anything. Had rumors of Reb troops moving west, but

44

didn't know for sure. Hadn't been in touch with their main outfit since yesterday. It looks to me as if Clark Mountain had seen Sedgwick and Custer heading west, as we'd hoped, and shifted some of his boys to meet them off there. If that's so, we're riding right clear round his right flank."

Dawn was fading the formless night masses into silvery shapes that slowly lost their last tarnish. Soon Kirk could make out raindrops on the square white pillars of Spotsylvania Tavern, outside which he and Pitler's troop were waiting. Other Maine units, followed by New Yorkers, were forming beyond Pitler and the road leading south past the tavern was thick with more cavalry, with ambulances, with the six guns and eight caissons of Ransom's Horse Battery. Farther up the road, Kilpatrick came out of the little story-and-a-half courthouse, pulling on long gauntlets, while Colonel Dahlgren followed, crutches under his arm. At the last step, Dahlgren paused, raised his hand, dropped it. Kirk nodded, gave a short command and the D.C.I.T. stirred, swung off down a side road that led away south and west. Behind him, Pitler's men were forming into column and trailing on after the D.C.I.T. Kirk looked back over his shoulder. Dahlgren was mounting, riding away from the heavy mass that still poured south past the tavern.

Jake clattered up from the rear and joined Kirk. "Well, here the real ride's beginning. How do you feel now about splitting the command?"

"Same as ever. It's always risky and sometimes it works. Just wish we knew more about Dahlgren. He's done a lot of spectacular things, but he's never served with a regiment."

"You mean he's not a real cavalryman?"

"Just that. He's always been staff, no regular job. He's borrowed men from this regiment or that and gone chasing off with them. I grant you that he's done some fine things, like capturing that courier from Jeff Davis to

Lee at Gettysburg, or taking and holding Fredericksburg with the odds five to one against him. But that isn't being a cavalryman. He's had no responsibility for his men and horses before starting, and when he's done, he turns them back to their regiment, says 'Thank you' to their commander and that's the end of it. And he can't have learned much about operating with other mounted bodies that way, like knowing when he can go ahead or fall back without hurting outfits to his right or left or behind him. Frankly, I'm worried."

Jake shook Kirk's shoulder. "Cheer up! We've got a lot of country to see and some nice rivers to cross before it's time to worry. From what they told us at the courthouse, we *have* got clear around and behind Bob Lee's right flank. So what's bothering you?"

"Telegraph wires that might be telling him just where we are."

Jake blew out his lower lip. "Those damn things! You never know when you'll come across a stretch with a Reb jiggling a key and tapping out, 'Hey, Marse Robert! Look what *I* found!'"

It was getting on toward eleven with the sun still lurking behind a thin overcast as Kirk brought the D.C.I.T. down the road that led from the clustered buildings known as Waller's Tavern and across the shallows of the North Anna. From the crest of the south bank he turned in his saddle to look back. Pitler's troop had forded about a quarter of a mile below him and was forming again according to plan. The high ground on the north bank was dotted with moving blue men, two here, five there, a dozen, all flowing south toward the crossings. Kirk whipped off his kepi, held it high above his head, swept it downward in a curving arc. A distant trooper raised and lowered his carbine twice, another repeated the signal from the skyline and soon red and white guidons began to wink along the north bank. Over the paths and along cartroads more blue streamed

46

into sight. Kirk replaced his kepi and nodded to Tom Latham. "We may not tot up to very much, but we sure look like an army."

Latham frowned. "Hope to hell the Rebs think so, wherever they are. Hey, watch it, sir! Here comes the Colonel!"

Dahlgren was splashing across the ford with a bugler and two lieutenants behind him. He waved to Kirk. "Keep pushing ahead. Pitler's to your left and a half troop of the Harris is circling to your right. The rest'll follow."

Kirk nodded in comprehension, set his right arm stabbing the air above his head as he put Roquefort into a trot. His eye caught a flash of brass at his elbow and he cried, "No, Music, no! No calls! The boys'll get my arm signals. Forget about that horn of yours till I tell you to use it."

Hoofs beat faster and faster behind him as the D.C.I.T. broke into a quick trot that carried it out onto a broken plateau, seamed here and there with the dark-shadowed gullies, spotted by ragged patches of woodland, weary-looking cottages in unkempt clearings. Kirk looked quickly left and right. There was Dahlgren and his group with Jake's State-a-Mainers trotting beyond it. There was the Harris detachment breaking out to his right. And every fold of land, every gully mouth, every rustling clump of trees spilled out more and more troopers.

Kirk settled himself in his saddle while eye and mind translated the scene to him. The whole command, in extended order, was across the North Anna, moving swiftly south. At first glance they seemed scattered, mere unrelated fragments. Then the whole course of the march, the features of the terrain showed him how, at a single order, the trotting lines could be massed, or set flowing to support any threatened unit or detachment. Dahlgren might be untried, but so far he was handling his mixed command very well.

There was another steep dip, shallow water, a climbing scramble up the far slope of Elk Creek and a repetition of the uneven plateau they had just crossed. The gait was increasing and the drill of hoofs louder and thicker in Kirk's ears. Off to his right he saw leading horsemen turning their heads uncertainly, as though asking the same question that was filling his mind. Where—where—

He gave a shout, pointed ahead beyond a thin line of trees. Dahlgren had seen it at the same time and was gesturing forward with wide sweeps of his kepi. Beyond him, Jake was standing in his stirrups, arm jabbing ahead as he called back to his men. Off to the right there was an assured surge and in the rear a suddenly quickened tempo. Kirk turned in his saddle and shouted, "Never mind about the others. Straight ahead to the job."

The trees were close now and beyond them the single-track line of the Virginia Central Railway, a huddle of grayish buildings not far from the rails. From a smoke-stained, two-story house, a thin line of wire reached out to flimsy poles, ran onto trees, flowed along the ground. Kirk pointed again, yelled, "Follow me," and drew his revolver. There were crunching cinders under the hoofs now, woodpiles close by the track. Two startled men in grayish brown sprang up almost under Roquefort's nose. Kirk saw eyes oddly pale and staring under the brims of battered hats, heard a shout of "Yanks!" He dropped to the ground, kicked over a stack of rifles and dived into the building under a sign whose flaky paint spelled out FREDERICKS'S HALL.

Someone yelled just inside the door and Kirk's knee sent a man spinning with his rifle under him. There were other boots pounding on the floor and Kirk shouted, "Take him, boys!" and lunged across a low partition where a very thin man clutched at a telegraph instrument and glared at him through stunned eyes. Kirk caught him by the neck, wrenched him aside. "No one's

48

going to get hurt. Keep your hands up and get in the corner." He raised the butt of his revolver, brought it smashing down on the instrument, four times, five times. Then he ripped it loose, flung it against the wall, yelling, "All right, everyone out. Get onto the next job."

He plunged through the door after his men. "Get the prisoners outside. The Harris looks after them. Get on with it."

Axes were whanging against the few telegraph poles, setting them swaying, then tottering, falling. Kirk picked up a hatchet that lay by a woodpile and hacked the wire in a dozen places. "That's enough. Maine'll take care of that end of it. Clancy, get busy on the west side. That's the stretch that runs on to Gordonsville and Orange Court House. Rip up all you can. Reel it in." A light wagon, the markings of the 5th Michigan on its sides, rolled up, and he sprang in front of it. "Get your oakum and your turpentine out. No, you won't need torpedoes here. Stack 'em in, on the double. Now back around. Clancy! Got the loose end of that wire? Make it fast to the tail gate. You, driver, get those horses moving. We want to coil in fifty miles of it if we can. Get 'em going."

The wagon lurched away east and the telegraph wire tautened, quivered, then gave. Far up the track Kirk could see trees and bushes stir as the wire played through them. He waved his kepi at the Michigan driver. "Get 'em digging! Follow along with your detail, Clancy. Don't let the wire get too taut. Ease the strain when you can. It's bound to snap sooner or later, but we want as much as we can get before that happens. Then reel it up and chuck it in the wagon."

He turned and ran around the corner of the station where thick, oily smoke had begun to coil. "Sure you got everyone out of there, Latham? Then hit any buildings the others haven't touched. They're all government-owned or government-used. Hey, watch out. Corporal Fein's job's about done."

Through the thickening smoke, the bulk of the water

49

tower on its spidery legs loomed twenty feet above the ground. Now it began to totter, sway, then pitched forward with a roaring, hissing crash and a torrent of chip-littered water rushed about the base of the station, along the tracks.

Kirk swished his hands together as though he had finished a dusty job. "That accounts for us. Now what?"

He stepped back out of the smoke and looked up and down the track. Far off, east and west, Number 4's were holding the horses of the troopers who were nosing on foot along possible avenues of approach, guarding against sudden counterattack. Someone had found repair tools in a shed and now they were being used to rip up sections of the rather flimsy rails. Details were running with the iron lengths to burning sheds, plunging them into the flames, drawing them out and bending and twisting them about thick trees. From a big building, west of the station, blue jackets were clustered, forming an aisle down which passed slowly a line of men in gray-brown, officers, to judge from the cut of their coats. A Vermont trooper came racing along the line crowing, "Snapped up a whole court-martial, a-settin' like a Rhode Island Red on its nest. Colonels and majors and Jesus knows what not."

Kirk looked west again. The Number 4's were still waiting with the horses far up the line and there was no sign of their dismounted fellows. So far it was obvious that Lee's army was unaware of Dahlgren's activity, to say nothing of Kilpatrick's far larger force somewhere off to the east. But sooner or later someone, somewhere must notice the rising smoke clouds. By the big building, now burning like the others, Dahlgren was talking with two Confederate officers. "Come on! Come *on!*" said Kirk between his teeth. "High time to get moving!" The Colonel talked on.

Kirk turned impatiently away, his anxiety somewhat eased by the sight of the D.C.I.T. cinching up under Latham's orders. At least, his troop would be ready to mount when the order came. His eye caught a slant-roofed shed half hidden among trees some fifty yards away. Its rear was toward him, but he guessed that it was just a carriage shelter, old and not worth burning. Just the same, it might hold government stores—

After a word with Latham, he walked toward it, revolver drawn in case the shed harbored fugitives. It was far deeper than he had thought and the entrance gaped wide and barnlike with utter darkness thick under the roof. The ground was soft and showed no footprints, nothing but the hoofmarks of a single horse and the thin ruts of a light carriage leading inward. Peering, he stepped inside and made out the rear of a hooded chaise. In the farther darkness a horse shifted its hoofs and sighed heavily. He called, "Anyone in here?" The echoes of his voice died unanswered.

Kirk moved on close to the east wall, taking high, slow steps with his arms stretched before him, letting hands and feet serve as eyes. His palms found the rear wall. Nothing. No stores. Just the horse and the chaise. He kept on toward the horse. Still nothing.

Something dark stirred, dodged, crouching, and tried to duck past him toward the door. He swept out his arm and caught a handful of strong woolen cloth. "Who are you? Now steady, sonny. No one's going to get hurt. Let's have a look at you in the light and then you can run on home."

His captive struggled and Kirk gave a firmer tug to the cloth. All at once the wool seemed to explode. Flying feet hacked at his shins and ankles and small, hard fists hammered at his chest. He recovered his balance, stowed away his revolver and hauled his small assailant against him. "This won't do, young feller. I'll have to carry you out." There was a convulsive struggle, a gasp and he set down his burden quickly, the memory of a rounded thigh, a firm breast lingering his palms. He gasped. "My God—" The vaguely seen shape made a gesture as though wrapping a cloak more tightly and scur-

51

ried for the door, only to be brought up sharply. A girl's voice, bravely icy, said, "Will you kindly let go of my cloak?"

"I think you'd do well to stay right here. Our troops haven't left. You'd de safe enough among them, but someone would be sure to pick you up for more questioning. Better get it over with now."

From the depths of the hood which she had managed to draw over her head she bit out the word "Yankees!"

Kirk edged closer to the light. "Yes. But you're no Reb, not by your accent."

She steadied a tremor in her voice. "That's no concern of yours."

With his free hand Kirk took off his kepi, tucked it under his arm. "My name won't mean anything to you, but I am Kirk Stedman, Captain, Union Cavalry. I'll be glad to let go of your cloak if you'll promise not to bolt, but I really must ask a question or two."

"You can't make me answer!"

Kirk moved into the gray light, bowing. "I don't think you'll mind what I ask. First, what is a neutral doing here?"

"I'll tell you nothing about myself or about my friends."

"Oh! Nothing *aboot* yourself or *aboot* your friends? How long is it since you saw Toronto? Or shall we just say the north shore of Lake Ontario? Please don't try to run. People are pretty busy out there and they *might* stow you with the Reb prisoners until they could find an officer to question you."

"Those prisoners are my friends. I'd be proud to be with them."

"But you're really better off here. In a few minutes we'll be starting out again—ah, starting *north*, that is. Then you can go where you please. But how about answering me, just as a matter of military routine?"

He caught the flash of her eyes under her hood. "You're really going back north soon?" Some of the

52

tenseness left her voice. "Very well, I *am* Canadian. Also, U.E.L. You know what those letters mean?"

"They mean United Empire Loyalists, the people who left the Colonies during the Revolution. You see, I've learned a little history."

She said sharply, "In Canada, children grow up with history, they don't have to learn it, and they know that everything bad that's happened to them has come from the Yankees. The U.E.L.'s were driven from the Colonies by your Yankee *patriots* for standing by the Crown. People remember how your Yankee army burned and looted our homes in 1814, my grandfather's among them. And Yankees came across the lake during the Mackenzie troubles and helped him against the Crown and burned and looted again. And that wasn't so long ago, because your people wrecked my father's lumber fleet. No, I'm not a neutral. Very few Canadians are, real Canadians, that is."

Kirk smiled. "I suppose not, since I can name a good dozen U.E.L.'s who wear the same uniform that I do. But we still have my question—what is this particular non-neutral doing here?"

She let her hands drop wearily by her sides. "Your duties can't be terribly exacting if they give you time to badger. Very well—my father's business is in Richmond, representing a British house owned by British cousins. We've been here since '61, importing things. He was asked to testify for the government at a court-martial here, something about supplies and—"

"He was with the court? Of course, he'll be turned loose as an alien citizen, but I might be able to hurry his release if he's being held. We captured the whole lot, you know."

She seemed somehow disconcerted by his suggestion and her tone was a little less edged as she answered, "Oh, he went west up the tracks with friends on a handcar after he'd testified. I got tired of waiting for him so I

53

came here to get a book from the chaise just when your men rode in."

"H'm," said Kirk. "You made very good time coming up here from Richmond, with the roads all crowded with Reb infantry."

"We broke the journey with friends at Ashland." Impatience came back into her voice. "Would you like to know what we had for breakfast?"

"Not very much." He paused, then went on casually. "But it must have been annoying, pulling up all the time for those infantry columns on the narrow roads."

She stamped her foot. "There *wasn't* any infantry or cavalry or anything. And a man I know—he just came in from Richmond this morning—said that the roads were still empty."

"He's an officer?"

"Why should you care? Very well, he *was* an officer— until your humanitarian army wounded him and sent him to that awful prison at Elmira in New York State. He was from South Carolina. He'd never seen snow before. You froze him up there until he lost a hand and a foot. You laughed at him when he and his friends asked for warmer clothes. You said if the uniforms and blankets were warm enough to rebel in, they were warm enough to be prisoners in. You starved him, and he and his friends could see great harvests being brought in from the fields around the prison."

"Elmira was bad," said Kirk gravely. "Very bad. There's been a change there and some officers have gone to jail."

She threw back her head and the hood slipped down about her neck. Kirk gave a quick, silent intake of breath as he saw a mass of corn-colored hair, deep blue eyes that snapped at him, a full, generous mouth and a firm chin. She went on, her voice shaking a little. "How very just that was! And has the great Mr. Lincoln written letters of sympathy to the families of those officers? Jail! You all ought to be there. You've killed my friends, lots of them. You're slowly killing the rest, starving them with your blockade." She moved a little farther into the light and Kirk saw a flush rising under her clear cheeks. "Old men and babies and sick women—you're killing them all. If they live out in the country, you burn the roofs over their heads, strip their storehouses. And your tenderhearted President frees the poor Negroes so that they wander off and starve, too. You call *that* war?"

Kirk nodded. "I'm afraid I do. It's the way it always has been and probably always will be. If it gives you any pleasure, I may tell you that there are a great many homes in mourning in the North, too. As for the rest, the devastation and so on—no, you won't find much of that in the North, mainly because the Rebs have never managed to establish themselves there."

Her blue eyes blazed at him and her lips drew back over small white teeth. "You *can't* say that! My friends would never—"

"No one's friends would ever. That's inconceivable. But so is war."

"Have you any more questions, Captain Stedman?"

"Just one. You seem to have been studying me rather closely. Why?"

She gave a cold little smile. "I've seen a great many Yankees going through Richmond on their way to Libby Prison. But they've just been faces. Someday you'll go to Libby, like the rest. I'll recognize you."

"And that'll make some Southern triumph less impersonal to you?"

"Just that."

"If I'm stupid enough to be caught, I shan't begrudge you your feeling of victory. I'll even watch for that Confederate gray cloak that you wear, I suppose, to show your sympathies. It's really very becoming, especially with its canary lining." He turned his head quickly. In the distance, men were shouting. "That means we're off. Please stay in the shed until we've left. And don't start south too soon. You might get tangled in our columns."

"But you said you were going north!"

"So we are. But it takes a little time and space to gather up seven or eight thousand men and start them home. Some of the outfits will have to circle to the south to reach the North Anna fords assigned them." He bowed. "Good luck. And since you know my name, may I know yours?"

"Thank you. You may not!"

Kirk bowed again, turned on his heel and strode off in the direction of the shouting. By a little path, he looked toward the shed. The girl still stood in the entrance, her back resolutely toward him. A gust of wind whipped up the hem of her cloak, showing a wide corner of canary lining. She bent quickly to arrange the gray cloth and a lock of corn-colored hair slipped from under her hood and across her shoulder. A small hand flew up and deft fingers tucked the tress into place. Her head turned with the gesture and Kirk's eyes met hers across twenty yards of winter-killed grass. Then she vanished into the shed with a flounce.

He stepped out along the path, his lips pursed in a soundless whistle. "Whew! That was a pretty girl! Don't know that I ever saw a prettier. And enough spunk for an Army Corps. Hope it did her good to get off that blast about Yankees. She sure had accumulated enough. Brought up to think of us all as having cloven hoofs and then living in that Richmond atmosphere since '61! I was the personification of everything she'd learned from her grandparents and everything she's heard in Richmond. Damn odd kind of a tête-à-tête. H'm, wonder if she'll remember to tell her Reb friends that we're heading back north right away. It may help us if she does. And she might at least have wished me a pleasant trip to Libby."

5

Lost Column

At the South Anna, Jake unerringly led the command through a black and streaming night to the secret ford that he had noted months before and the troopers splashed across, plunged on in dripping darkness. Miles later a wretched bivouac was made in drenched woods. Unsaddled horses, secured by picket pins driven into the soaking ground, turned their tails apathetically to the drift of the rain and stood motionless, heads down. Their riders lay under trees, by black rocks or simply in the spots where they had dropped after tending to their mounts, oblivious of the drip and trickle that fell on them.

Kirk tried to sleep, but the poison of overfatigue jabbed at his nerves, snapped his eyelids open, sent tingling waves up his back and shoulders. Groaning, he rose from his bed of soaking leaves. His knees buckled and his feet burned as he stamped about, blundering into horses, weaving past sleeping men. He began to walk with more assurance and his senses quickened until he felt that he could hear the patter of the smallest raindrop, detect the slightest smell, see quite clearly in the black woods. It was all deceptive, he knew, symptoms of increasing exhaustion, like the sudden lift of spirits that set him whistling softly, stepping out briskly with his head up and shoulders back. Later, he would pay for this unwholesome stimulation as a man paid for the exaltation of whiskey or a drug.

A few men were stirring uneasily under the trees. Fires would have been impossible, even if not forbidden, and some of the sleepless troopers were gnawing at raw bacon or chewing coffee. There were other people about, too, moving in a clearing just ahead. Dahlgren's voice, surprisingly buoyant, called, "Where's the Signal Corps officer? Oh, didn't see you, Mr. Bartley. All ready?" Kirk came out from under the trees and saw the Colonel moving toward a kneeling group and a droopheaded pack horse. Someone said, "We'll try it anyway, sir."

A shielded match flared, lit up a signal rocket in its propped-up trough. Sparks fizzed, then died. Another match. This time the fuse caught cleanly. There was a rush of sparks, a whooshing sound and the rocket soared into the night. Kirk held his breath, waiting for the burst high in the sky. Something far, far up made a faint plop, but there was no wide shower of stars, no red glow. A man by the trough stood up. "I was afraid of that, Colonel. Seems to be a kind of fog hanging up there. Saw the same thing in the Shenandoah."

"Is there a chance that General Kilpatrick's column saw it?"

"I'd like to say yes, sir."

"Thanks for the truth, anyway. You and your men better get some sleep now. And would you mind telling my orderly over there that I want Captain Stedman?"

Kirk came closer. "Present, sir."

"That's fine!" exclaimed Dahlgren. "I'm making a

58

change in your job. The command will move out well before sunrise. You'll leave a half hour ahead of it. Make for the same spot we've talked about all along. Drop markers the way Pitler did."

Kirk said incredulously, "A half-hour start? How will your command pick up my trail? I've not enough men to string out between here and where we're going!"

"You won't have to. You probably don't know this, but a scout overtook us after we left Spotsylvania. He knows the country around here perfectly and he'll be able to guide us to your first marker."

"A scout? Who sent him?" asked Kirk sharply.

Dahlgren called, "The dark lantern, Sergeant. Thanks." A thin yellow shaft cut through the rain and fell on a paper.

Kirk bent over the sheet. "Dear Colonel," he read. "At the last moment I have found the man for you. . . . Question him five minutes and you will find him the very man you want. Respectfully and truly yours, John Babcock."

The light was cut off and Dahlgren went on. "This scout, Eben Scudder, will take us right to you. You may have something of a wait, because we're going to scatter more Amnesties. And another thing you'd better know, though it won't affect you directly. I'm detaching Captain Mitchell, 2nd New York, with about two hundred men. He'll start after I do and take our prisoners, the wagon, the ambulance and Bartley's signal stuff and head for Kilpatrick. On the way he'll smash or burn those government depots we had marked out, so we won't have to bother about them. When my column joins you, the scout, Scudder, will lead the way. Is that clear?"

"Yes, sir. I hit out half an hour before you do. I forget about Mitchell's crowd. I get where I'm going, dropping off markers. Then I wait for you."

"That's it. No matter what happens, wait for us."

"Have you announced our objective to the command yet?"

"No. And don't you, until you begin your waiting. Then tell your men as much as you see fit. By the way, what do you think of the temper of the command?"

"Of course, sir, most of the boys were pretty well rasped at having their furloughs canceled. And they don't like marching blind and in the rain and for so long. They want hot food and they want to sleep. But they'll do."

"God, I'm glad to hear you say that. You're older than I am and you've seen more service. And—here's another thing and I'd like a frank answer. How do the outfits feel about my being in command?"

"They're old-timers. They know the job's too big for a major and too small for a brigadier. You're a colonel. *Ergo.*"

Dahlgren shook his head impatiently. "I'm damn young for a colonel and a lot of people say I got the rank because my father's an admiral."

"Your first steps came pretty fast. But everyone knows about the Jeff Davis to Lee courier you nabbed before Gettysburg. They know those papers let Meade know that Lee'd get no reinforcements. That was worth a couple of jumps in rank."

"Pah!" said Dahlgren. "Ever hear of any rewards given that man who found the lost Reb orders before Antietam? I never did. But since Gettysburg, people have been calling me a glory hunter, saying I'd do anything to change these eagles into stars."

"Not this crowd. They know about your leg. They've seen you up and down the column all through this march. They know you handled them beautifully at Frederick's Hall. You've played no favorites and dodged no chores."

"I came because I had to," said Dahlgren. "You know how it is when a beginner gets thrown from a horse. He's got to get right into the saddle, quick, or he'll be horse-shy the rest of his life. Well, when I was on the Old Gentleman's flagship off Charleston, I got thinking about the shot that mashed my leg and the amputation and all.

"Then I began wondering how I'd feel taking troops into action again with smoky fields and ripped-up horses and the Reb guns going strong. It bothered me badly. So when my stump healed enough and I got my new leg, I headed for Washington, looking for the first real job I could find. I heard about this and talked General Kilpatrick into giving me part of it."

In the dark, Kirk eyed the Colonel with growing respect. "Yes, it sometimes happens that way. You've got to find the answer to wonderings. I'm glad you've found yours."

"No," said Dahlgren abruptly, "I haven't found it and I won't find it just riding back of the Reb lines. It'll take a lot of Rebs and a lot of guns to give it to me. I—I wonder what it'll be."

Forgetting rank, Kirk laid his hand on the Colonel's wet shoulder. "So long as you've got this drive to keep looking, the answer's bound to be the one you want."

"Thanks. I appreciate that from you," said Dahlgren quietly. "I'll send word when it's time for you to start. Then I'll see you on the other side of the James."

Through a mist-filled morning, Kirk led his troop south down a deep, nearly dry watercourse. The ragged, red-walled gash twisted, slanted, almost doubled back on itself, straightened, twisted again. Kirk's eyes smarted as he stared ahead and his jaw muscles ached from the unconscious clenching of his teeth. He swayed in the saddle, looking ahead, looking right and left. Would the gully never end? *Was* it the right one?

Suddenly he threw an arm high in the halt signal and heard the clatter and shuffling behind him as his men reined in. Then he sat, frozen, in the saddle. The watercourse ended in a wide flare and a broad river lay before him. Arms crossed on the pommel, he studied it, and each detail that he saw seemed to light a flare of recognition in his memory. The deep-looking water, the clustered islets that trailed away east downstream, the low mist-crowned bluffs on the far shore, the dead road that ended short of the water over there. He muttered, "Done it, by God."

Just behind him Tom Latham's voice sounded. "Getting sort of ready to tell us *what* we've done, sir?"

Kirk gathered his reins. "Let's get the boys across. Then I'll give 'em the story." He swept his arm ahead—"For-*ward!*"—and set Roquefort splashing into the stream. Behind him a trooper yelled, "Big river! By Jesus, I bet it's the Potomac. We're Steveburg bound."

Kirk stifled a derisive laugh high in his throat. The Potomac! He pulled himself up quickly. Just another fatigue symptom. He would have to watch such impulses to sudden laughter or anger. They could lead to indecision, recklessness or even panic. He was among the islets, stirrups well above the water. There was the biggest islet. That must be skirted close to its west end. The little jagged one. The sandy spit with the shack on it. The bushy islet where the water looked smooth and deep. On he went, feeling his way across the ford that memory alone told him existed, that could not have been guessed from either bank.

Then the islets were behind him and Roquefort heaved and scrambled his way up onto the south bank. On the level ground beyond the bluffs Kirk dismounted stiffly and watched the troop clear the ford. There was no need to call roll as the troopers toiled on toward him. Twenty men. Add the six dropped off earlier as route markers for Dahlgren and the count was complete, the same number that had left Stevensburg on the night of February twenty-eighth. This was the morning of March first. How many units in Dahlgren's command could report "All present or accounted for" at such a stage of such a march?

He dismounted his men, told them to form a half circle about him.

Then he began to speak, slowly at first as he forced himself through the opaque shell of fatigue that always threatened to close about him. "You've done a fine job, every one of you, getting down here, and now I can tell you what we've come for. I've heard you guessing about where we were. Well, that's the James River we just crossed."

There was a stir among the troopers, mutters of "The *James?* What the hell we doin' way down here?"

Kirk went on. "Now listen carefully. Colonel Dahlgren and the rest are going to meet us here. Then we'll all hit east down the south bank. When we get opposite Richmond, we'll see an island. Maybe you've heard of it—Belle Isle."

A man muttered, "God damn hell-hole prison. My brother died there."

Kirk watched the narrowing eyes fixed on him. "All right. Those prisoners are what the whole expedition's for. We'll hit Belle Isle, smash the prison guards, release all the prisoners, arm as many as we can with stuff we know's there. Then, prisoners and all, we get back to the south bank, cross the James again over Mayo's Bridge and bust right into Richmond. In the city we'll meet General Kilpatrick with his three thousand men who'll have broken in from the north."

An awed voice said, "Right into Richmond? Jesus! What we do then?"

"Do? Why, we'll have done what we came to do, freed a good many thousand of our own people and brought them out with us. General Kilpatrick's force is strong enough to keep anyone from bothering us. That's the *only* reason he's there. We count on arming at least two thousand of the Belle Isle men. The job's done and we'll all hit back for Steve'burg, we and Kilpatrick and the prisoners. If we find that Lee's sent a big crowd down from Orange to cut us off, we'll slide southeast down the York peninsula where General Butler's got a lot of men waiting for us—just in case. And one more thing: When we get into Richmond, loot all you like, raise hell with the civilians—if you want your heads knocked off. Any man who wanders away isn't apt to see the troop again. He probably won't see sunset." He turned to Latham. "There's a shed and an abandoned house over there. Horses into the shed, saddles and bridles off, good rubdown. Pool all rations. Throw mine in, too. Smoke won't show in the mist, so fires'll be all right. Keep five mounted men circling the camp in a half-mile radius. Relieve them every half hour. Men off duty can sleep in the house."

"Right, sir," said Latham. Then his tone altered. "Better find a dry corner for yourself, sir. Clancy and I'll see to things."

"Can't settle down. I'm going to that rise there where I can get a good view of the north bank. Send me some bacon and coffee when the men have theirs."

Rain fell again before noon, a fine, drilling drizzle that hissed up the valley of the James and beat against Kirk's face as he sat crouched in the first sleep that he had known since leaving Stevensburg. He woke with a start, aware of the passage of time only by the slightly stronger intensity of light. He rolled to his feet, rubbing his eyes and staring across to the north bank. It and the wet lands back of it were empty as ever. Empty and— He snatched out his glasses, focused them on the broken ground that stretched away to the north. He swore under his breath, adjusted the lenses and looked again. He had lost whatever it was that had been moving off there. Much of the winding dirt road was hidden by dips and folds, but a column like Dahlgren's was too long to be swallowed up in the contours.

Then he froze, fingers biting into his glasses. There was no column. Just a single blue rider coming south at a labored gallop. A single rider! Kirk scrambled down to

64

the ford, shouting in relief as he saw one of his patrols close by. "Frazer!" he called. "Can you find your way back to the north bank?"

"Sure, Cap."

"Get over, quick. A marker is coming in alone. Bring him here!"

In a few moments Frazer was back, another trooper following. Kirk forced himself to stand quietly, as though waiting for a routine report. "Anything wrong out there, Goodwin?" he asked in an easy voice.

Goodwin dropped from the saddle, his chest heaving. "Orders were not to hit south till Lynch brought the column on. But I took a cast back to where you left Lynch. He wasn't there."

Kirk tried to mask the shock of the news. "You took a good look?"

"Long as I dared. And I found plenty along that track that forks off to the east, the one Lynch was supposed to keep the column from taking. But they took it. Hoof marks and wheel marks. A busted 1st Vermont canteen, a 1st Maine blanket, a wore-out blouse with 5th New York buttons. Lots of horse droppings."

"Many wheel marks?"

"Couldn't tell. The old ruts were deep and wheels wouldn't show in 'em like on new ground. I started back and went on to Carey's post, just below mine, and sent him back to stay at Lynch's, just in case I'd misread the signs and our crowd was still to come. But I tell you, sir, I had a good look at that turnoff when we dropped Joe Lynch and I swear there'd been nothing bigger'n a chipmouse on it then. Looks to me like the whole command took the wrong turn and snaked Lynch along with 'em. It all happened more'n a good hour ago, because the droppings weren't too fresh and the bushes under the wore-out blouse were dry."

"Good work. You used your head," said Kirk. "You'll find coffee at that house up there. Keep your news to yourself and tell the first sergeant I want to see him."

When Goodwin had gone, Kirk stood looking at the slow flood of the James.

It was obvious that Dahlgren had taken the east fork, far back there, and was now miles distant on the north bank. It was impossible to guess why he had taken that wrong turn, and why he had failed to send word to Kirk, and what had happened to Lynch. But the Colonel's orders remained unchanged. Cross to the south bank and wait for the rest of the column. No alternative had been remotely suggested. Mitchell, of course, would not cross the ford, but would continue east, as originally planned, on the far bank along the Goochland—Richmond road toward Dover Mills and the canal installations.

What, then? Dahlgren, for reasons of his own, might have ordered Mitchell to send word on to Kirk. Therefore, the only thing to do was wait until there was sure evidence that Mitchell, too, had taken the same wrong fork as Dahlgren. Any court-martial would uphold such a course, and damn any diversion from it.

Latham came skittering down the bank, jaws moving as though he had been disturbed in the midst of a belated meal. "Column sighted, sir?"

"Not yet. Patrols report anything?"

"Countryside all deserted, sir. Trooper Dingerdiesen says he spotted heavy smoke down-river on the north bank. I went to take a look, but it's hard to be sure in this mist."

"Smoke? Wait here." Kirk ran quickly up to the high point where he had watched earlier and leveled his glasses as he looked east. It *was* hard to be sure, as Latham had said. Mist rolled and eddied, now thick, now thin. Then a faint, sullen glow showed through, a low black cloud rose slowly, bellied out before the mist curtains closed about it.

Kirk turned. "Latham!" he called. "Pull in your patrols. Boots and saddles for the rest of the troop. When they're mounted, bring them down here to the ford. Make 'em step fast."

Latham raced off and Kirk raised his glasses again. He thought that he could make out another smoke bank beyond the first that he had seen. Dover Mills and the canal installations! That could only mean that the traces that Goodwin had seen by the turnoff had come from Mitchell's command as well as Dahlgren's. Now Mitchell's men were burning and smashing far downstream. And Dahlgren? He would be well beyond Mitchell on the Goochland—Richmond road and still on the north bank.

Kirk snapped his glasses into their case. "All I can figure is that Dahlgren got word of a better ford, closer to Belle Isle, and he's making for it." He frowned. "But who the hell did he get it from and why didn't he pull me in? 'Cross the ford and *wait.*' No if's or or's." When he heard the shuffle of tired horses heading for the ford, he dropped down to meet them. As he mounted Roquefort he was aware of curious stares from swollen-eyed troopers. Disregarding the mute questioning, he signaled "Forward" and drove his horse into the James again. On the north bank he watched his little command emerge.

"All right, Sergeant Latham, give Goodwin a fresh horse and send him back up the road north to bring in the markers. They'll pick us up on that track that runs east about a half mile above the river road." He scribbled a few lines in his notebook, tore out a page. "That'll be Goodwin's authority."

Riding into the drifting rain he watched his troopers, surprisingly alert after their brief rest, moving easily on, keeping twenty yards between each man. They looked big and formidable in their caped overcoats, with their carbines against their hips or carried across saddlebows. If trouble were encountered, Kirk could very simply draw them into column on the rutted path again.

He gave a start of surprise as he rode by a neat white house. He had probably gone past a good many during the dark hours, but the route from the night camp to the James had led through abandoned fields and empty, gullied lands. A curtain moved in the nearest window and a woman's face, pale and set, peered cautiously out. Kirk lifted his hand to his visor in a gesture that he hoped was reassuring and pointed ahead to show that no halt was intended. "Odd," he thought, "I've ridden across a good slice of Virginia this trip and that's the first civilian I've seen since—since—"

Then he remembered Frederick's Hall Station and a battered shed and a girl with river-blue eyes and a mass of corn-colored hair. "Canadian and both sides of my family U.E.L.! And I am *not* a neutral!" His memory recaptured her voice and he wished that he could have heard that voice when it was not hard with anger and defiance. Even so, it had been hauntingly pretty.

There were more houses showing dimly through the mist—a low cottage clinging to a slope among bare black apple trees, a cluster of chimneys and a wide roof above a ridge to the left. The ground grew rougher and his troopers were being forced back toward the old cart path. From a cabin door on the right a lean, bald old man in worn jeans stormed shakily into a fenced garden, fiddle in one hand, bow in the other. The fiddle snapped up under the withered chin, the bow swept and a thin, defiant melody cut into the air. The nearest troopers grinned and waved, then began to sing, "What matter if our shoes are worn? What matter if our feet be torn? Quickstep! We're with him before morn! That's Stonewall Jackson's way!" The old man shook fiddle and bow at them, struck up his air again. The men called, "Good for you, Grandpop! Keep a-sawin'." Kirk nodded to the fiddler and rode on, the last bars of "Stonewall Jackson's Way" following him.

The wind was blowing up from the river and the air was acrid with wood smoke mixed with a heavier, oily smell. Burning wood and burning grain! The sinister smell served as an infallible signpost. Kirk was abreast of and well above the first of Mitchell's demolitions, out of sight though they were.

Shouts and hoofbeats from the rear swung him about in his saddle. Goodwin was bringing up the markers as ordered. Goodwin panted that the country over which he and his fellows had passed was quiet. Carey had taken several casts about in the region of Lynch's old post, but had found nothing to explain that trooper's disappearance. Kirk sent the men on to join the extended line. When—and if—Dahlgren was overtaken, many mysteries as well as Lynch's ought to be solved. In the meantime, there was nothing to do but keep pushing on.

They were in column down on the river road with the canal at their left and a point of four troopers thrown out some fifty yards in advance. There was no questioning the evidence of the highway. Wheels and many hoofs had passed over it, headed east, not very long before. And here were two heavy canalboats canted crazily in the water and oozing out a loathsome porridge of scorched wheat and corn. They were closing in on Mitchell's rear. Kirk was about to signal a trot when he heard shouts from the men ahead. They had halted and were staring up into a grove of oaks.

Kirk broke away from the troop and cantered toward the four troopers. Close by them he reined in. A young Negro, his face horribly distorted and arms bound, was hanging from a thick branch. Kirk asked sharply, "Dead?"

"Dead'r'n hell, sir, and he's hanging by one of *our* halter shanks, the new kind."

Kirk stared in revulsion. "Why? In God's name, *why?*"

A worn, hard-faced trooper shrugged. "He ain't said."

Another cried, "I seen him before, at the last camp. He and a scout had a lit candle under a blanket, looking at a paper."

"What scout?" asked Kirk sharply. "Rowan?"

"New feller. I heard this'n', hangin' up in the tree, call him Mr. Scudder."

69

Scudder! The man sent to Dahlgren by John Babcock, best known and most reliable scout in the Army. Had the Negro been detected in some hostile act by Scudder? Perhaps the poor devil had persuaded Dahlgren to take that left fork with a false promise of a better ford over the James. Or the Negro may have been bona fide and, straying from the column, been snapped up by Home Guard patrols and hanged with the halter shank of his own mount. Kirk was inclined to doubt this, but if it were true, it could mean that local levies were between him and Dahlgren.

He split the troop into two columns, each keeping to the soft ground on either side of the plank road to avoid the noise of hoofs on boards, and pushed ahead. Normally it might have been sounder practice to form a skirmish line, but Home Guards, unused to combat, could be better brushed aside by a compact charge in column. The way wound on, entered a stretch of dense, high second growth that limited visibility to a few yards in any direction. The road dipped, straightened a little and he could look some fifty yards ahead.

Kirk reined in, holding up his hand, and the confused shuffle behind told him that the troop had halted with him. He loosened the flap of his holster, made another gesture and heard the quick rustle of troopers sliding from their saddles. There was really no need for those arm signals. His men could see as well as he could the stirring of sapling tops fifty yards ahead, could hear the growing crackle of underbrush, the ring of a hoof against a rock. And, like him, they heard one single new sound, the tiny unmistakable snick of a carbine being cocked.

6

Journey's End

From among the trees ahead came a shout, "Hey, for Chris'sake, what kep' you?" The woods and the plank road boiled with blue troopers loping along on foot, waving their carbines. The D.C.I.T. sent up an answering whoop: "What kep' you?" Kirk dropped from his horse and ran toward Jake, who had stopped at the edge of the road. "For God's sake, what's been happening?"

Jake shook Kirk by the arm. "Happening? Nothing, except the usual, which is D Troop getting sent back to pull you baboons out of trouble."

"I'm serious. How about that Negro hanging back there?"

"No one's hanging or going to get hanged, except maybe you when Dahlgren sees you. He's plenty mad at you for taking so long when he sent for you. He'd chewed up most of his sword blade when I left and he's probably starting on the hilt right now. Mount up and I'll ride with you and help you think up a story that'll

71

make him happy as a pinkle-tink in a swamp. What made you so late, anyway?"

Jake's grin vanished as he pulled in beside Kirk at the rear of the column. "Look, I've been acting like a Christmas carol just to keep the boys from slumping. But everything's spilled over like a bucket of hot pitch, gone wrong as hell. We're still on the north bank. Mitchell's crowd, that was supposed to circle up around the north of Richmond and join Kilpatrick, caught up with us and you ought to have seen Mitchell's face. He thought we were all across on the south bank where we damn well ought to be. God, here's daylight wasting and we should be hitting Belle Isle right now. I don't know the reason for anything, why we altered course or what. I don't know anything about a Negro getting hanged."

"You're sure Dahlgren hasn't found another ford?" asked Kirk.

"Ford? He's found nothing but deep water and an old, leaky scow that wouldn't stand the weight of a hop frog."

Kirk told briefly of his wait, of the news of the disappearance of the vital marker, Lynch, and of his own decision to cross to the north bank against orders and follow it east.

Jake pushed his kepi over his eyes. "Oof! So if we'd kept on to your ford, we'd be closing on Belle Isle this minute. Damned if I know what went wrong. We just kept marching and marching. I never saw your man, Lynch, but then, I was so puff-eyed that I could have ridden past a dozen saloons without knowing it. I never knew you weren't down the column somewhere till Dahlgren began sending word along asking about you."

"No sign of Kilpatrick?"

"Not that I know of. Bartley, the signal officer, sent up a rocket half an hour ago, but the rain and the mist kind of squidged it out."

"Dahlgren act worried?"

Jake shook his head. "That boy's a soldier. Rides

along easy, humming to himself, and the boys pick up just at the sight of him. We stopped near a big house up the line, carriage houses, slave quarters, barns, nice driveway and all, and damned if Dahlgren doesn't go in, *alone*, just a whoop and a holler from Richmond. Might have been ten Reb colonels on leave, sitting in the best parlor ready to grab him. We got worried, especially when he didn't come out and didn't come out."

Kirk whistled. "You'd have been justified in rushing the place."

"Some of us were talking about just that when the front door opened and he comes out onto the porch with a nice-looking old lady in lavender. They look like something out of a book, bowing and smiling, and then a colored man brings out a tray with a couple of silver cups on it and the two toast each other and he kisses her hand and comes down the steps real elegant and she waves a little handkerchief at him. All the boys had been watching him drink and there wasn't a one of 'em who wouldn't have done murder for a drop of day-old whiskey, but damned if they didn't give him a cheer. See? The whole picture made 'em feel kind of as if they'd had a drink and bowed to a nice old lady themselves. Heard later she's the wife of the Reb Secretary of the Treasury, Seddon, and Dahlgren's old man had been a beau of hers back when he was a midshipman or something."

"Catching the fancy of the men doesn't make a soldier, Jake. Remember McClellan."

"There's a hell of a lot more than that. Dahlgren's young, but he's learned, or figured for himself, the most important duty of a cavalry commander. See to the horses before the men, the men before the officers, and the officers before yourself. That's something that little Kilpatrick never found out, and a lot of others we've ridden under."

"Yes. But apparently Dahlgren's made one very bad

mistake on this ride, or we wouldn't be on the north bank of the James."

"Ever figure that maybe the mistake was made *for* him? You and I are just troop commanders. A courier may have caught up with Dahlgren, giving him orders you and I wouldn't know about."

Kirk nodded. "I hope that's it, Jake. I'd hate to have him stick his foot into something. How much farther?"

"Ought to be close to hailing distance. God, but it's getting dark fast. I wouldn't want to be taking a sloop up the Piscataqua channels in such dark. There we are. 5th Michigan pickets just ahead. I'll steer you to Dahlgren."

Having turned the troop over to Latham, Kirk found Dahlgren leaning against an oak, a crutch wedged under his arm. The Colonel acknowledged Kirk's salute. "I hope you didn't run into any trouble, Captain," he said pleasantly, though gravely.

"That's something I want to find out, sir," answered Kirk, studying the young face under the shadow of the kepi. Dahlgren's eyes looked desperately tired and his pale skin was more drawn than ever, so that his cheekbones stood out sharply, but his mouth, framed by silky mustache and goatee, was firm. Kirk went on. "I left markers and reached the ford. Then I learned that my first marker had vanished and that the road showed signs of your passage east, sir, not south to the James. I took it on myself to cancel your orders, cross to the north bank and follow the Richmond plank road east."

Dahlgren balanced on his crutch. "Vanished? But he had orders from me, personally rendered, to bring in the markers and your troop and follow that turning after me."

"He never delivered them, sir. And I had no way of knowing your change of route."

"Of course not. But it's extraordinary, really." His jaw tightened. "I'm afraid, Captain, that there's been treachery. A young Negro came into camp, after you left, with

74

news of a ford, better and closer to Belle Isle. The scout, Scudder, backed him up. I ordered your recall and took that upper road east. There is no ford, no ferry. Under military usage, I—I felt bound to hang the Negro, since his treachery was obvious."

Kirk started. "The Negro came in *after* I left, sir? Then I can tell you a little more about him. He was in camp well *before* my troop left. One of my men saw him. He was huddled under a blanket studying a map by candlelight—with Scudder."

Dahlgren's shoulders sagged so that the crutch pushed one arm higher than the other. Then he straightened himself. "Scudder's gone. I thought at first he might be taking a cast off by himself. You know how independent all those scouts are. But I do not believe that we'll see him again. And even if I did find him, what could I do? Just another hanging." He was silent for a moment. Then he raised his head. "No blame attaches to you, Captain. And we're still a combatant force, about as strong as when we started out." His voice gained power. "There's still no reason at all why we can't keep our rendezvous with General Kilpatrick—and in Richmond. I issued a lot of captured coffee a little while ago. Better see that you and your men get some. Just have them stand to horse, as the other outfits are doing, and—is that trooper looking for me? No, he seems to be after you, Captain."

Kirk turned and saw Trooper Lynch, still managing to look smart despite a mud-spattered uniform. "My missing marker, Colonel. Do you want to question him?"

Lynch's story was quickly told. After Dahlgren's column had passed him, taking the east fork, a trooper had ridden up to him with a written order, which he produced, telling him to wait and then join on to the rear of Mitchell's column when it passed him. The order had been given the trooper by a staff officer and was signed *"Ulrich Dalhgren."*

The Colonel dismissed Lynch. Kirk observed, "You

75

never wrote that, sir. Sounds like the work of some civilian trying to act military. And you'd never misspell your own names. Do you suppose, sir, that the staff officer who passed this message on happened to be named Scudder?"

"I should think it quite likely. Not that we can do anything about it. Now as for plans—I've conferred with Captain Mitchell and with Captain Myrick, commanding the Maine unit. We've mapped out a general course. You better close in on D of Maine as usual and—"

Both men turned abruptly, staring north and east. Faint but unmistakable, a muttering growl swelled somewhere far out of sight. A passing trooper cried out, "Christ, what a climate. Freeze your butt with sleet and then comes thunder!" A second snapped at him. "Thunder, you God-damn recruit. Won't you never learn? That's artillery, firing off Richmond-way."

"I think, Captain," said Dahlgren, "that you'd better join your command at once. That's got to be General Kilpatrick."

Dahlgren's whole command was flowing east along the plank road that ran across little plateaus, dipped down sharp grades to creeks, rose again. The country was fairly open and the D.C.I.T. rode beside Jake's men, followed by the four other Maine troops. Well out in front, Kirk saw the 5th Michigan moving in extended order, a screen of mounted and dismounted troopers ahead of it. They nosed slowly, almost timidly, Kirk thought, until his eye picked out regular masses of earth shouldering up right and left. Redoubts and trenches! They were unoccupied, but the next line might not be, or the next. Kirk tilted his head to catch the distant mutter of Kilpatrick's guns. They seemed louder and clearer.

Kirk rallied himself. Perhaps things were not going so badly after all. Dahlgren would attack the southwest defenses of Richmond, break through and meet Kilpatrick's far bigger force, battering down from the north

76

and northwest into the city. Once joined there, Belle Isle could be taken and perhaps even grim Libby Prison in Richmond itself. If matters were handled properly, a brilliant coup could still be brought off.

Jake called across, "Getting dark. About time to go home to supper!"

Kirk rubbed his reddened eyes. A thin gloom was filling the hollows, hugging the crests. He caught the attention of his men, rolled his right sleeve to the elbow. In a moment, the right arms of all his troop showed white against their uniforms. It was a precaution to lessen the chance of his rear rank's firing at their fellows ahead of them in the dark. Jake shouted, "Hey, it doesn't hurt much to ride with a man like you after all. D Troop! Roll up your curtains!" Bare arms showed in the Maine troops.

Dahlgren and Captain John Myrick, commander of the Maine contingent, rode out of a side path. For all the jingle of equipment, the churn of hundreds of hoofs, Kirk felt an odd hush settle down. He heard someone far in the rear cough sharply, caught the clink of a hoof against a rock. Dahlgren's voice, faint but clear, drifted back to him. "A little more briskly, 5th Michigan, if you please." Some clouds must have thinned off to the west, for a vivid glow spread over the terrain, unearthly, almost phosphorescent. Yet it did nothing to melt the shadows of late afternoon.

Through the numbness of fatigue, Kirk felt an inner tension grip him, tighten. By an odd trick of memory he was reminded of a time he had ridden over ground where the Rebels had buried torpedoes that the next drop of a hoof might detonate beneath him. He held his reins tighter as he saw a grass-grown redoubt loom just at his right. It was perfectly safe, of course, for he had seen Michigan men scaling its slopes a little while before. Just the same—His fingers clamped on his reins and he watched the skirmishers up the road. They had topped the long slope and were entering a stretch of woodland that bristled ghostly and unreal in the last touches of the livid glow.

He saw the flash before he caught the report, a reddish flame darting out of the trees to the Michigan right. Then the darkening woods erupted, right, left and front, stabbing toward the foremost troopers. Here and there men pitched to the ground. A riderless horse went tearing out of sight over the crest, stirrups lashing at its sides. Dahlgren left Myrick and galloped forward, bending from the saddle and gesturing to the men he passed. The Michigan files were moving slowly and uncertainly, probably because their mounts were spent from galloping about with Amnesties earlier.

Someone cried, "Hey! Looky!" and Kirk saw Dahlgren galloping back down the road, pausing for a word with Captain Myrick and then sweeping on in an arc that brought him close. The Colonel swung his kepi and his head went back proudly. Kirk braced himself against the thought of coming action. Then Dahlgren was calling and something lifted Kirk out of his tension and set him leaning eagerly forward in his saddle. There was an exultant, almost gay ring in the young voice. "All right, 1st Maine. In you go. Captain Myrick will take you. Briskly, now, briskly!"

The contagion of Dahlgren's *élan* was spreading. Troopers straightened in their seats, called to each other and there was a freshness in their tones as though they were recruits riding into their first, flushed action. Kirk shouted, "With you, Jake!" as he swung his men out to adjust to the line that D Troop was forming. He knew a hard, professional satisfaction as the left of the D.C.I.T. closed neatly on Jake's right. Just in front, Dahlgren was pacing his mount broadside to the line, swinging his kepi and laughing full-throatedly as the Maine men yelled, "Yo-ho, let's go! Richmond ahoy!"

Then Dahlgren gave way to Captain Myrick, who cut across the front, steady-eyed and calm as the whole line fanned out. "The command is 'Forward!' " he shouted.

"Pass through Michigan. They're expecting you. Captain Stedman, curve well out to the right. D Troop will conform. Keep closed up, everyone! Forward, State of Maine!"

Kirk was riding over open fields on the flank of his troop and rifles were spitting in the woods on the low crest. He shot a quick glance to the left. The whole Maine line, with two troops on the left of the road, was curving out in a great arc, a whiplash of blue with the D.C.I.T. at the far tip, as though Myrick were trying to flick that lash into the flank and rear of the opposition that Michigan was meeting. Without waiting for Myrick's command, Kirk signaled "Trot!", his eyes darting from the Maine line to the woods, back to Maine again.

There was no need to worry about Jake. D Troop was swinging in harmony with the D.C.I.T., conforming to every change of gait and direction. Again on his own initiative, Kirk ordered "Gallop!" Somewhere to the left Myrick was shouting, "Good, Stedman! But wider, wider!" The horses, intoxicated with the surge of mass movement, lunged on, pelted across a narrow run, broke into a stand of canelike trees that snapped and whipped at them. Kirk strained to hold Roquefort in, fought him back a little to the rear of his right flank. Out of the corner of his eye he saw brass wink and shouted, "Give 'em 'Left oblique,' Music!" The notes sang out and the whole troop veered slightly, burst from the light scrub growth onto open ground that was covered with running men who scrambled out of a shallow trench and raced desperately east.

Kirk was among them, seeing individuals as though by flashes of lightning—a fat, puffing man in beautiful new gray and a scarlet-topped gray kepi; a frightened boy who stumbled on, sobbing, holding his rifle butt-end first, an ink-stained apron flapping under his ragged uniform coat; another dandy in sleek gray and polished boots who fell flat on his face and lay there, hands clasped over the back of his head. Kirk yelled to his men, "Just disarm them. They're only city militia!" He bent from the saddle and twisted a rusty rifle from the hands of a red-faced whiskered man, tossed it aside as he slowed to a trot.

Out of woods to his left burst the rest of the Maine line, Jake closing its right flank. He waved to Kirk. "Myrick says halt and reform. New York and Vermont are coming up behind us."

Kirk checked his men, dressed them on the Maine troopers. "Have any trouble, Jake?"

"Not once we got among 'em. Office workers and draft dodgers and tradesmen and mama boys and dudes. E and F hit something different on the left of the road, though. Hear they got chewed up some."

"Funny. I don't remember hearing any firing after we started. What do we do about the fellows we rode over?"

"Michigan will pick 'em up. Jesus, I wish someone'd light the gas around here. What's that off yonder? Trees or troops?"

Kirk stared off to the east, then said, "Both. We're not riding into Broad Street yet. Look! Flashes off there! Bad fighting, Jake, when you can see the flashes plainer than the men that make 'em. Myrick up yet? I think we better hit ahead on our own say-so, break up that crowd."

As Kirk spoke, Dahlgren shot out of the woods to the rear, followed by Myrick. "Almost there, boys!" shouted the Colonel. "Clear out those woods ahead and we'll see the lights of Richmond. Take them in, Captain Myrick. Vermont and 5th New York are coming up on your left. In with you, now. It'll be just the same as before."

It was not the same as before. Steady volleys crashed out from the trees and Kirk heard heavy falls behind him. When he rode into the woods, the ground was a litter of fallen trees and rocks and ditches that threw the whole line into confusion, and the men back of the flaming rifles were lean, gaunt and ragged. They formed in little knots, back to back, and took the charges, firing, up. Mount, form column and hit west along the plank road. No need to observe silence any more."

"Hit *west?*" cried Kirk, his voice cracking. "What happened?"

A chunky shape near Kirk growled, "We violated four military maxims getting here, so we're going back to Dover Mills and do it all over again. Let's get it right this time, Kirk."

Myrick spoke calmly. "Colonel Dahlgren's found a better point of attack. Form up, Pitler, you and Stedman take the lead with your white-armed boys. That'll be easy for the others to follow in the dark. I'll go just ahead of you. I've a white handkerchief pinned to my back. Guide on it."

Bone-weary and bewildered, Kirk led his troop back to the plank road and headed west. There was no use in speculating on the reason for the withdrawal, though he had a sour certainty that Myrick's words about the better point of attack had been for the troops rather than for his and Jake. An arm reached out of the darkness and touched his shoulder. "Sir," said Latham, "twenty men present in ranks."

"How about the others?"

"Can't tell, sir. I know Dingerdiesen and Grenier and Cathcart got hit. The rest are K.W.M. until we know different. I'll report any stragglers joining us."

Latham dropped back. Six men, K.W.M., killed, wounded or missing. He shivered. The figure was not excessive at all for a confused action in twilight and darkness, but even so——He pushed the matter of losses from his mind. The immediate present was what counted.

When he reached the plank road, quick apprehension banished fatigue and set his mind working. The rough surface was jammed with troopers, who milled aimlessly, spilling over its edges, weaving back onto it again. He heard Michiganders, Vermonters, New Yorkers calling hopelessly for their outfits, cannoning into one another,

thrusting and parrying until Kirk thought he was back in the Shenandoah Valley or on the plains by the Rapidan. Someone must have combed the Richmond hospitals and sent out every man who could walk and carry a rifle.

The woods were clear and Kirk was in the open again, one more stage gained on the road to Richmond. At a brief halt, he ran his eye over the shadowy figures that made up the D.C.I.T. There was no time for a roll call, but he thought that he had about sixteen men with him and Jake's troop to the left looked badly thinned down.

He started over, hoping to find Jake, when Dahlgren appeared out of the twilight. "Pitler? Stedman? Right." The Colonel bent from the saddle and Kirk caught the shimmer of yellow wood lashed under the flaps. The young voice spoke quickly, cheerfully. "Earthworks ahead. I've spoken to Captain Myrick. Dismount your men. Push on. Get as close as you can to the works. They won't be able to see you ten yards away. I'm sending five troops in on each flank. When you hear their fire, hit straight ahead. The Rebs haven't many steady men out here, so don't be afraid of committing everything to the attack. I'll be at the rear of your line when the others go in. Good luck and thank you for fine work so far."

Lying flat on the trampled grass at the far end of the line of dismounted troopers, Kirk could make out nothing ahead save a dark blur that represented the works that he and the others were to strike when the firing on the flank should start. From the rear he could hear confused noises that told him of Dahlgren's other men coming up on the far right and far left. Then voices sounded along the front, apparently only a few yards away—Southern voices calling, "Keep cool! Fire low! Don't run! Just a few cavalrymen, that's all. Don't run!"

His breath went out in a silent whistle. John Myrick had certainly been faithful in carrying out Dahlgren's

84
81

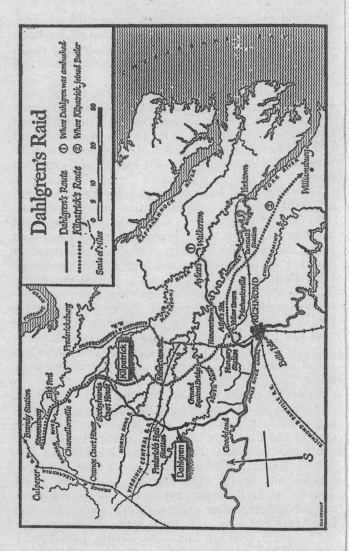

Dahlgren's Raid

① Where Dahlgren was ambushed
② Where Kilpatrick joined Butler

— Dahlgren's Route
······ Kilpatrick's Route

Scale of Miles
0   5   10   20   30

SAM BRYANT

orders to press as close as possible to the earthw
Kirk reached out a hand and touched little Music
suringly on the shoulder and heard his quick pan
grow slower and steadier.

Then he hugged the ground tighter and knew tha
own jaw was trembling. A sudden, furious burst of
ripped out from the defenses, lacing the night
reddish flashes. Experience came to his aid and he k
that the fire was far too high to threaten the waiting
tackers, lying so close in the darkness. A barely perc
ble stir to his left told him that his battle-wise men
reasoning as he reasoned and were relaxing, lister
with him for Union fire from the flanks. The Confe
ate fusillade died away, was renewed, faded again.
raised himself on one elbow, ears straining and h
beating faster. He had forgotten about Kilpatrick's
off in the northeast. Where was their thudding now
sank back, biting at his mustache. There was no so
but the drumming of his own pulses. Where were
guns? Where?

The minutes slipped silently by. Kirk kept bra
himself, relaxing, bracing, waiting for the burst of
that would send him against the works so close in f
Suddenly a hand touched his shoulder and som
whispered, "Captain Myrick's orders. Fall back t
horse holders at once."

"Oh, hell! What now?" thought Kirk as he t
and wriggled his way back to the Number 4's an
horses. "We could have been into the works, sho
before the Rebs could pull a trigger!" When he g
the long hollow where his and the Maine horses
waiting, he rose and saw a faint glimmer of white
as his men and Jake's followed his example. Ther
no white beyond D Troop and Kirk guessed th
other Maine men had rolled down their sleeves in
understandable wish not to make targets of themse

A horseman rode toward him. "That you,
Stedman? I'm Myrick. Good work, keeping your

thrusting and parrying until Kirk thought he was back in the Shenandoah Valley or on the plains by the Rapidan. Someone must have combed the Richmond hospitals and sent out every man who could walk and carry a rifle.

The woods were clear and Kirk was in the open again, one more stage gained on the road to Richmond. At a brief halt, he ran his eye over the shadowy figures that made up the D.C.I.T. There was no time for a roll call, but he thought that he had about sixteen men with him and Jake's troop to the left looked badly thinned down.

He started over, hoping to find Jake, when Dahlgren appeared out of the twilight. "Pitler? Stedman? Right." The Colonel bent from the saddle and Kirk caught the shimmer of yellow wood lashed under the flaps. The young voice spoke quickly, cheerfully. "Earthworks ahead. I've spoken to Captain Myrick. Dismount your men. Push on. Get as close as you can to the works. They won't be able to see you ten yards away. I'm sending five troops in on each flank. When you hear their fire, hit straight ahead. The Rebs haven't many steady men out here, so don't be afraid of committing everything to the attack. I'll be at the rear of your line when the others go in. Good luck and thank you for fine work so far."

Lying flat on the trampled grass at the far end of the line of dismounted troopers, Kirk could make out nothing ahead save a dark blur that represented the works that he and the others were to strike when the firing on the flank should start. From the rear he could hear confused noises that told him of Dahlgren's other men coming up on the far right and far left. Then voices sounded along the front, apparently only a few yards away—Southern voices calling, "Keep cool! Fire low! Don't run! Just a few cavalrymen, that's all. Don't run!"

His breath went out in a silent whistle. John Myrick had certainly been faithful in carrying out Dahlgren's

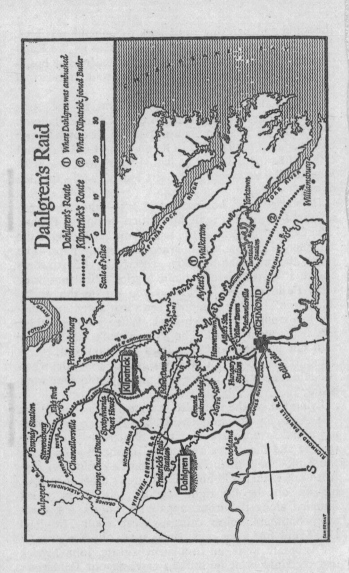

Dahlgren's Raid

Dahlgren's Route
Kilpatrick's Route

① Where Dahlgren was ambushed
② Where Kilpatrick joined Butler

Scale of Miles
0 5 10   20   30

SAM BRYANT

orders to press as close as possible to the earthworks. Kirk reached out a hand and touched little Music reassuringly on the shoulder and heard his quick panting grow slower and steadier.

Then he hugged the ground tighter and knew that his own jaw was trembling. A sudden, furious burst of fire ripped out from the defenses, lacing the night with reddish flashes. Experience came to his aid and he knew that the fire was far too high to threaten the waiting attackers, lying so close in the darkness. A barely perceptible stir to his left told him that his battle-wise men were reasoning as he reasoned and were relaxing, listening with him for Union fire from the flanks. The Confederate fusillade died away, was renewed, faded again. Kirk raised himself on one elbow, ears straining and heart beating faster. He had forgotten about Kilpatrick's guns off in the northeast. Where was their thudding now? He sank back, biting at his mustache. There was no sound but the drumming of his own pulses. Where were the guns? Where?

The minutes slipped silently by. Kirk kept bracing himself, relaxing, bracing, waiting for the burst of fire that would send him against the works so close in front. Suddenly a hand touched his shoulder and someone whispered, "Captain Myrick's orders. Fall back to the horse holders at once."

"Oh, hell! What now?" thought Kirk as he turned and wriggled his way back to the Number 4's and the horses. "We could have been into the works, shooting, before the Rebs could pull a trigger!" When he got to the long hollow where his and the Maine horses were waiting, he rose and saw a faint glimmer of white arms as his men and Jake's followed his example. There was no white beyond D Troop and Kirk guessed that the other Maine men had rolled down their sleeves in a very understandable wish not to make targets of themselves.

A horseman rode toward him. "That you, Pitler, Stedman? I'm Myrick. Good work, keeping your sleeves up. Mount, form column and hit west along the plank road. No need to observe silence any more."

"Hit *west?*" cried Kirk, his voice cracking. "What happened?"

A chunky shape near Kirk growled, "We violated four military maxims getting here, so we're going back to Dover Mills and do it all over again. Let's get it right this time, Kirk."

Myrick spoke calmly. "Colonel Dahlgren's found a better point of attack. Form up, Pitler, you and Stedman take the lead with your white-armed boys. That'll be easy for the others to follow in the dark. I'll go just ahead of you. I've a white handkerchief pinned to my back. Guide on it."

Bone-weary and bewildered, Kirk led his troop back to the plank road and headed west. There was no use in speculating on the reason for the withdrawal, though he had a sour certainty that Myrick's words about the better point of attack had been for the troops rather than for his and Jake. An arm reached out of the darkness and touched his shoulder. "Sir," said Latham, "twenty men present in ranks."

"How about the others?"

"Can't tell, sir. I know Dingerdiesen and Grenier and Cathcart got hit. The rest are K.W.M. until we know different. I'll report any stragglers joining us."

Latham dropped back. Six men, K.W.M., killed, wounded or missing. He shivered. The figure was not excessive at all for a confused action in twilight and darkness, but even so——He pushed the matter of losses from his mind. The immediate present was what counted.

When he reached the plank road, quick apprehension banished fatigue and set his mind working. The rough surface was jammed with troopers, who milled aimlessly, spilling over its edges, weaving back onto it again. He heard Michiganders, Vermonters, New Yorkers calling hopelessly for their outfits, cannoning into one another, cursing, scuffling as they tried to re-form. Kirk saw the white patch on Myrick's back glide along the near edge and followed it, telling his men to link arms to keep their formation from being broken up by stray troopers.

But how about Kilpatrick and the six guns of Ransom's Battery? There was no hint of thudding in the night air now. Of course, Kilpatrick might have broken into Richmond and managed to get word to Dahlgren to join him there. Kirk tried to focus his thoughts on this possibility as he eased past a mixed knot of troopers, but his head rode lower and lower on his shoulders.

Then Dahlgren called from a field to the left, "Who's that with the bare arm? Stedman? Just the man I want." The Colonel rode closer. "There's a column formed just ahead. It's all mixed up, but we can't take time to straighten it out now. Get up to the head, string your men right back to the rear. I'll have Pitler link up with you. Captain Mitchell's got the 2nd New York in pretty good order and he'll act as rear guard. Pitler'll connect him with the rest of us. We've got to get going. I'll join you up front in a few minutes, but if I'm at all delayed, take the column up the first turnoff to the right."

In a few moments, Kirk had found the column and spaced his bare-armed men as widely as he dared along it. When he had word that his last file had connected with Pitler. he tried to size up the formation beside which he was riding. The troopers were keeping quite good order, but a few quick questions told him that they were from several different units. If Dahlgren really meant to attack again, there would have to be a halt to sort out the various commands, to put the men among known comrades and under officers whom they knew and who knew them.

Just in time he sensed a break in the trees to the right and turned the column into it, glad to find soft dirt underfoot instead of the echoing planks. Soon hoofs sounded a weary trot from the rear and Dahlgren pulled in beside Kirk. "That was the correct turn, Stedman. Thank you."

Kirk leaned toward the Colonel. "Going to try a new spot in the Reb lines, sir?"

"No." Dahlgren dropped his voice although the two were well ahead of the leading files. "I called the last attack off because the Rebs were bringing more men into their lines, especially at the right. And two of our units got confused in the dark. You'd have had no support. It's obvious Kilpatrick hasn't been able to break into the city. There's no chance of our getting to the south bank now and hitting Belle Isle. So we'll circle north and east around Richmond and join the General. Then we'll cook up something together. You know the country about the city?"

"Pretty well. From maps, of course. The way we're heading ought to bring us to the Richmond and Fredericksburg Railway below Hungary Station. We cross it bearing about east and we'll pass below Yellow Tavern along the pike that hits Atlee's Station on the Virginia Central, well north of Richmond."

"Perfectly right. I've got the maps in my head as well as in my saddlebags. And somewhere between Yellow Tavern and Atlee's, we'll pick up the General's trail, probably at the Chickahominy Crossings. The river's just a trickle this high up, so we won't have any trouble getting over." Suddenly the confident tone went out of his voice. "Oh, my God, my God! Why the hell did I listen to Scudder? If I'd stuck to the original plan, we'd be on the south bank now with all the Belle Isle men free."

Kirk laid a hand on his shoulder. "You had no reason to doubt Scudder, though we'll probably find out when we get back that Babcock's note's a forgery, like yours to Lynch. You had what looked like a good chance to save time and lives and you took it. No one can blame you for that. And if we *were* on the south bank now with the Belle Isle boys, what good would it do us? Getting ahead from there depended on Kilpatrick's being able to break into Richmond and meet us. He didn't break in. Perhaps he'll be able to when you bring him some four hundred fresh men, now that Captain Mitchell is back with you, to add to his force."

"Of course, of course. That's the immediate thing. Keep the boys in hand and closed up and be ready to hit when we have the chance."

"Right. I'll drop back down the column and see how they're coming along."

Kirk pulled out to the side of the narrow road and watched the leading files float past him, black amorphous shapes. The horses were beginning to stumble with fatigue and the troopers were swaying in their saddles. Kirk called in a low voice to each of his men as they pushed along in wide-spaced single file on the flanks. A bare arm showed in the darkness and someone called, "That you, Cap? This is Clancy. Better drop back and have a look. Flannery passed word up he's having trouble."

"Thanks," said Kirk, wearily turning Roquefort about. He found trouble long before he reached Flannery. Troopers were sleeping as they rode, their mounts blundering on unguided. Here eight or ten riders were tightly bunched in an irregular clot. Then came a stretch of road, ten yards, twenty yards quite empty, a single rider, chin on chest and reins trailing, four or five troopers in the next fifty yards at a dead halt, asleep on their motionless horses.

Kirk rode among them, kicking at horses' rumps, shaking riders' shoulders that sometimes bore an officer's epaulet. All ranks roused willingly enough, pushed on ahead, tried to re-form as best they could. Kirk could only hope that the wakening would last as he pushed and butted and shoved among them. There was no point in trying to save his strength or that of his own troopers. Soon enough the effects of the unscheduled rest that they had all enjoyed on the south bank would wear off and they would be reduced to the state of the others.

There was a wide gap behind a couple of squads of Vermonters who rode on in very fair order. Kirk checked Roquefort and sat listening. The weary shuffle up the road was slowly fading, but he could catch no fresh sounds coming from below. He dropped his hand quickly to his holster as he heard hoof beats swelling from the rear. Then he saw a blur of white and relaxed. "Step it out, back there," he called. "Who are you?"

A hoarse voice answered, "Can't you see our plumes? We're the 10th Royal Bashi-bazooks, who the hell did you think?"

Kirk started Roquefort toward the voice. "Jake! Can't the outfits back of you walk it out a little? There's a bad gap here. Tell 'em to keep right on and they'll strike some Vermonters. Dahlgren's up ahead."

Jake Pitler cantered to meet him. "Sure, sure. They'll close up. Something's gone wrong with my cinch. Mind dropping off and taking a look at it?" He called to a dark mass behind him. "Pick up the step, boys, and you'll ride right up the Green Mountains."

Kirk dismounted by Jake's horse as a succession of half-seen men pushed on up the road. Jake leaned from the saddle. "See what I mean? Keeps slipping out of the ring." He bent lower. "Keep this to yourself. All hell's to pay and no pitch hot. We've lost Mitchell."

Kirk gripped the stirrup leather. "His whole crowd?"

"Yes! The boys have been straggling cruel. I've been casting back and forth keeping things linked up. My last cast, there was nothing to link. We scoured back a mile, two miles. Not a Goddamn sign of Mitchell and more'n two hundred others. They must have curved off down some trail and Christ alone knows where they are now. I had to give up and bring along what I could find, maybe twenty, thirty men and only about a dozen of 'em mine. The rest of D Troop trailed off with Mitchell."

Kirk slowly remounted. Somehow the news brought

88

no particular shock. It was something to be accepted and met along with other mischances of the day. "Perhaps thirty men with you, Jake? Then when we report to Dahlgren, we've got to tell him he's got at most a hundred officers and men."

"How's he going to take that, Kirk?"

"He'll take it. I doubt if he's slept since we left Steve'burg. His stump's galling him badly. I can tell by the way he shifts in the saddle. He's about sick from the trick Scudder played on him and what it led him to do. Missing Kilpatrick's cut him deep. But he'll take this and go on and he'll make these hundred men worth five hundred. He's a soldier, as you said. Now let's go up and give him the news."

The march went on under a drive of icy rain, first west to shake clear of the Richmond defenses and any possible sallies by their garrison, then north to make sure of not getting entangled in the outer fringes of the city, and at last east in desperate hope of overtaking Kilpatrick, who must surely have broken off his attack and be heading east toward Butler's Union lines.

A railroad track was crossed, a small stream, a bigger one, and still the remnants of Dahlgren's command lurched on east. There were excited shouts when a trooper picked up a haversack, a canteen, marked with the insignia of one of Kilpatrick's regiments. They were on the right course! Nothing to do now but drive on until the New Jersey general's rear guard was met.

Then the night was stabbed with the orange flare of rifle shots, scattered at first, slowly thickening, crashing out to the right, the left, in the front, in the rear. Church bells were clanging in the distant darkness, calling up the Home Guards to fall on the raiders. Alarm guns boomed and unseen hoofs beat as the warning was carried to every village and hamlet.

Eyes blurred by the rain and head throbbing with exhaustion, Kirk led squads and platoons against shadowy formations that materialized ahead and on the flanks. The enemy was badly led and badly equipped and there was little trouble in breaking them up, but always fresh outbursts of fire told of more threats to be beaten off, driven away. Dahlgren ranged up and down the column, keeping it superbly in hand, speaking in a quiet, confident voice. Time and again Kirk heard him saying, "Just a few more miles, boys, and we'll be back in our own lines." But Kirk was uneasily certain that these constant rushes out of the night, the growing volume of fire were nudging the command slowly but surely northwest, herding it away from the southeast track that would bring it to the York peninsula between the York and the James Rivers.

There was a dawn halt and a couple of hours' sleep in wet woods somewhere far east of the Chickahominy that Kirk could not remember passing. Then the command was mounted again, round up its take of prisoners that now almost exceeded the captors in numbers. Spent men on spent horses rode out into the rainy morning trying to forget the cries that had followed them through the night, the agonized cries of their own wounded. "Sweet Christ, don't leave me, fellers." . . . "Jack! Jack! Gimme a hand. My leg's near shot off. Don't leave me."

Low hills ahead showed a fringe of mounted men circling toward the column and Kirk had to rally himself to lead tatters of his own men, stray Vermonters and New Yorkers against hard-shooting sprays of Home Guards and local levies. What he did was done mechanically, guided by nothing save past experience and training. Somewhere ahead lay the Pamunkey and a road that swung south to safety. The river and the road! Drive and drive and drive toward them! Nothing else mattered!

But when the slow roll of the Pamunkey was sighted, the fields to the south and east were aswarm with the enemy, on foot and mounted, and once more the head of the column butted northwest, not daring to risk its shrinking numbers against the fresh masses. Very well! Ford the Pamunkey higher up, strike across country to the Mattaponi a few miles beyond. The far bank of the Mattaponi would hold safety and a clear ride south toward the York and Butler's lines, with an ever-increasing chance of overtaking Kilpatrick. The Mattaponi!

Dusk, and tall buildings lifting through the drizzle off to the left and a thick growth of pines along the near bank of the Mattaponi at Aylett's. Dahlgren balanced himself on his crutch and stared at the sluggish flood before him, at the treeless far bank that shimmered, mocking and unattainable, through the rain that had started an hour ago. "The map doesn't show it anywhere near as wide as this, Stedman," he said in a flat voice. "You found a six-foot depth close to the shore?"

Kirk leaned against a pine. "At least. And it seemed to get deeper farther out."

Dahlgren braced himself. "I wish you'd take ten men and scout downstream. You might be able to find a better place to cross. It's impossible here, with the state the horses and men are in. You'll have time. We seem to have shaken off the pursuit."

A trooper's head popped up around a tree close by Dahlgren. "Hey, Colonel, sir! We used to have one of them at home."

Dahlgren turned impatiently, but Kirk saw that he managed a smile. "We're a little busy just now, boy."

"But they're real good. Sam Crane and I found it up the bank. Look. The one we had'd ride the Kennebec in white water." He pointed and Kirk gave a start as he saw a dim bulk gliding downstream, close by the shore. "Lumber scow, sir. Pole her in here, Sam!"

The Colonel's arm shot out. He dragged the trooper from behind the pine and then hugged him. "Be sure I get your name and outfit!" He released the startled man. "That'll hold twenty troopers easily. We'll swim the horses. Four round trips and we're across. Captain

91

Stedman, please call the other officers together. We'll load right away."

Kirk ran back among the trees, cupped his hands about his mouth. But before he could utter a word, a voice roared away in the gloom. "Here they come! Fire at will!" A ripping smash of rifle fire drowned out the rest.

"Think they'll try another rush?" asked the Vermont captain crouched close by Kirk among crumbling rocks.

"That's the trouble with these militia crowds. You never know *what* they might do. They got hit hard last time, but they may be too green to realize that they were hurt," muttered Kirk, gripping the carbine that he had taken from a dead Michigander.

"They got hurt, all right," said the Vermonter. "It was the cross fire from the left. Who's in command there? That New Yorker?" Kirk shook his head. "Dahlgren pulled all that lot back to the river. Latham, my first sergeant, is looking after that part of the line." He slowly raised his carbine, then lowered it. "Thought I heard a stir out in front. Guess it wasn't anything. So dark they could run a brigade of artillery over us without our seeing it. Hey! There go more horses, taking to the river. Hear the splashes? It's sure to God that the Rebs can hear them. You'd figure each splash would tell them they've got fewer men in front of 'em."

The Vermonter dropped his voice, "We're the last to leave?"

"The damnedest and lastest." Kirk stiffened. "Now they *are* stirring. Did you catch that? 'King William County men, form here.'"

The Vermonter cleared his throat softly. "Well, I don't reckon you and I'll miss much, not seeing the other bank of the Mattaponi. It's probably about like this. Hey, what is it? See something?"

Kirk had risen to his knees and swung facing to the rear where faint crackling sounds grew louder. A hand dropped on his boot, gave four sharp tugs. "It's all right," Kirk whispered. "They're calling us in, back to the barge. Send your messenger to warn that Michigan lieutenant off to the right. He'll know what to do. I've got a man to bring Latham in."

"Steady," said the Vermonter. "Rebs are getting a little more agile out in front." As he spoke, a rifle cracked and its flare lit up a vista of wet tree trunks, then faded abruptly. "Get as many of the boys back to the river as you can. I'll cover you. Hurry! I can hear the Rebs ramping and stamping off there. I doubt if their intentions are benevolent."

There were more rifle flashes, then carbines began to answer along the last line that Dahlgren had thrown out to cover his embarkation. "Going to get pinned right down here, sure as hell," muttered Kirk. "No! By God, I've got an idea. It may work with militia." He flattened out on the wet pine needles that carpeted the ground, began wriggling off to the right, one hand reaching out ahead of him. At last it fell on sodden cloth that stirred convulsively to his touch. "That you, Music? Still got your horn? All right. Forget your orders about keeping quiet. Sound the charge." The little bugler struggled to his knees, fumbling with his instrument. The notes came out blurred and discordant. Then they cleared, soared high under the dripping trees. Kirk cried, "Good!" then pulled himself to his feet and roared, "B and H Troops, oblique more! No, God damn it, F Troop! Close on G. That's it. Bring in all the prisoners you can! Horse holders, follow close! Keep the path clear for the gun teams!"

Rifle fire died abruptly. Carbines ceased to snap out flame. Soon the dark woods about Kirk were astir with half-seen troopers who moved at a running crouch. One of them veered toward him. "Latham, sir. Two killed, one slightly wounded. None of the D.C.I.T."

"Good," answered Kirk. "Take the boys right down this path. You'll find the barge waiting. Step it out.

Even the militia'll see through that old trick in a minute or two and come a-booming after us." He turned to the Vermonter. "The Michigander and his crowd coming in all right? Good. You and I'll bring up the rear."

The Vermonter sighed. "That was downright deceitful, what you did with that bugle, but I don't think the Lord'll hold me to be an accessory to a falsehood if I just walk along with you. There's the last man. Let's go. I guess I am getting a mite curious about that other bank after all."

Horses were floundering in the water about the barge as Kirk and the little rear guard emerged from the trees. From the bank Dahlgren called, "In with you! That's it. Better stand up. There's not too much room. Save me a place in the stern, Stedman. Fine! I'm aboard. Push off, polemen! You men along the gunnels, keep a good hold on the bridles or the horses'll head downstream." The barge slid out into the slow current and the Colonel slapped Kirk's shoulder. "Journey's end! You know, once or twice back there I began to wonder if we'd make it. But we're clear now. Hi! There are our friends, just too late to wish us *bon voyage.*"

Kirk heard angry, frustrated voices, clattering among the pines. "Wonder how well they can see us, sir," he muttered.

"Quite clearly, I should think," said Dahlgren cheerfully. As he spoke, a ragged fusillade broke out along the shore and bullets slapped into the water. Kirk was quite sure that he could distinguish at least two men creeping toward the end of a fallen tree that stretched out into the river. He dropped to one knee, drew his revolver, then felt a heavy Colt jump in his hand as he fired. Answering flashes burst from the shore and someone in the barge swore between pain-clenched teeth. A revolver slammed above Kirk's head and he looked up to see Dahlgren, still erect and propped on his crutch,

94

sending out coolly spaced shots, his head thrown back and kepi rakishly atilt.

The barge shuddered, grounded, and Dahlgren wheeled about. "Here we are! Horse holders off first and lead straight up the bank. Stedman, you and Captain Rugg see to the others. The column is fifty yards inland with the rest of the mounts."

The horses splashed and snorted their way ashore while the men spilled out over the bow with Dahlgren pegging nimbly along on his crutches. "Smash up that barge!" he called. "There's an ax and a maul in the bow. I want one good man for the job."

A stoop-shouldered trooper in a battered slouch hat came forward, arms dangling awkwardly. Dahlgren laughed. "Are you the good man I called for?"

The trooper shifted his feet. "Maybe I ain't what you'd call godly good, but I was counted a good man on a farm back in Michigan."

"You'll do. Stave in the bottom. Follow this path up the bank when you're done. We'll wait for you. Come along, Stedman."

As the path leveled off, Kirk's mind went back to the route still to be covered, as Dahlgren had described it at the last halt—or was it the next to last?—before they reached the Mattaponi. He could visualize the terrain as though a map were unrolled back of his eyes. Straight south down the left bank through Walkerton; a sharp turn to the right just before King and Queen Courthouse; across the Mattaponi again at Frazer's Ford; then a clear run down to West Point where the Mattaponi joined the Pamunkey to form the York River. But long before the point was sighted, the countryside would be thick with General Benjamin Butler's blue-coats and there would be white-topped wagons crammed with bacon and coffee and hardtack. Above all, there would be sleep, profound and unbroken sleep.

The stir of men and horses ahead broke into Kirk's thoughts. Dahlgren was calling for his mount and the

Michigan trooper, maul still in his hand, was stumbling up, croaking, "Smashed her good, b'God." Then Jake's voice came through the dark. "Where's Captain Stedman? Anyone seen him? Hoy! Kirk! What kep' you?"

The road that ran southeast down the right bank of the river was filled with the subdued jingle and thud of the little column lurching wearily along. The sounds and the soft patter of the rain beat into Kirk's ears, dulling his senses, clouding his consciousness as he fought against sleep. Time and again he recovered just before pitching out of the saddle, and he was almost grateful for Roquefort's stumbling gait that kept jarring him awake.

High banks lined with scrub growth pressed closer and closer on either side and it was hard to keep the command formed in fours. Horses on the outer flanks lost their footing on the slopes, pressed closer back onto the narrowing road. Kirk found himself forced into the column itself, riding between two troopers. The man on his right suddenly bent forward, fell sidewise against him. Kirk managed to throw out an arm, shove the man back into the saddle. Jake's voice growled, " 'Course I'm awake. Got to get over to Brandy Station—God damn! I was near gone then. That you, Kirk? What you doing, riding in the column?"

Kirk shook him. "Try biting your tongue, Jake. It helps. I'm here because there's no room on the flanks. Where'd you go after the column started?"

Jake straightened, rubbed his hands hard across his face. "Tried to play sheep dog in the rear. No use. The boys are dead." He dropped his voice. "A lot have straggled. Doubt if we've got more than forty riding with us."

Forty! Kirk tried to grasp Jake's news, but his mind kept slipping away, just as the horses slipped from the steep sides of the road. When another of Roquefort's stumbles cleared his brain a little, a Michigan trooper rode where Jake had been and there were only two sets of fours looming ahead in the night.

All at once Kirk was wide-awake, standing in his stirrups and his ears questioning the darkness. The sound came again from the wet black fields beyond the second growth. "Yeh! On the Walkerton road, headin' downstream!" The distant voice was sharp and penetrating. "Downstream!"

Kirk jabbed his elbows into the ribs of the troopers on either side of him. "Trouble coming! Be sure your carbines are loaded!" He forced Roquefort on into the next four, slapped the nearest rider on the shoulder. "Rebs! Get ready to smash ahead!"

A familiar voice answered. "Thanks, Stedman. I heard that, too. King and Queen County must be raised against us. Pass the word back. We'll just have to cut our way through." Dahlgren's tone suddenly sharpened. "Who's that by the side of the road? You, there, by the big tree. What outfit?"

Kirk saw a dismounted man move uncertainly halfway up the bank. Then came a hesitant reply: "Tainth N'Yawk!"

Dahlgren shouted, "Damn you for a liar," and fired two quick shots.

In the light of Dahlgren's revolver flash, Kirk had a quick vision of the sham New Yorker crumpling against the tree. Then the road was filled with a bright, horrible clangor. Rifles flashed left, right and front. There were empty saddles on both sides of him. In the rear, a horse screamed and someone fell heavily. In another series of flashes, Kirk saw Dahlgren fling up both hands, pitch forward, then crash to the ground among milling hoofs.

Kirk yelled, "The Colonel's hit. Form about him," and dropped to the ground, reins over his arm and revolver out. He jammed Roquefort against a maddened dancing horse, dodged a stumbling man who ran blindly to the rear, hands clutched to his belly. He thought that he could just make out Dahlgren, lying very still near the edge of the road, and fought toward him, still calling, "Form about the Colonel!"

A plunging horse nearly knocked him off his feet, was followed by another. He tried to catch at the nearest bridle, then saw that the riders were firing up the road, shooting from the saddle and yelling. There were more hoofs pounding toward him and he pushed Roquefort closer to the bank as he fired at a new knot of half-seen riders who yelled, "They're a-bustin'! Herd 'em up in the fields!" He drew his saber and thrust at the nearest man. Something deflected his blade and he stumbled out into the road. More riders were sweeping along. A horse's shoulder sent him reeling. His kepi flew off. A hand caught at the cape of his overcoat, held it for an instant and then lost it in a ripping of cloth. Kirk recovered, lunged again. A revolver cracked close by and Roquefort let out an agonized whinny, plunged up the bank at the left, dragging Kirk along by the reins still looped about his wrist.

Kirk tripped, fell flat, then lay panting on the soaking turf, still clinging to the reins. He heard rifle fire up the road, interspersed with the boom of fowling pieces. Horsemen were still galloping below the bank, hallooing and shouting to each other. Then the road was empty. He fought for breath, wriggled forward, peered through the brush.

A riderless horse was grazing quietly a few feet away from him. Another lay motionless on its side. A man was sprawled here, another there, anonymous in the darkness. Kirk's eyes picked up a glint of bright wood by the far edge of the road, made out a body beside it. Dahlgren's crutch! But the body, it didn't have to be the Colonel's. The Colonel could have—Then he saw that one leg was angled grotesquely out, the artificial leg. There was no mistaking the ghastly immobility of that figure. Everything that Ulric Dahlgren could have done had been brought to an abrupt end in the first wild out-burst of the ambush.

Kirk rose to his knees, raised one hand in salute. "Jake said you were a soldier, Colonel," he muttered. "The rest of us found out he was right. Let's see if we can help you finish the job."

He got to his feet. There was still firing off up the road, the nearest flashes not more than a hundred yards away, scattered shots to the far right, the far left and the front. It might be possible, by keeping to the fringes of whatever fighting there was, to pick up a few men here, a few there, form some kind of a body and keep on toward Butler's lines. "I'll find Jake," he thought. "Jake and I can brew something out of this. There couldn't have been many in that ambush party, not so many that Jake and I and some troopers can't handle them. I'll find Latham, too."

He sheathed the saber that dangled by its cord from his wrist and began gentling Roquefort, running his hands carefully over legs and flanks in search of the wound that had sent the blue roan darting up the bank. His right hand found the spot, a long, scoring gash in the nigh haunch, but not deep. Roquefort whinnied softly and rubbed his nose against Kirk's sleeve as though trying to tell him that the blue legs could still cover a good many miles.

There were flashes not fifty yards away to the right. An unseen man called wearily, "All right, Reb. I'm done. Carbine's fouled and my pouch is empty." Someone was giving orders to the surrendering trooper, but Kirk was deaf to them. He stood, reins still in his hand, looking down at the suddenly fallen Roquefort. The horse lay quietly, even though the bone of its foreleg showed white, shattered by a stray bullet from those last dis-charges. "Compound fracture," he thought numbly. "Nothing to do about it." Under his breath he said, "Sorry, boy. Got to leave you. Some Red'll do the job that's got to be done for you." He wrestled his saddlebags free, slung them over his arm and walked slowly away. Roquefort gave a long, shuddering sigh. Kirk dropped the saddlebags and reloaded his Colt. There was a chance that a single shot this night would not be noticed. Carefully he pressed the muzzle against the blue roan's head and pulled the trigger. Then with a set jaw he picked up his gear and moved carefully off. His best chance, he reasoned, was to head north toward the Rapidan and Meade's lines. To try to go back along the road toward Walkerton would only invite capture or worse. Pressing on by night, lying up in woods and swamps by day might bring him within sight of blue pickets in a week or less.

Two days later Kirk, mounted once more, rode steadily on. But he rode south, not north, and all about him were lean, gray men, hard-bitten South Carolina troopers of Wade Hampton's command who had caught him at the edge of a marsh by dawn. They were rough, desperately weary men but treated Kirk good-naturedly enough and shared their rations with him.

As the troop pushed on south, Kirk listened to snatches of talk from the troopers. By their account, regular Confederate cavalry had overtaken Kilpatrick's main force and cut it to pieces somewhere between the lower Pamunkey and the Richmond–York River Railroad. This might or might not be true. He had learned long ago not to rely on news brought by scattered units. Small groups usually knew only what their members had actually seen and hence were apt to view an extended action simply in the light of their own experience. Thus they could report a crushing defeat as a major triumph, or vice versa, depending on their own particular fortunes.

About Dahlgren and his command, the lieutenant in charge of the troop, a prematurely wearied boy from the High Hills of Santee, had known nothing until he had seen some Richmond newspapers of the third and fourth of March. Where Dahlgren had gone and what had happened to him the lieutenant did not know but told Kirk that press comment had been mild. "Just said something about his officers' being a fine-looking lot," observed the man from Santee. "Seems they halted at Major Young's house north of the city and had been right civil, their men too. That was in the *Examiner*."

Kirk wondered which of the many halts had been at Young's, but details of the ride that had ended so fatally at Walkerton were dim in his mind. At least, Dahlgren seemed to have inspired respect in Richmond and that respect seemed to be reflected in the attitude of Kirk's captors toward him, as a participant in a gallant failure.

It was with a real shock that Kirk saw steep hills and houses and spires rising off to his right. They had to be part of Richmond, and yet they couldn't be. The city had come upon him far too quickly. Then he knew that he must have circled and doubled far more than he realized after his escape from the ambush on the night of March second. The flats that he and the Carolina troopers had just been crossing must have been the terrain of Seven Pines and Mechanicsville and all the useless blood that McClellan had spilled there in '62. The nearest heights, if he remembered his maps correctly, were called Chimborazo, and the railroad tracks ahead could only be the Richmond and York River line, and the sheds and open platform its terminus. A train must be due, for not only was the platform crowded, but civilians were trailing out of the east end of the city toward it, on foot and in carriages.

The trooper on Kirk's right grunted, "Sure is a passel of folks 'thout a God-damn thing to do but gape."

Another said, "Lot of 'em look able, powerful able. Could recruit a purty smart regiment just on thet thar platform." He spat. "Must be prime, not havin' nothin' to do but hang around a depot. It may be the Holy Sabbath for them bastards, but it's just March the sixth for

101

us. Hey, Slim. They sound kind of riled. Maybe some-one's menaced 'em with a uniform and a gun to tote."

The road was slanting close by the platform and Kirk heard an angry buzzing. Men and women and children were spilling out over the tracks, pushing and shoving as they tried to force a way onto the jammed platform. The buzzing swelled to an angry roar and fists and sticks were shaken at the thickest clump of people. The roar had an angry undertone that sent uncomfortable chills up Kirk's spine, but he could make out no words.

There was a stir at the edge of the crowd and infan-trymen were using rifle butts, none too gently in some cases, to clear a way for themselves. Kirk saw them butt up onto the platform, a peg-legged captain with a long gray mustache leading them. He was shouting, "Every-one off! Provost marshal's orders. No one allowed up here."

The crowd gave way sullenly but still massed along the tracks and the high ground by the sheds, yielded still more as Kirk's guards clattered on, skirting the far side of the platform, slowing to a walk to avoid trampling people. A trooper cried, "Hey! Chrisamighty! Who thet?" Kirk turned toward the platform, then clutched convulsively at the arm of the trooper on his right. He was looking directly down at the face of Ulric Dahlgren.

The young colonel's body lay in an open pine coffin. The fine features, still smeared with the mud of the Walkerton road, were contorted, probably in the same expression that they had worn when the fusillade struck him. A white cotton shirt had been drawn down over the torso to meet the rough, nonuniform blue trousers, whose right leg lay limp and shapeless. Kirk suddenly gagged. More than the artificial leg was missing. The left hand, lying across the white cotton of the shirt, was torn and ragged and a dried blood clot had formed over the spot where the little finger had been clumsily hacked off. That simple gold ring, the only jewelry that Ulric

102

Dahlgren wore. Where was it now? Had the owner of the clumsy hacking knife already sold or pawned it?

Kirk tipped back in the saddle as the trooper angrily shook off his hold. "Look, Yank, I'm peaceworthy, but if you're lookin' for a coffin that's all your'n, you're goin' about it just right." Kirk recovered himself and rode on, head down. Yet somehow, as the shock wore off, he found his anger and disgust at the yelling, staring crowd ebbing rapidly. There had been no doubt of Dahlgren's death the moment he pitched forward in his saddle. The scene at the station only repeated to Kirk the known fact that hatred and hysteria always run far hotter and keener among the noncombatants than among fighting men. But why the sudden animus against Dahlgren? A newsboy went running by, holding up a sheet with smeary black letters: "ULRIC THE HUN! SHOT LIKE A THIEF IN THE NIGHT!"

In the crowd a man was calling, "Mr. Stockdale! Better get Miss Lynn out of this crush. Never tell when horses'll take a scare!"

Kirk looked up incuriously. Then he clutched the pommel of his saddle. A very shiny barouche was trying to turn in the crowd and a big, handsome man with a square, iron-gray beard was standing up against the rear seat, directing the coachman with sweeping waves of his arm. And beside the man, deep blue eyes wide and troubled, sat the Canadian girl of Frederick's Hall Station.

"Looks scared of the crowd," thought Kirk. "Can't say I blame her, but she isn't one who scares easy!"

Their glances met and Kirk knew that she had seen him before he had caught sight of her. He raised a hand to his kepi in salute and she half rose, steadying herself by the rail of the vehicle. The barouche swung sharply, the big man settled himself beside the girl and the carriage bowled away, a hint of green bonnet just showing above its curved rear.

"I'll be damned," Kirk muttered to himself. "So her name's Stockdale—Miss Lynn Stockdale."

His escort turned down a side street and halted. A fattish, gray-faced major in a buggy drew up by the lieutenant, spoke to him briefly. The latter rode back toward Kirk. "You were part of Colonel Dahlgren's command, sir?" he asked.

"As I told you, Lieutenant. Troop Commander, D.C.I.T."

"Just wanted to be sure. Colonel Dahlgren's men, all ranks, go to the Pemberton Building, just across the street from Libby." The new orders apparently did not please the South Carolinian.

"Not Libby? Do you know why?"

The lieutenant shook his head angrily. "I don't know anything. Just the way I didn't even know that was the Colonel's body on the platform back there." His tired face grew paler. "But I *do* know that's no way to treat a soldier killed in honorable action. Come on. Let's get to Pemberton. My boys and me, we want to clear out of this God-damn city and get back to the army where we belong."

7

The Sentence

The prison guards pushed Kirk along a dark corridor in the Pemberton Building and flung open a door. Muzzles prodding his back, he stood for a moment on the threshold, looking into a huge room eerily lighted by sunshine that filtered in long bars through the cracks of boarded-up windows. At first he thought the place was empty. Then he heard a shuffling and shifting, saw a confused blur of faces that floated toward him from the front, right and left, as the door slammed behind him.

The slow drift stopped and he began to pick out details—a thin shaft of light falling on a blue kepi; light blue trousers topped by a homespun coat; a bearded mouth; a bandaged forehead; a glint of brass buttons. A frightened voice cried, "It's a Reb spy, put in to listen at us! Grab the bastard!"

Kirk called, "Captain Stedman, D.C.I.T. Who are you?"

There was a sudden stir as a man broke forward, crying. "It's him! Cap! Hey, Cap! What the hell they trying to do to us? Don't you know me, sir? It's Trooper Lynch!"

Another voice spoke. "First Sergeant Latham, sir. I've got a list for you of all the D.C.I.T. I could locate, so far."

Then everyone began shouting. "I'm Sergeant Mason, 1st Vermont. Have you seen my brother?" . . . "Look here, Captain, I want to know what happened to the connecting files after we crossed the Chickahominy." . . . "Sir, heard anything about C Troop, 2nd New York?" . . . "All I ask is a reasonable explanation of why we're herded in here. They won't tell us." . . . "God-damn Reb doctor took my boots. They was made special for me in Biddeford and I only just got 'em in the last mail before we dragged out of Steve'burg." . . . "Sir, what the hell the Rebs got against us?"

The words rained down on Kirk, the latest arrival from the outside world, the man who *must* know everything. He held up his hands. "Easy, please! Maybe I know less than you do. We were ambushed the night of March second across the Mattaponi. Colonel Dahlgren was killed and I'm afraid a lot of others. I was picked up this morning somewhere to the north. Something damn funny's happening, but I don't know what. If you tell me what you know, maybe we can piece out what's going on. But I've got a question, first of all: Has anyone seen Captain Pitler, 1st Maine?"

A voice came from behind a beam of sunlight across a broad chest. "I'm from his troop, sir. No one's seen him. He was near the tail of the column at the ambush. He was on foot because he'd given his horse to Mark Freeman from Machias. Mark had lost his and then got hit in the knee ferrying across the Mattaponi."

"Thanks," said Kirk. If Jake had been on foot at the rear of that mixed-up column, his chances of getting clear must have been quite good. The Maine man was tough and resourceful and very likely was safe inside

106

Butler's lines by the York. On the other hand, Jake was not the type to think just of his own skin in a *sauve-qui-peut*. He would think of less tough and less resourceful men who needed a hand in stormy going. Time would have to tell the rest of Jake's story. He turned to the others. "Let's try and put the pieces together," he said.

The men in the big room had been taken at different times, some during the attacks on March first, some during the long ride around Richmond. Others had been picked up just after the ambush or two or three days later, like himself. All those made prisoner up to the fifth of March agreed that they couldn't complain about their treatment. Even the prison guards had viewed them with grudging admiration. Then, on the fifth, details had swooped down on the officers in Libby Prison just across the street and on the enlisted men on Belle Isle and herded them, regardless of rank, into their present quarters. They had been handled roughly and crowds in the streets had yelled, "Assassins! Murderers! Hired cut-throats!" at them. No one could account for the sudden change. It was merely a fact. And they were quite sure that more of Dahlgren's men were in other rooms of the Pemberton Building.

That was all that Kirk could learn, beyond the fact that no prisoners from Kilpatrick's main body had been subjected to the same treatment. And, for what comfort there might be in the news, Kilpatrick had not been cut to pieces, but had gained Butler's lines with quite light losses, as had Captain Mitchell and the two hundred-odd who had strayed away from Dahlgren after the attacks of March first.

"Well," said Kirk as the flow died away, "a lot of that's illuminating, but it doesn't tell us much. We still don't know why we've been culled out. We don't know why Kilpatrick broke off his attacks when he did or how Mitchell got separated. I've got nothing that'll add to any of it, except that Dahlgren was killed, and some of you knew that, anyway." He thought of telling about

107

that open coffin on the station platform, the hacked hand and the missing artificial leg, but decided not to. Such details would either depress the others further or anger them and he saw nothing to be gained by adding to their disquiet. "One more question of my own," he went on. "When do we eat?"

Someone laughed harshly. "We ate slim but regular in Libby. We were formed into messes and rations issued us each day for us to cook. Here—hell—this morning the guards brought in a bucket of warm water with a little corn meal floating in it and some shreds of sour pork. Also one dipper. No lights allowed. No fires. Twenty-one blankets so thin that if you heaped them all onto a titmouse, he'd freeze in midsummer."

Kirk sat down, leaning his back against the wall. "This isn't like the Rebs."

A man said, "Not like the ones we fought against. These are powerful different. Most of the prison lot ain't fought and don't mean to."

Kirk sighed. No doubt the Confederate prisoners in camps like Elmira were voicing those same thoughts at the same moment. "So you've got twenty-one blankets. How many are there in this room?"

"A sight more than twenty-one."

A hand touched Kirk's arm. "I took a count, sir," said Latham's voice. "We've got forty-four men, all ranks. In the morning we'll get close to one of the biggest cracks in the window boards and I'll show you the list, along with the D.C.I.T. roster."

Kirk reached out, found Latham's hand and shook it. "Thanks—for a whole lot of things. I suppose they'll wake us when they bring the next rations."

"They won't have to, sir. It'll be morning. And don't worry about Captain Pitler, sir. He's not one to get lost."

Light flashing in his eyes tore Kirk out of a trancelike sleep, dreamless and numbing. A hand shook his shoulder, and Kirk's eyes blinked in the glare of a lantern that shone on gray-clad legs and battered musket butts. A harsh voice said, "Stedman, District of Columbia Independent Troop. Up. Major wants to talk to you."

Kirk got up dizzily, rubbing his eyes. "What time is it?"

"What you want to know for? You ain't goin' anywheres."

Kirk saw ragged chevrons on the sleeves of the speaker. He looked slowly at the bayonet-tipped muskets of the escort. "If you were a sergeant in my outfit, you'd be using those stripes for gun wadding. What have your men been doing with those bayonets? Cleaning fish with them?"

"Talk big while you can, Yank. Git moving, now. The boys ain't afraid to prod."

In the front office where Kirk had been questioned on arrival, a lamp burned brightly, its china shade spattered with peculiarly offensive greens and reds that were supposed to represent rose sprays. Back of the lamp, by the paper-stacked table, was a puffy-faced Confederate major. A little behind him, partly in the shadows, a tall, thin captain in worn gray sat, his right hand shading his eyes as though to avoid looking at the ghastly shade. His left sleeve was pinned neatly to the front of his threadbare coat. His head did not move as Kirk entered, but the captain was probably watching him from between his fingers. Kirk noted the old uniform, the hollows and angles of cheeks and chin that were thrown into high relief by the lamplight. "Infantry," thought Kirk. "Looks as though he might have been one of Stonewall Jackson's men. Invalided and on staff work and doesn't like it."

The major barked, "The prisoner will report his presence!"

Kirk answered evenly, "That's up to the sergeant of the detail who brought me, sir."

The captain's lined mouth contracted as though hiding a smile. In almost a whisper, he said, "Captain Stedman is correct, Major Pleasants. And may I suggest that we dispense with formalities? General Bragg won't be pleased if I take too long with this."

Major Pleasants's soft, petulant face creased in sulky lines. Then he growled, "All right. We've got some questions to ask the prisoner."

Kirk inclined his head. "Anything that does not go against regulations, ours or yours, sir." He drew a chair out from the wall and seated himself. "I am ready, sir."

Pleasants flushed, thumped the table. "The prisoner will remain standing until otherwise ordered."

The captain's hand still shaded his eyes, but Kirk knew that the tired eyes were fixed on him, not unsympathetically, he thought.

Kirk remained seated. "I do not recognize the term 'prisoner' as applied to myself. You appear to be confusing the paragraphs in your own regulations concerning prisoners of war with those dealing with courts-martial."

Pleasants popped up from his armchair. "You'll stand on your God-damn head if I tell you to. I'm in command." The captain lowered his hand, showing deep-set eyes, a beaky nose and tough chin, and reached out to touch the major's sleeve. In the same low voice as before he murmured, "Captain Stedman is correct, sir. And may I repeat, General Bragg is not a very patient man?"

The major sat down huffily. "Very well. But you must be aware that I shall report your interference to General Winder."

"Quite, sir. Shall we proceed?" He shaded his eyes again.

"Now, Stedman," snapped the major. "Will you tell me and Captain Archer if you recognize *this*?" He flapped a sheet of very stiff, glossy paper onto the table.

Kirk picked it up, wonderingly. "Why—this is a photograph! I didn't know you could photograph handwriting."

"Never mind what you know or don't know," barked the major. "Read it and answer my question."

Kirk ran his eye over the sheet, a sense of utter bewilderment filling him. It began, "Headquarters Third Division, Cavalry Corps," in bold type that was very familiar to him. Then came the script: "Officers and Men: You have been selected from Brigades and Regiments as a picked command to attempt a desperate undertaking . . ." There was no need to read more. He laid the sheet on the table. "I recognize the letterhead and the orders. They were issued by Colonel Dahlgren to his command once it got under way."

Pleasants popped to his feet, flushed and crowing. "That's all we need, Captain. You can report back to General Bragg that this prisoner acknowledges the orders to be genuine. We can proceed now as the General and the others propose. I'm told that the President concurs, as does the Secretary of War."

The head behind the shading hand shook. "I can't report that, Major. Captain Stedman has only seen part of the evidence. I must insist that you show him the sheet that bears the rest of the order."

The major threw back his head, making gobbling noises of dissent. Captain Archer lowered his hand again, extended another sheet. "Would you mind telling us about this, Captain?"

"Glad to," replied Kirk. The second sheet began familiarly enough. Then Kirk stiffened in his chair. "We will cross the James River into Richmond," he read, "destroying the bridges after us and exhorting the released prisoners to destroy and burn the hateful city and to not allow the Rebel Leader Davis and his traitorious crew to escape."

Pleasants was leaning far across the table, eyes on Kirk. "Well?" he snapped.

Kirk glanced up at him, then kept on reading. When he had finished, he handed the sheet back to Captain Archer. "You can tell General Bragg there's nothing in

111

this, sir. I saw every order that was issued. I was present at nearly every conference that was held from the very inception of the plan."

Pleasants pounded the table. "*I* am asking the questions, not this captain."

"Very well. The whole plan was to get in quickly, get out quickly. Richmond was not to be burned. We had neither the time nor the equipment for the job. As to the rest, nothing was ever said or written about your President and his associates. We weren't supposed to take them prisoner."

"Of course not, of course not," said Pleasants softly. "There was another paper found on that Dahlgren's body, a sort of summation in his own writing, to wit: 'The Belle Isle prisoners being released, once in the city of Richmond, it must be *destroyed*, and Jeff. Davis and his Cabinet *killed*.' What have you to say to that?"

"Just what I said before. If such a plan had been contemplated, I and my fellow officers would have had to know about it. Now another point, Major. I'm not familiar enough with the late Colonel's handwriting to swear that this is *not* his. But I can tell you this: He was a well-educated man and would never have written 'traitorious.' I have seen his signature on a good many documents and I don't recall his ever abbreviating the 'Ulric' to 'U.,' as this sheet shows. Oh—and one more point which may have escaped your sharp eye, Major. A man in a hurry *may* misspell a word. But he will never misspell his own name. And this so-called signature reads 'D-a-l-h-g-r-e-n,' not 'D-a-h-l-g-r-e-n.'"

"Damn your impudence! Do you mean to accuse General Bragg and Secretary Seddon of forgery?"

"Not in the least. Someone cooked up these papers and they were bound to make inquiries about them. That's all I can tell you."

Captain Archer rose. "I can see nothing to add, Major. Other officers have said what Captain Stedman did, though only one other caught the slip in spelling of the name. I must say that the stories all agree with what the officers of our army whom Colonel Dahlgren captured and later released have told us. A quick in-and-out raid."

Pleasants smiled sourly. "They might have been tampered with. That damned bandit had gold with him."

Archer's voice took on a chilly edge. "Several of those officers are personal friends of mine. More than that, Major Mayhew, who was taken at Frederick's Hall, is a cousin of Mrs. Archer. I suggest respectfully that you choose your words a little more carefully. Now with your permission I shall take the papers back to General Bragg's office. Good night, sir. Good night, Captain Stedman. You may count on me to give General Bragg my honest opinion: that you told a perfectly frank and straightforward story."

"Good night, Captain Archer, and thank you."

When the captain had gone, Kirk turned to Major Pleasants. "If this is all, sir, I'd be glad of permission to return to my quarters. You appear to find my request amusing."

Pleasants was rocking back and forth in his chair, laughing high in his throat. "That God-damn supercilious one-armed son of a bitch! He's going to be about as popular as a man smoking in an open powder magazine! Bragg says those orders are genuine. So does Fitzhugh Lee. So do the President and Secretary Seddon! But most of all Bragg! Christ, just wait till he tells Bragg that he believes you. By God, he'll get sent to defend some North Carolina sandbank with green recruits against the whole Union Navy! That General Bragg, he ain't one to cross."

Kirk forced a yawn. "He'll cool off. After all, Richmond's still standing. Your President and his Cabinet are still alive."

Pleasants showed his yellowed teeth. "Yes. *They* are still alive. Sergeant, take this prisoner back to Room C where he was."

113

Kirk went back down the corridor, his guards clumping after him. "Pleasants!" he thought. "What a name for a man like that. He's typical of prison officers in any army. Seemed to be threatening me, too, and meaning it. How did those words go?" A cold chill went along Kirk's spine as he remembered. "Yes. *They* are still alive," Pleasants had said.

The door banged behind him and the flow of faces, unreal in the half-light, came toward him, questioning the man who had been outside. "Find out anything?" . . . "What they going to do with us?" . . . "What did they ask?"

He said, "I don't know anything new. They wanted to know where we crossed the South Anna. Now, has anything been done about organizing the room? Who's senior here?"

A tall shape spoke. "No one here higher than captain. While you were out, we decided to ask you to take charge, being the last come. That'll save trying to find out the dates of commissions."

Kirk reflected for a moment. It was apparent that only he knew of the forged orders and Pleasants's veiled threat. So the less contact the other prisoners had with prison officers the better. A hint could throw the room into a panic or precipitate some violent action that Pleasants would probably welcome. If he himself served as buffer between the captives and the authorities, he might be able to fend off such a danger.

He said slowly, "If that's what you want, I'll take the job, but I've got to be in absolute charge. Agreed? All right. In this light we can't see very well who is who, so if the officers will appoint one of their number to act as adjutant each day, I'll accept their choice. First Sergeant Latham of my troop will look after the enlisted men, reporting to me."

Later Kirk sat with his back against the north wall, trying to keep awake in the heavy, fetid atmosphere while men stirred, whispered, snored all about him. His

114

mind tormented him by starting to formulate infallible plans for bettering conditions in Room C, Pemberton Building. When he tried to follow them through, they faded out, reappeared vaguely, vanished again, only to be replaced by still sounder plans that evaporated like the others.

At intervals he worried about Jake and a persistent inner voice kept muttering that he had had his last glimpse of his friend at the Mattaponi Ferry. And what was so surprising in that? Other close friends had stepped out of column and gone down a dark road to fall in with a never-seen army whose ranks were growing every day. Why not Jake Pitler? But Jake was Jake, solid and indestructible.

A man was saying, close by his ear, "Say, Cap, it's me, Hank O'Day, 2nd New York, the old Harris Light. Look, Cap, I'm scared my foot's festering. Will you come over where you can see good? Jesus, I'd hate to get anything festering in this place." Another voice joined in. "Can't you do nothing about the rations? My guts won't go that stuff. I been doubled up with squitters since last sundowning."

Kirk wrestled himself to his feet and back into the realities of his task. "Come over by that shaft of light, O'Day, and we'll get your foot fixed up. I'm doing the best I can about rations and I'll keep prodding the Rebs."

At some unmarked hour of the night, Kirk rose stiffly, wondering sourly about the adage, "He who sleeps, dines." But what if you didn't sleep? He straightened, cursing the trembling of his knees, then stumbled. A tattered blanket lay across his feet. So he had been asleep and someone had spread a blanket over him! There was no point in rousing the whole room to find out who had taken that thought from him. At least he could see that someone else shared his luck. The night outside must be bright and clear, for threads of silvery light lanced

115

through the cracks in the boarded windows. Not far away he saw the whitish blur of a bare foot with a dark band across the instep—Trooper O'Day of the old Harris Light, and the band was the filthy rag that Kirk had bound about the festering spot while assuring O'Day that it would clear up by morning. Pleasants would surely have some doctor within call and that foot needed attention right now, would need it worse in the morning. As gently as he could he spread the blanket over O'Day. The trooper stirred, mumbled, "Must kicked covers off. Thanks, Rosie," and was silent again.

Kirk rubbed his own knees. Was Rosie Mrs. O'Day or some less decorous memory? Whoever she was, she lived in an ailing soldier's mind and was called to in the darkness of a battered Richmond building.

It certainly was bright outside and the filtering light showed men stretched out under torn blankets, huddled uncovered with their knees drawn up to their chins, lying rigid with hands clenched on their chests. And there was more than night radiance beyond the brick walls. Men were tramping by the north side and the west, two companies or even more, Kirk guessed from the noise. There was sound in the corridor, too, like many men shuffling along with a rustle of equipment. Light framed the outlines of the big door in the east wall, yellow, artificial light.

A sharp creaking, a sudden flare of lanterns dazzled Kirk. He could see little beyond the new strong light, a huddle of men clumping in through the open door, the glow of musket barrels and bayonets. Then from behind, Pleasants's cawing voice rasped, "All prisoners up! Form single line along the west and north walls. Then sit down, legs out in front of you, hands on the floor. Jump, all of you! My men have orders to shoot."

Now Kirk saw some twenty men, rifles at the ready, lining the east wall. Four or five more of them held lanterns. In the doorway stood Major Pleasants, revolver in one hand, lantern in the other. Behind him, more heads

116

and bayonets stretched right and left along the corridor. Kirk came forward. "I'm in command in this room, Major. It may be easier if you pass your orders through me. But first I demand to know the meaning—"

Pleasants snapped, "You're demanding nothing. Get over there with the others. You know what to do, Sergeant, if he resists."

Kirk shrugged and joined the half-awake, stumbling mass that reached the walls indicated and dropped down between O'Day and Latham.

The major came slowly forward, revolver dangling. "You'll all stay just where you are and my men'll be here to see you do. And I've got four companies surrounding the building if they're not enough. Now quit talking about prisoners of war. You're not prisoners of war, you're just plain land pirates and you know it."

"Just think of that!" A voice spoke in mock awe somewhere off to Kirk's right.

Pleasants wheeled about. "Who said that?"

From the left someone crooned. "*Wouldn't* you like to know!"

Kirk called, "Easy, boys. That won't help us any. Now, Major, how long must we stay here?"

"I said I was doing the talking," barked Pleasants.

"I heard you. But you're not talking enough. Some of our men are sick. What if they have to use the latrine buckets?"

Lantern light threw twisting shadows across the major's pudgy features. Kirk suddenly remembered a certain Union provost marshal who set a definite quota of offenders for his men to bring in, who destroyed valid passes, dragged men from the very ranks of units moving to the front on pretext of past misdemeanors, impounded convalescents trying to rejoin their regiments. That provost and Pleasants would have been either bosom friends or deadly rivals had they found themselves in the same army and the same area.

The major said grudgingly, "If you got to, you got to.

But four guards'll take you there and bring you back." He turned to his men. "Understand that, Sergeant Treat?"

Watching the major, Kirk said, "My men will observe your rules, sir."

"Damn right, they will," growled Pleasants. Then he bristled and his face was livid in the shifting lights as a falsetto voice beyond Kirk chirped, "Oh, mister, can I leave the room, please?"

The major took two quick steps forward, bending from the waist. "You think this is God-damn funny, don't you? By Christ, you're wrong. You men might as well know this now as later." He paused, then went on in a rasping, lowered voice. "Every God-damn one of you—every man in this building that came here ready to carry out Dahlgren's orders to burn and murder—is under sentence of death and that's final. Get it? And all we're waiting for now is to find out if you get hanged or shot." He drew himself up. "Now let's see some of you minstrel-show end men laugh at *that!*"

Pleasants had gone and the heavy slam of the door melted away into the stunned silence that hung over Dahlgren's men seated on the floor. The guards along the east wall grounded their rifles uncertainly and stood watching, their hands resting on their bayonet sockets. One of the detail sneezed and his fellows started as though the expulsion of air had been a warning shot.

Kirk sat fighting the waves of exhaustion and hunger that swept over him, deadening his thoughts and his senses. He raised his head. "Steady, boys. You've only got Pleasant's say-so and that doesn't mean anything. Just hang on to this: we're prisoners of war and we're damn well sacred so long as we don't butt too hard against the rules." Inwardly he wondered, while his pulses still hammered from the impact of the news, just how far such a restraining influence would go, particularly as he remembered the temper of the city outside the walls of the Pemberton Building.

Someone said dully, "They hanged a lot of Andrews's raiders back in '62 and they were prisoners of war just like us."

Another man spoke and Kirk recognized the voice of a Captain Spier. "We're all soldiers," Spier said. "We could wink out anytime in some little two-bit patrol that didn't affect the war any more than snail grease along a brick wall. Or we could get tumbled in something big that still didn't mean anything. Like Fredericksburg. Thousands of men fired their last shot at the damned stone wall and for all the good it did they might as well have stayed on the left bank up by the Lacey house."

"Shut up talking about folks winking out," said a hoarse voice off to the right. "For all the good *we* done, we'd better stayed at Steve'burg."

Spier went on: "A combat soldier always plays with marked cards against him. But this won't be like getting plugged in a Rapidan swamp on patrol and nothing to show for it. If the Rebs are crazy enough to send us to a firing squad, we'll have given them the worst beating they've had since Gettysburg and Vicksburg. Seems to me that's what we came to do in the first place."

"Sure, win the war by getting stood up against a wall and letting these prison-guard bastards use us for targets," snapped another man.

"If they do, they can't keep it quiet," said Spier calmly. "The Reb Army won't like it worth a sham dollar and lots of Rebs at home won't, either. We hold a lot of prisoners ourselves. There'll be a chance for reprisals, but I think our government's too smart to take it and that'll put the Rebs in a very bad light."

Someone laughed sourly. "I bet the Rebs are shivering right now, thinking of the nasty editorials our papers'll print."

"They ought to shiver. And there'll be editorials in England. Jeff Davis and his crowd are just hanging on, hoping that England'll declare for them and come right into the war on their side. I've lived in England. News like this would finish up any government there that even hinted at recognizing the Rebs. And another thing, up home the recruiting offices'll be swamped, just the way they used to be in '61 and '62."

Close to Kirk Tom Latham said slowly, "There's one feller that's got a lot to say on the Reb side. Unless I been hearing wrong about him, he'll spout like a heavy mortar *for* us. Feller named Robert E. Lee."

One of the guards yelled in a high-pitched, nervous voice, "No talkin' amongst your midst."

Kirk said quietly, "I heard no orders about that."

"You're hearin' 'em now. I'm in command. Shut up, or we'll move in with rifle butts and Major Pleasants will back me."

8

A Visitor at Libby

Somewhere by the east wall Kirk could hear the loud ticking of a watch in a guard's pocket, ominously marking the passage of minute after heavy minute in the cold, rank air of the room. The men about him were silent after the sharp warning, and when he closed his eyes, he could have thought himself alone, except for the occasional shifting of a foot or the breathing of those nearest him. Some seemed almost to be panting as the impact of Pleasants's statement bit deeper, while others drew in air laboriously as though stunned by a blow on the head. He himself was shivering as cold seeped through his worn clothes from the brick wall and the fetid atmosphere kept him in a state that was neither dozing nor awake.

The tinny watch ticked on. The guard was relieved with a deal of stamping and waving of lanterns and a new detail took up the uneasy vigil. A barely noticeable light began its chill flow through cracks in the window boards, and Kirk began to think beyond the walls of the Pemberton Building. He suddenly felt an odd consolation in the memory that, before he left Stevensburg, he had remitted to his mother a good part of his arrears of pay in addition to the usual allotment that he had arranged long ago with the Paymaster's office. She would be spared a lot of governmental red tape whatever the future held for him.

On his right, O'Day stirred, moaned, slid over against him. As gently and quietly as he could he straightened O'Day, propped him against the wall. His hand brushed the other's cheek and the skin was hot and dry. Heedless of orders, he called, "Officer of the guard! There's a very sick man here. Under military law you're required to provide medical care."

The bull's-eye dazzled Kirk's eyes, then snapped off. "You're not under military law and you'll keep silent."

The reply was curt and brusque, but Kirk had a feeling that the officer disliked intensely the role he had to play. Kirk began again. "It's a septic foot that's getting worse."

"I've got my orders," said the officer. "You'll help no one by making a scene. Stay quiet and don't move."

Kirk closed his eyes as he tried not to read an implication into the reply—why waste a doctor's time over a man who would soon—

The room was suddenly brighter and Kirk realized that he must have dozed off, for daylight was edging in around the cracks, a new guard relief was filing through the door and there was reflected sunlight in the corridor. Boots thumped importantly, a saber jingled and Major Pleasants stood in the entrance, some kind of colored sash about his waist. He scowled, then puffed out his flat chest.

"All commissioned officers will fall in along the south wall when I give the command. You will keep your hands clasped behind your necks and you will communicate in no way with each other. Any deviation will have serious results. All right, now, fall in!"

A few guards moved forward to insure compliance and Kirk got dizzily to his feet. Somehow the pressure of his own hands on the back of his neck steadied him and he felt a cold confidence as he took his place against the wall. It would have been the last humiliation had he stumbled or wavered on his weak legs under Pleasants's hard stare.

The major shouted again. "Form in column of twos. Now—forward! Through the door. Column right!"

Kirk found himself making up the leading pair with Captain Spier. As he turned right through the door, he managed to nudge the captain and brought his feet down as firmly as he could on the flooring of the corridor. Spier gave a slight cough as though in acknowledgment and fell into step with him. One by one the following pairs picked up the cadence. Down the long corridor the rhythm of the march echoed, sure and crisp as though passing in review. Spier's mouth shaped the words, "Good for you. That'll show the bastards." Pleasants scuttled along, shouting, "Break up that step. You ain't soldiers any more." Kirk slid his fingers under his ear, indicating that he could not hear. The major yelled, "I said to break up the step."

But Kirk had forgotten the major. He was through the main door and out onto the narrow sidewalk with clean, fresh air filling his lungs, spring sunlight in his eyes, a blue sky above and the sparkle and shimmer of the James at his left. Behind him the cadence beat on, unbroken. The sense of relief vanished as he saw the double line of guards along the cobbled street. He was aware of them as he was of the long brick bulk of Libby Prison ahead on his left, the cobbled street and the hill that rose beyond it, crowned with the colonnaded Capitol, clean and proud in the new morning. What he saw and heard had nothing to do with him. It was all like unimportant sights and sounds about his troop when he

123

formed it for attack, dimly realized in the tension and fear of the moment.

He knew that he was passing the first great door of Libby with its bare marquee frame jutting out. There were other guards, backs to the street, looking up at the barred windows, rifles cradled in their arms. There was a wide middle door, then another marquee frame at the far end of the building, and a sign that he unconsciously spelled out: LIBBY AND SON, SHIP CHANDLERS AND GROCERS. All that he saw meant no more to him than an over-turned churn in a farmyard that he had seen as he pulled his men together for the tragic charge under Farnsworth at Gettysburg. Yet he and many of his men had come out of that charge untouched, whereas now— he fixed his mind on Spier's words the night before: "We'll have given the Rebs the worst beating they've had since Vicksburg."

The guards were shifting, blocking Cary Street with a hedge of bayonets. A voice that was not Pleasants's shouted, "Column left! And for God's sake, drop your hands. You look like a lot of gals putting up their back hair." Kirk marched on unheeding until a rifle was jammed lengthwise across his chest and a guard growled, "Ain't you heard? Column left and drop them hands." Kirk's arms fell by his sides and he made the turn with mechanical precision. He stepped over a high curb, across a narrow sidewalk and under the marquee frame where a wide door yawned. A single thought filled his mind: "No public execution. No witnesses."

He was inside the door and a one-armed captain with a worn, bony face was nodding to him. "Forget about everything in Pemberton, Captain Stedman. There are no charges against you or the others. Keep right on up those stairs."

A voice that Kirk dimly recognized as his own answered, "Thank you, Captain Archer." His mind grappled with the news as the stairs seemed to rise under him, pushing his feet from tread to tread. It was

124

true. It *had* to be true. Archer was calling out the same words to the rest of the group as it entered.

Kirk was at the head of the stairs and a guard was throwing open a massive door, motioning him inside. He hesitated on the sill, gazing into a seemingly endless room. Then a wave of men in nondescript clothes broke toward him, shouting. He took a step forward and hard hands fell on his shoulders from behind. His knees buckled and the hands pulled him upright and there was Jake Pitler thumping him and yelling, "What kep' you? What kep' you?"

Kirk panted, "Jake, how'd you get here?"

"Some friends of mine thought I needed shore leave from the war."

"But all Dahlgren's men were—wait a minute." He pushed his way to the door, called down the stairs, "Captain Archer! What about the enlisted men who were with us?"

Archer answered, "Don't worry. They're clear like you and on their way to Belle Isle. I sent a surgeon along with them."

Kirk cried huskily, "Thanks—for a lot of things!" and stepped unsteadily back into the room. Jake caught his elbow. Kirk muttered, "Got to sit down. Knees gone. Can you spare anything to eat?"

Jake shot a quick look about. "We've been fed. You ease down by the wall here." He bent over Kirk, whispering. "Feel in the lining of my right coat pocket. Chunk of hardtack. Don't let the others see it." He raised his voice a little. "What's been happening to you? You look like something that dropped off a butcher's scrap wagon."

Kirk palmed the square of hardtack. "You're too damn close to the truth. Until we saw Archer downstairs we thought we were all going to be shot."

All trace of raillery left Jake's face. "No! Not *shot?*"

Kirk nibbled furtively at the square. "The only alternative we were told about was hanging."

125

Jake squatted beside him, one hand on his shoulder. "No wonder you look frayed out. But what was it all for, if you feel like talking?"

"Long story." Kirk chewed slowly. "Claimed to have found papers on Dahlgren's body saying we were under orders to burn Richmond and murder Davis and a lot of others. I saw photographs of them. Forgeries. Even spelled Dahlgren's name wrong in the signature. But enough people up there on the hill believed them, or wanted to. Said we were all outside the laws of war. Going to be shot or hanged. Then something changed all that. Got scared of reprisals or public opinion here and abroad. Maybe someone wondered if the orders *were* genuine. One thing's sure: They'd have had to consult General Lee, and if I know anything about him, he told them not to be damn fools."

Jake studied him, eyes narrowed. "So you've had to live a spell with *that* hanging over you. God damn it, they ought to send you back to our lines under a flag of truce and a hell of a big apology, not that the apology would help much."

Kirk, still busy with the hardtack, said, "I'd about given up on you, Jake. Time went by and you weren't brought in with the rest of us and no one knew anything about you. How'd you get in here?"

"Because the authorities are so damn literal-minded. After the ambush I wandered off south and came across some of Kilpatrick's stragglers and then we all got picked up. When I told the Rebs I'd been with Dahlgren, they wouldn't believe me. See? I was caught with Kilpatrick's men, therefore I *must* have been in his command. When I kept saying I'd been with Dahlgren, they got suspicious, figuring I had some sea lawyer's reason for lying, and they questioned me for hours." He began to grin. "I see why, now. Who ever heard of a man wanting to go boogie-boogie at a firing squad? That's the only funny side to the whole damn business."

"Glad they didn't believe you, Jake. They weren't

very courteous to us in the Pemberton Building. Well, that part's all over now. What I'd like to know is *who* did that forgery and why. And how they got Davis and Bragg to believe in it. They must be mighty jumpy up at the Capitol these days."

He broke off as a man in a tattered dressing gown with major's leaves pinned to the shoulders bent over him, holding out a rusty tin can. "You've just come in with the others?" said the major through a dense beard. "Try some of this soup, sir. It'll strengthen you."

Jake's hand gently pushed the can away. "Too rich for him, Major Timms. He's been on starvation diet and it'd make him sick."

The major backed away. "Thoughtless of me, thoughtless. If I may be of service to you later—you understand—don't hesitate—" He shuffled off, worn carpet slippers flapping at his heels.

Kirk sighed. "Maybe you know best, Jake, but I think I could have used a drop or two of real soup."

Jake lowered his voice. "That major. Indiana Infantry. They say he used to be the damnedest skinflint east of the Mississippi. Been in Libby most a year now and he's beginning to slip his cable. Gives everything away if the others don't watch him, because there are some here mean enough to meach him out of everything he gets. And don't worry about that soup. It was some of the rice and water we had for breakfast. He'd saved out a tot just to keep him going till we get more rice and water at noon. We all try to piece out our rations that way."

Kirk eyed Jake. "The way some people cling to a little square of hardtack, for example?"

Jake flushed. "Oh, hell, that damned stuff was so moldy and rotten that it'd take someone fined down like you to swallow it. I was going to throw it away. Well, beginning to get your bearings?"

Kirk turned away from Jake's embarrassment and fixed his attention on the room. It was well over a

127

hundred feet long and a good fifty across and the gnawed floor seemed carpeted with heads and shoulders of squatting men, seated men, men who lay at full length. Halfway down, a six-foot table cobbled out of scrap lumber shouldered above two even rougher benches. Two or three board bed frames sagged drunkenly. The side walls of the room were pierced with five barred windows each, and many of the panes were plugged with rags.

A dull buzz over everything and Kirk could see some of his fellows from Pemberton talking with wan animation to close-huddled groups. Desultory card games, played with nearly black, tattered cards were in progress. Off to his right, two men moved roughly whittled checker men over squares scratched on the floor. Farther down, a gray-mustached colonel scowled at a chessboard balanced between him and a gaunt captain. The colonel's hand played unsteadily over the crude chessmen, settled. The move seemed to delight him, for he cried in a high, cracked voice, "And your bishop's mine!" Then he shivered, collapsed to the floor.

Kirk started up, but Jake laid a hand on his arm. "Colonel Fabyan. Always faints when he makes a good move. A lot of the boys get hit like that when something excites them. Been on scant rations too long. He'll be up in a minute." He looked carefully at Kirk. "Maybe you better get some sleep or you'll be keeling over for any reason that happens to strike you."

"Can't sleep," said Kirk. "Feel as if I had red ants running up and down my legs. What's the routine here?"

"Hard to describe it. Mostly, we try to keep alive, or so the boys who've been in longest tell me. We're bust up into messes of twenty men. There are only sixteen in mine, so you can come in with us. Mess Number Nine. One man does the cooking each day. The stoves—just four of them and so rickety they wouldn't be worth fishing out of a creek—are down in the basement. When you're cook, you draw rations for our mess from the commissary and you've got to watch the portions they give you or you'll come out short. Not that it's much to keep track of. Each day there's supposed to be three quarters of a pound of corn bread, a gill of rice and a half pound of meat for each man, and sometimes, by God, there is. There'll be days when they'll issue you corn meal instead of bread and you bake your own."

A bearded, hook-nosed man in an officer's worn frock coat and breeches basted together from several pieces of blanket eased himself down beside Kirk. "Better warn him about sifting the flour," he said in a hollow voice as he clasped gnarled hands about his knees.

Jake nodded. "Lieutenant Fitts, 4th New York Cavalry, the Count di Cesnola's outfit. Captain Stedman, D.C.I.T."

Fitts said, "How-are-you?-Warn-him-about-sifting," all in one breath.

"I will. I was on yesterday and found enough sticks and twigs in the meal to start a fire and there was a mouse. At least, I think it was a mouse, judging by what fur was left on it."

"Cockroaches are worse," observed Fitts to the room in general. "Dried out proper they ain't so bad, but a fresh one squishes when you bite on it. Have you taken the captain to admire the view out our windows?" He rose and slouched absently away.

Jake snapped his fingers. "Thanks. It's about time I did. Listen, Kirk. The windows here are nice and big and the view's what I'd call elegant. You can look out and see people moving in the streets and birds flying by and horses and kids, just as if there weren't things in the world like bars and walls and guards. But it doesn't do to get too close to the windows. It's against rules and if the guards down below see you looking out, they're apt to break more panes shooting at you and we can't spare rags to plug up more holes. So here we are. I wonder who in hell it was who said, 'Stone walls do not a prison

129

make/Or iron bars a cage'? Maybe he was right, but they do sort of make a reasonable facsimile thereof."

Kirk stretched out at full length on the floor. "I'll remember about the windows. Got one question: When do you and I start figuring on getting out of here?"

Jake looked quickly at him. "Hey! Don't even whisper about that unless we're absolute complete alone! You'll get us—" He paused. "H'm, looks as if the red ants had got tired of doing squadron drill up and down your legs." He slipped off his jacket, wadded it and slid it expertly under Kirk's head, frowning down at his sleeping friend. "You old bastard, I sure was worried when you didn't turn up. Guess we'll start figuring on that escape about as soon as you're awake."

Slowly the routine of Libby settled about Kirk like a murky cloud. The rough floor that stayed gritty no matter how often it was swept became the focal point of his life. There he slept, sharing part of a torn blanket with Jake. There he sat among his messmates to eat the scant, often spoiled, always monotonous rations, using rusty tin plates, bits of shingle, broken knives for table ware. Lying, sitting or standing he came to accept the sudden waves of weakness that swept over him, the rarer periods of steadiness as his body tried to adjust to the new diet, accepting them as he did the floor or the bits of shingle or the verminous life that swarmed in the cracks in the boards. It seemed natural to wake shivering each night after sunset had chilled the spring air or to sweat as sunrise heated it again.

At all hours the cavernous room echoed to racking, rending coughs as tuberculosis made its slow way among the prisoners, weakened by the starvation rations, by previous hardships or half-healed wounds. The sounds were always in Kirk's ears and became as much of the routine as dawn break or sunset, something that always occurred and always would occur. Soon he could smile with the others when a particularly resonant cough was greeted with bantering shouts that hid deep anxiety: "Hey, you're getting a real nice volume into that, Art. We'll have to shift you down with the bassos at the other end of the choir." He came to look with something like reverence on the Confederate Army doctors who wore themselves into wraiths in their hopeless battle against malnutrition, filth, official blunderings and an almost total lack of medicines and drugs. In a similar light he saw the few Union medical officers who refused the exchange that was theirs by law to stay in Libby to carry on their work. He learned to keep silent when lanterns burned at midnight and shadows went dancing over the cobwebbed ceiling while a surgeon from Virginia and a surgeon from Ohio whispered yes, it is essential that a patient be moved to the ground-floor hospital, quite concur, pity he didn't mention these symptoms before. Nor could he entirely close his ears to rumblings and shouts in the street below: "Here's the dead cart! Stack your dead Yanks in the dead cart!"

He bowed to the discipline of the senior officer in the room, Colonel Daniel Coryell, Pennsylvania Infantry, and strictly observed Coryell's rules about sanitation, the allocation of floor space, the use of the few bits of rough furniture, the sharing out of any rare windfalls of extra food or clothing that came into Libby. And he realized the need for the law that any attempt at escape must be first talked over with and approved by the Pennsylvanian.

Kirk drew the pay of his rank, according to military law, but drew it in filthy, tattered, mended Confederate bills whose value slipped from day to day. A man could only look forward to accumulating an ill-smelling mass of them to make it worthwhile to stand by the prison commissary and read the schedule of Libby prices: "Potatoes (per bu.) $50; Onions, ditto, $60; butter, per lb., $12; coffee, ditto, $16." Sometimes it was possible to send out into the city and buy a book or even a musical instrument, but such favors depended on the mood of the

131

prison authorities. One night Kirk paid a Michigan lieutenant ten dollars for some forty soiled and torn pages
from *Adam Bede*. He had always disliked that book, but
at least he had something to read. Then he found a plu-
tocrat with a private library whose volumes could be
rented at a high figure. Other old residents had acquired
and on some evenings the room echoed to "Neeeeta!
a creaky bass viol, a dejected violin and a tinny banjo
Wa-ha-ha-neeeta! Ask thy soul if we should part." When
a fiddle string snapped, the impromptu orchestra, bank-
rupt by its great outlay, had to take up a collection to
replace it.

Early in the history of Libby Prison, captured officers
had formed school groups, each with its qualified lec-
turer, for the study of Greek, Latin, French, Spanish,
German, mathematics, literature and the sciences. As
pay accumulated, in fast-depreciating Confederate cur-
rency, the prison authorities allowed the purchase of
textbooks in Richmond and a respectable library had
been built up. Kirk found himself assigned to teach al-
gebra and, using an out-of-date book, guided some
twenty officers through elementary problems. "If A can
complete a given piece of work in four days and B can
complete it in five, I demand to know how long said
piece of work may be completed by both, working together." Jake took over a small but enthusiastic class in
navigation to which he expounded the mysteries of
clawing off a lee shore, heaving to and lying to, or jog-
ging off and on.

The big room, one of the six that made up the Libby
quarters, was far too crowded for exercise. One night
Kirk went down to the basement kitchens to look for a
piece of Mess No. 9's makeshift cooking equipment and
found some seventy officers going through a meticulous
foot drill under an Iowa major. He fell into step, rejoic-
ing at the chance to stretch his legs, to feel that indefin-
able surge of strength that comes from marching in
well-drilled unison. But the commands and the *"One-*

132

two-three-four's" of the squad leaders attracted the attention of the authorities and armed guards drove the marchers to their quarters. After that, about all a man could do was to stand well back from the south windows, well back to avoid a chance shot from a guard. From there it was possible to look out onto the James and the play of light and shadow on the water and the ripple of the little sailing vessels and the bridge that led to Mayo's Island from Manchester and the houses and the brown roads on the south shore and people walking and riding and wagons rolling, free to go where they wanted and when they wanted. But a look too far to the west showed a corner of Belle Isle and the wretched huts and leaky tents of the captive noncoms and privates.

The outer world set men to muttering about escape and Kirk heard of ruses that had worked in the past. You smeared your face and hands with soot and mingled with outgoing Negro laborers at dusk. If you rubbed your cheeks with Croton oil, eruptions like smallpox followed and you were rushed to the hospital; once there, you took the place of a corpse awaiting the dead cart (never a difficult feat, it was said) and rolled from it as it rumbled through Richmond. Men still spoke in awe of a man who had been a tailor in civil life and who agreed to make a coat, complete with insignia, for a Confederate officer; when the coat was finished, the ex-tailor slipped it on and simply walked out of Libby, unchallenged and within a week was inside the Union lines. And there was Colonel Streight's tunnel, so skillfully dug from the subbasement and on under 20th Street past the guard posts. Over one hundred officers had broken out from it just last February. It was a pity that most of the escapees were recaptured, the tunnel discovered and sealed up. At least, it was something to talk about.

And there was endless speculation about the treatment of Dahlgren's men, the forged documents, the threat of execution and then the abrupt dropping of the whole matter. Kirk thought that the plot had been brewed up suddenly by men fairly powerful in the Confederacy, though not big enough to carry it through by themselves. But *why* had such a plot been concocted in the first place? Perhaps those back of it had counted on world opinion damning a plan that contemplated the wanton burning of Richmond and the assassination of Davis and his Cabinet, ostensibly proved by the forged papers.

A wave of resentment against such brutal prosecution of the war might have swept the North. These, and a dozen other hypotheses, were earnestly debated in Libby, but none of the theories satisfied Kirk. Nor could he explain to himself why the executions, which undoubtedly had been planned, were canceled. It seemed likely to him that the whole truth of the episode would never be known.

One afternoon in mid-May Kirk and Jake stood watching the stir of free life across on the south bank while patches of bright sunlight chased little rain squalls down the valley of the James. Jake suddenly began shaping barely audible words out of the corner of his mouth and Kirk bent his head quickly toward him. It was necessary in Libby to talk like that when escape was the subject, since the least hint of a plan was sure to bring a dozen others crowding about, pathetically certain that at last they were to hear in detail the one, infallible, sure-fire route out. "Damn it," Jake was saying, "there's *got* to be a way of getting out and mingling with all that." He waved his arm at a string of farm carts, minute on the distant shore.

Kirk copied his tone. "There are plenty. The trouble is, we don't seem bright enough to clamp on to even the easiest one. God knows we've talked enough."

"I've made a cover of gray cloth for my kepi," Jake went on. "And I've got that set of Reb Navy buttons that that lousy guard Magoffin sold me, thinking that he was swiveling me. I'd take a chance on just walking out with you in your gray, but Coryell won't hear of it. I'm still thinking, though." He dropped his voice lower yet. "Been thinking about the tunnel that Streight dug."

Kirk shrugged. "So's everyone. But it's sealed up. We know that."

"Sure we know it. But the Rebs never filled up the full length, so far's I've heard, just the two ends. Suppose maybe someone broke into it from the side and bust out the west end. They won't be watching the ends, figuring they're all watertight and Pitler-tight. I got down into the subbasement just below where our stoves are, that day Coryell sent me to inspect the rice the boys were howling about. There's a little empty room just under our chimney. If we could bust into the chimney on our kitchen level, drop down a floor and get into the empty room, I bet we could chew our way into Streight's boulevard."

"It's worth thinking about," said Kirk slowly. "But, Lord, we'd need time and a lot of tools and more luck than's been running loose around this continent since it was discovered."

Jake sighed. "That's it. The tools. Give me them and I'd do without the rest. Maybe something'll turn up, though."

The stoves of Libby kitchen demanded highly skilled management. Top plates were cracked, lids were missing and broken legs were propped on crumbling bricks that canted each structure at an awkward angle and allowed loose-hinged oven doors to swing open at the least convenient moments. Smoke seeped in stinging coils from stovepipes, blurring the lanterns that hung from the basement's blackened ceiling and settling about the heads of the mess cooks. In this gloomy, soot-daubed dungeon there was not even the consolation of the smell of cooking food. Thin gruels of rice or corn meal, watery slabs of johnnycake do not give off the same

135

aroma as roasting joints, fresh-baked bread or bubbling coffee.

Yet in this dark cavern where half-seen men moved about the stoves, Kirk was actually humming to himself as he wiped his eyes with a blistered hand, humming, "An' I'll be in Scotland afore ye." This was a lucky, lucky day for Mess No. 9.

When the guard had escorted him downstairs, the ground floor had been crowded with civilians engaged on repair work. They were being issued rations in lieu of wages and Kirk, indistinguishable from them in his worn homespun, had been carried along in the press. To his surprise, a harried sergeant, flanked by boxes and barrels, had thrust double handful of peanuts, or pindars, as he called them, into his pocket, shoved two squares of corn bread with a slab of salt beef between them into his hands and told him for Chris'sake to step along and give the next man a chance. The guards had been too concerned with extricating him from the jam to notice the unauthorized issue and had hurried him into the basement kitchen.

Now some of the peanuts, chopped as fine as possible with the edge of a tin can, were mixed in with the cornmeal ration and were slowly roasting on an iron sheet. Kirk spread the blend about with a splinter, sniffing eagerly. Then he slid the brownish mass into a tall pot in which water was hissing. It would be, he thought happily, the most zestful, tangy coffee that Libby had known for a long time.

He turned to the scarred table behind him and the mound of chopped salt beef, peanuts, boiled rice and corn meal that he had prepared earlier. He scooped the mixture into a crusted iron pot, added water and a sparing pinch of the meager salt ration. He waited while a New Jersey lieutenant shifted a potful of some gluey stuff on the stovetop, then fought the oven door open and pushed in his dish. He called down to the murky basement, "Who's holding the watch today? Pete

136

Loomis? Hey, Pete, tell me in twenty-five minutes, please."

He leaned back against the table to rest from his struggle with the oven door, his eyes on the simmering coffee. The time allotted for the main dish ought to be enough, if the wood ration held out. He remembered that the winter his father died and money was very scarce in the Stedman house, his mother had contrived a vaguely similar dish for him and he had eaten two huge platefuls. She had laughed over her product, calling it Wonderland Pudding, and had said that she wished that she was hungry as he, but really she couldn't touch more than a spoonful. He had been surprised then that anyone could stop at a taste or two of such memorable food. Later he understood, but at that age a boy didn't stop to wonder about other people. At least with her teaching at the Botsford Female Seminary and his arrears and remittances, she would not have to watch someone else eat Wonderland Pudding, or make it, either, for that matter.

He opened the oven door, closed it. The pot did smell good and he stifled an urge to taste a bit from the top, just to make sure that it was fit for No. 9 Mess, of course. Then he remembered, across the deep absorption of his cooking, that there was more news, perhaps even more important than the added bulk and flavor that luck had given him for the prison rations. Barrels were stacked high and thick about the base of the chimney concerning which he and Jake had whispered so earnestly the week before. And there was . . .

The coffee can was bubbling and other cooks paused to sniff in envious wonder at the steam. Kirk smiled as he visualized Jake and the others getting their first taste of the corn-meal and peanut brew, their first whiff of the big pot. It might help perk up young Reardon, the Rhode Island gunner, whose sores did look like scurvy, and if they had anything to do with the swellings below Reardon's jaw muscles—well, Kirk had known of men strangling to death from scurvy settling there. Were there no antiscorbutics in the whole Confederacy? No vinegar or pickles or green stuff? Jake needed watching, too. He surely had not been on prison diet long enough to show scurvy symptoms, but once or twice Kirk had seen him prod furtively at a tooth as if it were sore or loose or both.

The guard at the foot of the stairs bawled, "Captain Stedman! Wanted at the Commandant's office!"

Kirk called, "Tell him to come here, if he's in a hurry. Against his own rules to interfere with a cook's work. He knows that."

"He says it's for your own good," shouted the guard. "Two men from your mess are coming down to relieve you."

Boots thumped on the stairs and Jake, followed by stoop-shouldered Lieutenant Mason from West Virginia, stormed into the basement. "What's all this?" called Jake. "You in trouble, Kirk?"

"I must be. They say it's for my own good and that sounds like something more than ordinarily nasty."

Jake pushed back his kepi. "We'll go with you."

"No need, Jake. Now look. That's our coffee in the pot beyond Mess Number Five's. And when Pete Loomis hollers, 'Twenty-five minutes,' snake our main dish out of the oven."

"This our coffee?" Jake began to sniff. "What the hell you got in here? *This* isn't our usual brand of calking pitch! Mason, bend the beak of yours over here. Kirk, you're permanent cook. No one's ever made corn-meal coffee like this since Libby was opened."

"Maybe I was just lucky. Here, take these." He handed Jake the squares of corn bread and the few remaining peanuts. Then he started reluctantly up the stairs, wishing that he could be present when the main dish came out. Would peanuts really add to the flavor? He turned into the wide central corridor and saw clear sunlight through the open main door, the brick fronts of the buildings opposite, the sloppy array of guard tents

138

in the vacant lots beyond. The outdoors beckoned to him and for a moment he clung to the illusion that he could walk right on and out into the clean April air. The guard behind him threw open a small door at the left and Kirk crossed the sill, then brought up short.

A young girl, pretty and cool in sprigged green muslin, was seated by the barred window, a chip bonnet, green-ribboned, on her bright hair. Kirk recovered himself, whipped off his hat, acutely conscious of his blistered, blackened hands and the flecks of soot on his face. Across the room from Lynn a very sleek lieutenant in well-cut gray was obviously enjoying Kirk's discomfiture. Kirk read the man's insignia—PRISON COMMISSARY—and mentally abolished him. "I hope I haven't kept you waiting, Miss Stockdale," said Kirk. "I was only told that I was wanted here and as it's my turn to cook for the mess, I didn't hurry. I—I hope there is something I can do for you."

Lynn was on her feet, one hand partly raised and her blue eyes very wide. "Captain Stedman," she said, almost in a whisper. "You've been ill. I—I hardly recognized you."

Kirk bowed. "I don't blame you. It's mostly due to kitchen work. That, and the fact that when our uniforms wear out, we have to take what we're given, like this civilian stuff that I've got on now." It was hard not to stare as she stood there in the dusty office. The gold of her hair and the deep blue of her eyes and the clear bloom of her cheeks and the red of her lips and the white of her throat and the slimly rounded poise of her figure were an almost unnerving contrast to his Libby surroundings. She started to speak, but he went on hurriedly, fearing that a few brief words from her would end the scene. "I thought civilians weren't allowed in Libby. This is very kind of you." (Anything, say *anything* just to prolong it.) "I hope you've been well." (And stand straight! Look her in the eye! Rags and soot don't count. You're a captain of Union Cavalry and some pretty good horsemen have been glad to ride with you.)

She seated herself. "Do sit down too, Captain," she said. "Father got permission at the Capitol to come here. Of course, Lieutenant Fyfe must be present."

Kirk took a chair, and Lynn went on, hands stirring uneasily in her lap. "I wanted to come here before," she began hesitantly, "but we've been in Wilmington." She paused, eyes on the gritty floor, then went on hurriedly. "At Frederick's Hall Station—I was very angry with you and it really wasn't your fault. I said I hoped I'd see you marched through Richmond as a prisoner." Her blue eyes met his. "But I didn't really mean it. I felt so badly afterward and it *was* a nasty thing to say. I just—"

Kirk spoke gently, surprised at how moved he was by her apology. "But it was only natural for you to say that, feeling as you do about the war."

She flung out a small hand. "It wasn't natural—I hope. I didn't want any such thing! I just wished that you and all your people would go back where you belonged and let my friends alone. And then"—her forehead wrinkled—"then I *saw* you, just as I'd said I hoped I would, a prisoner and that horrible crowd jeering and that poor dead colonel in his coffin on the platform. I tried to call to you, but then the horses were frightened. But I did try, tried to tell you that I didn't mean it, and you must have thought that I was gloating over you, and believe me, I wasn't."

"I saw you," said Kirk. "I knew you weren't gloating. Your expression told me that, but I'm very glad to hear you say it." She colored lightly and seemed about to rise. Kirk spoke quickly. "So you've been in North Carolina? They say it's fine country there, especially along the coast. Had you been there before?" (Go on talking, *please*. About anything. What did you see? How long were you gone? Where did you stay? Your dress is the color of young apples in the orchards around Dunbarton, and do you know how dark your eyelashes are against your cheeks? Don't go. Not yet!)

Lynn spoke quickly. "I hope you won't mind. Father—he's in the next office with the Commandant—well, Father and I brought you something from Wilmington, just something for yourself and your friends. We talked with a Captain Archer at Headquarters—he says he knows you—and he advised us about what you might need. It's over there in the corner by the little window." (Make that gesture again with those slim white fingers and that rounded wrist. Don't you know that just *being* here, you, a girl, is the greatest gift you could bring—except freedom?) "And I do hope you'll accept, for yourself and your friends."

"But of course I accept, and most gratefully."

She rose and Kirk got to his feet. Now it was really over and he felt as though a cloud were passing over the sun. "I must go now," she said. "We'll send over more things later, if we can get permission." (Send, not bring. The cloud deepened.) She looked at him steadily. "And you understand that I feel just the same about the war and about my friends here."

"Of course I understand."

She inclined her head in its chip bonnet, gave a grave little smile and was gone.

Kirk looked after her, but a chevroned arm in the corridor closed the door. He sighed, then mechanically turned to the corner she had indicated. His breath went in sharply. There were some noncommittal packages, a stone gallon jug marked VINEGAR in runny black letters, two quart jars of pickles and four smaller ones. His mind jumped to the room upstairs. Reardon's scurvy would clear up quickly and Jake could forget about his teeth. There would be enough to spare for other messes, like No. 7, where the Wisconsin major's gums were turning black. Jars of peaches beyond the pickles. How the sugar-starved men would rip those tops off! He pushed

141

his hat forward. "I'll have to have help to lug this stuff upstairs."

Fyfe stepped between him and the supplies. "I'll save you worrying about that. Reckon I'll impound the lot for the commissary."

Kirk studied the sallow face, the reddish fox eyes and the little, thin-lipped mouth. "No," he said slowly. "I don't think so."

"You couldn't be a hell of a lot wronger," laughed Fyfe.

"Oh, use your head, Fyfe. A man who's got influence enough to get an interview with a prisoner has got enough to light a fire under your tail if the stuff he sends doesn't get where he wants it to go."

"And just *how*'ll he know where it goes?"

"I'll let you sit back and fret over that."

Fyfe chewed nervously at his thumb. "You two must have worked that through the Capitol. Look here, Captain, I been here long enough to know some damn funny things happen in this town. There's channels where you wouldn't think they'd be. How you got word out's your own business, but if you could drop a hint—I wouldn't be knowing where—that Lieutenant David Fyfe'd be mighty pleased to get shifted to the prison at Salisbury, North Carolina, why I wouldn't forget it and it'd do you no harm, maybe a lot of good. Remember that? Fyfe to Salisbury."

"Well," said Kirk reluctantly, "I can't *promise* anything. Now how about sending upstairs for a couple of men to help me with this truck?"

The other stared at him, half suspiciously, half respectfully. Then he said, "I'll go myself!" and plunged through the door, only to pop his gingery head around the jamb. "The full name's David Fithian Fyfe."

"I've got a good memory," said Kirk, lifting the vinegar jug.

Word had flown about the big room that something

was in the wind, and when Kirk, George Hilliard, a limping Massachusetts gunner, and Jon Ek, a Minnesota engineer, reached the top of the stairs with their loads, the doorway was blocked by milling, buzzing men. Someone croaked, "Peaches! Got an iron spoon, a real jim-dandy, I'll trade for a scoop of that jar!" . . ."Here's Volume Two, Headley's *Napoleon and His Marshals*, hardly a page missing. It's yours for enough vinegar to fill this little tin. My cousin in Twelve's getting swollen glands." . . . "Two pair shoes that are almost mates and a spare heel you can cobble to fit either. Five slices of pickle will buy 'em." . . . "Hurry up! The old man's getting suspicious and if he—oh, Christ, here he is!"

Colonel Coryell pushed through the crowd. "What's all this, Stedman? Oh, I see. Set it all down right here. Pickles and vinegar count as medical stores. So does the white bread. I'll issue it to those who can't hold down johnnycake. *Chocolate?* I doubt if there's a crumb in all Richmond. Salt. That's for the common pool, too. So are those bolts of homespun."

Over the heads of the crowd Kirk saw the members of Mess No. 9 quietly sitting a circle, dipping busily into the big pot with apparent satisfaction. He felt a warm glow. So the peanuts and the extra meat *had* helped. Coryell went on. "Now these preserves and things, there aren't enough to go around and since I gather they were sent for your mess, you can keep them. And the vinegar jug belongs to Number Nine when it's empty. You'll find it useful."

"You'll see that Tim Reardon and Jake Pitler get some of the antiscurvy stuff, sir? Reardon needs it particularly."

"There'll be plenty," said the Colonel. "Now about this chocolate—" He raised his voice. "There's not enough for a nibble in any one mess. Now, gentlemen, you all know Lieutenant Clay of the Prison Guard. Of the whole Libby lot, he's the one man whose hand I'd

143

be proud to shake when this damn war's over. He's got a ten-year-old daughter lying in a bran box with a fractured hip and I'll bet she hasn't tasted anything better than brown sugar since '62." He sniffed the package wistfully. "Genuine. Best-quality Swiss. Gentlemen, I'd be *very* sorry to hear any objections raised."

There was a heavy silence. Then someone called, "That's a hell of a way to put it, Colonel. But—God damn it, *yes!* Any bastard want to argue about it?"

The crowd broke up grudgingly, Kirk, Hilliard and Ek brought the jars to the mess. Jake waved a wooden spoon. "The stuff's still hot, Kirk, and you ought to get a medal for this dish. Drop your jars in the middle here. By God! Peaches, raspberry and damned if this isn't honey drip! We'll issue the stuff a dollop at a time and make it last."

Kirk was given a shingleload from the pot and someone pushed the communal coffee can toward him. Feeling suddenly famished, he began to eat, realizing delightedly that he had been successful. The peanuts tied the whole mixture in together and the corn meal and rice were nicely crusted. He drank from the can, grinning across at Jake. Later, he would top off his meal with a sliver of peach.

Then he saw that his mess was surrounded by other officers. Some, their backs turned, were looking over their shoulders at the shiny jars. Others were frankly staring. Jake cried, "Oh, Jesus!"

Kirk set down the coffee can. "Right. It won't work. Mess leaders, fall in! We'll keep one jar. You draw lots for the rest."

Later Kirk carefully spread a film of honey drip on a morsel of corn bread and met Jake's questioning eye. "It all came from that Canadian girl I told you about. Her father got permission."

"Must have knocked on some pretty high-polished doors to get it. I'll see if I can't horse-trade for a sheet of paper and the mess'll send her a round-robin letter."

"Yes and it'd go right from here to Winder's secret police and they'd wear it out hunting for codes and invisible inks. And it might not do her and her father any good, a letter from us to them."

"M'm. Maybe safer to say nothing. Your friends might land in Castle Thunder." Jake munched solemnly on a pickle. "Just the same, you've got a damned unchristian suspicious nature. Now take me. I *love* the guards and the noncoms and officers in Libby. They want to see me smiling and happy and singing at my work. If they do give me bad news, it's just because they don't understand."

Kirk sat up. "What bad news?"

"After you ran away to play, leaving me to tend the stove, I needed a rag to open the oven door. The guard gave me a wad of newspaper. Richmond *Examiner*. So I examined it. Couldn't make out the date, but it must have been last month sometime. Been changes in our home port. Some may be all right. It's too early to tell. We've got a new papa, for one thing. Name of Ulysses S. Grant. Georgie Meade's still running the Army of the Potomac, but Grant's going to run him and about everyone else except Father Abraham. Grant's going to berth in Virginia and see if he can spoil Bob Lee's sleep for him. And there was another change. The Union Cavalry's going to be reorganized by—now get a good hold on your lifeline—by someone named Philip Sheridan."

"There's no cavalryman in the Army by that name!" cried Kirk.

"There is now. He was commanding a division, one whole *infantry* division under Grant. Now he's coming up here to tell Torbert and Merritt and Averill and Kautz and Custer which end of a horse is which."

"My God!" exclaimed Kirk. The Union Cavalry would be set right back where it had been in '62. Great strides had been made in '63, giving the Union horsemen the upper hand over their Confederate rivals.

Then in the past months that advantage had been frittered away under Meade, the engineer, who did not understand the role of cavalry and had been steadily relegating it to riding patrol and carrying messages. Now an *infantryman* who had never been in charge of more than a division was to be placed in supreme command of the Cavalry Corps of the Army of the Potomac!

Though they still had no concrete plan of escape, Kirk and Jake sought out Colonel Coryell. There was vital information available, they explained, concerning what escapees should do in the event of a successful break. Oh, yes, they were well aware that such details were usually given only to the leaders of a group who had an approved and matured scheme afoot, but how about men who saw a sudden, unexpected chance and seized upon it? Surely the Colonel could see that such prisoners would be helpless without some idea of where to go and what to do. Colonel Coryell refused at first and then, to Kirk's great surprise, agreed to instruct them. There would, he added, be heavy mental work ahead for them and they would do well to pay attention.

There was, said the Colonel, a surprising number of active Union sympathizers in the devotedly Confederate state of Virginia and in Richmond itself. Messrs. Stedman and Pitler would have to learn by heart the names, locations and descriptions of as many of these as possible. No, it would not do to count on one sympathizer alone, for an escape route, no matter how well planned, might have to be abandoned in emergencies and escapees *must* know alternate people to whom to turn for advice, shelter, supplies or concealment. Sometimes a definite address could be furnished, but more often the person sought could be found only by following up a specified creek, an old wagon road or a distinctive ridge.

Yes, there was a good deal of detail to remember, so the Colonel would divide up the task. They both must

146

learn all the places in Richmond. Then let Captain Pitler memorize the havens to the east of the city and Captain Stedman those to the west. This did embrace a very wide area, but in some sections Union sympathizers were scarce and that reduced the number of points to be committed to memory.

Now for Richmond ...

9

Jake Pitler Takes Charge

One morning, after a breakfast of the thinnest of rice gruels, a sliver of corn bread in which maggots had been baked and a swallow of bitter acorn coffee, Kirk stood looking moodily out a south window, standing well back in case of a chance shot from a guard below. The late August sun was bright on the far bank of the James and the roofs of Manchester just across Mayo's Island. A locomotive was lazily shunting flatcars west along the Richmond and Danville line, its hopper stack sending great balloons of burnished smoke to the blue of the sky. Bright glints showed from the flatcars, telling of shovel blades and picks carried by a working party bound on some unguessed errand. Kirk thought of the men on those cars, the sun strong on their backs and the wind off the James sweeping over their tanned faces. They would be singing, joking, squabbling, swapping tobacco out in the free air. When the cars halted, they would drop over the sides, drink from a spring or a well, pick late berries while listening for the creak of turning wheels. The more crafty would hide, spend the rest of the day roaming the countryside, then innocently hop on the train on its return trip, hoping that their non-coms had not noticed their absence. Free men, immersed in a rich, full life, and men to be envied, even if their rations were probably little better than those in Libby.

The panes began a faint chatter in their frames and there was a vibration, almost too slight to be detected, in the air. Kirk glanced down the James. Off by Petersburg, heavy Union and Confederate guns were firing, but they sounded no closer than when he had first heard them back in June. He looked south again. A Negro, head back as though singing, was prodding a yoke of oxen along a dirt road. Up a cottage path a scrap of a girl in a pink pinafore ran bravely on unsteady legs, arms wide. A sunbonneted woman knelt, perched the girl on her shoulder and went lightly around the corner of the house, a small animal, puppy or cat, racing after.

From the floor a thin voice called, "What you looking so glum about?"

Kirk saw the flushed face of Karl Hofstra, a Delaware lieutenant, grinning at him over the edge of a tattered blanket. "Hello, Karl," he answered. "How are you feeling?"

Hofstra's grin spread his sunken cheeks wider. "Hate to say it, with so many of the boys down with fevers and scurvy, but, by God, I'm feeling damn fine!" Unnaturally bright eyes shone. "Plain damn fine. Give me a few days and I'll be taking my turn at the stove again. Maybe even tomorrow, if I can just get my legs under me. Say, did you hear they took off two of Bill Delaney's fingers in the hospital yesterday?"

"Just two fingers? Bill's lucky, if he heals clean. That Alabama doctor was afraid the whole hand would go. Yes, Bill's damn lucky." Hofstra raised himself on his elbows. "*Lucky?* Didn't you know Bill was heading to be a real concert pianist? By God, he was *good!* I don't mean

150

this tinkle-tinkle stuff. I heard him play in a bar in Washington when we were on pass. Something by someone with one of those damn German names. Not what you'd call a tune to it, but right away two fights stopped, the bartender forgot to close the bung of a beer keg and one of the bar girls started crying. He'll never play concert now. Christ, I hate to think of Bill, and me feeling so good." He broke into a paroxysm of coughing.

Kirk knelt by him, rubbing him between the shoulders. "Take it easy, Karl. Yes, that's tough on Bill. I never knew he played. There, that better now?"

Hofstra lay back, panting. "Thanks. These damn barks used to scare me, but they've felt kind of different the last few days, just as though I was all healing up. Like to do something for Bill. He could have two of my fingers, if the docs could find some way to hitch 'em on. A lawyer like me don't need 'em, but Bill sure does, concert playing. Oh, and look! Did I show you the letter I got from my kid in that mail they let us have last week?"

"Mail?" Kirk had forgotten about that trickle of letters. There had been nothing for him in it, or in earlier ones. "Oh, no. I don't think you did."

Hofstra's smile widened again and he slipped a wasted hand into his jacket. "The first letter she's ever written. 'Course, she used to make scrawls on what Kitty—that's my wife—wrote, but this is a *real* letter and she's only six last May. Here, you read it."

Kirk smoothed out the crumpled sheet, where shaky script staggered up and down with fat-bellied *b*'s and wobbly, long-stemmed *t*'s. He read:

Dearest Papa,
    I hope you are well. I am. We all miss you. Aunt Madge made a dress for my Mary Ann doll, that's her name, that you sent me and she has got a cape and a hat, too. And the dress Aunt Madge made for her. Last night my gray kitten ran away and I cried

151

and he came back this morning aren't you glad?
Come home soon and my love and Mama's,

Patty

Hofstra watched him anxiously. "Pretty good for a kid just past six? 'Course, I guess Kitty wrote it all out for her, good and big, just the way Patty'd say it, and then she copied it. What you taking so long for? That's not hard to read, six or no six."

Kirk handed him the sheet. "No," he said slowly. "It's easy to read. Mighty easy. Thanks for letting me see it. I *was* a little down in the mouth, but this certainly helped me." (Was some Virginian, dreading the coming of winter over Lake Erie to a prison on Sandusky Bay, hoping for news of the pink-pinafored mite in the cottage yard across the James?)

Hofstra chuckled. "Cute, wasn't it, about that doll? I sent it from Washington last year. You know, I'm mighty positive I'm going to get exchanged real soon. Got a feeling about it. I'll get leave and back pay and I'll bring a brooch for Kitty and the biggest doll in Washington for the kid. Wish I had an ambrotype of the two to show you. She's got curly black hair just like Kitty's, but some folks think her eyes are like mine. You'd see—" He went rigid, clutching at his throat and gasping.

Kirk slipped an arm under his shoulders. "Get your breath. Slow and easy." The thin body shook as though in answer to the distant concussions that still rolled up the James. "Now you're getting it better. And thank God, here's that Alabama doctor." He called, "Dr. Penn! Mind coming over here a minute?"

Tall but frail, the Alabamian came quickly from the door and dropped his bag by Hofstra, who lay panting, propped against Kirk's knee. "Mean to tell me you aren't up and about? Seems like you're just naturally malingering."

Hofstra's breathing was easier as he said, "Honest, I

152

feel tiptop, except for coughing, and that's nowhere near as bad as it was."

Kirk looked at the doctor, but he was peering into his worn bag. "Mm, no, won't give you this. It's for really sick folk. Nor this. Let's see now. Might as well get rid of this dollop of pine balsam. Won't hurt you, and I can use the bottle for real medicine. I'll pick it up empty on my next rounds. By rights I ought to send you down to unload that lumber schooner just outside. Let him lie back, Mr. Stedman. If we keep on babying him, he'll fix to have every soul in Libby waiting on him."

Hofstra beamed delightedly. "Guess you found me out, Doc. Hey, Sted, Major Shane's hollering for you."

Again Kirk tried to meet Penn's eyes, but the tall doctor was intent on his bag. Kirk crossed the room reluctantly. Behind him, Hofstra was saying, "Did I show you that letter from my kid, Doc?" Penn answered, "No, but I'd be right happy to see it."

Major Shane, acting as Coryell's adjutant, apologized for bothering Kirk. Blankets had been received from the United States Sanitary Commission and there was some discrepancy in the count. Would Kirk go to the subbasement and help Captain Pitler verify the lot? Kirk could look at the invoices at the office on the way down.

It took Kirk nearly half an hour to go through the smeared sheets with their endorsements and surcharges. As he left the office he saw Dr. Penn coming down the stairs, one step at a time, holding on to the rail. Penn looked up and then sank to the lowest tread, his bag dangling from slack hands. Kirk stood over him, worried. "Doc, if you don't take care of yourself, who's going to see to your patients? Why don't you stir up Dr. Grigsby? He only comes in once a week."

Dr. Penn nodded vaguely. "I've sent for a stretcher."

"Well, you tell the bearers to lug you to the nearest doctor."

Penn swayed back and forth like a slow gray metronome. "Stretcher's not for me. Guess I've seen too many patients die. Too many for one man to see. Just hit me, coming down the stairs. Like a revelation." He pointed an unsteady finger at Kirk. "Know what's going to happen? The biggest, most beautiful doll in Washington's going to sit on a shelf and rot and rot and rot because the only man in the world who knows about her is never going to come in and point at her and say, 'I want her for Patty.' " He pried himself to his feet. "Seen too many die. What did he have to show me that letter for? Seen others like it here in Richmond. And why'd I care anything about *him*? Seen *hundreds* like him. Just another dead Yankee prisoner. I wade amongst 'em hip-deep and they reach out for me. 'Doc, my hip wound's suppurating. Fix it up for me, will you?' 'Doc, I puke up everything I eat. Can't you get me something to soothe my innards?' 'Please make my gums quit turning black, Doc.' 'I feel real good, Doc, but I keep coughing up blood.' So what's one more?"

He suddenly lurched forward and blundered on, one hand scrabbling along the wall. Kirk called, "Dr. Penn! Wait a minute." But the bent figure shouldered around a corner and Kirk heard a clanking of chains and a rasping of bolts as a heavy outer door was opened for Dr. Penn. Then the doctor's voice sounded, a little brisker. "I'll be here tomorrow, same time."

Kirk wiped his forehead. Hofstra was gone, of course. He had seen other consumption cases and had learned the meaning of that high surge of optimism, that feeling of well-being that marked the last stage. But Dr. Charles Penn, of Selma in Alabama, was going too, killing himself working over enemy prisoners. And his going would lay a heavier burden on the other doctors, until one by one they too would see the death of one patient too many. Kirk ran down the stairs, his feet drumming out the words, "Got to get out—somehow—got to get out!"

In the storeroom Jake called from a pile of blankets, "About time you got here. I never learned to count above ten and I've run out of fingers."

"Listen, Jake, Karl Hofstra just died."

"Jesus, that's tough. But it was tomorrow or the next day, if not today. I've been watching him."

"And Dr. Penn's getting worn mighty thin. He'll be around tomorrow, same as usual, though."

"He's the best of a good lot."

"They're all good. Say, isn't there a guard around here?"

"Was. But I haven't seen him in the last twenty minutes. Hell, they don't need a guard down here. Nailed up so tight a teredo couldn't bore out. What do you think of my new coat?" He puffed out his chest. "Only about five people wore it before me and it ought to last two months at least." It was a Union officer's frock coat, originally blue, but now faded by wear, washings and dyeings to an indeterminate grayish hue.

Kirk grinned. "Don't get feeling so grand that you start giving me orders."

"I wouldn't bend that low. You look like a Reb dock worker. Gray-green coat, horn buttons, brownish pants!"

"How about *your* buttons? Marked with an anchor and c.s.n.! I don't believe they're even regulation!"

"At least they're brass. Do you smell smoke? Hate to get trapped down here. One thing, the Rebs'd give me a military funeral on account of the c.s.n. They'd just shovel you into the James. Damn, it's getting stronger. Wonder where that door leads to." He walked across the room, tugged at a knob.

"Smoke must be from the kitchens. Where'll I start my count of the blankets?" He bent over the pile. "I said, *where* do I start?"

But Jake was gone and the door was ajar. If Jake went too far beyond it, he could run into serious difficulties. Kirk started forward, then recalled a Libby law: if a prisoner takes a course that you don't understand, let him alone; if he's in trouble, you may make it worse; if he's not, you may spoil what he's trying to do. He went

155

back to the blankets and began a careful count, his mind taut with suspense as time slipped by.

He heard many voices outside, arguing angrily. They faded, came closer, topped by Jake's, though Kirk could not make out any words. He counted on. Suddenly Jake's head, crowned with a flat cap, showed around the jamb, sunlight from beyond touching a miniature brass anchor on the cloth just above the visor. Jake raised a cautioning finger, then barked, "For Christ's sake, Carey, get out here and get to work!"

With anyone else, Kirk would have hesitated. But this was Jake Pitler, who once led his troop and the D.C.I.T. through a sleeping Confederate camp. He moved forward and Jake nodded, pointed at Kirk and slumped his own shoulders. Kirk's breath caught in his throat and his mind fixed on the immediate present, not reaching beyond the limit of each step. Jake had found *some-thing* worth doing and that was enough for him. With another snarl at Kirk to look alive and follow him, Jake went *south* down the corridor. Kirk stepped out of the storeroom and, with an impulse that was almost mechanical, closed the door gently behind him, found a key jutting from the outer side and turned it. Then he waded on through thickening smoke that dimmed the bright sunshine. The shouts grew louder and a clunk-clank, a splashing of water and a harsh hissing enveloped the voices.

Kirk was outside the walls of Libby with the narrow ship basin before him and the blue of the James beyond. To his left, a long line of men passed buckets of water to a group on the deck of a listing schooner. More men manned a pump that shot a wavering stream into the ship through a leaky hose. Black-edged flames darted through welling smoke.

Jake pointed to the right, snapping, "Stand by the barge horse's head!" Living from moment to moment, Kirk slouched away toward the far end of the basin where a blunt-nosed barge lay with two anxious-eyed civilians running about the roof of the low deckhouse. On the pavement a horse sidled nervously, its hoofs tangled in a tow rope. Kirk shuffled on, repressing a start as he saw the letters C.S.N. painted on the bow of the barge, and began gentling the horse. He set his whole being to the task, stroking its neck and clearing its hoofs from the tow rope. He was just a laborer, vacant-eyed and slack-jawed, and what went on down the basin had nothing to do with him. Let those who got paid for looking after such matters worry about the fire.

He managed not to look round as Jake's voice boomed, "I'm telling you for the last time I'm not going to risk Navy property. That barge goes out now! Go ahead and report me and be God damned to you! If you had a brain in your head, you'd get some hands forward to cut those halyards. Flames'll run up 'em like a 'coon climbing a 'simmon tree. I told you! for Christ's sake, whistle up some axes and chop away that foremast. The way you're listing, you'll pitch a mess of burning canvas and wood right through the windows, and how the hell will you explain that, with a lot of God-damn Yanks jumping around inside?"

Inwardly taut, Kirk made his fingers fumble over the worn harness. The shouts meant nothing to him, nor the clank of the pump nor the whack of axes. They were as meaningless as the stacked muskets of the guards who sweated in the bucket line. Jake's voice sounded nearer. "No! If what I told you's too much for your thick head, my staying around wouldn't do any good. And have your men stand clear when that mast topples!"

Kirk heard a thump as boots landed on the barge, then an unknown voice said, "Sure am obliged to you, Lieutenant. I had to sign for this barge at the yard and if anything—"

Jake cut in. "That's all right. God-damn Army thinks it's running the country. Huh! Trying to tell *me* I couldn't move a Navy barge! I'll go up with you a stretch in case anyone asks questions. Better cast off. Those baboons will probably get the fire out, but if they don't, well, everyone knows Libby is mined and just one spark'd send up the whole town from Chimborazo to the Capitol. I'll take the tiller and you two stand by with the poles. My man Carey'll see to the horse, but you better watch him. He's so damn stupid it takes four men to tell him what to do and eight to see that he does it." Jake's voice soared. "Carey! Cast off that horse and steer him along the tow path." Kirk tried to look bewildered. Jake's tone dripped with patient sarcasm. "Yes, that string that's tied to that piece of iron on that piece of stone. Just untie it. Then lead the nice horse straight ahead. Keep to the pavement. Nice horse can't walk on water. Now, for Christ's sake, have you got *that?*"

Kirk blinked at him, then slowly freed the halter shank as he clucked dully to the horse. The animal leaned into its breast band, fought against the dead weight of the barge and began to amble west along the edge of the basin. Kirk still held his thoughts in check. He and Jake were out of Libby. How it had come about, he didn't try to guess. He was merely an unskilled laborer, probably unfit for military service, employed by the Confederate Navy and, at the moment, under the thumb of a most overbearing, unsympathetic officer of that Navy. Out of the corner of his eye he could see Jake lounging by the tiller while the two civilians from the Navy Yard tramped back and forth with their poles, adding their strength to the tugging of the horse. He was at the end of the basin, crossing to its outer edge over a plank draw. The men on the barge cast off the tow rope, then made it fast again, as the barge slid under the draw and out into the James. In the rear, men were still shouting and the pump clanked on. There was a rumbling overhead and Kirk stopped to gape up at heavy carts passing over Mayo's Bridge, like a yokel on his first visit to a city. His acting was rewarded by a howl from Jake and a wooden block whizzed past him.

Jake was still yelling angrily as Kirk guided the horse under the arches of the Richmond and Danville Railroad bridge, but Kirk only bobbed his head several times, showing a placating, open-mouthed grin.

He let his attention wander and peered north at the city rising on its hills above him, at the bulk of the Gallego Flour Mills, the Shockoe Tobacco Warehouse. Tilting his head, he could see the Capitol, its roof soaring on high pillars over everything. He wiped his sleeve across his forehead as though bewildered. Another chunk of wood buzzed into the ground at his feet and he turned to see Jake leaning over the side of the barge shaking his fist at him.

There was no need to feign surprise. The bow was well past him and the tow rope dragged slack. The barge was only a few feet away and the two civilians were dropping the end of a battered ramp ashore. Jake bawled, "Now, Carey—" Then he threw up his hands in disgust, ran down the ramp and led the horse aboard. Kirk shuffled his feet. "You want I should come?" he asked.

"No! God damn it, I never want to see you again, but I've got to account for you somehow. Get aboard. Walk around if you want to, but if your feet begin to splash, it'll mean, you've stepped into the river." Jake turned on his heel and went aft to the tiller while one of the men made the horse's halter shank fast to a ring.

Kirk rubbed his sleeve across his face again and shambled forward beyond the end of the deckhouse out of eyeshot. The barge was nosing slowly along, keeping close to the north bank and weaving through a maze of wooded islets that broke the blue surface like high clumps of green feathers. He couldn't understand *how* the barge went upstream, aided only by the poles. Then he recalled that the James was tidal. The tide must have set in soon after they left Libby and its strength had been enough to outpace the horse. Now tide and pole did the work. He wondered what Jake's thoughts were,

159

or rather, what they had been when he first went out to the edge of the basin. He must have seen some chance play of circumstances that had dictated the subsequent moves. Kirk knew that there were few to equal Jake in snatching at the one split second that could be turned to rich advantage. From the moment of pushing off, though, there could have been no planning. Therefore, Jake must be improvising each step. It would be up to Kirk to maintain his present role and at the same time keep his mind alert to fall in with whatever move came next.

There was another railroad bridge, the Richmond and Petersburg, Kirk guessed, and then a heavy smell of burning charcoal and chemicals from the land side. Low, sprawling buildings with black-spouting chimneys loomed and dirty wharves heaped with scrap iron. The stunning smash of trip hammers was loud in Kirk's ears. Negroes were dragging a shattered gun trail out of the nearest pile and he had a queasy feeling as he read the letters "—USETTS LIGHT BTY" on the blistered paint. His fingers worked as he realized what he was seeing. The Tredegar Iron Works were the very heart of all Confederate armament manufacture. If—*if* a few of Dahlgren's troopers, armed with explosives, could have worked down to this point, it would have been worth every man and every horse lost on the expedition.

The Tredegar wharves were behind and the barge was easing along the sloping north bank. Kirk looked south, then turned away. There lay long, high-crested Belle Isle with its squalid tents and swarming prisoners and guard posts, nothing for a man precariously out of Libby to see or ponder over.

The barge stopped close to the bank and Jake was calling, "You didn't need to bring me this far, but thanks all the same. You can pole back to Tredegar and tie up there. You'll probably find Major Mason in Building Number Three. Don't let him overload you.

160

He doesn't know much about boats." He raised his voice. "Carey! We're going ashore here."

Kirk scrabbled to his feet and pointed uncertainly. "You mean here?"

"Yes! Get going."

Kirk plopped over the side. The slope was steeper than he thought and he went up with conscious awkwardness on all fours, heading for a deep grove. In its shelter, he stood and looked back. Jake was walking easily along, whistling to himself. Kirk went deeper into the grove until the trees hid the river. Then he caught at a low bough, looking forward with unfeigned blankness. Improvisation would have to be swift from now on. Perhaps Jake had figured at least one more step. He stood clinging to the bough, waiting for him to catch up.

Jake's footsteps were no longer assured. He was stumbling on, blundering into boles, tripping over roots. Close by Kirk, Jake's knees buckled and he sank to the ground, his face a gray-white. Kirk reached out, but Jake waved him away, was shaken with a spasm of futile retching, then slumped forward, head in his hands. "I'm done! Can't think a step ahead."

Kirk said quietly, "Get your breath. You've done ten men's work today. In a few minutes we'll figure out what comes next."

Jake's hands were shaking. "Got to. Fast. But my brain's quit on me. Legs are gone. Not going to trip you up. If you can figure something and I'm still in a dead calm, hit out for yourself. I'll make for the city when I can and cover your tracks. Here, take this. From the barge." Without lifting his head, Jake fumbled under his coat, tossed out a deep, narrow canvas bag, rope-handled, with c.s.n. stenciled on it.

Kirk looked intently at him. Then he said, "About time I did some of the work. I'll go on patrol. Wait right there." He moved on through the trees, sinking to the ground as he neared the far edge. Just before him was what seemed to be a park, climbing a steep slope. To the left, carefully tended grounds, a maze of carriage paths and a shimmer of white marble on another hill could only be Hollywood Cemetery, which he remembered from maps. And at the base of the two hills was a wide ribbon of blue-green water, reaching out from the city on the east and stretching away and away to the west. He thumped the ground with his fist. Lord, but he must be stupid with fatigue to have forgotten it, he who had studied the bends and turns and locks of the James and Kanawha Canal on many maps back in Stevensburg before the raid. He lay, chin in hand, eying the far bank. A few carriages rolled through Hollywood. A woman in black with a blur of bright flowers in her hand knelt by a gravestone. A child's hoop bowled crazily down a park path, a shouting boy in pursuit. A parade of lazy ripples, pushed by a slow wind, moved west up the canal. Kirk looked east toward the city, eyes narrowing, while several minutes passed. Then he got stiffly to his feet and went back into the grove where Jake still sat, head in his hands. Kirk said quickly, "Got something figured."

Jake made an uncertain gesture. "Maybe the less I know, the better."

Kirk knelt beside him. "You've got to hear everything. We've a good ten minutes, maybe more. Listen. You're still in the Reb Navy. You've had James fever, and you've got leave to lie up for a couple of days. Then you're bound for the blockade-runners' base at Wilmington. Now for me, I'm still civilian, but I'm an expert on ship's machinery and they need me badly at Wilmington. I'm independent as hell, got no use for officers' gold braid and it's your job to get me down into North Carolina."

Jake's head was still sunk, but a flicker of life crept into his voice as he asked, "Who do we tell that to?"

"Never mind just now. Start picking up some of the

chunks of wood lying around here, short, thick ones. Then we're both going to shed our underclothes."

Slowly Jake rose; his eyes seemed to clear. "All right. You're the bos'n."

In a few minutes the canvas bag bulged with solid pieces of wood, wrapped in underwear. One end of a drawer leg dangled from the mouth. Kirk examined the pack, stuffed the leg a little farther in. "That's enough for show. Wish I could find something that'd clank like a tool kit, but this'll have to do. Now let's go."

Jake gave a low exclamation as he saw the canal. "Begin to get the idea now, Jake?" asked Kirk, pointing east. Out of the first hints of dusk, a canal boat glided on, a pair of horses in tandem plodding heavily along the tow path. "Lynchburg-bound, Jake. South and west, just the opposite direction the Rebs'll expect us to take when they miss us at Libby. And that barge'll be empty, because everything comes into Richmond, nothing goes out, nothing that'd need guards. No bargeman is apt to refuse a lift to a Navy officer, Wilmington-bound. And we can hop off where we like."

There was no sag to Jake now. He said slowly, "You've found us something that's worth a try. One thing, we've got to have a name for you. How about James Harpell? That was your old troop guidon and you'll remember it all right." He gave a hitch to his coat. "I can handle this talk. I've *got* to. Stay here on the bank till I call you."

Jake dropped to the towpath.

Leaning against a tree, Kirk watched the tandem hitch thump slowly along while the barge glided gently on the mirror surface of the canal. Jake nodded to the Negro by the lead horse. "All right, boy, rest your feet a minute." Then he hailed, in a strong, confident voice, "Ahoy, the barge!"

A bent man with a stubble of beard masking his cheeks swung the tiller over and the canal boat nestled close by the bank. "Evenin', sir," said the canaller.

"Got room for a couple of passengers?" asked Jake.

The man spat reflectively into the canal. "I'd say so. Ain't the swiftest travel in the world, though."

"It's that or renting a rig at the livery by Westham—and Jesus, I hate horses. I'd walk, only I've got a blistered heel."

"Seems you'd 'a' taken the steam cars."

"You ridden 'em lately? Engines break down or you get pushed onto a siding and wait all night. Or the God-damn Army grabs the train and dumps the passengers off plumb in the middle of nowhere."

"Where you bound?"

"Wilmington, but I'm stopping off to see some kin in Fluvanna County."

"*You* ain't from these parts."

"Cambridge, Dorchester County, Maryland," answered Jake evenly.

The bargeman jerked a thumb toward Kirk. "Who's him?"

"He's a marine-engine expert, Baltimore born, that I'm taking to Wilmington. They sure need him, the way those blockade-runners pound their engines to pieces. But he can fix 'em. Hell, he's Jim Harpell, the man who put the machinery in the *Merrimac*, back in '62, when all the bigwigs said it couldn't be done."

"Reckon you can come aboard all right."

"Obliged to you," said Jake. "Oh, Mr. Harpell! He'll be glad to take us. I think we better go right aboard."

Kirk slowly shouldered the canvas bag, growling, "Hurrying all I can," and slouched down the bank, muttering to himself and kicking at pebbles and weeds as he came.

"Say!" said the bargeman. "S'pose he'd take a look at the tiller? Been acting skitterish and can't no one seem to fix it."

Jake made a weary gesture. "These God-damn mechanics. Touchy as a new-minted Army lieutenant.

I'll ask him. Oh, Mr. Harpell, would you be willing to see what's wrong with the tiller?"

Kirk stopped, surveying the barge with obvious distaste. "Where'm I going to berth?" he grunted.

The bargeman said eagerly, "Anywhere suits you."

"I'll cast round and choose."

"And you'll fix the tiller, Mr. Harpell?" Jake's voice was soothing.

"Maybe I'll think about it. I'd figured to eat some, first."

"Oh, I'll eat you good," cried the bargeman.

"What you going to eat us?"

"Got real bread and bacon and ham." He looked anxiously at Kirk. "And brown sugar and milk. Can spare a toothful of real coffee, too."

Kirk's brows drew down. "Had my mouth kind of set for greens."

"Got beet tops and snap beans. All that truck's in the deckhouse. Good firebox, too."

Kirk turned to Jake. "Tell him if I do take an idea to see that tiller, I ain't wearin' out my own tools for him."

"You'll fix it?" The bargeman's face glowed under its stubble. "There's tools aplenty in the cuddy beyond the vittles. Here, I'll tote your bag for you."

Kirk eyed him sourly. "I lost tools before, letting strangers tote my bag, lost store clothes, too." He threw a leg over the side of the barge and dropped onto the deck. Then he looked at Jake. "Who's going to hand me the tools I want, s'posing I do take an idea to look at things?"

Jake turned hopelessly to the bargeman. "God damn if *I* know what's rilin' him now. I'll try and nurse him along." He pulled out two tattered notes. "Will this cover what we eat?"

The other waved the money away. "Worth thribble to get that tiller fixed. Besides, I'm heading for country where food's plenty. I'll be bringing a load back to

Richmond and it always seems like a few bags leak when they get on board."

"Obliged to you. Better get your team started or Harpell'll be taking shore leave." The horses leaned into their harness and the barge resumed its slow glide west up the canal, the bargeman standing in the bow, an anxious eye on the tow rope. Jake found Kirk staring gloomily into the deckhouse. "Well, Mr. Harpell, found what we need?"

Kirk barely glanced at him. "Never was much of a hand to cook."

Jake forced a jovial grin. "I'll stand galley watch."

"Reckon you will. I'll take a look at the tiller first, so while you're down there, just prize up the lid of that tool chest."

Jake dropped into the low cabin while Kirk kept up a steady flow of directions. "That. Yes, and that one. No, next to it. Now what the hell you think I want with *that*? Pull out that drawer."

Jake emerged with a load of tools that Kirk fingered disparagingly. "Don't say as how I can make do with 'em. Let's see what's wrong." He clumped aft, Jake following. When they reached the stern, Kirk muttered out of the corner of his mouth, "Find out what the matter is and tell me what to do. While I'm doing it, I'll figure out how we can get to Union people. We're west of Richmond, so it's my job."

Jake bent over the sternpost. "H'm. Ringbolt's about worn through, but there's a spare one in the tool chest. Too much play in the tiller shaft. Take this wrench and loosen that nut."

Kirk adjusted the tool, threw his weight against it while his mind ran on feverishly. "We're in Goochland County. Next comes Fluvanna with the Rivanna as boundary. James Maxwell, planter, two miles west of Bryant's Ford on the Rivanna. George Hildebrant, small farmer, on Little Byrd Creek, about five miles west of the Rivanna. The main creek, Byrd's, flows into the

166

canal beyond the only really big bend. Hildebrant and Maxwell." He said aloud, "Here comes the damn bolt. Rotten wood under it."

"Huh!" grunted Jake. "All this needs is sound timber in the post. Now act mad and point to the deckhouse. I saw a solid chunk of wood we can fit right in here. Don't think our man's watching us, but we better act as if he was. Jesus! On the canal! Can't believe it."

"Maybe *I* will, when you tell me how it all happened."

"You still won't believe it." Jake trotted off to the deckhouse, calling, "Sure, Mr Harpell. I know just what you mean."

Kirk's thoughts went on. "Byrd's is more than thirty miles from Richmond and we're making about six miles an hour. Guess that's the best place to jump off. It'll be at night and the bargeman'll never be able to say when or where we left him. Find Hildebrant, then hit east, three or four days' travel, ought to hit into Ben Butler's lines, down the York peninsula. Hildebrant'll give us our route and tell us whom to look for."

Then he heard Jake calling, "Where do you moor for the night?"

"Don't. Pick up a fresh relay of horses near Goochland Court House," answered the bargeman.

"Mean you're at the tiller all night?"

"Kind of got to be, but, Jesus, mister, do I need sleep!"

"Hell, I'll stand a tiller watch for you. I'm all slept up."

"You *will?* Man, but this is my lucky day."

Kirk's heart beat faster. The change of horses at Goochland would give him a bearing—a big bend in the canal beyond, then a wide, shallow, U-shaped turn a couple of miles across at the base. Byrd Creek came in where the canal straightened out again. And Jake at the tiller and their host asleep!

Kirk looked up grumpily as Jake knelt beside him,

handing him a wooden post. "Take the auger and drill here," Jake whispered. "This'll fix easy. Uh—figured out anything?"

"Yes. You be sure and take the tiller after Goochland. I tell you, your thinking of steering makes things a hell of a lot simpler for us."

"Knew you'd come up with something. Let's see that post now. Just right. Rip out that rotten wood, slide this down and bolt it into place."

Kirk gouged away with a chisel. "Why be so careful? This is a Reb barge."

"And we're on it. When you tell us to go ashore, I can lay this craft along the bank so smooth that it wouldn't wake a baby. Take up more on that nut. There, she's good as the day she was built."

Kirk walked away from the stern, leaving Jake to gather up the tools. Over his shoulder he called irritably, "I've done the job. Now I aim to smell something cooking."

Jake picked up his load and came forward, shouting. "Ahoy there in the bow. Tiller's better than new."

The bargeman looked about, face split by a vast grin. "Obliged to you, Mr. Harpell, powerful obliged."

Kirk scowled. "If you hadn't treated it like a playtoy, I wouldn't have been put to all this trouble." He tramped sulkily down into the deckhouse.

10

The Right Sort of People

It was almost worse than not eating, Kirk thought, this sitting asprawl on the deck with the tin plate between his knees and the cup of hot, strong coffee and the thick glass of milk at his elbow. Men playing his role and Jake's should not have Libby appetites, and men with Libby appetites dared not plunge into such fare as the barge afforded. The coffee and milk must be sipped sparingly. The fresh corn bread, heated on the sand-box stove, had to be chewed very slowly and it did not do to add more than a touch of golden butter. Ham slices demanded a cautious approach, as a man might face raw whiskey on a long-empty stomach. The crisp bacon was best taken in fine bits on the bread. To have eaten too ravenously might have awakened suspicion on the part of the bargeman. Worse, it could have brought on violent cramps, crippling diarrhea and paralyzing weakness that would have chained him and Jake to the barge as surely as though all the Libby guards patrolled the decks.

It was no help to watch the north bank slide by. It had been dark when Kirk had last seen it, but he was sure that that unmanned redoubt just beyond the woods was the same that he had attacked on that February raid. And he was agonizingly certain that if he had extended his line a little more toward the canal and river, he could have swept into the position from the rear. A little later he thought that he could pick out the tree where the Negro guide had been hanged. And if it hadn't been for that guide and those who had used him for their own ends, Dahlgren's command would have crossed over Kirk's ford to the south bank, and he had heard enough of conditions on Belle Isle to believe that the one-legged young colonel would undoubtedly have brought off a mass rescue of Union prisoners.

Chewing carefully at a bit of ham, he started, shaken out of his concern for the present and regret for the past by Jake speaking in the lipless Libby voice. Kirk tilted his head a little to catch the words.

"This is how it happened—" Jake had pushed through the unlocked door, gone a few yards down a corridor, opened a second door and stepped out into swirling smoke. It had been so thick that for a moment he had not grasped that he was on the edge of the ship basin and that a schooner was burning at the east end. Half-seen figures were running, shouting, getting in each other's way. He was about to duck back into Libby when a man burst out of the smoke, caught his arm and asked for help. There was the burning schooner and farther up the basin lay a Navy barge. The man, obviously a civilian, was in a panic. He was responsible for the barge and the damned Army wouldn't let him move it! Slowly Jake realized that he was being taken for a Confederate Navy officer, possibly from the color of the coat, for the man could hardly have noticed the c.s.n. buttons so soon.

"Maybe I was just a plain, God-damn fool," muttered Jake. "But I thought I saw a chance opening for us, one of those chances you have to grab right off or miss them forever."

"You weren't a damn fool," said Kirk. "Go on."

Jake had told the man to wait, then had ducked back into Libby, dragged the gray cap cover, complete with anchor and c.s.n., over his kepi and returned to the basin. The smoke was still dense and he butted ahead till he found an Army officer trying desperately to organize the available guards into a bucket line. Jake was sure that the officer and men were from a unit newly assigned to Libby, which, along with the smoke, made recognition a very slight risk. He had stormed up to the officer, demanding that the barge be moved into the James. It was bound for the Tredegar Iron Works to pick up heavy mountings needed by naval guns at Drewry's Bluff far down the James. If that officer thought *he* could interfere with Navy plans . . . The argument raged on. Jake felt that his effort might have failed if the fire had not been getting out of control. As it was, the man was torn between the challenge to his authority and the increasing menace of the fire. At last the officer wilted for a moment and in that pause, Jake had dashed back to the storeroom, bawling for his man "Carey."

"That's all there was to it," concluded Jake. "I knew you'd tumble into your role and, by God, you did, right to the hilt. So here we are, up the canal, with nothing but the clothes we wear, a couple of hundred Reb dollars between us and a canvas bag with some wood chunks in it. Jesus, I've wished a dozen times I'd slammed that outer door and stayed in Libby."

"You did just right. Let's look at it the way the Rebs will. There'll be hell to pay over the fire. Roll calls will be late. When they do miss us, they'll figure we're hiding somewhere in the building, or that we've got into the hospital or the deadhouse. It'll be hours, maybe tomor-

171

row, before they know we're really gone and they'll never link us up with that barge and that damned, overbearing Navy officer. Unless—where was the barge going after Tredegar?"

"Riding the down tide to Drewry's Bluff. Yes, if I was boss at Libby, I'm damned if I'd know where to start looking. They'll comb the city and they'll be watching the east exits, thinking we're heading for Butler or Grant, while we're sailing west. It's—" His voice grew lower. "No. They're onto us right now, and it's my fault. Of all the damn, stupid, clutch-brained things to do!"

"How do you mean?"

"The Rebs'll start looking. Where were we? The records'll show we were in the storeroom counting blankets."

"What's wrong with that? There's no way out, except right back into the prison."

"*Isn't* there? How about that door in the storeroom where I went sashaying out? The one worst thing for me to miss! It'll be unlocked, maybe wide open, and it'll lead them right out to the basin. See? Easy enough. What ships left the basin during the fire? Just one. Ours. If Turner's got half a brain, he'll put a couple of steam-launches into the canal and come pounding down after us."

"No," said Kirk, "he won't, and just *because* of that door. I don't know why I did it. Sort of a reflex. But I closed the door very quietly and turned the key in the lock. It was on the outside, of course. Now how will Turner read that? The one door in all Libby that could lead him to us is the door that we *couldn't* have left by. He can't reason any other way. But someone may start wondering about your uniform. A real Reb Navy man'd give one look at you and then hoot."

"Kirk, the smoke was so thick that I could have said I was a Belgian hussar and *someone* would have believed me. The important thing is that, so far as I can see, I *acted* like a Reb Navy officer. And the uniform isn't so

172

bad. This cap cover mashed my kepi so flat that I began to think I'd served with Semmes on the C.S.S. *Alabama*. No smoke and no excitement and I wouldn't have fooled Punch's dog Toby. But there was smoke and there was excitement."

"How about the boat crew from Drewry's?"

"Hell, they're the ones that picked me out as Navy. You know what civilians are like about uniforms. No, it looks to me as if we've got no old things to worry about, just new ones."

"Don't look so discouraged," said Kirk grimly. "We've plenty of those."

A hint of still-distant dawn drifted out of the east, but night hung dark as ever over the canal. Kirk stood in the stern, hands on the thwarts as he strained his eyes to read the riddle of the slow-passing north bank. "Still don't see anything?" muttered Jake from the tiller.

"Might as well be looking at a brick wall. But that *had* to be the Cartersville bridge that nearly scraped us back there. Then we made a sharp turn north. We're going west again now. After that—" He leaned still farther out, listening. His hand closed on Jake's collar. "We're right! Bring us close to the bank!"

When a bare two feet of water shone below, Kirk snatched up the canvas bag, poised on the edge of the barge and jumped. He landed on a sloping, sandy bank, struggled erect and worked higher.

A soft thud behind him and a scramble brought Jake up beside him. "Tiller's set," panted Jake. "She'll swing right into midstream. What did you see that made you jump?"

Kirk shouldered the bag. "Nothing. It was what I heard." He moved carefully on, his head thrust forward while tormenting thoughts plucked at him. Had he jumped too soon? Too late? In a patch of underbrush he stopped, listening. But the sound which he had been so sure about on the barge was no longer in his ears. Ten steps ahead, a halt, a dozen steps. Just in time he caught at a branch, checked himself with one foot out in space. "Look, Jake," he whispered. Just below, a broad creek slid south, silent, shimmering faintly. Behind him Jake breathed, "This it?"

"Got to be. I heard the ripple it makes joining the canal while I was on the barge. Ashore, I lost it. But this is it."

"Might be some other creek."

"Couldn't be. This *is* Byrd Creek, the only one this size that feeds into the canal between the big bend and the Rivanna. We follow up the east bank now till we hit a double fork, and the right fork is Little Byrd Creek. Then we cross the main Goochland—Columbia road and the house we want'll be about a mile farther up the east bank of Little Byrd. Keep close behind me. You'll be able to see the white of the bag in the dark."

The going was rough. Patches of scrub wood crowded up to the creek, forced them inland. Rock outcroppings threw them so much off course that Kirk twice lost the stream and used up precious darkness in finding it again. The twin forks showed plainly in a tumble of white water and soon the Goochland—Columbia road was before them. They darted across it and took shelter in a pine grove. Somewhere off to the east a dog began to bark and they froze, listening to the swelling *row-row-row*. They edged closer to the creek, ready to kick off their boots and wade if the din came nearer. But the dog apparently was off on some absorbing mission of its own, coursing a rabbit—or just being a dog.

"Safe enough to go on," said Kirk. "I've lost all count of distance, but we can't miss Hildebrant's place. The creek edges his land." They came out of the pine woods and Kirk suddenly crouched. "Done it!" he said between his teeth. "A roof, just over that high ground to the right. It shows against the sky. Come on."

After a hundred yards or so of scrambling, Jake touched Kirk's arm. "That's not Hildebrant's place, not the way you described it back there. It's too big. And

174

there are cabins at the edge of the hollow. You said Hildebrant's a small farmer, not a planter. You said Hildebrant raises chickens. This man doesn't."

"How do you know he doesn't?"

"I just know, that's all."

"This is no small-farmer's layout, anyhow. We better cross the creek and work up the other bank."

They met brushwood across the creek, then a long stretch of plowed land that forced them back into the stream to avoid leaving footprints. On dry land again, Jake said suddenly, "Drop so you can see the sky line."

Kirk tried to focus on the almost indistinguishable meeting of earth and sky. "Can't see anything."

"Look left of that big oak on the sky line, fifty yards off."

"Still don't see anything. Just a big box on a post, that's all."

"Big box, hell. You've seen hundreds like it, riding over Virginia. It's a marten house, a six- or seven-story one. Martens chase off hawks. Chicken farmers kind of like to have martens around, so they build houses for them. See? Chicken farmers, same as Mr. Hildebrant. His house must be close by. Let's go look for him."

Kirk gave the lead to Jake and followed along, eyes on the dim outline of the oak. A quarter of a mile more, perhaps, to go and then—The dog burst out of the underbrush without warning, hurled itself at Kirk with short, vicious snarls that welled up deep in the animal's chest. Kirk swung hard with the bag, knocked the dog off its feet, but it scrambled up, darted in again, retreated, came on. Kirk felt Jake's back close against his, knew that Jake was lashing out with his boots. "Easy, Jake," Kirk called. "If you miss your footing he'll rip at your throat. There—nearly got him that time. Stand steady. He's circling again. Look out! What's he up to?"

The dog had dropped to the ground and lay, a crouched, snarling menace. Then something hard jammed into Kirk's ribs and a harsh voice snapped. "H'ist them hands! Got a double barrel here."

Kirk held his hands high, his knuckles hitting against Jake's as the latter obeyed. The surprise had been complete. The man had crept up while they were fighting off the dog and now stood at Kirk's left. The harsh voice went on. "Going visiting this time of night ain't healthy. Was you looking for someone in particular?"

"We're looking for the—right sort of people," replied Kirk.

"What's your idea of right sorts?" asked the man, omitting Kirk's pause.

Jake spoke quickly. "You're asking a lot of questions, mister. Maybe it's time we asked one or two. Who are you, ramming a gun at peaceful folks?"

"I'm a landowner that don't like trespassers, midnight or high noon."

"Just 'landowner' doesn't tell me much," said Kirk.

"My name's Hildebrant and that means enough for me."

"We heard there was a George Hildebrant up Little Byrd Creek who was the—right sort of person," said Kirk. "If you're he, it could mean a good deal to us, too."

Slowly the twin barrels dropped. "Ease your hands," said Hildebrant. "I wasn't looking to meet any of the—right sort of people tonight." He took off his hat, swept his arm across his forehead. "Chrisamighty, you two have been wading in luck hip-deep and all of it good. Was a big patrol riding these acres not an hour ago, hunting deserters and them as ain't taken kindly to conscription. They wouldn't 'a' minded netting you. It was them that brought me out tonight. Patrollers take to lingering near chicken runs and smokehouses and I didn't feel like losing to them. You up from the Carolina coasts?"

"Libby," said Jake.

"*Libby*? How'd you ever get—No. You'd best not tell me. Dawn's a-nearing and I better get you hid. We go this way. Maybe you'll make me acquainted with your names and outfits. Heel, Race." The dog followed on.

"One more thing," said Kirk. "We nearly hailed a big place downcreek from you. Whose is it?"

"Ow!" exclaimed Hildebrant. "You fellers ain't just lucky, you got a kind of guiding star set in your heads. Place belongs to old Judge Slade. He seceded way back in '55 and he's built a jail for runaway slaves and escaped Yankees, only he ain't caught any yet. He'd 'a' been proud for you to be his first guests. Now 'bout us getting acquainted—"

"Here's where you'll bide," said Hildebrant, kneeling to light a lantern in an old wagon shed.

The flame slowly showed the interior. Pale stars shone through gaps in the roof. The walls sagged and bulged as though ready to drop the crossbeams down onto the flaking, decrepit carts that stood dispiritedly on the dirt floor.

Jake cleared his throat. "Got a cellar or something dug here, Mr. Hildebrant?"

The other shook his head. "Dug dirt talks too much, even if you tamp it down good." He reached under a cart, drew out a short ladder and set it against the left wall. Kirk held his breath as the old boards quivered, but Hildebrant went up a few rungs, swung out a cunningly hinged section, showing solid wood in the gap. Another push and the newer wood turned inward and Hildebrant wriggled out of sight. Jake rubbed his chin, staring. "Now it'd stump a good ship's carpenter to rig something like that. Hildebrant never built that alone, either."

"That shows he's got neighbors he can trust."

"Don't say how close neighbors, but, by God, he trusted them. Now he's beckoning. Don't know what we're getting into, but if he's there, it's enough for me. You go first. I'll lug the bag."

Kirk went slowly up the ladder. The lantern shone

down the wall, showing weary, gray wood that looked as though he could crumble it between his fingers. Hildebrant called softly, "Don't get scared if it 'pears bustable. It ain't given yet and many's used it." Kirk reached the opening and swung himself into it. There were firm planks under him and along both sides of a very narrow room that ran half the length of the shed. He stood up, found inches of clearance between his head and the roof. Jake scrambled in, dragging the canvas bag, and Kirk saw his eyes bulge as they took in the construction. "Bet all my back pay that a seaman rigged this," panted Jake.

"Ain't growed out of the earth," said Hildebrant, lifting the lantern. "Don't mind my staring. I got to know what you look like well as what you sound like. Won't hurt your getting a study of me."

About fifty, Kirk thought, lean and sallow with a drooping mustache above a good chin. The eyes, flanking a bony nose, were weary-looking but steady and filled with a sort of grave sadness. Hildebrant set the lantern down. "Reckon we done looking. Here's where you bide and don't fret about the old wood. That's for show. A body can stand mighty close to this shed and never guess the double walls. The bulges and sags help some and the far end of the room's built into a hillside. Daytimes you'll get light and air through slides in the roof. Ain't likely anyone'll bother you, but come a scare, there's a dead space under the roof where you can crawl. Bedding's stacked to the far end. For your needs, there's a privy cut into the bank. I'll show you the door before I go. I'll feed you best I can."

Jake swept up the bag. "There's rations in here and no need for you to know where they came from. We'd be obliged if you'd dump them in the common pool, share and share alike."

Hildebrant inclined his head gravely. "That's kindly in you." His voice dropped to an awed whisper as he sniffed, "Coffee, real store-boughten coffee."

178

"That's for you," said Kirk quickly. "Share and share alike, as Jake said, and we've had ours."

"Common pool," said Hildebrant firmly. "And I'm beholden to you. Now I've got to ask it of you that you don't show so much as a whisker outside without my say-so."

"You've our promise," said Kirk. "And—there's not much we can say, Mr. Hildebrant, but Captain Pitler and I will never forget you."

"We're all fighting, sirs, you in one way, me in mine. You got any plans you'd feel easy to tell me about?"

"Just to get back as soon as we can. We'd like to find some route that'd take us east to the nearest Union lines. Swinging north around Richmond seems the best way from what we know, but we're not set on it."

Hildebrant narrowed his eyes. "Got Union posts on the North Carolina coast. Union ships lie close in where they ain't posts. Could be you could make a set for Sherman, it seeming he's like to take Atlanta down in Georgia pretty soon. East? No. A while back I'd 'a' started you out next sunfall, but the country's thick with commissary parties and thicker yet with troops hunting deserters and them as is dodging the draft, like I told you about before. You'd last about two days going east, if your luck kept running good."

"What's your advice, then?" asked Jake.

"Lie up a day or two and let me figger." There was a scrabbling at the ladder and the dog Race's muzzle showed in the opening. Hildebrant pushed the animal gently back. "Dooryard, Race. Watch for Sam." The muzzle vanished. Hildebrant sighed. "Sam's my brother. I was shaving when he put on his first breeches. Kind of partial to Sam. We fixed to send him to the college to Williamsburg, but the war came. He got hurt bad, twice. Now he's hurt again, but mending. Lives down the road with Pa. Don't sleep too good since his hurt and sometimes he comes to help with early chicken chores. Sam's

179

a sergeant, 3rd Virginia, but don't fret on that. Race'll bark and give me time to seal up here."

"*You've* got a brother in the 3rd Virginia?" exclaimed Kirk.

"Times is peculiar and they sent me and Sam on different ways, not that we don't cleave like we always did. Peculiar it is. Here's me, believing in slavery that the Lord God Almighty ordained and I can show you plenty lines in the Book that proves it. But the Union, that's what I was born under and what I'll live and die under. Now Sam, he hates slavery but he stands firm by his state. I ask him, 'Sam, what's any state but a part of the Union?' and he says, 'It was states made the Union and therefore states can unmake it when that Union gets unrighteous.' But we can still shake hands same as ever, Sam and me."

"What if he knew what you're doing?" asked Kirk.

"Why, then I reckon he'd feel he had to shoot me, bad as it would grieve him." He turned toward the opening. "I'll leave the lantern with you. It'll show you bedding and privy. I'll look to you later in the day." The Unionist slipped down the ladder into the pitch black below, but somehow a brightness went with him.

Kirk slowly closed the sham door and the true one. "That's a mighty good man, Jake, and not just because he's on our side."

"Yes," said Jake thoughtfully. "He's a man you could ride beside."

They found a few sacks loosely stuffed with corn husks, turned out the lantern and lay down. "One more stage in the journey, Jake, thanks to you," muttered Kirk.

"Thanks to us both. Safe—so far."

Rain drummed on the curling shingles of the wagon shed and the long, narrow compartment became dank and cheerless. Strong sun dried the shingles and the hidden chamber was an oven that sealed in its heat from dawn to dawn. On especially dark or stormy nights, Hildebrant took them on careful walks across country with the dog Race casting in wide circles about them. The fare that their host brought after sundown was usually sufficient, but there were days when he apologized for meager slices of salt pork and shriveled potatoes. Such shortages followed sudden descents of commissary patrols who seized what they could find to forward on to Lee's army, still battling desperately about Petersburg. On one such foray a prolonged search was made and the refugees lay in the cramped loft hardly daring to breath while troopers tethered their horses in the shed and later lounged inside, eating their rations and cursing the rain that hissed down. It was another hour before they finally clattered off.

Hildebrant occasionally brought Richmond papers up the ladder and they read how Grant was held as in a vise before Petersburg, how Sherman was bottled up in Atlanta while General John Hood massed an army to snap the slender Union supply line and then sweep Sherman in ruin toward the Florida line. In the Shenandoah Valley, the new Union Cavalry general, Sheridan, was said to have met a stunning reverse at Winchester. Kirk and Jake took in the news philosophically. For over three years they had read the press of the North and the South and were quite aware that these Union "disasters" were probably being hailed in Philadelphia and New York and Chicago as Confederate "debacles," for a while at least. They could be sure of only one thing—that the war still went on—and that, in itself, could be taken as a sort of triumph for the government of Jefferson Davis.

One day Jake passed Kirk an *Examiner*, saying, "Something here about some friends of yours," and Kirk was vividly reminded of another carriage shed up by Frederick's Hall Station as the smeary type told him that among guests at a reception at Secretary of State Benjamin's were Mr. Ian Stockdale and his daughter, Miss

Lynn Stockdale, escorted by a Captain Charles Fentress, 4th Georgia Infantry.

The corn-colored hair and river-blue eyes were vivid in his mind as he handed the paper back to Jake. He could see that slim, rounded figure in the gray and canary cloak, standing poised, almost on tiptoe, as she had defied him on that February day along the Virginia Central line.

So she was still in Richmond, she and her father. What did it matter? He was not likely ever to see her again and even if he did, by some freak of chance, he might not remember very much about her if he had met two or three reasonably attractive girls in the meantime. And who the devil was this Captain Charles Fentress, and what was a captain of the 4th Georgia doing, mincing about at Richmond receptions when every able-bodied man was needed in the lines to hold off Grant or drive Sherman out of Atlanta?

One night toward the end of September, Kirk and Jake were waiting by the loft door, listening for steps on the ladder that would announce Hildebrant's arrival with food and, perhaps, word that they could walk in the open for an hour or so. Boots crunched on the rungs and Kirk swept Jake away from the door. "Under the roof!" he whispered. But Jake, too, had heard more than one pair of boots, had caught a sound as though still another man had hit his foot against the bottom of the ladder. Kirk caught at the edge of the opening under the eaves. Then Hildebrant's voice sounded, low and steady. "Got friends coming."

The door swung open and Hildebrant climbed in, set his lantern on the floor, beckoning. A tall, very thin man in a broad-brimmed hat marked with crossed sabers crawled in, followed by a short, wiry man in a Cavalry kepi. "Vouched for," said Hildebrant. "The big one is Lieutenant Jabish Kell, 5th U.S. Cavalry. The other's

Captain Mark Furber, 1st Massachusetts same. They've mealed. No walking tonight. The roads is uneasy."

Later, seated on corn-husk mattresses, the four talked in low, eager tones. Kell and Furber had been captured in a reconnaissance far up the Shenandoah Valley. Somewhere near Lynchburg they had escaped and, by a stroke of luck, had stumbled onto Union sympathizers. Then they had been passed on in slow stages south, finally arriving at Hildebrant's, buried in a load of hay.

"Don't know who did all this or why," Kell concluded. "Guess it's the same at home. I've heard that a Reb, breaking free of Camp Douglass or one of those places, can get passed right down the breadth of the Union and into his own lines. No business of mine. I want to get the war over and pick up my law practice in Milwaukee again. When can we start? I'll want one good night's sleep before going on again."

Jake laughed. "You'll get plenty. We've been here close to a month. Hildebrant's waiting for a sign that it'll be safe to turn us loose."

"A sign from whom?" asked Furber suspiciously.

"From the—right sort of people," answered Kirk. "The same kind that brought you here. You'll have plenty of time to find out, as Jake said. Now, what's going on in the Cavalry Corps? Whose brigade are you with? Where's Kilpatrick? What's become of Custer and Gregg and Devin? Have they really begun to issue repeating carbines to all the Cavalry? Are you getting good remounts? Where is . . .?"

"Just doesn't smell like October to me," said Jabish Kell, stretching his long legs before him in the darkening loft. "Doesn't feel like it, either. At home, leaves'd be starting to turn and we'd get that steady wind hitting down across Superior and ruffling Michigan. It'd make a man want to take a gun and make for the country around Winnebago and watch for duck."

Jake yawned. "Give it time. October's only two, three days old. Maybe tonight Hildebrant'll snap leashes onto

183

our collars and take us out for a walk. My coat and pants are so thin that it'll feel like plumb December to me."

"Wish he could do a little more about rations," said Mark Furber. "I know he does ten times what any reasonable man could expect, but you'd think in farming country there'd be more around."

Kirk settled his folded jacket behind his head. "There are plenty of supplies, all kinds, in the Confederacy, but the Reb railroads never were geared to handle them and nothing's been done to improve the system. Jeff Davis doesn't seem to have any good railroad men. To feed a city like Richmond, you just can't bring in enough by rail, so the country nearby gets stripped and food that's out of reach is left to rot."

"The Reb papers say that people who've got the money are heading down into parts where rations are more plentiful," observed Jake. "Can't say I blame them. Some seem to have gone for good. Others stay long enough to fatten up and then come home to starve a bit more."

"Having Lee's army just about next door at Petersburg uses a lot of stuff and a lot of cars that the city'd normally get," put in Jabish Kell.

"Don't forget Libby and Belle Isle," snorted Jake. "I've wondered what beetle-brain thought of penning thousands of prisoners of war right in the city. Every new prisoner they get means that much more food that has to be brought in, just so much more car space that could tote stuff for civilians. Steady now! Here comes Hildebrant with our rations. I'd hate like hell to have George think we were mollygrubbing about them."

Steps sounded on the ladder, Hildebrant gave his usual staccato knocks and the door swung in. "Evening, gentlemen," he said, dumping softish bundles onto the floor. "Country clothes for you. They won't fit good or look good, but no one on the road'll look at 'em twice."

Kirk sprang up. "The road's clear, then?"

Hildebrant pawed over the bundles. "Your rig's all right as it is. Here's Captain Pitler's and Captain Furber's. I reckon Lieutenant Kell'll find his short in the legs and sleeves. The road? Why—oh, here's the hat to go with Captain Furber's kit."

Kirk studied Hildebrant. The lean man seemed unduly preoccupied with his bundles and kept his head turned away. "Something wrong?" asked Kirk quietly.

"War times is always wrong. It's—" he squatted over the clothes and looked up at Kirk—"Sam," he said. "At nooning he allowed it might be a good idea if this old shed got burned. Said it'd save me the trouble of ripping it down and I could sift the nails out of the ashes to build a new one. Nails are scarce and Sam's a saving man, like me."

Furber laughed. "We'd stew like clams in a seawood fire. Hope you'll give us warning."

Hildebrant's eyes turned toward Furber. "What I'm doing," he said softly, "ain't only what Sam said. A neighbor came by with a load of oats for the commissary. Told me a man we both know was took sudden to Richmond at night by soldier police. A woman east from here ain't had word from her husband since he was seen talking to horsemen close to Deep Creek crossroads. Maybe Sam heard the same things."

"He was warning you?" asked Kirk.

"Looks so. Now I always held Sam'd fire up real quick, did he have a hint about what I was doing. But he ain't. Reckon we're closer'n I thought for, Sam and me."

Jake scrambled up. "We're lighting out as soon as it's dark. Is this the first you knew about all this?"

"It's the first time I was real sure."

"We'll be glad if you've any suggestions about our route," said Kirk.

The other, still crouched, shook his head. "I ought to 'a' been able to do better by you. Some place, somehow, I must 'a' got shiftless. Now I been plaguing my mind

185

all day for a route. East? No, don't let it even tickle at you. North? Just as bad. Lor-*dee*, gentlemen, we're in a fix. But this is what keeps stubbing into my mind like a nail in an old shoe: Far it is, but you'd best make south and west for the North Carolina mountains. You'll strike a sight of Union folk, so thick in some places the gov'ment don't dast send soldiers to pick up them as wouldn't answer the draft. It'll be killing going, but I'd push on into east Tennessee, trending for the French Broad or the Holston. That'll lead you right to Knoxville and Union troops and the old flag." He was silent for a moment, head bowed. Then he spoke. "I'll set you on your way and tell you a stream to seek and a house to look for. The man in it'll have to point you after that—if *he* ain't been visited, too."

"Don't you go a step farther with us than you know to be safe," said Kirk. "Or maybe it would be better if we just struck out by ourselves without your knowing when we left or where we headed. We're all used to looking out for ourselves and if we do meet trouble, well, we'll only be four runaway prisoners of war—who never heard of a man named George Hildebrant."

Hildebrant rose. "There's food for you in this pack here. But I'm setting you on your way, heading you right. It's more fitting."

11

"Unquietsome Times"

The sun had set while the rickety train was laboring over the bridge of the Richmond and Danville line spanning the Roanoke River in the far southern reaches of Virginia. Now, for all Kirk saw through the grimy coach window, he might have been moving through an endless tunnel, though some inner sense told him of masses of steep-rising land off to the west. He shifted forward on the wooden seat and rested his weight on the musket that jutted between his knees. The fat civilian who shared the space with him mumbled in his sleep, stirred, worked an irritable elbow against Kirk's ribs. Kirk slid the clumsy cartridge pouch and haversack away from his neighbor and looked down the coach.

The single hanging lamp gave off a smoky glow that accentuated rather than dissolved the darkness, but he could make out Jake's head a few seats away. Behind Kirk, Mark Furber and Jabish Kell stood in the aisle among other passengers and a litter of boxes and bags

187

and crates of chickens and a dog or two. There was no point in turning to exchange glances with Kell and Furber or to make his way forward for a short word with Jake. Their thoughts would be the same as his and the same questions were in their minds: when would their next helper or pilot pick them up and where would he head them?

Kirk hoped that whoever the pilot might be, he would be more like George Hildebrant than some of the last had been. Hildebrant risked his neck out of a deep love for the Union. The others seemed motivated by a hatred of life in the Confederacy or of men identified with it. One had been ridden by a frenzy against Jefferson Davis that arose from a real or imagined slight inflicted by the President on a close relative. Another railed against the Congress for upholding a War Department ruling that his owning a mere fifteen slaves did not exempt him from military service. The fact that he was manifestly unfit for soldiering and had never been called up seemed to have no bearing on the case. His pride had been affronted and to hell with the Confederacy! Such men were dangerous allies, since a sop to pride could have set them waving the Stars and Bars beside the most selfless patriot. "These 'agin-ers' scare me," Jake had said. "The man we're always looking for is a 'for-er.'"

Then there was the question of "where." Kirk had never been sure that Hildebrant had been right in feeling that the best route lay through North Carolina and Tennessee. He had argued for a course that would not commit them so definitely, mapping out a way that would take them on foot through southwest Virginia, whence they could strike into the Shenandoah Valley where Sheridan's successes were assuming increasing importance, or into West Virginia. There would also be a chance to hit across the central part of the state to the Potomac. If all these avenues were blocked, they could still swing down into eastern Tennessee.

188

But each pilot had nudged them away from routes that could lead to the Army of the Potomac. Their progress reminded Kirk bitterly of the last wild ride under Dahlgren that could so easily have led to safety but which was always headed off by swarming Home Guard bodies until the final tragedy of Walkerton. So, as matters stood, they were riding south through the night toward the Virginia-North Carolina border. And they rode alone, faintly buoyed up by the assurance of the man who had armed them and given them forged papers that the next pilot would meet them on the train.

Down the car a hen squawked furiously. A dog floundered along the crowded aisle, yipping an obligato. A baby wailed monotonously and Kirk's fat seatmate leaned more heavily on him. Kirk rubbed his forehead. "Maybe Jake was right when we slept in that sty last night," he mused. "Maybe Libby *was* a pretty good old spot after all."

The train ground to a swaying halt and lanterns waved along the track. The forward door opened and a tall young man with lieutenant's loops on his gray sleeves pushed his way in. Kirk's hands tightened on his musket as the officer paused by Jake and jerked a thumb toward the door. Then he was standing by Kirk. "Fall in with the rest outside. Shake your feet. The train won't wait forever." He was past Kirk and calling to Furber and Kell.

There was nothing to do but obey. The coach was a trap, but out in the open with a loaded musket in his hands and three armed, experienced soldiers with him, something might be attempted if matters took a bad turn. He hurried along the aisle after Jake, then felt a chill as he saw other men filing out of of the car ahead, shabbily dressed, some in tags of uniforms and all hugging muskets as antiquated as his own. On the platform he took heart a little as he saw Jake below, standing slouched and helpless, the very picture of a man not used to moving in concert with other men, a lost civilian bewildered by the simplest matters military.

On the ground a sergeant was growling, "Get into two ranks!" Kirk shuffled uncertainly beside Jake, standing a half pace ahead of him. The sergeant shoved him. "In rank, I said! God damn it, you look like a passel of shotes tryin' to get into a trough." Kell's tall form showed against the dim light of the car, halted just in front of Kirk. Furber stumbled up ahead of Kell. The sergeant screeched, "God's ribs! *Two* ranks! Oh, my bleedin' guts, you don't even know what a rank is." He dragged Furber off to the left, rushed back to herd Kell into formation.

The train groaned off south while the sergeant scuttled along the ragged lines, muttering, "He's one, he's two, he's three, he's four—" Another lantern bobbed into sight and the lieutenant called, "How many, Sergeant?"

"Eighteen's good's I can count in the dark, sir."

"Eighteen's right. Now, you men, you're under military discipline until your tour's over."

A voice beyond Kirk whined, "When we get paid?"

"You'll find out later. Some of you men have been in the army before. Steady down those who haven't. Every man give a half turn in the direction I'm holding my lantern." The two lines did a sketchy right face. "Now start off, following Sergeant Racker."

The way led west along a soft road where the sound of boots was muffled as though by thick snow. Water gurgled off to the right and presently the boots rang in a hollow drum across a bridge. Kirk listened to the cadence, thought that he could pick out the firm, light tread of a few men accustomed to marching standing out clean and assured over the shamble of the others. Such knowledge might be useful if trouble came. He was unable to reason out any possible mission for such a body and he could not guess how the officer, now off on the flank, had picked him and his companions out of

190

the crowded coach. Lights showed ahead and the column was in a village street where vague shadows moved jerkily across drawn curtains. Lanterns showed on the steps of a general store and a fat man in uniform clumped down. "That you, Mr. Brewer?" he called.

The lieutenant shouted, "Step 'em somehow, Sergeant, and make 'em stand. Lieutenant Brewer reporting, Major, with eighteen men."

"All right. Take four men and go on up to Captain Hecker's post. And tell Hecker he's to send any whiskey he finds right down to me."

"Very good, sir." Brewer saluted and walked down the line. Kirk heard him say, "You—you—" Brewer's hand touched his own shoulder. "You." Then he was past and Kirk caught a final "You," followed by the curt order, "Leave ranks. Follow me."

Kirk hesitated, then saw Jake and Kell leave the line. He hurried after them and was not surprised to find Furber trotting up beside him. But the pilot who was to meet them? Would he be able to find where they had left the train and pick up their trail? For the moment, that was the chief worry. The four could handle Mr. Brewer without trouble, though something would have to be done before Captain Hecker's post was reached.

After a couple of miles Brewer left the road and struck out across a meadow where tall grasses whispered. Kirk gave Jake a warning nudge, passed him his musket, then leaped suddenly onto Brewer's shoulders and wrestled him to the ground. "Give me two musket slings," he panted. "That's it. Make one fast around his arms. He seems to be stunned. Hasn't moved since I hit him." Kirk cautiously eased the pressure on Brewer's throat, held out a hand, felt another sling being pushed into it. Then the body under him stirred and the prisoner said faintly, "Take your muskets and pitch them into the lake just ahead. They'd be easy to trace through their numbers and they might lead back to the—right sort of people."

191

Kirk rolled to his knees in utter surprise. Jake, musket still poised, said, "What the hell?"

Brewer sat up, rubbing his neck. "Something must have gone wrong. Didn't you spot me on the train? You were supposed to have my description. I had yours, right enough."

Kirk slid a hand under Brewer's elbow, helped him to his feet. "Maybe we shouldn't have jumped you, but to us you were just a Reb officer. Like to tell us about yourself and what *you* call the right sort of people?"

"I'd rather talk about you. Two nights ago you hid in a tobacco loft owned by a man whose name—well, it isn't Pythias."

"Go on," said Kirk, remembering the tobacco grower, William Damon.

"Last night you were in an outbuilding near a high waterfall. You had neighbors who did a lot of grunting. Their owner was supposed to have told you about me."

Furber leaned on his musket. "I'm satisfied. But we had no description of you. We were just told we'd be met on the train."

Brewer flexed his shoulders. "It wasn't your fault that that swine merchant got careless. Someone will pay him a call in a day or two and show him how mistakes like his can hurt people bad."

"A lot of people," said Kirk. "Want to tell us anything about yourself?"

"No need to tell too much," said Brewer. "Then tongues don't do damage without meaning to. I'm a Union man, like lots in my part of North Carolina. I was under arrest for a while at first and was watched pretty close after that. Then the authorities let up on me some and I took a Quartermaster commission with North Carolina home troops. That was easy enough, my family having influence. And that way there wasn't much chance of my ever having to fight against the Union. Of course, I just *might* have been able to slip out and join the Union Army, but I've plenty of kin

192

and friends in the Confederacy and I didn't feel like pulling a trigger against them any more than against the Union. As it is, I can move about pretty free and sometimes I get a chance to help people like you."

"Wait a minute," put in Kell. "You hold a North Carolina home commission. How does that let you work in Virginia?"

Brewer gave a short laugh. "What I and some others are supposed to be doing is helping Virginians run down deserters and draft evaders who shift back and forth across the border. We're just a few miles from it here. Those men I took off the train with you are part of a short-time levy who'll work under that major back there. *I* don't care anything about the deserters and the others and neither does Hecker, my boss. What we're really trying to do is break up some gangs who lie up in the mountains and raid the farms and plantations. They're a damned, murderous, vicious lot and we don't care if the places we protect are Union or Reb."

Jake said abruptly, "That's good enough for me. You're a 'for-er' Now where's this pond of yours? I'll dump the muskets in it."

"Let me give you your directions first. Go back to the road we were on. It'll begin to climb pretty quick and you'll have to hit a good three-mile-an-hour clip. That'll bring you near the crest about sunrise. You'll see a big split rock hard on the sky line. Get into the woods at its foot and lie up there. You'll see a little farmhouse about half a mile to your left front. When it's dark, go down there and say you're looking for John Hart. That's not his name, but it'll open the door for you."

"You said 'crest,'" observed Kell. "We must be pretty close to Danville and all the maps I've seen show mostly flat country around there."

"You're not close to Danville. Your train swung off on a branch line not long after you crossed the Roanoke and you've been heading west and south. It's a kind of spur that's not been used much lately and I hear they're going to rip it up and take the rails somewhere else. Of course, you won't be hitting into real mountains yet, but you'll have a climb."

"How are you going to account for us four?" asked Furber. "You reported eighteen to that major."

"Oh, these short-time levies have a habit of melting away, so he won't be surprised if four men don't show up to draw their pay. Now, good night, gentlemen, and good luck." He turned and was lost in the darkness.

Jake waved his arms. "Poof! Just like that. Rub the lamp and he's here. Rub it again and he's gone. I'll dump the muskets. And the pouches. If we do meet anyone, we'll look funny with ammunition and nothing to feed it to."

"Empty your pouches into your pockets," put in Kirk. "We're going into wild country and maybe cartridges'll buy us more than gold dollars would."

Jake scurried off with the equipment. There was a series of splashes and he rejoined the others. "Real deep water, the way that stuff sank," he panted. "Wouldn't surprise me if four little mermaids were using our pouches for sewing baskets right now. Take the lead, Kirk. Your turn to command began at sundown."

"Come on, then. You know, that was another good man and he's hurting inside a lot more than he lets on. Half the people he knows are calling him either a traitor or a skulker and they won't forget it after the war, if he lasts that long. One wrong word or one slip of his mind and he'll have bayonets around him and they won't be held by short-time levies, either. My hat's off to him."

"Mine, too," said Jabish Kell. "But come to think of it, if he lived up in my state and was helping Reb prisoners, we'd call him a traitor bastard and start yelling for twenty feet of rope and a tall tree."

"That's part of the glory of war," said Kirk. "Your enemies can't do anything right and people who help you get halos issued to them."

194

The four went on in silence, increasingly aware of wooded land shouldering up higher and higher on every side. Hidden rocks jarred their feet as the road climbed and the slopes were heavily gullied. Now and then gaps in the night showed distant lighted windows whose glow only emphasized their own isolation. Kirk began to fear that he was not setting the three-mile-an-hour pace that Brewer had prescribed. He was sweating profusely and knew that Jake, too, was suffering from the ascent. Mark and Jabish, who had not known the scant rations and enforced idleness of Libby, were in better shape, but they were panting and glad of each halt.

Night wore on. There were false crests where Kirk was sure that he would sight the split rock, but they always led down steep pitches or into flumelike funnels where the narrow road was crowded by white-topped streams that sooner or later had to be forded. At one spot a waterfall plunged in a silver column from the very treetops to thunder into a pool close by, while spray turned the footing into ankle-deep morass. Mark Furber groaned, "How'd you like to guide a battery of Parrotts along here with Reb sharpshooters up on the clifftops?"

Jake, stumping along valiantly, wheezed, "I'd love it. Think of those limber seats and those nice caissontops to ride on. But all I'm really thinking about is what a God-damn fool Mr. and Mrs. George Pitler's oldest boy was ever to get off that lovely barge on the Kanawha Canal. Kirk! You sure you haven't lost the road? The ground's climbing under my feet sheerer than the steeple of the First Baptist Church back home. And Brewer saying we wouldn't be hitting any real mountains yet. Like to have a picture of what he calls a real mountain."

"It's the road, all right, and worse than you said," answered Kirk. "God, but it's black as the Earl of Hell's boots, what with the trees and the cliffs. I'd like to know

195

what they use for horses in this part of the country. I'm damn near on my hands and knees right now."

The blackness grew thicker and thicker, until Kirk was forced to pull himself along by overhanging branches, feeling for the rocky surface of the road with an outstretched foot. He began to wonder dizzily if an eclipse were smothering the dawn. It would be perfectly possible to toil right past the landmark that Brewer had described to them—how many hours ago?

Kirk gave an involuntary lunge forward. The road had flattened out unexpectedly and his poised foot, reaching for the slope, came down with a thud. He recovered himself, went on a few paces and then stopped short, one hand clutching at a pine bough. Ahead of him the night was melting as though a gas jet were being slowly turned up and he looked along a fairly level stretch where rocks and trees showed faintly luminous. Off to the right, a high crag stood, vague and shimmering in the first rays of the sun that had finally cleared the high ridge in the rear. And the new rays struck into a deep, wide cleft that ran from foot to summit. "Made it!" he said thickly. "There's the split rock." The others crowded up beside him, staring. "Made it!" he said again. "Woods at the left. That's where we lie up. Come on."

Their passage made the dark tracks across the long, dew-soaked grasses as they headed for the woods and plunged in among the trees. Jake mopped his forehead. "Always did want to see the Rocky Mountains," he panted. "Where d'you suppose we are, Kirk? Pike's Peak?"

"Maybe we better find out. We'll make a reconnaissance. See if you can spot the farm we want. Cast about for drinking water, Mark. Jabish, see if there are any paths or trails coming into the woods. We'll have to have one man standing guard all the time and I'll take the first shift. The command passes to Mark at sundown. Next night'll be Jabish's turn, you remember."

196

The others scattered and Kirk walked to the east edge of the woods, curious to see what the killing terrain over which they had passed really looked like. At first he stood frowning, unsure of himself and thinking that he must be facing the wrong way. There was no mistake about direction. The country to the east was hilly and broken, but the four had scaled nothing more rugged than, say, a lower shoulder of Monadnock, back there in New Hampshire. By day the climb would have been fairly easy, but night and fatigue and accumulated tension had vastly magnified every difficulty. The route led over a poorly sited road that finally shrank to a trail, but he had taken the D.C.I.T. over far worse country in the Shenandoah and thought nothing of it. Why had Brewer sent them, guideless, in pitch darkness on such a course? Then his eye picked up a real road a couple of miles to the south, nearly parallel with last night's tangle of deep ravines and sheer ascents, a broad road that flowed easily over rolling fields and woodlands.

Brewer had been no fool. They could have moved easily and swiftly along that road, but so could others, others who might stop four men afoot with awkward questions. Their route, possibly laid out in colonial days and butting straight ahead regardless of slope or torrent, was not likely to attract other travelers. He turned back from the edge and saw Jake waving to him. "Found the farm, all right, Kirk, just where Brewer said. And look, if you think we were playing mountain goat last night, wait till you see what lies west of us. This hill's just something that a couple of lazy moles could pile up in a night."

"So I found out. Where are the others?"

"Mark spotted a spring and lugged our haversacks to it, but no one will want to eat before they've had some sleep. Jabish says no trails except one that leads down to the farm. I'll take the guard shift after you. Give me a shake when you want relief. I'll be by the spring over there."

"Jake went limping off and Kirk began a slow circuit of the woods. From time to time he stopped to watch that yellow-brown road flowing west. There were groups of tiny horsemen on it and slow-moving ox carts. A carriage that looked like a barouche turned out of some side road or drive and rolled west. A herd of cattle formed an ambling ribbon along the road, then vanished behind a masking hill. A light chaise whose bright paint shone in the sun went smoothly east, two horsemen keeping pace. "You're a very smart man, Mr. Brewer," thought Kirk. "That road's a good place for us to keep away from, even at night."

A morning mist was beginning to close in over the west as the sun climbed, but Kirk could see enough of what Jake had reported to make him stand, thoughtful and somberly brooding, for a good quarter hour. Range after range of shaggy mountains rolled away, close-packed, with treetopped peaks or bold rock faces lifting higher and higher as though striving to rise above the golden haze of the new day. Upland farms lay oak-embedded, like islands in a tossing green sea. Brown ribbons led to big houses in parklike valleys behind which cliffs and towering rounded shoulders hung poised as though to break, wavelike, on field and meadow and barn and house. Bright mountain lakes lifted like deep blue mirrors to the sky above. A cottony cumulus cloud drifted south to reveal the long gray-brown scar of some ancient rock slide. "West and southwest," thought Kirk. "Gets worse the longer I look. And we'll have to dodge all the better going and daylight travel. Wish we had a medic with us. That's going to be hard on knees and ankles. As for a broken bone—that could mean a long stay in the mountains for a man, maybe for as long as the mountains last."

Slowly the great panorama withdrew behind its mist curtain and Kirk looked for the farm. It was in plain view, a small story-and-a-half whitish house with a few outbuildings and a barn, set in a desolate grassless patch. A man was swinging an ax by a woodpile and the *whick-whick* of the blade was startlingly clear in the still air. A sunbonneted woman came out of the house and scanned the countryside for several minutes. Seemingly satisfied, she picked up a covered basket and went into a barn. In a few moments she reappeared, sitting sidewise on a saddleless horse, and rode south over meager fields to vanish in distant woodlands, the basket slung from an arm. "Wonder why she took that look around," Kirk mused. "None of my business, Just the same, we'd better watch that house. The more we know, the fewer roots we trip over."

Short and wiry, Mark Furber knelt in the woods, a dim figure in the swift-flowing darkness. "All right," he said crisply. "We filled our bottles at the spring. We've got two days' rations each if we go light on them. Here's what happened at the farm when Kirk and Jake were asleep: On my shift, the woman rode out of the woods and went into the house about two. No one's seen her since. The man butchered a cow or something, then worked at salting the meat. After Jabish relieved me, four armed men rode into the yard with a wagon following. They came from the southwest, so there's some kind of a road off there. They chucked what looked like hams and grain sacks into the cart and went off the way they came. No telling yet whether it does us any good to know all that. Let's go."

The four followed a deep-worn path across the fields, guiding by one faint light in the rear of the house. A dog barked somewhere indoors as they came into the yard, then ceased abruptly as though by command. Mark rapped on the weather-gnawed door. There was silence for a moment, then cautious footsteps. A muffled voice said, "Who's that?"

"We're looking for Mr. John Hart," answered Mark.

"None such in these parts. What sort of folk's he supposed to be?"

"The—right sort."

Rusty bolts slid and the door swung open and a high-held candle shone down, giving a brief glimpse of a small, bearded man. A gaunt woman stood just behind him, a shotgun in her hands and a dog growling at her side. Then the man blew out the candle. "Be welcome," he said.

They filed into the room, bowing to the woman, who was hanging the gun on a peg in the wall. The few chairs, the backless bench and the pine-topped table that stood on the splintery floor were homemade, but floor and furniture were spotless and a smell of crude soap was strong in the air. The woman inclined her head gravely. "Sit by," she said, edging the bench closer to the hearth. "I'll stir the fire and set a kettle for you."

"That's kind of you," said Mark. "But we've had our rations."

The man seated himself on a low stool. "Well, if you've et—'course, I ain't pressin' guests—but maybe you'd like to talk some. Say, 'bout how you come here and who you be."

Mark glanced at the others, who nodded. "We came here because someone who holds to the Union told us to."

The woman, on a stool across the hearth, eyes him approvingly.

"That's spoke spare but fair. Reckon the who'll sound just as good."

"Hope so," said Mark as he began a brief account of the group, the others adding details from time to time. Before he had finished, the dog rose from its corner, growling again. Their host opened the door and let it go howling into the night. His wife's hand reached slowly toward the shotgun. Kirk, nearest her, started to his feet and gripped the stick that he had cut in the woods. She muttered, "Stay froze, all. If I say 'Git', you climb them pegs to the loft above. It's dark there."

"And then?" asked Jabish Kell.

200

"Do what seems fittin to you. But don't tangle in our miseries. You could make 'em worse. Hark, now." Then her worn hand fell away from the gun and her husband, crouched by the door, swung it open. The dog came pattering in, tongue lolling, and curled up in its corner. The woman sighed. "Ascairt, I was. He stayed out so long. Must have heard some varmint crossing the barnyard. Had it been folks, he'd 'a' told us quick enough."

"Do folks mean trouble to you?" asked Jake.

The host resumed his stool. "Our boy. Four months, now, he's been lyin' out in the hills to the south, hidin' from them conscriptioners. Never can tell when they might swarm the house, hopin' to catch him a-settin' with us. But he ain't been home since he lit out. We take him food and dry powder. He's got the Deckhard rifle, the same that one of his name lugged to King's Mountain in the war against the Britainers. No conscriptioner'll lay hands on him alive."

His wife reached down to pat the dog. "Our guests got their own troubles. We'll tend to our own."

"I misspoke," said the man contritely. "Now I've heard all that's safe to hear 'bout you gentlemen. You know where you are?"

"No," said Kirk. "Nor where this house is nor the names of the owners."

"I knew you right off for safe folk, not questionsome. You're trending toward Knoxville?"

"We want the quickest route to Union troops," said Mark.

"Knoxville is surest. You'll travel hard and rough. Sure to God, folks'll get wind of you and you'll need limber legs and spry minds to get shed of them. You'll find the mountains creepin' with soldiers lookin' for deserters and conscripts. And you'll find a devil's brood rangin' the hills that'll slit a throat for a pair of boots or drill a man's head for a two-bit piece. You'll have an unquietsome time."

201

"What'll we have to watch most?" asked Jake.

"You got to watch everything most. You'll follow an Indian trail that looks like a body had never set foot on it since the last redskin lit out. Sudden it'll cut into a highway and that's when you got to walk most delicate. Watch the little back roads if you think a wheel could turn on 'em, 'cause some folk'll risk a road like that, takin' five rough miles to save thirty smooth, folk who might wonder 'bout you where it wouldn't do you good. Or you could get embrangled with soldiers escortin' a commissary party."

"I wouldn't expect much travel deep in the mountains," said Jabish.

"There's always stirrin', farm to farm, settlement to settlement, town to town. Been thicker lately. Folks livin' where the armies have been find they eat better where soldiers ain't. Folks in the gov'ment that got big plantations in mountain valleys hanker for a taste of their own crops. Some clear from Richmond ride the steam cars down to Greensboro in North Carolina and then carriage out to their places, three, four days on the road. Yep, there's always stirrin', 'specially now."

Mark looked up quickly. "You said 'Greensboro in North Carolina.' Then we're still in Virginia?"

Their host looked mildly reproachful. "I ain't a surveyor, but them as is ain't never too sure just where a county line lies, nor a state line. Was I to say 'You're here' or 'You're there,' I could mislead you, not meanin' to."

Mark flushed. "Sorry. We're under your roof and that's all we need to know."

"It's a roof you rightly belong under," said the woman.

Her husband reached across and touched her hand gently, nodding. Then he said, "You'll lie up in my barn till next sundown. Come full dark, I'll set you on your way with a good pilot."

Jake coughed. "If the pilot's anything like a twin of

either of you, we'll travel with easy minds. Sound taps, Mark. We're burning up sleep for our friends here."

A biting wind whistled down the valley that was a cleft in a vast rock ridge with a mountain stream roaring over its floor and trees scaling the five-hundred-foot sides, up and up, clinging to the steep walls until their greenish tops bent and danced against the sky. Kirk huddled a blanket about his shoulders in the lee of a boulder close by the stream and uneasily watched Mark as the latter perched on a boulder in a mid-current, surveying the gorge with frowning intensity. At last Kirk called, "You're pretty conspicuous out there. We're supposed to keep under cover. Better get some sleep with Jabish and Jake under the trees over there. We've had five miles of this and there may be five more ahead."

Mark sprang ashore. "Sorry. I was trying to figure how you could blast and dig into the sides enough to lay rails through here."

"Don't you ever stop thinking about railroads?"

"Not often. Soon as the war's over, I'm going west. There'll be big building jobs going on there and I want to work on them."

"Wish I could cast ahead like that. When I see tough country, all I think of is how I'd get cavalry through it. Right here, you'd have to lead your horses. You couldn't have wagons, either."

"Wagons? How about that Reb commissary team we nearly stumbled over two days ago? It was on a road not much better than this tangle."

"Was it only two days? Then it's a full week since we left that first cabin. Say, seems to me that Cherokee pilot of ours has been gone a long time."

Mark grimaced. "If a pilot's gone more than a minute, I get jumpy. Like that rainy night when—" He broke off, staring amazedly with Kirk.

The Cherokee had materialized soundlessly among the trees, a coppery finger beckoning. "You come," said the pilot, pointing up the slope.

The night's shelter was at a valley plantation whose owner, a tall, silent man, hid the four in the loft of a chapel which he had built for his freed slaves. Then he left them with the promise that by next sundown he would have a fresh pilot for them to take the place of the Cherokee, who had drifted off, wraithlike, at the plantation's edge.

Later that evening there was a subdued murmur from the neat cabins about the chapel, a murmur of rich Negro voices. Kirk, bathed and full-fed, caught snatches of talk as he lay drowsily by the loft door. Hogs had been butchered and would end up miraculously on Mr. Jeff Davis's own table in his palace at Richmond. A man chuckled delightedly over a haul of catfish. Kirk sat up suddenly. A little girl was calling, "Henny's a bad-girl-bad-girl-bad-girl! Says there's Freedom sojers to the chapel loft!" A chiding voice cried, "What truck *we* got with Freedom sojers? Us all free since old master died. No Freedomers here!" He relaxed. That babble of child talk would be forgotten before morning. He drew his blanket about him, for the air was chill, even in this broad, sheltered valley, and settled himself for sleep like the others.

He dozed off, half roused, dozed again. Then he was fully awake, listening intently. A soft intoning came through the locked door from the stairs leading to the loft. "Oh Lord God Almighty," the muted, mellow voice chanted, "we is your children and most respectfully hopes you'll hear us without delay, oh Lord. We's in a right smart of a hurry. These here gen'men wants bad to get back North and they ain't got much time to wait. If it be 'cordin' to the destination of Great Heaven to help 'em, it do be necessary for that help to git here right soon, oh Lord. The hounds and the Rebels is on their track, so mebbe you'll take the smell out the dogs' noses and blind them Rebels with 'Gyptian darkness. Send a Moses, oh Lord, to guide these gen'men far from the Red Sea of 'fliction and into the Promised Land. Let help come soon, oh Lord, 'cause your Yankee servants is sure goin' to need it."

The voice died away. Kirk edged toward the door and whispered, "Amen. The servants of the Lord'll meet Him halfway." Then he wriggled toward Jake and woke him. "No noise. We're leaving. Carry your boots in your hand."

Jake roused the others silently. Kirk rolled his blanket, wrapped it about his waist and then stood by the door, waiting. Soon he felt a gentle push from Jake as a sign to take the lead. Slowly he turned the key, swung the door open. He could just make out a short, stooped man on the stairs. Laying a hand on his shoulder, Kirk whispered, "We're trusting you."

"Trust in the Lord that opened your ears to my words, suh," the Negro breathed. "They was loud as I dast make them." The half-seen shape moved down and Kirk followed, boots in hand and aware of the pressure of Jake's fingers on his arm. At the foot of the stairs, the Negro pressed a fat glass jar into Kirk's grasp. "Hands and faces. White skin show too good."

Kirk set his boots down, dipped his fingers into an oily mass in the jar, smeared his face, hands and wrists, passed the jar back to Jake. In a few moments Jake whispered, "Everyone fixed up. You take the helm till we know what we're going to do." Kirk nodded and slipped on his boots. The old man guided him cautiously to an open side door and stepped through. Kirk's feet had barely touched the ground when he jammed his arm back, blocking Jake in the doorway. The nearest cabins were dark, but beyond the last a couple of torches burned murkily. The old man caught his sleeve. "Rest easy, suh. Sat'day night. Master always lets the young folk go spear-fishin' then. We'll make company with them. And, suh, it ain't no use the Lord hustlin' Himself to help if you don't hustle with Him."

Kirk stifled his doubts and went on toward the lights.

In the open field he asked under his breath, "Can't you tell me what happened?"

The old voice wavered. "Sojers come for the master. Took him to the county seat."

"No! They took *him?* Then it was on account of us!"

"Them sojers don't know 'bout you. But they's others that does and they aim to harry you with dogs."

"You're sure of this? But how?"

"My people cain't read and cypher like white folk, mostly, but word do travel swift amongst us. Jason, head houseman, and me, we warned master 'bout the first lot, but he say he ain't never showed his back to folks lookin' for him. Then they come for him. After that, we hear 'bout the other sojers and the dogs, so I come to you, not darin' to make much noise, like thumpin' on your door. Maybe two, three plantation hands it ain't safe to trust."

The torches were close now and their muted lights showed a cluster of shifting forms, some of them carrying long fish spears. "How can we be sure about all these people?"

"Sure? Who goin' to spec'late 'bout five, six more trompin' off in the dark, spear-fishin'? You blacked your hands and faces. Just don't talk amongst 'em. And others'll join in on the road 'fore we ever gets to the fish pools."

"And what do we do when we get there?"

"I aim to find a mighty wise man from the nex' plantation and we'll study on what to do. He always at the pools."

The leading torch moved off and the Negroes followed it, laughing and talking. Kirk frowned. "They seem pretty happy for people who've just lost their master—for a while, anyway."

"Reckon a lot ain't heard or just plumb don't understand. The master lef' quiet and Jason he told the house servants they wasn't to talk none."

"Just hope it's all right," Kirk thought. "Maybe I'm

running us all into a trap." Then he reached out, caught the old man gently by the arm. "Off there to the right," he whispered. "Someone moving."

The latter winced. "Oh Lord, look down!" he whimpered. "That ain't none of our people."

12

The Hostages

A man detached himself from the shadow of a young live oak and spoke in a low clear tone. "You come."

The Negro threw his arms into the air. "Now praise the Lord. He sent you a Moses. The same Cherokee as brought you here. You just go with him, with the Moses the Lord done sent."

"Moses might have had quite a time finding us if it hadn't been for you," said Kirk, gripping the clasped hands. "We won't forget you or your master. We'll be praying for you both."

"Pray good for him! Pray *real* good. And God bless your steps in the dark wilderness."

The Cherokee said, "Take this," and shoved a soft packet into Kirk's hands, then moved on to the others. "Take this. Now you come quick."

They moved off through the night, away from the torches. "Wish we could do something about our host," muttered Kirk.

"We can help him most by getting off his land," said Jabish. "We left nothing in the loft, no trace that we'd been there. What's in these packets, pilot?"

"Pepper."

"What do we need pepper for?"

"The dogs," said Mark. "It'll kill any scent we leave if they're tracking us. Then they'll sneeze their fool heads off and it'll be hours before they can smell again. Do we start scattering it now, pilot?"

"I tell when."

Kirk turned back to Jake. "Better take up your command again."

"Right. And the first thing I want to find out, if I can, is how Big Chief Talk-a-heap happened to be waiting for us." He lengthened his stride, caught up with the Cherokee. In a few minutes he dropped back beside Kirk and the others. "He told me in about a dozen words, but damned if I can squeeze it up like that. He hung around in the hills after he left us. He found ten soldiers, *real* ones, not levies, cooking a quick meal. They had a brace of dogs with them. He begged food and then combined eating and listening, found out they knew where we were and were coming after us. Then he melted away and you know the rest."

"Any proof he really ran into them?" asked Jabish.

"Enough to convince *this* jury, Lawyer Kell. He brought away one belt buckle stamped C.S.A., two Colt-pattern revolvers from Tredegar with twenty rounds each. Better not give away these cartridges the way we did Brewer's, because we may need 'em for something different. My idea is that the man in command lugs one Colt and his relief has the other. That suit all hands? Then here's your gun, Kirk, and cartridge pouch. Now we better strap on our Seven League-Boots, because our friend says we've got real climbing ahead. We've got a good start and it may be that no one will catch up with us."

The Cherokee went on, tireless, scaling steep hogbacks

as easily as a weasel going over a log. A precipitous dry watercourse where Kirk had to guess and fumble his way among eroded boulders was seemingly as simple to the pilot as a broad street. There was easy going for a while along a deep-worn deer run and the party swung on at a good pace. Clean forest showed on either side, with trees towering to the black sky and a swift stream foaming and chattering off to the left. A few more such miles would soon make up for slower progress on slopes.

It was Kirk, bringing up the rear, who heard the sound first, a distant ghostly baying far off to the east. He doubled ahead to warn the pilot, but the latter's quick ear had just caught the sound and he was halting. "They take short cut," he said. "Maybe they broke into two parties." He raised a hand, nodding, as more barking came from the north. "Yes. Two. Later they meet. Go on together if not find us by then."

It all seemed logical enough, Kirk thought. There must have been two probable trails, converging somewhere off in the west, and the pursuers were covering both of them, planning to meet at the junction. "That barking in the east sounds louder," he said. "Will they be carrying lights?"

"No lights." The Cherokee stood for a moment, chin on chest. Then he threw back his head. "Better we run," he said and started up the deer trail at a smooth, loping trot.

"How does he think we're going to outrun dogs?" panted Jabish.

"He's a boy who doesn't make many mistakes," answered Jake. "Now dig for it!' They raced on, barely able to see the pilot's bobbing head and shoulders. At the end of a few hundred yards they veered to the right, off the trail, and kept on over more broken country until the Cherokee stopped them with a warning hiss. Kirk found himself staring down into deeper blackness, a cliff edge with an ocean of darkness beyond it.

"Do this," said the pilot. He rubbed his hands along

the lip of the cliff, lowered his body halfway over, hauled himself up. Kirk obediently wriggled and twisted until his legs dangled over what might have been ten feet or a hundred feet of empty dark. Levering himself back on the cliff, he whispered, "Want a hand, Jake? You all right, Mark? Sure, I see what he's doing, leaving a scent trail that seems to go right over into nothing, but what comes next? My God, there he goes. Nothing for us to do but follow."

The pilot had started *back,* trotting over the identical ground that had been covered before and turning into the deer run. At the foot of a great oak close by the stream he stopped and began rubbing his hands along the bark. "Pepper now," he said. "On ground, too." He watched while the others smeared the powder about. "Now come." He swung himself into the tree by a bough some six feet off the ground, patting more pepper about. It took frantic scrambling, especially for the shorter ones, before they were all in the tree.

"Can't stay here," muttered Kirk. "We'd show up big as vultures."

But the pilot was going higher, reaching for a thick, lateral bough and beckoning. For the next few moments Kirk could only pray for a steady head and sure feet. Step by step, gripping an overhead branch, he and the others worked along with the rush and toss of the stream below them. If he could only take his eyes off the headlong sweep of the water that seemed to be dragging him along with it! But when he tried to look away, his feet scraped on the rounded sides of the bough and he had to clutch madly at the branch above to keep from pitching among the rapids.

He gave a gasp of relief as he saw ground below him and the pilot standing waiting. He let himself drop and stood by to ease Jake's fall and Mark's. When long-legged Jabish thudded down, the Cherokee hurried them all into a thick growth of laurel whose waxy,

212

spined leaves ripped at faces, hands and clothes. "Very quiet," he whispered.

Kirk settled himself as comfortably as possible so no involuntary movement would snap or rustle the dead twigs about him. He cleared away dead grasses before his face, remembering a night a long year and more ago when a blade had tickled his nose and nearly forced a sneeze that could have betrayed him to passing Rebel troopers. The wind was blowing through the trees and across the stream toward their laurel clump, so there was no danger of their scent being carried to dogs over there on the old deer run, a good thirty feet away, he judged. The endless churning of the current gave off a faint luminescence, but their hands and faces could hardly show, since they still wore the greasy stain that the old Negro had given them.

Kirk's fingers dug into the ground. Barely visible, just a little lighter than the background, ghostly figures moved along the run. He heard their soft tread, a crisp patter that must have been a dog's paws. The group slowed down by the oak and Kirk held his breath. There was a sharp "Chiff!" and the figures moved on. When the last light footfall had died away, Jake whispered, "Did he get enough pepper to put him out of action?"

"Not get much," answered the pilot.

Fresh baying broke out and Jabish stirred, muttered, "Now he's left the run. Now—" The Milwaukeean kept up a low stream of comment as though he could actually see the dog. The animal was running in circles. It was at the edge of the cliff, puzzled.

"You know dog good," said the Cherokee.

"Hunted behind a few." Jabish's account went on. The pursuit was being led back to the run, up along it, then back to the cliff edge, the dog telling his masters that the fugitives *must* have gone down it.

"What'll they do now?" asked Jake.

"People know country good. Go much north. Circle back to foot of cliff. Find no scent. Come back to oak."

"How long'll all that take 'em?" asked Kirk.

"Enough." He rose, slipped out of the laurel. "You come. I find next pilot."

With hardly a halt, the four labored on south, away from the stream. There was meadowland where they moved swiftly. There were tumbling creeks up which the pilot waded, sure-footed, while the others floundered, slipping off glasslike rocks, getting entangled in rotting driftwood. Steep slopes rose ahead of them and they had to dig their boots into the ground to keep from pitching backward. They went up wall-like rises of sheer stone, while the Cherokee, hanging in the dark above, whispered, "Hand here. Catch root. Hand here, foot there."

Among tumbled boulders the pilot said, "You wait," and vanished. Kirk stretched out, panting, on the dew-soaked pine needles. Never had he felt so utterly lost in time and space. He could not have given the vaguest estimate of the direction of the night flight or of the hours that had passed. And time—time was flowing away like the mountain streams. How much more of their route lay ahead? Days, weeks—or months? His only sure knowledge was that they were well into North Carolina. It was growing lighter and all at once the Cherokee came drifting back among the rocks and trees. Something of the quiet assurance, the cold confidence, had left the man and Kirk felt a sudden qualm of fear.

Jake sat up, instantly alert. "What's wrong?" he asked.

The Cherokee leaned against a pine. "Next pilot gone. House burned."

"My God!" exclaimed Mark. "What do we do?"

The man said wearily, "Maybe know one more pilot." Uncertainty crept into his voice. "Only—only—this not my country."

Jake rolled to his feet. "We'd trust you to find your

214

way on the moon. Take the lead and we'll follow and not a worry in the lot of us."

The pilot's head slowly lifted. He gave himself a shake, hitched at his worn breeches and moved off toward the south. "You come," he said.

The sparse pines were beginning to stand out, black against a dark gray sky. Kirk caught up with Jake. "At least I know our direction now. South and a bit west. See how much lighter it is off to the left? Hope our lie-up place is close."

Without turning, the Cherokee said, "Not lie up."

"What? We're going to travel by daylight?" cried Jake.

"Not my country. Maybe walk over cliff in dark. Got to see."

Jabish hurried up. "We've been warned and warned not to travel by day. Best thing to do is find a good, high spot, study the land from it and then hit out after sundown."

"Bad country," said the pilot, not breaking his stride.

"I rather like Jabish's idea," said Mark.

"I said before, this boy of ours doesn't make many mistakes," said Jake firmly. "As long as I'm in command, we follow him. Anyone wanting to get left behind's free to follow his will."

"That's even worse," grumbled Jabish. "But it doesn't make what we're doing sound any better."

The west was still dark, but a steady glow was spreading over the east. Then a long finger of light reached across the dome of the sky, fell on a rocky crest far, far to the west, began to trace a brightening line downward. It lit up savage scars, deep, lateral valleys, the flat gray faces of cliffs. A broad ribbon of silver shone as it hurled itself from a granite lip to fall hundreds of feet into some unguessed basin. Light flooded through a gap that the centuries had ripped out of a rock barrier and glittered on a narrow river bend purling past jutting cliffs. Range after range of lower ridges took the new day on their crests, heaved up out of the darkness. Jake

215

pointed. "Look at all that. And there's probably just as bad country lying beyond that last high mass. Anyone here want to try getting over there in the dark, without a pilot who knows every seam and fold?"

Jabish muttered, "Might be better than moving by day. Hi! Watch out. Must be people close by. Smell the smoke?"

The Cherokee pointed to the left. There was a cart path, fields as gray and meager as "John Hart's" and a heap of blackened wood about a cat-and-clay chimney. "Next pilot," he said. He ran toward some bushes and caught up part of a linsey-woolsey shirt with a hole in one shoulder and dark stains spreading from it. "His," he said. "Two, three day ago. Not know country beyond here. Go careful." He waved an arm toward the west. "My people here, long ago. Had villages and fields in valleys. Now all gone, all forgot. They make this trail before white man come, long ago." He struck out toward the south, keeping below the shoulder of an endless ridge that the sun was just topping.

Kirk, close behind Jake, could see no trail, only a smooth matting of dead leaves and branches, but his feet sank into a trough, deepworn, that ran on and on, dipping into hollows, slanting up steep inclines. Off to the west the eternal surflike lift and toss of the ranges grew brighter, then slowly dimmed. Streaming banners of cloud frayed out from their crests, and along the tree-clad slopes whitish bands stretched right and left as though a hundred infantry regiments had opened fire. Swirls of mist clung to the east side of the valley and the fugitives moved ghostlike through them. Thick spats of rain began to fall.

The morning wore on through an intermittent downpour that washed most of the black stain from the hands and faces of the four. The ancient Indian trail bent west along a snoutlike spur that jutted from the main ridge, and Kirk noticed that the Cherokee was moving very cautiously along it, shaking his head and stopping from time to time to sniff the air. In a stretch where rock walls rose high on both sides he suddenly braked with his feet, then stood still, pointing ahead. The four closed on him, staring at the bare expanses of earth some fifty yards in front. There was no need to explain. A rough road cut the trail at right angles. "Where does it go?" whispered Jake.

"Not know. Got to cross it."

Jake nodded briskly. "We'll rush it. There'll probably be no one on it, but if there is, they're not going to follow us down the slope beyond, from what I can see of it. If they do, well, Kirk and I'll bring up the rear with our Colts. Take the lead, pilot."

They crept down between the rock walls that rose higher and higher. Then the pilot darted out, crossed the road and plunged into the trees on the far side, Mark and Jabish close behind him. Jake followed. Then Kirk poised, dropped to the road. A low branch flicked off his hat and he turned, mechanically, to pick it up. At the same moment a horse neighed, high and quivering. Kirk whirled about. An enemy patrol? No! Civilian travelers, so often mentioned, moving from army areas to more bountiful parts of the country, for in a long, deep scoop in the hillside below the rock bastion was a horse and buggy. A tall, iron-gray man with a square beard stood frozen by the horse's head. And on the seat, one hand clutching the frame of the hood, was Lynn Stockdale, blue eyes wide, cheeks flushed and lips compressed into a button of startled amazement.

Kirk thought that during long nights and long miles he had schooled himself mentally and physically to meet any contingency. But now he stood numbed, hat in one hand, Colt in the other. He could not take his eyes from Lynn, so feminine with her crown of bright hair, her thrown-back shoulders emphasizing the tightness of her bodice above the billow of wide green skirts.

Then she cried, "Why, it's Captain Stedman!" and to Kirk's further bewilderment, her eyes were suddenly

217

dancing and her lips curved in a warm smile that he had never seen before. She swung herself to the ground in a whirl of green skirts and a distracting flash of slim white-stockinged ankles. "We read about your escape in the papers. How ever did you manage it? Of course, a lot of our friends were furious, but we couldn't help being glad, somehow."

Kirk bowed. "This really is a pleasure. About our escape—" Then his mind flashed a warning and all the implications of the presence of Lynn and her father on that desolate road swept over him. He moved quickly back to the trees at the far side. "I'm afraid I'll have to ask a few questions of you and your father. Were you to meet anyone here? Where does this road go to?"

Slowly a trace of the old, familiar hostility crept over Lynn's face. "Really, Captain, you're in Confederate territory, and as for questions—"

Ian Stockdale came out onto the road. "Best leave this to me, Lynn. You've every right, in your position, to ask questions, Captain Stedman. We're waiting for no one and expect to meet no one. You've nothing to fear from us. As for this road, I'm afraid I don't know much about it. Really, I was terribly relieved when my daughter recognized you. We've heard stories of rather odd people in the mountains, marauders, armed gangs and so on. You've met no one like that?"

"No one, sir. But surely you found out about things like that when you took this road."

Stockdale looked a little sheepish. "I must admit we're not where we expected to be. We'd been staying with friends over in Lost Valley and were on our way to visit other friends farther south. Our host told us of a short cut, rough but safe, he said. He would have come with us, but his gout was too much for him and I was very sure I could find the turn-off without him."

"I see," said Kirk, eyes on Lynn. "You risked five rough miles to avoid twenty smooth ones. You came by train from Richmond to Greensboro in North Carolina.

218

Then you've been moving west, town to town, plantation to plantation. Yes. It's a route many Richmond people seem to be taking these days, or so we were told in the mountains."

Lynn tossed her head. "Just why should you be so interested in our travels?"

"In your most recent venture, anyway." He studied the surface of the road, trying to gauge about how long the horse had been standing in that deep scoop. It was very odd that the Cherokee's quick ears had not picked up the clank of hoof and grind of wheel as the party came down from the ridge above.

Lynn gave an audible sniff, but her father nodded in understanding. "I see. You're escaping and it's only natural that you want to know about any movement on any road. We're on a short holiday and our next stop's to be our last. Then we go on to Wilmington, where I must see some of the masters of the blockade-runners. Luckily, I know just where I took the wrong turn, about five miles back. But when I tried to turn around, the horse shied when he saw the steep pitch across there, became quite unmanageable. So I decided to let him quiet down by himself."

"Yes. They will shy," said Kirk absently. The wait must have been quite long enough to account for the pilot's having heard no sound.

Lynn tapped her lips gently with a small hand. "You'll have to run to catch up with your friends, Captain," she remarked.

Kirk hooked the Colt onto his belt and smiled at her. "I shan't have very far to run." He gave a low whistle. " 'These be Clan Alpin's warriors true and, Saxon, I am Roderick Dhu.' "

Lynn gasped as the bushes rustled and Jake came onto the road, followed by Mark and Jabish. There was no sign of the pilot. Kirk eyed the trio as they stood, hats in hands, obviously trying not to stare but as obviously still rather overwhelmed by the sight of Lynn. Then

Jake grinned. "Never thought I'd have the chance to thank you, Miss Stockdale. You saved at least four bad scurvy cases in Libby. And that pot of honey drip healed up one boy who had a putrid throat on top of a sawed-off arm and he's back with his folks in Pennsylvania right now."

Lynn's eyes were suddenly bright and her lips were soft. "Back to his own people," she said, and her voice was gentle as her glance. "And some of the others were really cured? It seemed so little to do. We wanted to send more, but the authorities told us that the prisoners had everything, and besides, so many of our own friends needed so much. I'm grateful to you for telling me." Her tone changed a little and she glanced coldly at Kirk. "It's the first that *I've* ever heard of what became of—" She left the sentence unfinished.

"We didn't figure it was safe to write you from Libby, what with the secret police and all," said Jake. "Well, let's see what we can do now. This is a mean place to turn, but we're all horse soldiers and I guess we can manage. We'll unhitch your horse and head him back. Then we'll swing the buggy around and hitch up again."

"That would be very kind of you gentlemen," said Ian Stockdale.

"You and Mark handle the beast, Kirk," called Jake. "Jabish and I'll see to the buggy. Catch hold, now!"

Kirk gave Jake's shoulders a light shake from behind. "What's the matter with you? Getting scared of horses or something?" Under his breath he muttered, "Not yet. Couple of things I want to find out. Just keep fussing around till I get back." He released Jake, slipped off into the woods, swinging himself a few yards down the slope from branch to branch. He found the Cherokee standing by a great lichened rock. "Who?" asked the pilot suspiciously.

"They'll do us no harm. You've been on a scout? What did you find out?"

220

The pilot had worked south along the slope, it seemed, and although in strange country, had spotted a few landmarks that he knew by sight and had pretty well oriented himself. The road south was safe and a few miles farther on was a settlement of which he had heard, a cluster of houses belonging to Unionists, perched in a forgotten cleft. "Right people," he concluded. "Not good if wrong people know about." His eyes flicked toward the road.

"We'll see that wrong people don't," said Kirk slowly. "You come along where you can watch, but keep out of sight." He worked up the slope and onto the road, where Jabish and Mark were looking soulfully at Lynn while Jake was picking up one of the horse's hoofs as seriously as though he were on his own picket line. Lynn and her father were laughing at something that Jake had just said. Ian Stockdale nodded pleasantly to Kirk as he emerged. Lynn did not even look at him. "She will in a minute," thought Kirk, bracing himself. Then he said quickly, "I've bad news for you."

Jake dropped the hoof and Mark and Jabish turned quickly. "What's wrong?" asked Jake.

"Nothing, if we can help it. Mr. Stockdale, I'm afraid that you and your daughter will have to go back on foot."

Lynn turned on him in a swirl of green, her eyes snapping. Then they grew cold, half veiled by the lids. "We should have expected that from the first, I suppose. We've seen Yankee raiders before."

Her father said, "I'm afraid I don't quite understand. This rig belongs to our host in Lost Valley."

"It'll get back to him," said Kirk. "We're not interested in it. But we are interested in relative speeds. The horse would take you far quicker than your feet to people who'd like nothing better than to run us down."

Jake burst out, "Oh, look here, Kirk. They won't say anything about us. You can't make a girl tramp over

221

these roads. Look at her shoes. She'd cut her feet to pieces."

Ian Stockdale's face turned a dusky red. "Now I do understand and it's a most damnable outrage. Certainly you have my word and my daughter's that we'll say nothing of this meeting, but we're not knuckling under to any threats in giving it. Stand aside, sir. I'll turn the buggy around myself."

"You won't have to, sir," exploded Jake. "Kirk, you have chucked your wits overboard? I'm in command and *I'm* taking their word. All hands get busy and slue the rig around."

Mark Furber shouted, "Jake's right."

"I'm standing by him," cried Jabish, moving closer to Lynn.

Kirk shook his head violently. "I've got my wits, all right. I'm not doubting anyone's word. But we've all been in service long enough to know how often information gets out without anyone meaning it to. Something's overheard that doesn't mean a thing to the person saying it, but it can mean a whole damn lexicon to someone hearing it. Like the time we got wind of that Reb ambush below Kelly's Ford. No one ever *meant* to tell us about that. I know Mr. Stockdale will say nothing and I'm equally sure of Miss Stockdale, but just the same—"

Lynn linked her arm with her father's, her chin stubbornly lifted. "*Are* you so sure about Miss Stockdale? I don't mind walking and I've a nice stout pair of boots in the little trunk in the buggy. When we get back to Lost Valley"—she gave a cold smile and her tone became bantering—"*wouldn't* you like to know the very first thing I'm going to do?"

"Not very much," said Kirk. "Now about the horse—"

"Not very much!" mimicked Lynn. "You aren't interested that there's a command of about seventy-five men, looking for people just like you, not ten minutes' ride away from the valley? Not militia, Captain, but regular

222

troops who were born around here and they've got all the horses and dogs that they need."

Kirk looked steadily at her, but her eyes never wavered. "I'm quite sure that you're inventing nothing. No, keep quiet, Jake. You would have done better not to have mentioned them, Miss Stockdale. Now I'd be glad if you and your father would get into the buggy."

Lynn laughed derisively. "So the seventy-five men frighten you!"

"I must confess that they do. I only hope that your next host won't worry too much when you don't appear. I wish I could see some other way out, but I can't. You'll have to come with us, both of you."

Ian Stockdale grew even redder and his beard jutted. His voice was surprisingly calm as he said, "My daughter and I will do nothing of the sort. You've suggested a hard way back for us, but we shall manage it, I can assure you."

"It will be a pleasure," said Lynn coldly.

Jabish turned to Lynn. "I don't know what this is all about. But the only man giving orders is Jake and you heard him tell us to turn you about and get you started. Ready, Jake?"

"Not quite yet," said Jake slowly. "I've never known Kirk to alter course without a good reason. Maybe he knows something we don't."

"Get over here out of earshot," said Kirk. When he and Jake were a few paces off, Kirk told him quickly what the pilot had said. "So you see," he went on, "if the Stockdales get back to Reb people, they're bound to let *something* drop, even without meaning to. They'll have to have a story to account for their lateness, just in common courtesy. That'll bring search parties up here. They've got good trackers—remember how quick the hounds picked us up after we left that chapel?—and they'd be bound to spot this old trail. If they don't catch up with us, at least they'll watch it from then on and it'll be useless to the right sort of people. And you can't

223

tell what else they might run onto. The hunt could lead them to people who've sheltered us."

Jake nodded somberly. "That's good figuring. I ought to have moused out something like that myself, even without the pilot."

"Hell, you were dizzy looking at the only pretty girl you've seen since a brunette got onto our car at Amelia Station. And you were looking at *her,* all right. But there's more than just what I've been saying. That settlement, a few miles up the road. Even if patrols miss our trail, they're apt to push right on to those houses. From what the pilot said, the area hasn't been bothered in a couple of years and it must be crawling with deserters and conscription dodgers. Maybe a few people like us. A patrol up here'd mean more burnings and killings."

"I still think it's safe to turn the Stockdales loose on foot. They've both promised they wouldn't mention us."

"Kelly's Ford, Jake, Kelly's Ford. Don't forget what innocent little words warned us about that. Why, a scout like Chris Rowan could just chat with them for five minutes and piece out everything they've seen or heard. And they haven't *both* promised. The girl's so boiling that the Spanish Inquisition couldn't wring a pledge out of her."

Jake rubbed his knuckles across his forehead. "Damn it, it just isn't *decent* to drag a girl along with us."

"Did I say it was? Our lives were table stakes when we started out, but now a lot of others can suffer if the cards fall wrong. We can't take chances. Those two have got to come with us."

Jake hitched his coat. "Yep! It's got to be the way you say. But, holy hell, it's going to be a rough trip from now on, and I'm not thinking just about the Stockdales' end of it. Let's get back. You do the talking."

Kirk strode across the track. Lynn was tight-lipped, the pallor of her cheeks offset by the hot anger of her eyes. Her father was calmer, rather ominously so. "Will you please get into the buggy?" began Kirk.

"And if we refuse?" asked Stockdale in a level tone.

"We'll have to use force, I'm afraid. That, or shoot the horse and pitch it and the buggy down the slope."

"There may be another answer." A short, double-barreled derringer seemed to leap into Stockdale's hand. "I hope you won't make me use it. Travel would be difficult if two of you had a heavy ball in a leg. Don't reach for your Colts. I'm quite accustomed to firearms."

Lynn gave a brittle laugh. "How about force now, Captain? I remember from Frederick's Hall that you enjoy mauling people smaller than you."

"That would hardly include your father. By the way, sir, I am sure that you're used to firearms, but you seem to have forgotten that a derringer has to be cocked. Both your hammers are flat." The other's eyes dropped for an instant and Kirk sprang forward, wrenched the weapon loose. "Search him, Jake. See if he has more hardware on him." Jake slapped deftly at Stockdale's clothes but found nothing.

Lynn planted herself before Kirk. "I suppose you're going to search me to!"

"If we have to. I'd prefer your word. You *are* unarmed? Thank you. Now I want to know where that pistol came from. I'm damn well certain he didn't have it before."

"I gave it to him," said Jabish sullenly. "It was in the buggy. You've got no right whatsoever—"

"This isn't a law court, Jabish. This is something that could mean life or death for us and some others. You're going against orders. If you want to drop out, go ahead. I don't think you'll get far alone."

"I don't like this either," muttered Mark. "But we agreed about discipline." He bowed to Lynn. "I'm afraid you'd better obey."

"Kirk's been speaking for me," said Jake. "I hate to

225

put it this way to you people, but I've got to. Are you getting into the buggy or—"

Lynn flared. "Not while I can use my hands and feet!"

Her father spoke wearily. "We've no choice. But all of you are going to regret this bitterly, most bitterly. Please mount, Lynn. It will be only a matter of hours before people begin looking for us and they'll find our track without much trouble."

With a swish of her green mantle, Lynn brushed by Kirk, head high, and climbed nimbly in. Her father followed her. "The reins, if you please," he said.

"Sorry," answered Jake. "Kirk, you take 'em and walk by the horse's head. And I better have that whip. A quick cut across the face could be as bad as a saber slash. H'm. Yankee whip, from Greenfield, Massachusetts. Lead out, Kirk."

Kirk started the horse, aware of a thunderous silence from the buggy.

Off to the right an occasional stir among the branches told him that the Cherokee was paralleling the road, always watchful. The way grew narrower with frequent gullyings and potholes and rock domes. The iron wheel rims clashed against stone, the buggy shook as it thumped into deep troughs. Twice the horse stopped, straining, until Jake's hail, "Cannoneers on the wheels!" set the others pushing at the spokes until the vehicle was freed. On a fairly level stretch, Mark Furber caught up with Kirk. "All serene back there?" asked Kirk.

"What do you expect? Look here, Stedman, I really don't know a hell of a lot about you and there's something I've been wondering. So has Jabish."

"Go on," said Kirk, easing the horse around an out-cropping.

"You knew this girl before, didn't you?"

"Can't say I *know* her. I ran into her on the Dahlgren raid. She came to see me in Libby. That's all. I don't

226

think I'm exactly a favorite of hers. What's all this getting at?"

"She's damn pretty."

"Lots of girls are."

"But she's being pretty around here. I don't say this is so, but a man *could* figure you've got reasons of your own, dragging her with us."

Kirk turned quickly. "What do you mean, reasons of my own?"

"You haven't gone soft on her, have you, or figured that if she saw a little more of you, you might be a bigger favorite than you say you are? Now don't start balling up your fists. On a job like this, not knowing you too well, I've got a right to ask. You'd do the same in my place."

Kirk clamped his jaws hard. Then his mind cleared and he nodded. "Yes. You've got a right to ask. Here's my answer. I'd give anything to have her mincing up 9th Street on her way to a levee at the Reb Capitol instead of here. There are other complications, too. Kidnaping that pair would be bad enough if they were just plain Rebs. But they're Canadians, neutrals."

"They told us." Mark studied Kirk's expression. "Yes, I can see you mean that, about not wanting either of them here. I don't know if you can convince Jabish. He's mulish sometimes, and that girl's got him in a vertigo, not that she means to. I'll get back to my post now."

Kirk plodded on, his head bowed. Mark's suspicions had shocked him, but he had to admit their logic. And so Jabish was mooning stupidly at her, had probably armed her father to gain favor in her eyes. Jabish would have to be watched. And there was still more to be watched. Lynn was a clever girl and if she decided to use her striking good looks to set the four at loggerheads, to ration out her smiles and undoubted charm, decorously, first on one man and then on another, an ugly situation could be created. "Damnation!" he

227

thought. "Why couldn't she have been a dumpy little mouse with buckteeth and a squint. Wonder how they're doing back there in the buggy."

A shrill whistle sounded off to the right and Kirk turned, shouted, "That's the pilot! Making port, Jake!"

The road, now little more than a rocky path, grew more level and the trees fell away on both sides. Not far off, a dozen shakeroof houses with whitewashed slab sides and worn, shallow porches clustered about a vast oak. To the left lay upsloping fields whose soil was meager but well tended. Beyond the fields, stunted cattle grazed and, in the background, a towering rounded mountain shut off the south, its tree-shrouded heights looming darkly over the little settlement.

From the porch of the nearest house a tall man with a sweeping white beard came slowly forward, patriarchal staff in hand. At the rail fence that marked the northern limit of cultivation he stopped, waiting, ageless and impassive. As Kirk drew near, the old man lifted the gnarled staff head to his hat. "The Cherokee's spoke for you. What we got's yours."

Almost unconsciously Kirk raised his hand in salute. "We're glad to find ourselves among the—right sort of people, sir. We don't want to be any trouble, but we'd be glad of a few hours' rest, a little food if you can spare it and a pilot to take us on to our next stage tonight."

"Reckon we'll make do. You can bed down in this empty house." He turned and walked easily over the worn brown grass as though the land that was his and his people's demanded no effort from his old legs.

At first the settlement seemed deserted. Then doors slowly opened, heads peered cautiously out. Old men came onto porches, gray women close behind them. Younger women appeared, some with children in their arms. Two girls, one fat and plain, one slim and darkly pretty, edged shyly out from behind a house, hand in hand. The patriarch observed, "You're the first strangers to come this way in nigh six months."

Jake raised his hand to his hat brim as he passed an elderly couple who had ventured, step by step, onto the grass. As though his gesture had been a signal, people poured from all directions, hands reaching toward the strangers. Hobbling, limping, walking heavily, skimming gracefully, the settlement descended on the fugitives. "Real Union folk!" "Look, Uriah, they got a Yankee gal with 'em, a right pretty one." "Bright be the day! We got Unioners amongst us." An old man close by Kirk wiped his eyes with the back of his hand, croaking, "Oh, glory, glory! The old flag's come back to us!" A gaunt matron hid her face in her worn apron and walked beside the horse, tanned fingers gripping the shiny shaft. Something small and soft slipped into Kirk's free hand and he looked down through a sudden blur at a mite of a girl with sun-whitened hair, skipping beside him.

He had a sudden flash of memory, a mental picture of Confederate prisoners being marched through a village in eastern Maryland. There, old men had wept and women had broken through the guards to thrust loaves and pies into gray-clad arms and someone had shouted from a window, "We'll be free yet and you with us and God damn the Union!" And the Cavalry escort had felt awkward and out of place. There, in eastern Maryland, the blue coats were *not* the right sort of people, not to those grimly cheering villagers.

Faces swam before Kirk's vision, old men, old women and young and a swirling dance of children, most of them clad in long yellow shirts and apparently not much else. But the younger men—where were they? Then far on an upland field he saw a gliding figure moving toward the settlement and carrying a long musket as easily as a matchstick. Another was leaping a stream by a mill wheel. A third, a fourth, a fifth came ghostlike out of the eastern woods. A boy in his early teens, dwarfed by an ancient musket, slid from a copse close by Kirk, muttered, "Howdy," with a shy, sidelong glance as he loped away. It was evident that something, perhaps the passage of Kirk's own party, perhaps the noise of hoofs and wheels, had been noted earlier in the day by watchers in the high reaches, who had sent word back. Then the able-bodied men had gone out to investigate.

The patriarch held up his hand and the procession halted before the last house, a shaky mass of grayish wood whose empty window frames stared blankly. "You'll bide here. The women'll fetch blankets and hang deerskins in the windows. The loft's dry and'll do for him as is wedded to the young lady, for him and for her."

There was a light thud by the buggy and Lynn marched up. "The young lady is wedded to no one. Welcome *these* people if you like, but my father and I are not here as guests!"

Stockdale joined Lynn. "The circumstances are most unusual, sir. We've been dragged here against all law. I appeal to your sense of justice and ask that we be allowed to rest here and then resume our journey. You surely have enough young men under arms to prevent any interference."

The old man looked sharply at Jake. "You done all that?"

"Didn't the Cherokee tell you?"

"He just said what you was."

"You must have known him pretty well to take his say-so," put in Kirk.

"His face was strange but his signs was known."

"This has nothing to do with us," said Stockdale. "We were on our way to Mr. Ashby's plantation, Mr. Charles Lillington Ashby, down in an upper valley. You must realize that it's your clear duty to see us onto the right road."

"We don't hold with lowland folk. Their hands has always been turned against us and their ways ain't our'n. Just the same, it ain't always right, molestin' peaceable folk on the road." His keen gray eyes probed Jake's face

230

again. "Your words could be straight whilst your intent was crooked as the heart of Judas."

A young man spoke. "I seen 'em from on top Smoky Knob. Them in the wagon was farin' along quiet." A growing mutter arose and Kirk, suddenly uneasy, saw men in homespun edging closer, fingering their weapons. A woman murmured, "Purty li'l thing! We'd ought to send her home to her ma!" Another cried, "Purty, all right, and, land, but she don't scare good!"

Jake planted his fists on his hips. "Here's what we did and why we did it. Right or wrong, we'll leave for you to say."

"Your words had kind of better be convincin', friend," growled a tall man near Kirk as Jake began his story.

Lynn looked about with a warm, easy smile that brought an answering ripple from the crowd. "Don't worry about us," she called. "We can take care of ourselves. But thanks for your good will anyway." One hand strayed to her green bonnet and coolly tucked back a wisp of bright hair. "In the meantime, Father, we might as well find out how far we've been dragged." She bent to a round-eyed child who had been staring at her, edging up a step at a time, a grubby finger in her mouth. "Little girl, can you tell me where we are?"

The young eyes grew rounder and the tousled head nodded vigorously.

Lynn waited, still bent over, but the child stared on silently. Lynn knelt, "Just tell me, dear. Where are we?"

Blank astonishment spread over the little face and the finger left the mouth in utter bewilderment. "Here!" she said, very distinctly, as though explaining something to a dull child. Lynn flushed, then laughed, gently touching the girl's cheek. "Why of course that's it! We *are* here, aren't we?" She rose, smiling. "Father, when this lecture is over, won't you ask one of the men just where—"

The patriarch rapped his staff on the ground. "You've all heerd what was spoke. Now this I say: what was

231

done was hard doin', but it was right doin'. We been talked straight to."

Stockdale burst out, "Do I understand that you approve of this outrage? I warn you, I have some influence in the Confederacy. I'm not threatening at all, but people are bound to start looking for us."

Lynn slipped her arm through her father's. "I know you mean to be fair, sir. But just think a minute. We came up that road and other people can come up to it, looking for us. You won't be able to justify helping these men who kidnaped us."

"No." The long white beard shook. "Folks won't be comin' up that road. There's rocks as will be rolled and log bridges tore up, so's the best trackers in the Smokies'd swear they ain't been a hoof nor a wheel on it in the full span of a moon."

Stockdale asked tightly, "How much farther is the next real town?"

"Some'd say about ten mile."

"And how long would it take to get here from it?"

"Four day, with good luck laughin' right out loud every step of the way, not just smilin' down. Now you folks are kind of Britainers. The first ax laid to a tree on this mountain was by men who'd fit the Britainers. What you're doin' here I don't rightly understand, but your hearts are with them Confedruts in the lowlands, with them as'd come and take our young men and our flocks and our goods for their war. We aim to git let alone."

Lynn's mouth set. "Wait till you've had Yankees here. Then you'll wish your young men had gone out long ago with those other North Carolinians whom I've seen in Virginia. Oh, I've seen plenty of them there. I've also seen what Yankees can do to a peaceful place like yours."

"The Yankees ain't bothered us. The Confedruts have. But we ain't a-warrin' on folk like you. We wish you well. What we got's your'n, like I said before. We'll see you on your way, easy as the Lord'll allow, but that way's got to lie so it don't bring ruin to us or to these Unioners."

Lynn's glance was searing. "You still say that we've got to go along with—*these?*" One small hand swept out toward the fugitives in a gesture that was scarcely affectionate.

"So it must be. There's a road your wagon'll weather through safe country to the next safe people. One of my boys'll guide you. Now, seein' you ain't wed to none of these folks, I reckon it ain't decent to bed you down in that loft. Widow McCaskie'll see to you."

Stockdale drew out a notebook and pencil. "Do I understand that we are to be held prisoners?" His hand poised over the paper.

"Roam fur's you like. Some of our people'll be with you, just to make sure you don't get tuckered or lost, maybe."

"I see, We are in custody." He wrote rapidly. "I'm setting down a record of all this. You can see it before we leave and if you feel I've overstated anything, it's only fair that you have a chance to note down any exceptions you may take."

"They ain't a soul to the mountain can read, write or cypher. No matter what taxes we paid, schools ain't never reached up here. By the time the lowlanders got looked after, they was nothin' left for us. But set down your words as you see fittin', and if they come a mite hot, I ain't one to blame you. Now I'll take you to the widow's. Her brother, Lachlan McQuorkodale, shares her roof, so it'll be seemly for you and your daughter to be together."

From the porch of the house assigned the four, Kirk watched the Stockdales following the old man. The father strode on, head erect and back unbent, meeting an unpleasant situation with dignity. The angle of Lynn's bonnet and the swish of her skirts showed that she, too,

233

was keeping the flag flying bravely, but a brisk toss of her head from time to time hinted at repressed explosions. Jake, standing on the doorsill, leaned a forearm on Kirk's shoulder. "Damned if that family isn't quite a family! Wow! Seems to me our trip's just about starting. At least, they weren't on the canal boat or at Hildebrant's."

Jabish Kell, astride a gaping window, burst out, "They shouldn't be with us now! We're making a hell of a bad mistake."

"Sure we are," agreed Mark Furber. "But it would have been a worse one to have turned them loose. Where's the Cherokee? We ought to thank him. Could we spare him a few cartridges?"

"Cherokee?" said Jake. "Come to think of it I haven't seen him since we met Old Testament at the edge of this township. Here's one of the ranger boys with his artillery strapped to his back. Maybe he can tell us." Jake stepped off the porch as a tall, bearded man in homespun shirt and buckskin breeches came on at an easy pace, long rifle slung from a shoulder. "Good afternoon. Have you seen the Cherokee?"

"Good evenin'," said the hillman. "He's like to be clear t'other side of the mountain by now."

"Damn it, we wanted to thank him and he greases off before we get a chance to."

"It's the way of his people. Reckon it's time to talk some. I'm pilot. We'll vittle you for two days' trampin' and—" In sparing words he told of what the settlement could do, spoke of the road ahead, of precautions to be taken. The four listened intently, asking equally sparse questions. When the discussion was over and the pilot had gone, Jake blew out his cheeks. "Now, there's a boy who knows country and how to stay alive in it. I've known damn good Cavalry colonels he could make fools of. Not to mention Cavalry captains. Well, the next thing to do is go see the Stockdales and tell them about reveille, march orders and the rest." He rubbed his forehead ruefully. "Guess that's up to the leader for the day."

Jabish rose quickly. "I'll go if you like."

"Better for the leader to do it, the man in command," said Kirk.

To his surprise, Jake reached out and gave his hand a firm shake. "Now I knew you'd figure right along with me on that. That's just fine." He unbuckled his Colt, handed it to Mark Furber.

"What's this for?" asked Mark.

"Why, you're in command at sundown tomorrow. Haven't you been watching the west? The sun set back of those clouds a couple of minutes ago, so the command passes from me to Kirk, the same as it'll pass from him to you tomorrow." His hand fell jovially on Kirk's shoulder. "Just want to tell you that we've all got complete confidence in the way you'll put things up to Mr. Stockdale and Miss Stockdale. Yes, *sir!* You'll do just fine and we'll stand back of every word you say and every order."

"Hold on!" cried Kirk. "*You* were the one who was going to see them!"

"Oh, no, Kirk. Why, I'd never even think of saying that *I* was the man for a delicate job like that. Didn't you agree that the leader was the one to go?"

"But I'll never be able to get within shouting distance of her," protested Kirk. "Her father doesn't like me any better than she does. Back there on the road she was talking and laughing with you others, but she'd have pushed me over the brim of that last waterfall if I'd been standing close enough to it."

"Exert your authority," urged Mark, grinning. "That's the true test of leadership. Anyone can get easy orders carried out, but it takes a born commander to make people swallow the tough ones."

"You've got no legal basis for giving them *any* orders," growled Jabish.

Kirk rose reluctantly. "Legal or not, I guess I've got to give them. Wonder which house is Widow McCaskie's."

"We'll just watch from here," purred Jake. "When we see a roof fly off, we'll know that's the widow's." He settled back comfortably on the porch.

13.

Mountain Village

Kirk's task rode heavier on his shoulders as he went down the lane to the widow's house. It would be easier if he could talk to Stockdale alone, explain the measures that had been taken for the safety and the comfort of the pair. He saw himself builidng up a frank, common-sense, man-to-man atmosphere that would solve every-thing. But Lynn—Kirk had never been much of a ladies' man and he found himself envying various deft men he had known who seemed to have the gift of winning over, with a word or two, the most stubborn and con-trary girls. For his part, no matter what he said, sooner or later Lynn began throwing off sparks, sailing away with chin lifted and head erect. He was uncomfortably sure that a more knowing man could even make her for-get the present situation.

He left the lane and cut across a small field, making for the north side of the house where stacked tools, a wagon wheel and two drying raccoon pelts suggested the hand of Lachlan McQuorkodale. The father would be settling himself there while Lynn was in the widow's care in the south part of the house by the flower beds. He checked his pace, frowning, as a fearful din of shrill, high voices and thumpings and stampings set the slab walls quivering. Then he took hope from the tumult. Lynn would never stay inside with that avalanche of sounds beating about her. Very likely she was in some other house where women were heating water and scooping out soft soap so that she could freshen up after her day on the road. He rapped on the window frame that was flanked by the raccoon pelts, but the noise only swelled. He rapped harder, then shrugged, walked round the corner of the house and onto the porch.

His hope died quickly. A babel of children's voices enveloped him and he looked dizzily at a swirl of little girls who danced from room to room, joining hands, breaking up into couples, weaving in bobbing lines that formed, melted, formed again in uncertain imitation of their elders. Young voices rose higher and higher and little feet, bare or moccasined, drummed on the plank floor.

> *"Little red wagon painted blue,*
> *Little red wagon painted blue,*
> *Little red wagon painted blue,*
> *Skip to my Lou, my darling!"*

And by the open window sat Lynn, silver flashing in her slim hand as she brushed out the flaming red hair of a delighted six-year-old. A small trunk that he remembered seeing strapped to the back of the buggy stood gaping on the floor and a mass of bright ribbon trailed out from it. The children whirled on, some of them with bits of gay silk already shining from their hair or knotted about their necks.

> *"Gone again, what will I do?*
> *Skip to my Lou, my darling!"*

238

Lynn's silver brush plied on and her foot tapped lightly in time with the song. "There. Almost done and here's a lovely soft green ribbon to set off that hair of yours. Just a few more strokes and—"

The dancers caught sight of Kirk and whirled toward him.

> *"Yankee soldier come from far,*
> *Skip to my Lou, my darling!"*

Without looking up, Lynn called casually over the racket, "Am I being allowed too much liberty for a prisoner?"

Kirk smiled. "You're giving these kids a day they'll remember forever."

"Well, it's nice to think that *someone* will want to remember it. There we are, my pet. My, what hair! A lot of people will envy you that before you're done. How do you want the ribbon? Braided in? A nice big bow behind? Around your neck?"

The girl jumped up and down, stiff-legged, chanting, "Around my neck, around my neck, around my neck!" Lynn knotted it deftly, flared out a great falling bow and the girl darted out among the dancers, singing:

> *"Pretty lady with eyes so blue,*
> *Skip to my Lou, my darling!"*

Lynn clapped her hands. "Now you, little girl, with your soft brown hair and here's a yellow ribbon that'll suit you exactly. Have you come with orders for us, Captain Stedman?"

"Not orders, exactly. If your father—"

A child's piercing scream cut through his words. Lynn rose from her stool, staring past Kirk. Then she cried, "Oh, no! Not *that* one! The very first ribbon I fixed!" Before Kirk could turn, she darted past him and off the porch, catching up a child with black curls who lay sob-

239

bing on the hard ground. He was beside her in an instant, looking down in deep concern at the little whittled crutch, the bare withered leg and the one sound knee from which blood spouted. "Oh, the poor little scrap!" Lynn cried brokenly. "She was standing by the trunk and I was so afraid that she'd be jostled by the others. I don't know when she slipped out. It's a dreadful cut! I should have watched all the time!"

"Take care!" warned Kirk. "Look at the way you have her!"

"Don't interfere! No, don't try to take her. She's better off with me."

"Then don't hold her so that you're pressing her leg. You're just squeezing out more blood." A small, grimy hand reached out, trembling, and a finger hooked itself through a frayed buttonhole of his shirt. With a quick, gentle motion he took the child before Lynn could protest. "H'm. Clean cut across the kneecap. Didn't reach the bone, I think. Nasty, just the same. There, there, soldier, take it easy and we'll have you fixed up." The child's cries had stopped, but the bony little chest was heaving and quivering. "This must hurt a lot, soldier, but we're all looking after you. Miss Stockdale, will you please get hot water and clean cloth for a bandage? I'll want something to make a pad over the cut and that'll have to be cleanest of all. No! I *am* holding her properly and will you stop arguing and find those things! Get the other kids off the porch. Use 'em to run errands."

Lynn drew herself up as though for another outburst and her blue eyes snapped through the mist that had gathered over them. For an instant she met his gaze, then turned and ran into the house, herding a few girls ahead of her. There were thumpings and bumpings, quick ripping sounds, the slam of a lid closing, a few muffled words. Lynn reappeared, lugging a steaming black kettle and holding a mass of white cloth against her side with one arm.

240

"Set the kettle right down there," directed Kirk. "Sure that cloth's clean?"

"*Clean?*" Lynn's eyes widened indignantly. "Seeing that it's from my own—yes, it's clean! Now I'll do the rest." She held out her arms. The child pressed tighter against Kirk, whimpering, "Stay here, stay here!"

"It'll just upset her if we move her. Please slip my coat off. Yes, my *coat!* Thanks. Fold it under her knees while I sit on the edge of the porch. Some of that soft stuff now. Ouch, the water's hot. Steady, soldier. This'll help you feel better. Another pad, please, and fold more of that stuff into a square to cover her kneecap. And get closer so you can catch the other end of this."

Lynn's voice was almost in his ear. "Is this the side?"

Kirk looked up with a start, his forehead nearly grazing Lynn's cheek. She was kneeling beside him, apparently had been there for some time. "Sorry," he said. "I can't move much, the way she's hanging on to that buttonhole. Hold the corner down. Catch that loose end. See, soldier, we're getting things into shape again." He chuckled. "She didn't even wince that time. Once more around. That's wonderful linen. Where did you ever find it in this house?"

"It was lying about."

"Good thing for us. And here's luck. Buttonholes in it. Run that tag through that hole. Tie it good and tight."

"Is that enough? Oh, look! She's stopped crying."

"It was mostly scare and shock. Hope I didn't snap out too many orders at you. I was just thinking about fixing this knee."

"You snapped a great many and you snatched her right out of my arms," said Lynn. Then her voice softened. "I'm glad you did. You managed better than I could have."

"I've had to look after accidents like this, though they usually happened to rather larger children. How's it feel now, soldier?"

Still kneeling by Kirk, Lynn looked down at the grubby little face, smoothing out the black curls that fell over Kirk's shoulder. "Why, she's dropped off to sleep!"

"Someone better carry her home. I'd like to keep her quiet like this for a bit longer, though. Will you hold her? I've got to be moving."

Lynn laughed softly. "You'll never get her finger out of that buttonhole without waking her. If you want her quiet, you'll have to stay just as you are." She looked past Kirk. "Why, it's still quite light. I never knew that day could last so long, here on the western slopes."

"Sometimes you get an hour or two extra. I've seen it often, up in the White Mountains."

"Is that where you come from?"

"No. With all due regard for our host's feelings, I'm a lowlander. My home's in New Hampshire, but down by the Merrimac. The river just slides along there, wide and pretty slow with riffles showing through, and the meadows roll down to meet it. In summer everything's green and blue and brown and you look north and there are the mountains, way off, but somehow hanging over you, and they're bluish and purplish. Then when you get up into them, you look back and there are the river and the meadows showing between granite shoulders and maybe a thunderstorm drifting through a deep valley. And you can see little white villages and steeples and red barns, very plain sometimes, but so small you can cover them with the end of your finger."

Lynn reached out and adjusted an edge of the bandage. "I'd never seen real mountains before. There's something frightening about them and yet they're peaceful. At home, there's just Lake Ontario and the country sloping away north from it. But somehow you never get tired of Ontario. I do miss the lake. How that child is sleeping! You must have the healer's touch, Captain Stedman." She bent forward again and a wisp of her hair brushed against his cheek as she straightened the little pinafore.

"Hope I'm not called on to use it too often, assuming that I do have it," said Kirk, keenly aware of the touch of the golden tendril. "How about the other children? They seem suspiciously quiet to me."

"Rummaging in my trunk, I suppose. I told them they could. They can't harm anything."

Kirk started. The trunk! It would have to be repacked and— "That reminds me, Miss Stockdale. I came here looking for your father to tell him about early reveille tomorrow."

As though a spring had been touched, Lynn was on her feet. "Oh, all that wretched business! I'd been able to forget it for the moment." Her head went back. "Do you really need to consult with your prisoners, Captain? Aren't simple orders enough?"

Before Kirk could answer, a swarm of little girls poured onto the porch. "Ooooh, Miss Stockdale! What's all this truck for?"

Whatever the true nature of this truck might have been, Kirk had only a glimpse of something very white and soft and trailing, with a good deal of frothy lace on it. Lynn gave a shocked cry, caught at what the girls were holding and scurried through the door.

On the porch, the injured child slept on in Kirk's arms, the white bandage sharp in the growing dusk, the withered leg stretched out on the rough boards as though grateful for their comfort and support.

Kirk touched the black curls with the red ribbon tied about them. "Guess we've got a few minutes before any bugles blow, soldier," he thought. "Damn it, why did I mention the trunk? We'd been talking along like real people. I ought to have told her about some of those little towns like Contoocook or Sunapee instead. Or got her talking about what it's like in upper Canada and what people do there and if she's ever seen Niagara or a big storm on Ontario. If I had—what difference would it have made? We've still got to start in the morning and a lot of other mornings and she won't like them or us or

243

me, no matter what happens. She isn't the only pretty girl in the world. Doubt if anyone would look at her twice if there were a few other fairly attractive girls around. Wonder if she'll come out again."

A voice off in the dusk called, "Is that you, Mr. McQuorkodale?"

Kirk's mind whisked back to his work in an instant. "It's Captain Stedman, sir. I came looking for you, Mr. Stockdale. Your daughter was amusing the children and one of them fell and hurt herself a little. Miss Stockdale's in the house now."

Stockdale loomed closer, peered at the bandage. "Scraped her knee, did she? Good of you to look after her." His manner changed. "Now I want to make one thing perfectly clear to you. When we are at liberty, I shall submit a statement of the case to whatever authorities I can find. Her Majesty's Minister in Washington must hear of it. I shall not neglect your own government I may even write a letter to the London *Times!*"

"No reason why you shouldn't," said Kirk.

Stockdale went on: "I have taken it upon myself to ask some of the older men in the village if they would permit us to stay here a reasonable length of time after you have gone. You couldn't object to that, since they seem to be on your side of the war. They were damnably stubborn and won't allow strangers here. Very well. For myself, I've never flinched from a challenge in my life. But it's different with my daughter. In all humanity and decency you can't justify forcing a young, inexperienced girl to go along with a group of men. I'm still sure that I could persuade them to shelter her here. Then when I reach civilization, I could come back for her, properly equipped. You couldn't object to that."

"H'm. There's a lot in that," said Kirk thoughtfully. "Perhaps I can help make the people agree. And I'd have to consult my friends. Yes, it would be a lot easier in a great many ways to leave her here."

There was a light rustle on the sill and Lynn stepped

onto the porch. "Save your breath, Captain, much as I'd like to make things easier for you, of course. Dad, dear, it was sweet of you to try to get me out of this, but I've not the least intention of being left alone on a mountaintop while you're carted off the Lord knows where. We shan't have many easy moments, I suppose, but I shouldn't have even one, wondering about you, if you left without me."

The child stirred against Kirk's shoulder. "That's the purty lady," she murmured. "She got the softes' whites' breeches in her trunk, all raggedy like, same as lace flowers in the spring."

Lynn's breath went in sharply. Then she said, "Well, after all, I *did* tell them they could rummage, but I didn't expect—Little girl, won't your mother be worrying about you? I think you ought to take her home, Captain. The others have gone, but they told me she lives in that house by the well sweep. Her name's Mary Ogilbie." Kirk rose, careful of the bandaged knee. Lynn bent over. "Good night, Mary. You'll be all better in the morning."

"All better," murmured Mary Ogilbie. Suddenly she reached out, twined her free arm about Lynn's neck. Lynn swayed forward and for an instant her cheek was smooth and cool against Kirk's as the child clung tighter. Then it was no longer cool and she was pulling back, freeing the little arm as gently as she could. Her skirts swished and she was gone, the door closing behind her.

Kirk recovered himself, realizing that Stockdale could have seen only the child's sudden move. "I'll take her along. But I do want a couple of minutes with you, sir. I'll be right back."

"Very well," said Stockdale resignedly.

"Purty lady," said Mary Ogilbie.

The road was far worse than it had been on the other side of the settlement, which the party had left two hours ago. Now it dipped down an incline that slanted even more crazily than the last which they had faced. Kirk, in the lead beside the pilot, was thankful that the sun was beginning to melt the gloom in the deep valley. Looking back, he saw Jake, bridle in hand, walking by the horse's head as he guided the buggy down the long, rocky slope. He could just make out Lynn, sitting very erect beside her father while her slim body yielded gracefully to the sudden angles and pitches of the road. Stockdale held himself rigid as though unwilling to make the least compromise with the wretched terrain, accepting each bump and tilt as though they were tests of his character. Jabish and Mark, muddy-handed, were at the rear wheels, ready to snatch at the slow-turning spokes in case of need.

"Stream ahead," said Kirk as he caught the too-familiar gurgle.

The pilot, Hatton, known as "Midnight" from his blue-black hair, nodded. "Little trickly crick a hop frog could span without sweatin'."

Kirk caught the glint of water through the trees below. Just a brook. No trouble there. He followed the pilot, taking the stream with an easy leap, and started up the ascent on the far side. It was a relief to be able to walk more freely as the light slowly grew. Off to the right twin peaks stood high, aglow in the morning sun. In an hour or so the party would be moving through full day, able to see well ahead and prepare for any difficult going. The slope grew steeper. "Ropes," said Midnight.

Kirk shouted, "Ropes, Jake!"

Jake waved acknowledgement as he called, "All hands on deck to man the capstan! Mr. Stockdale, will you unhitch the animal?"

"Much of this?" asked Kirk.

"Tol'ble," answered Midnight.

Jake came trotting up, a long coil of rope slung about his shoulder. "I'll take a turn around this pine, Kirk.

Haul the buggy up to it and then go ahead to the next good point."

"You're the rope expert. How are things back there?"

"I wouldn't say they'd been what you'd call voluble. Not a word since we left the settlement. But I keep telling myself that they're just brimming over with love and gratitude for all of us. Just too bashful to say so." He knelt by the pine and unslung his rope.

"You won't need me," said Kirk. "I'll go on and see what's ahead."

"Sure, get an idea how many times we've got to haul. When we hear you running back with a glad little patter of feet, we'll know you've found level ground."

Kirk started up the long, twisting grade, wondering who had thought of it as a practicable ascent back in the far-off past. It certainly had been little used since, for seedlings and some saplings bristled ahead of him. After a few minutes he came out onto a shoulder. The ground dropped sharply away to his right, down and down until he found that he was looking onto the tops of trees far below him. He turned and looked toward the buggy. Lynn and her father were already seated. Kirk caught Jake's eyes, made a throwing motion ahead and the latter acknowledged the signal. "Come on, pilot," said Kirk.

The road was fairly level compared to some of the slopes that had been met earlier, but the surface grew worse. Limestone ledges were hidden in brush and where there wasn't undergrowth, the soil was gullied as though spring freshets had flowed over it. From a rise, Kirk looked ahead and his eyes narrowed. Off in the distance, two or three valleys away, a great rounded crest shouldered up, masked by clouds. The haze thinned, but the high dome remained white. White! It had to be limestone, he told himself. But stunted trees do not thrust up through limestone. "Snow!" he muttered. The Stockdales couldn't have many changes of clothing in their two little trunks, and he and his friends were worse off. He shook away his fears. "We'll not be going over mountaintops. Roads seem to run along the sides or in the valleys. Cold weather could be tough on that pair. But I didn't have any choice. Everyone agrees I didn't. Damn it, if everybody disagreed, I'd still say I was right."

There was a long slope ahead of him, and at the bottom, Midnight stood, leaning on his rifle and studying a broad black stream that cut across the route. Kirk ran down the grade, picking his way carefully among exposed roots. Midnight nodded to him. "Used to be logs acrosst here. Floods must 'a' dumbled 'em away."

Kirk watched the swift waters that were rippled by boulders just below the surface. The stream was not very deep, perhaps three feet at the most, but it was a good fifteen yards wide and the boulder-strewn bed promised treacherous footing. The far bank looked solid and the ground rose gently from it. The horse could probably get across if carefully led, and the buggy—He shook his head as he visualized one wheel striking a big boulder while another dropped into a pothole. Passengers and supplies would slmost surely be tipped out. He said quickly, "We'll have to manhandle all our truck to the other side. The buggy too. Everyone will have to wade. We'll run a rope from this tree to the other side, like a lifeline."

The pilot raised his eyebrows. "The gal got to go patty-foot over the rocks? October's dyin' and the air's got an edge to it."

"You and her father carry her."

"Not him and me. He's big-thewed, but he ain't used to work like this. And he's past his summer. His leaves is turnin'."

"Ye-es. A slip could give us broken bones. Here they come." He called, "We'll have to empty the buggy. Unhitch, Jabish. Jake, we want a line across the stream."

The Stockdales got stiffly out while Mark and Jabish busied themselves. Jake took one look at the water, then slid off his shoes and socks, rolled up his trousers. "A

248

hitch around this tree," he said, uncoiling his rope. "Make fast on the other side." He deftly secured one end of his line and stepped into the current. "Jumping Jeeeezeeboy! Colder'n Casco Bay." He fought his way across, slipping on glassy rocks, stepping into potholes, until he emerged, puffing, on the far side. "I'll moor it right here, Kirk. Then I better come over for the animal. I've got so I can talk his language." He tested the rope now spanning the stream and worked back, hand over hand.

A voice by Kirk's shoulder said coldly, "Do I understand that my daughter has got to wade that stream?"

Intent on getting the crossing under way, Kirk glanced absently at Stockdale. "No. We'll chair her over." He called, "That's it, Jake. Jabish and Mark, start on the trunks. Miss Stockdale's first. Keep a free hand for the lifeline. Follow after Jake; he's learning the potholes and boulders. Pilot, do you want to start with the provision bags? Good. Don't overload, though."

Midnight, a heavy sack on his shoulder, took the current, unhurried and sure. A hand pulled at Kirk's arm. "I'll carry my daughter myself!"

Still watching the passage of the stream, Kirk shook his head. "We're used to this life. You're not. A fall out there could be very bad." He cupped his hands. "Fine. Now the other trunk. Jake, you and Midnight get the rest of the food. Then we'll all work on the buggy."

Fifteen minutes later the buggy stood on the far bank. It had nearly tipped over twice and the off shaft had lodged in a rock crevice, but it was safe. "Mr. Hatton," called Kirk through chattering teeth, "you and I are about the same height. Want to team up with me carrying Miss Stockdale? Jabish, if you can stand the water again, you might come with us and give her father a hand."

Jabish scowled at Kirk. "I'm tallest. I can carry Miss Stockdale alone."

249

"And what'd you hang on to the lifeline with? Your teeth? We'll do as I said. Come on, now."

Back on the other bank they found Stockdale talking earnestly to Lynn, who kept shaking her head. Kirk interrupted, "Now, Miss Stockdale, Mr. Hatton and I are going to chair you across. He'll lock my left hand with his right. We'll each have a hand free for the lifeline. You'll sit on our wrists and hook an arm about our necks. You won't even get splashed."

Lynn looked coolly at him, then turned to her father. "Dad, you're not going to break a leg or strain your back carrying me. And I'm *not* going to have my arms around those necks. Captain Stedman, you're in command. Take your people across and make them keep their backs turned. Yours, too I'm wading. Dad, you'll follow right after me and I'll be perfectly safe. I'll take off my shoes and stockings and truss up my skirts and we'll start. Captain *Stedman!* Please go."

For the first time on the journey, Stockdale smiled, though icily. "You can't threaten force now, Captain."

"Force could be used. We've all of us handled reluctant people before."

"Don't count on me for anything like that," said Jabish.

"Thank you, Mr. Kell," said Stockdale. "I might add, though that I was once boxing champion of the Blue School at Toronto."

"The point's academic," cut in Kirk. "The main thing's to have you on the far side. Miss Stockdale, there's a little ridge across there. We'll all be out of sight on the other side until you call. Come along, Mr. Hatton, Jabish."

As they regained the far bank, Midnight shook his head. "Reckon you went up the wrong trail there, Cap'n."

"She's not good at being scared," observed Kirk.

"Times a body's safer, do he scare the right amount at the right time. Maybe they wasn't anything you could 'a' done. Was I her pa, I'd 'a' turned her up and smacked her little bottom."

"We've got no right to interfere with them," snapped Jabish. "We had no business bringing them with us."

Kirk hailed, "Jake, Mark! Get over that little ridge. We stay put there till Miss Stockdale calls. How about a little fire to dry out by, pilot?"

"Nope," said Midnight. "One twisty finger of smoke c'd look mighty beckonin' to some folks."

Kirk eased his feet into his shoes, wrung water from his trouser bottoms. "We must be sure to tell the Stockdales that they better do some running up and down while we harness and hitch or their legs'll break off."

"You treat 'em like half-witted kids," said Jabish shortly. "They'll know what to do."

"Did you, the first six months you were in the Army?" asked Jake. "I know damn well I didn't. In camp at Augusta, State-a-Maine, I remember—God's chowder! What was that?"

Kirk was on his feet, racing up to the low crest, the high cries loud in his ears. He shot down the other side and the cries came again, unmistakable and unbelievable. *"Kirk! Kirk! Quick!"* He ran on through the trees, took a rock in a flying leap, plunged into the stream in a cloud of water. Halfway along the lifeline, Lynn was clinging desperately with one hand while the other clutched at something that floundered in the icy current. The rope bent downstream and Kirk caught a flash of white as Lynn's bare legs were swept from under her. Slithering off rocks, battering his feet against boulders, he hauled himself along. Lynn cried, "Quick! Help! I'm losing him.

With a final lunge Kirk whipped an arm about Lynn, felt the tug of the current as it dragged at her. He panted, "Keep hold of the rope! Brace against me!" He felt her body ease as he took some of the strain from her, but her legs in the trussed-up skirt still thrashed and beat. Kirk leaned as far as he dared, caught a sodden collar,

251

and Stockdale's head, hair and beard dripping, appeared above the surface. Kirk hauled harder, got a knee forward under the broad shoulders.

He gripped Lynn tighter, wondering if she, too, had seen the blood that oozed from a gash on her father's left temple. "I've got him," Kirk called through water that splashed about his face. "You let go of him. Catch hold of me with that hand. I'm all right. Got my arm over the rope. Hang on to me and kick your feet under you. Try to get a footing. Jake! Thank God! Get hold of her! Midnight! Give me a hand with Stockdale. Good man, Mark. Go on there with Midnight."

Close to him, Jake panted, "Hell's fritters, Jabish, you're only in the way. Get on the other side and brace Kirk."

Lynn's arms were tense about Kirk's neck and her fingers dug into his flesh. "That's it. Get an arm around Jake's shoulders."

Midnight spluttered through frothing water, "We got him. You two h'ist the gal ashore. Me 'n' Mark'll handle this."

Kirk slowly released his grip on Stockdale. "Jabish, stand by Mark."

For the first time he looked down through spray-clouded eyes at Lynn's upturned face on his shoulder. He said encouragingly, "Only a few feet to go. Never mind about the footing. We'll carry you."

Lynn's streaming face looked very white and her teeth were clenched. "Father! I've got to get to him."

"Don't worry. The others have him."

"But he's hurt. He slipped and I made a lunge for him. His head struck a rock. He's bleeding."

"Stunned, that's all," said Kirk, hoping that he was being truthful. "We're going to lift you now."

She was surprisingly light, even in her drenched clothes that clung to her figure like skin. He could feel the curve of her back under his arm. She wriggled, turned a little as Jake stumbled, and a bare knee, ivory-smooth, pressed against Kirk's hand. "No time to be delicate," he thought. "Damn these boulders. Nearly went that time."

Jake shouted, "Ashore. Heave with me, Kirk!"

They gave a final lift, dug their way up the bank, Lynn hanging between them. Under the anesthesia of shock and fright she seemed unaware of her tight-clinging dress and her legs, bare to the knees. She tried to stand, but her knees doubled and she sank again, arms still about their necks. "I can't feel anything," she said faintly. "Turn me around. I want to see Father."

"Midnight and Mark have got him," said Kirk. "You've got to move around. My God, have we anything dry to wrap her in?"

Jake bent, picked up a pair of blankets. "Figured we'd need these. Now listen, lady, you must look after yourself or you'll be in a bad way. We'll carry you to the buggy, cover you with the blankets. Then we'll get more, make a regular little cabin out of it. You'll be all shut away there and no one'll come near you. Shuck off your clothes and give yourself a good, hard rubdown."

Lynn's head shook, as though impatient with trivia. "I don't see Father."

"You do what Jake said," urged Kirk. "If you don't give yourself a rubdown, someone'll have to. Lord, why didn't Midnight bring a wife or something with him to help out?"

"Up with her," said Jake cheerily. "Catch her under the knees." He fell into step with Kirk. "There we are. Onto the seat. Sling that blanket around her waist right down to her feet. I'll cover her shoulders."

Kirk struggled with the blanket, but Lynn kept turning toward the stream. He was reminded oddly of a little girl neighbor long ago trying to put a doll's dress on an unwilling kitten. "Please hold still. And you're looking the wrong way. Here's your father now, walking between Jabish and Midnight." Lynn gave a deep sigh and sank back on the cushions. "Hi!" cried Kirk. "You can't go to sleep, Miss Stockdale. That's it, Jake. Keep shaking her. I'll see about her father."

Stockdale was standing on the bank, hanging rather limply between Midnight and Jabish while Mark sponged his temple. "Now what the devil can we do for him?" thought Kirk. "We'll need every blanket for Lynn." He called, "Midnight! We'll want a fire right away, a lot of fires, and damn the smoke!"

"You ain't much wrong," said Midnight.

On the far side of the ridge where the party had waited for Lynn to cross, Kirk shook warm ash from his shoes, touched his breeches that hung on a rack of branches near the fire. "About right," he observed. "How about the rest of you?"

"Dry as kelp on a sandspit," said Jake.

"If the Stockdales come out of this in good shape, there's no harm done," said Kirk. "Except time wasted. We've been here two hours. I'm going over to see how soon the Stockdales can start."

He climbed the ridge and headed for the two blanket-screened fires beyond the buggy, noting that some part of Lynn's dress that had been hanging on a branch had vanished. He raised his voice, "Hello, Mr. Stockdale! We better get started or night'll hit us on the trail before we reach the next pilot."

14

Shots among the Ridges

The mishaps at the stream seemed to set a new pattern for the march. The road dwindled as it climbed and sometimes even Midnight lost it in a maze of waist-high seedlings that forced him to make casts right and left to find its true course. Limestone gave way to hard rock and the wheels slammed and jarred until the mountain rang as though ghostly blacksmiths were hammering on hidden anvils. The slope grew worse and several times Kirk, well in advance, looked back to see the buggy halted and Jake trotting on indefatigably with his ropes to rig his never-failing tackle.

Light dimmed as mountains towered on either hand, shutting in the narrow pass. A cold haze formed and Midnight in the far lead had to slow his gait to keep within Kirk's sight. Then a new wind, keen and bitter, swept down. Kirk hunched his shoulders as he faced it. It was a good thing that at earlier stages of the march he and his companions had picked up heavier garments,

255

bit by bit, through gift or barter. The Stockdales were well sheltered back of the curtain of blankets that Jake had rigged for them. In any event, the father's clothes, aggressively British and heavy for the low-lands, would stand this sudden drop. As for Lynn, wearing a buckskin coat and a homespun skirt, bought at the settlement, under her gray and canary cloak, she would be all right even with a sharper bite in the air.

Then out of the fading light a single dot of snow sailed down the path to settle against Kirk's forehead. Another brushed his ear. The air thickened, filled with darting white flakes. *"Just* what we needed!" he groaned to himself as he lengthened his stride to catch up with the pilot. As he came abreast, Midnight remarked, "I ain't beginnin' to like this."

"We keep on, though?"

"Kind of got to. You and me'd better close back on the little wagon. Too easy to get losted, turnin' this-a-way-that-a-way, not seein' good."

Kirk shivered as he remembered how Dahlgren's command had broken up like quicksilver in the night woods west of Richmond. "How far to the next pilot?" he asked.

"Been lookin' for a landmark, but so fur the country ain't told me."

Kirk glanced over his shoulder. Already the road was powdered with white and his tracks and the pilot's stood out dark against it. He scuffed snow under his foot. It was not slippery and a few inches' fall might even help cushion the buggy wheels against the unmerciful pounding of the rocks. The vehicle had been skillfully built to stand rough going, but its designer could hardly have foreseen these conditions. Midnight's elbow nudged Kirk. "Sounds like someone wants you kind of sudden," he remarked.

Kirk turned quickly. The buggy was behind a bend in the road and he could hear nothing but the beat of the wind and the light hiss of the snow. Then he saw a stocky man running desperately up toward him. Heedless of snow-masked rocks and hollows, Kirk raced to meet him, calling, "With you in a minute, Jake."

Jake stopped, shouted. "Bring Midnight, too. It's Mark! His knee's gone!"

They found Mark Furber lying in the snow, his left leg stretched out and Lynn bending over him. He managed a smile as Kirk knelt by him. "Sorry. Clumsy of me. Slipped in the snow. Same knee my horse rolled on at Catlett's Station."

"Bruk?" asked Midnight.

"Ligament's torn again, I guess. I can get up now."

Lynn laid a light hand on his forehead. "You stay where you are. You probably don't know it, but you fainted when you fell."

"These things always hurt at first, but walking around will fix it. Mind giving me a hand?" Jabish and Stockdale levered him to his feet, but his knee buckled. "Then boost me onto the horse. I'll ride the stiffness out."

"The horse is carrying all it can. Jake, Midnight, catch hold with me," ordered Kirk.

"Yep," said Midnight softly. "Right easy to know what to do when they ain't but one thing left."

"Sure is. Into the buggy with him."

"There isn't room!" cried Lynn.

"I know," said Kirk between his teeth as he heaved with the others. "Quit fighting, Mark. It's either this or leave you. There we are."

Stockdale stroked his square beard. "Ah, quite. I understand."

"Father! You simply can't—"

He laid a hand on her arm. "They've no choice. I can step out just as well as these young fellows. Please get in. I'll walk right by your side of the buggy."

With a flounce and spring, Lynn settled herself.

"Thank you, Mr. Stockdale," said Kirk. "Take Mark's stick. It's a good solid one. Midnight, any idea where the sun is now?"

"Close to roostin', I reckon."

Kirk unbuckled his Colt, held it out to Jabish. "Mark can't take command, so it passes to you."

Jabish backed away. "I'm not in on this. I'm standing clear. Give it to Pitler."

Jake, by the horse's head, spread his palms downward. "No time for a town meeting to settle this. Kirk, I'm busy all the time with the animal and the ropes. The command's yours."

Kirk strapped the Colt on again. "Then take the other gun from Mark. It's no good to him in the buggy. Now lead out. Come on, pilot." Midnight by his side, he worked on up the pass. The wind blew keen as ever and snow sifted through the trees, settled in the folds of clothes, worked insidiously inside collars. The two toiled on, stopping every now and then to try to see through the white curtain that was closing in on all sides. On a fairly level stretch Kirk said, "Hard to be sure about anything in this light, but haven't we got open fields either side of us? Look off to the right."

"Open that-a-way, all right. Open a plumb thousand feet below. I can smell distance. 'Pears purty clear and level to the left, but it don't tell me nothin'. The country ain't wantin' to be read. Right now, you're a-knowin' of it as I be."

Light steps sounded behind Kirk and he started as Lynn's head, swathed in a bright scarf, suddenly materialized between him and Midnight. "Don't jump so," she said, wiping snow from her eyebrows and lashes with an end of her scarf. "Everything's all right back there. I told Father I was cold and made him get into the buggy. I caught up while you two were moon-raking by those rocks. Keep on going. I can stay with you. What I want to know is, do we go on like this forever?"

258

"Till we hit the Union lines. Then we'll see about transportation for you and your father to wherever you want to go and he can file his report against us."

One of Lynn's stout little English boots came down smartly in an impatient stamp. "I mean now, today." Her gray cloak billowed as she flung out her arms. "We're just going from nowhere to nowhere. We haven't much food and only one day's bait for the horse; our clothes are giving out. Are you going to march us till we drop?"

Midnight shifted his rifle. "Mebbe all this ain't too comfortsome for a lady that ain't mountain-bred."

"Thank you, Mr. Hatton, but I can follow every step the rest of you take. I just don't want any more steps than there have to be."

Kirk studied her as she walked along. In the dim light her cheeks seemed ruddy as ever and she moved briskly, but he thought that her lips were pale. "Still no sign, pilot?" he asked.

"Nary."

"There's level ground to the left. We'll camp there for the night."

Lynn said quickly, "Not on my account, we won't." She had been facing into the wind and now wore a white snow mask. Kirk reached for the tucked-in end of her scarf and brushed it lightly over her eyes, cheeks and chin. "No need of turning into a snowman," he said.

She stepped back quickly. "Well, Captain, as for camping in this blizzard just to show your chivalry, I'll thank you to forget it."

"All I want is a place to stretch Mark out and go to work on his knee. We can melt snow and get hot water onto it. We'll build brush shelters for you and your father, apart from us. Let's pick out a site, pilot."

As he turned away, a small voice at his elbow said, "I've some very strong linen in my trunk. You can have it to make bandages for Captain Furber if you like."

"All right, all right," muttered Kirk, eyes still tight shut. "I'm awake. Tell Tom Latham to have the troop on the Raccoon Ford road in—"

A voice that was not the least military said, "Yes, yes. Always the commander! I'm going to flick your face with a wet cloth if you don't wake up. How many times do you have to be shaken?"

He sat up with a start, his head knocking aside the brush lean-to under which he had been sleeping. Lynn, the hood of her cloak drawn over her head, looked suspiciously down at him. "It's day already. Four by Father's watch, ten after by mine. Let's get on the road."

"Four?" He tossed off his blanket. "Are the others up? I told Jake to call me when he came off guard."

"No one's up but Father and Captain Pitler and me. I've got acorn coffee boiling and ash cake baking, and I changed the bandage on Captain Furber's knee. Don't go to sleep again." She moved gracefully toward a small fire, dusting her palms together as though she had accomplished one more tiresome detail in the day's routine.

Kirk scooped a handful of snow, scrubbed his face briskly. The storm seemed to be over and a few stars hung in the dome of the sky. "It'll be good to get an early start. Just the same, she's got to understand that she can't go round giving orders without clearing them with me first." He saw Midnight emerging from his lean-to in slow, lank sections and went on to Mark, who seemed listless and depressed. Kirk patted his shoulder. "Lie back and take it easy. I'll bring your rations after I've roused Jabish."

At the fire Jake grinned broadly, whanged an iron spoon against a tin plate. "Kirk, ever read that book, *Swiss Family Robinson?* Remember how the mother was always hauling stuff out of a bag in the nick of time, stuff the others didn't know she had? Well, you ought to see what's been coming out of the buggy! Miss Stockdale, if we come to a nice, wide river, think you can find a fifteen-foot dory with two sets of oars?"

Lynn appeared from behind a wall of branches that had been woven for her. For an instant Kirk thought that she looked, somehow, touchingly like a schoolgirl playing at camping out as she sipped daintily from a tin cup. She answered, "If it's a river that'll take us anywhere, I'll see what I can do. Have you tried the ash cake? I made it just the way you told me to."

Ten minutes later the buggy was repacked and Jake led out the horse. "Hi, this animal must like mountain air! Skittish as a moses boat in a crosscurrent. Steady now. Oh, jumping *Christ!*"

Hoofs had lashed out in a crash of splintering wood. Jake managed to get the horse clear, but the damage had been done and Kirk looked down on a wrecked off shaft and a cracked horizontal bar. "Gone, isn't it, Jake?" he asked wearily.

"Done. Guess the cold made the wood extra brittle."

Kirk turned quickly. "Midnight, think you can find the next pilot?"

Midnight, still munching one of Lynn's ash cakes with evident relish, nodded. "It'll dawn clear."

"Want to find him and bring him back with any tools he has?"

Lynn planted herself before Kirk. "Why wait for all that? There's enough wood here to build a whole navy and Captain Pitler can make ropes do anything he wants them to."

Jake shook his head. "We need saws, augers, planes—"

"And hatchets!" cried Lynn. She whipped a little ax from Midnight's belt and began hacking away at the base of a tough sapling.

Jake shouted, "Well, Mother Swiss Robinson! If you can do that, I guess I can make my ropes sing *Annie Laurie!*"

Jabish came heavily over. "Better let me do that, Miss Stockdale. I've been around lumber camps at home."

Lynn gave up the hatchet, flew off to another sapling, shaking it to test its toughness.

"Burn me, Moses!" muttered Midnight. "Maybe she ain't mountain-bred, but she must 'a' been borned mighty close to a peak!"

Midnight had gone, and after him, another pilot, a fat little man who talked endlessly in a high whine, detailing over and over his grievances that seemed based on some squabble about land, dating back to pre-Revolutionary days. Now still another man, even leaner and taller and more fiercely bearded than Midnight, led the party through a knife-slash valley. The air was wine crisp, its edge mellowed by the sun that played down out of a high blue sky. Lynn, walking beside Kirk some fifty yards behind the pilot, Cotesworth, threw back her head and clenched her slim hands. "It's like mid-September at home. I felt sure we'd find something like this after we got over that ridge last night. And I knew we were going to get over it, I knew it, I knew it!"

"Then you knew more than I did," observed Kirk. "Twice I thought we'd have to turn back."

"Never! I wouldn't have given up as much as a step. We've got to get through and that's all there is to it! And we're headed just right, now. Southwest. I can tell by the shadows. And if we'd turned back—or if you'd even hinted at it—I'd have—I'd have—"

"I'm sure you would have. But please, once for all, I *don't* want to have you pushing at the wheels with the others. I've told you that before. You could get badly hurt."

"Yes, but we kept the buggy moving, didn't we? And anyway, two nights ago I heard you and Captain Furber saying that the test of a real soldier was if he knew just when to disobey orders."

"That was just theory."

"And I put it into practice. Maybe Dad and I have got to stay chained to your chariot wheels while you

262

parade us through these Unionists like Roman conquerors, but we're going to do everything we can to keep those wheels rolling, Mr. Commander!" She pulled forward the slack of the silk scarf that bound her hair to make a visor against the sun.

"That's a very pretty shade of blue," said Kirk. "But I think that green bonnet you wore yesterday would be more useful."

"Oh, that. I gave it to the woman who took us in last night. She said she'd never had anything "store-botten' before."

He glanced sidewise as she adjusted the blue knot under her chin. For the last two or three days she seemed to have lost some of her sharp hostility toward him and the others, was less apt to burst out with cutting comments. And yesterday, as today, she had walked with him, wrapped in a mantle of armed neutrality if not amity, saying that she liked to keep as far forward as she could, to be among the first to see new scenes and vistas.

"We'll be in the valley all day, Mr. Cotesworth said," Lynn remarked. "Out of the peaks and the snow. I wish we knew what was happening in the rest of the world."

"Last sure word we had was that Sherman was still sitting tight in Atlanta, but that couldn't have been anywhere near up to date."

Lynn tossed her head. "Just a rumor. Maybe he's surrendered. I'll tell you what's really happening. Dad and I talked about it last night. England must have come in with the Confederacy. The war's over. You've lost."

"Thanks," said Kirk dryly.

"Oh, we went way beyond *that!* I do hope you'll like this part. The North and the South have realized that they can't exist separately, so they've come back under the Crown and North America's British from the North Pole right down to Mexico. *That's* what's been happening."

"Sounds fine—to a Britisher. It'd last about ten

minutes. Why, what Jake calls that 'jury rig' he put on the busted shaft's more solid than those ideas of yours."

"That rig!" said Lynn with a toss of her head and a sniff. "If I hadn't started hacking down a tree to show you how, we'd all be sitting on that mountaintop, waiting for Mr. Hatton's friend to bring us a carpenter shop!"

"We don't do much sitting around. As a matter of fact, we were just going to—" He wheeled about as a sharp crash sounded from the rear. Then he began to run, unaware of Lynn pelting after him, crying, "Wait for me!" The horse was down on the road among splintered shafts. The off front wheel and the nigh rear were tangles of splintered spokes and one iron tire still spun, held up by its own momentum, before settling with a muffled clang among brown-edged rhododendron leaves. The buggy was tilted sharply to one side and Stockdale was helping Mark Furber to the ground. As Kirk arrived, Jake had extricated the horse, which stood trembling. "Can we fix this, Jake?" asked Kirk.

Jake shook his head. "Not even with a full-fledged blacksmith shop. Wouldn't you know it? The damn thing sails through gullies and ledges and then tumbles in a heap on a soft, level road. Kind of like that poem Mark was repeating once about 'The Wonderful One-Horse Shay."

Kirk took a last look at the wreckage, then called, "Mr. Cotesworth! Can you whittle a decent crutch for Captain Furber?"

The pilot, who had come running up, drew out a long hunting knife. "Won't be like a store-maden one, but it'll prop him."

"Fine. Jake, help me figure on how we can sling the trunks on either side of the horse. You know, like the packs of the jackass batteries."

Stockdale edged past the buggy. "You propose to use that horse just to carry *our* things?"

264

"Why not? Your horse, your trunks. We'll rig some kind of a pad so Miss Stockdale can ride sidesaddle."

Lynn darted past him. "Not the trunks. They'll rub sores onto the horse. Dad, make what you want into a soft bundle and I'll fix mine, too. We'll leave the trunks for the rabbits and squirrels."

"Look here, Mrs. Swiss Robinson," cried Jake. "We've been counting on your stuff to get us through tight places, like in the book. You're going to jettison too much. You can ride with the trunks, all right."

She knelt, threw back the lid of her trunk that had been spilled from the buggy and her small hands went patting among the contents. "I'll want this and this and this. Wrap it in this. What did you say? *I* ride? Fiddle-faddle and moonbeams. Captain Furber's going to ride."

"No!" cried Mark. "I can walk just fine!"

"Mark's right," began Kirk.

Lynn deftly passed twine about a bundle. "Please put your finger here while I knot this, Captain Stedman. Can't you see that we'll save time with Captain Furber riding?"

It was another day and the knife-slash valley and the wrecked buggy were far behind as the party wound up a long, grassy pass with a bristle of high crests on all sides. Cotesworth was a slow-moving black dot, working toward the misty blue summit of the corridor. Lynn, a green scarf about her hair, marched briskly on between Kirk and her father, a half mile behind the pilot.

Ian Stockdale was saying, "You understand, Captain, that I shall have to include the loss of my friends' buggy in the report that I'm keeping of this whole affair."

"You gave us fair warning, sir," said Kirk.

"And also we have not the slightest obligation to help you on this journey, except when it may be to our advantage."

"Precisely, sir."

265

"How nice that we all understand each other," observed Lynn, her eyes on the summit of the pass.

Kirk glanced at her, but her face held only the gravest of innocence. Her father went on: "In all fairness I shall have to stress in that report your complete reasonableness, despite the fact that I disagree utterly with your choice of sides in this whole war."

"Still, it's rather hard to understand just why you should feel so keenly," said Kirk.

"I told you a long time ago that we were United Empire Loyalists, that our family was driven north for standing by the King," said Lynn.

"I know, but a good many U.E.L.'s came back later and became Americans," argued Kirk. "You'll find a good many Canadian-born men in the Union Army, too."

"The view of myself and many of my friends is entirely logical," announced Stockdale. "There's the 1775 business, to begin with. We were abominably treated. Then in the war that you started in 1812, your people burned what's now Toronto and carried out what I can only term wantonly destructive forays across the lakes. My grandfather was ruined by all that. When that idiot, William Lyon Mackenzie, began his damnable rebellion against the Crown in 1837, Americans came in droves to help him, trying to tear down what we'd built up since our exile. It's hard for a Canadian to think of the border as a friendly one. Trouble's always come to us from south of the line."

Kirk smiled. "Don't blame us Yankees for all your troubles. I seem to remember that in the War of 1812, an American army was headed toward Montreal under command of one General Wade Hampton, of South Carolina. I've heard you both speak admiringly of his grandson, General Wade Hampton, head of Lee's Cavalry since Jeb Stuart's death."

"Thunderation! General Hampton's grandfather tried to invade us? Well, Ah—" He broke off as Kirk stepped

266

suddenly in front of Lynn, half crouching. Somewhere off to the right a rifle shot rang out, faint, but clear. Another followed, barely audible, another closer, then a steady fusillade in which he thought he could pick out the flatter sounds of muskets. Up the pass, Cotesworth had turned and was running toward them.

"Kneel. Right where you are," said Kirk, then started up to meet the pilot. "How do you figure this?" he asked as Cotesworth joined him.

"Could be Lance Ritchie's boys."

"Who's Ritchie?" asked Kirk.

"A bad-turned man, hard and mean as they make 'em. Him and his lot's been actin' up lately, but I ain't heard of 'em comin' this far south, molestin' and marodin'."

"That's no marauding," said Kirk, as he sorted out the distant sounds. "Two bodies are banging away at each other." The noise seemed a little closer now. Two bodies, not in actual contact, possibly exchanging shots across a steep, narrow valley, but unable to come to grips. "Who'd be apt to interfere with Ritchie's men? Confederate troops?"

"None such to these parts. More like, it's someone cut out the same hide as Lance, playin' king over them from both sides that's wearied of fightin' reg'lar. Go after cattle, crops, fixin's, money. Could be one's tryin' to tell the other they ain't welcome."

"Any chance of that fight drifting this way?"

The pilot's keen, lined eyes searched the terrain. "I ain't never pressed fur that side the pass, but I'd say, did they swing down off'n Ransome's Spur or Chilhowee Bald, it could be they'd cross our trace."

"That's something we've got to know."

Cotesworth adjusted the sling of his rifle. "Reckon I'll go hang my nose over the next crest and see what's there to see."

"We need you to keep us rolling."

Cotesworth nodded. "Then we'd best step quick and delicate."

All through the rest of the day, Kirk pushed on with the pilot, his shoulders hunched as though expecting a sudden blow. The world was empty, save for the little party, but the hidden horizon to the north and to the east rippled uneasily with that same sporadic rifle fire. Twice Kirk was sure that he caught the echoes of stray bursts dead ahead in the west or off to the south.

Close to sundown the air was suddenly still and Kirk threw back his head, swinging his arms as though a great burden had been lifted from him. From the crest of a ridge he looked into a deep valley with a stream, a grove of trees beside it and a towering mountain range, gilded and flaming in the dying day, closing it off in the west. "We'll camp there, pilot, if it looks all right to you. There's good grazing for the horse and plenty of wood and water." He looked back over his shoulder. The others were strung out along the slope, working slowly toward the crest, with Lynn in the lead, apparently urging the others to hurry. "Wood and water," repeated Kirk. "We'll want hot food and a good fire when we halt. They're about done."

But before the grove was reached, the firing started up again, thin in volume and sharper. "Sounds closer," said Kirk, unconsciously lowering his voice.

"Is closer," said Cotesworth. "Someone's sure to God gettin' chased. Down one valley, 'cross another. Ain't no tellin' where they'll end up."

"Still think we can camp here?"

"One spot ain't no wiser'n another. The grove'll do."

"Then we'll have a cold camp, no fires. And no hot food. Here come the others. Hope they weren't counting too much on frying bacon and baking ash cake."

268

15

Troop Train!

The low, rolling hills through which they had been toiling for the past two days were melting into the night. The west wind was cold in their faces, sharp yet somehow flat, lacking the tang of the Great Smokies. Cotesworth, walking in advance with Kirk, breathed as though he found the air heavy and dead. "Ain't even got nigh to a notion where we are," he grumbled. "Them last directions I got don't follow true to the land. The feller was held trustable, but it do look like he'd mazed me, done a-purpose."

"At least we're well out of the mountains and into east Tennessee," observed Kirk.

"Sure, and somewheres 'twixt and 'tween the Little Tennessee and the Hiwassee. But that don't tell us how to find the roof and the vittles as was promised us. The land gets flatter and flatter. Ain't no dome or bald a man can take a sight on and say, 'Howdy, friend, and thanks for pointin' the way.' And the lady needs sleepin'

269

and vittlin', though she ain't sayin' so. Me and her paw, we had nigh to chuck her onto the horse to ride a spell, Cap Furber's knee bein' loosenin'. Says she ain't one to be kitten-coddled."

"The country's safe. We can camp if we have to and scrape enough from our pouches to see that she gets a meal, anyway."

Lynn's voice, quick with excitement, sounded unexpectedly just behind Kirk. "I saw it! From the horse. A light, a funny kind of light." She darted between Kirk and the pilot. "Hurry! Get on that high ground ahead. We can see from there."

From the low rise Kirk saw an evenly spaced string of lights that glowed steadily. Then a sudden flare broke out, dimmed the bright points, was gone again. "That's it!" cried Lynn. "The quick glow that fades out and then comes back again. It *must* mean something for us."

The pilot cupped his hands about his eyes. "Them little lights could be folks with lanterns. Can't figger the other."

"We better get ahead and find out," said Kirk. "Miss Stockdale, please get back on your horse and tell Jake double time. Come on, pilot." He started down the trail at a brisk trot. A hand hooked sharply onto the back of his pistol belt.

"I will not be left behind," cried Lynn. "Go as fast as you like, but you'll still be towing me. Yes—I—can—too—keep—up—very—easily!"

Kirk nearly stumbled through sheer amazement as, frighteningly unexpected and shrill, a locomotive whistle split the night air. Lynn jumped straight up, clapped her hands high above her head. *"We've done it!"* There was a ring of sheer triumph in her voice. "We've beaten them! We've beaten the mountains!"

The strange light flared again. "Opening the firebox!" panted Kirk. "Chucking on more fuel. The other lights are the cars. Oh—no, no!" Wheels ground on iron rails and the line of lights began to slide off toward the south. The grinding stopped and the lights were stationary again. Then the lights began to flicker.

Lynn's hands clamped onto Kirk's arm. "That flickering. People are getting off the cars. Oh, will you *please* keep going? The train may start again any minute."

Kirk resumed his steady trot. "They'll be Union people, you know."

Her fingers linked again about Kirk's belt, Lynn cried, "I don't care if they're Cossacks! They're on a train and trains don't run through mountains! We've won! We can ride home on it."

The cars were not far off now and Kirk could see the steady flicker of people passing by the lighted windows. He heard boots thump down wooden steps and then—he jerked back his head as though someone had struck him—the unforgettable sound of hard hands slapping against rifle butts. "No need to hurry now!" he cried. "That train won't move for a long time. Let's take it easy. I don't want to get there out of breath."

At his side Cotesworth spoke dryly. "Reckon the lady ain't goin' to fall down if you let go of her."

"Let go—?" began Kirk. Then he realized that one of his arms had fallen across Lynn's shoulder, that she, still skipping with excitement, was holding tightly to his free hand.

She gave a little bounce to one side. "Thank you, Captain Stedman. I assure you that I was in no danger of falling." Her voice had the familiar edged ring. "Oh, listen! What's that man shouting off there?"

A harsh rasp sliced the night. "First Provisional Company—fall in!"

Kirk snatched at Lynn's hand, drew her swiftly along with him. As he ran he shouted, "Ho! Army of the Cumberland! Hold that train! Escaped prisoners from Virginia! Army of the Cumberland!"

A bull's-eye lantern shot a hard, round beam toward the runners and Kirk stopped, Lynn cannoning into him from behind. He hadn't thought that the troops

271

were that close. Other lanterns lit up a double line of men shuffling into ranks, men in kepis, in slouch hats. Someone shouted, "Wow!" as the bull's-eye played on Kirk and Lynn, standing hand in hand in its light, blinking like sleepy children who have blundered out of a dark room. The single "Wow!" swelled into a heart-deep "Ooooooowheeeee!" that ran along the lines from end to end.

Lynn flushed, glanced downward and started as though seeing her fingers for the first time. Then she gave Kirk's hand a hasty toss, spun about and ran off into the dark, calling, "Dad! Do make them hurry!" the troops snickered and someone sang:

> *"Oh, why did she flatter my boyish pride?*
> *She's gone and left me now!"*

The bull's-eye flicked off, leaving Kirk and Cotesworth in the dark. The harsh voice that had been giving commands snapped, "Quiet, you gandy dancers!" He faced the pair. "And who the hell might you be?"

"Captain Stedman, escaped from Libby Prison. Three other officers are back there. This is our guide. We've two neutral civilians with us. Who's the senior officer present?"

The man drew himself up and Kirk caught the blur of worn chevrons. "Major Millard, sir, in the last coach. This is the First Provisional Battalion, out of Knoxville, Chattanooga bound."

Kirk glanced at the half dozen cars from which infantrymen were still pouring. It would be wise to assume that the Major, in command of a scratch unit, would not be pleased with his assignment. The halting of the train in the middle of nowhere would not add to his amiability. And he would be operating from cramped quarters with a makeshift staff, if any. Thus it would be best to have the initial interview with him alone and hold back the rest of the group till later. Then he shook

272

his head. The Stockdales had to be taken care of first of all. "Jake!" he shouted. "Hold the party right there. Mr. Stockdale, will you and your daughter please come with me?"

The rear quarter of the last coach had been roughly partitioned off and several seats had been ripped up to make room for a board bench or two and a table. Major George Millard, Missouri Infantry, pushed aside a heap of papers with the hook that did him clumsy duty for a left hand as he listened to Ian Stockdale's statement. His weary, reddened eyes seemed younger, though not necessarily rested, as they flicked from time to time to Lynn. At last he said, "I understand your status, sir. But I can't accept your complaint about Captain Stedman. What he did's no concern of mine. You'll have to go to Corps or higher. Now just where do you want me to send you and your daughter?"

"Why, to Richmond, of course," replied Stockdale, surprised.

A ghost of a smile played behind Millard's full beard. "A lot of our people have been trying to get there since '61 and plopped flat on their faces every time. Still, they belonged to the Army of the Potomac and I never did think much of that outfit. Guess you can get passed north, all right, but it'll be a roundabout way. After that it'll be the Potomac boys' job. Maybe they can get two people into Richmond, even if they can't get fifty thousand."

Lynn, sitting on one of the remaining seats, hands folded primly in her lap and little feet very close together, spoke suddenly. "If trains can run south on this line, they can run north to Knoxville. We could be passed straight into Virginia from there and back to our friends."

Millard was startled. "Eh? What? I mean, there'll be nothing going north on this line for some time to come."

273

"Stuff!" exclaimed Lynn, and Kirk masked a smile as he noted how the sudden snap in her blue eyes seemed to force Millard onto the defensive. "If trains can run south, then they can run north!"

The Major's hook scrabbled among his papers and his glance dropped. "No. They can't. This line's like a river. Flows just one way."

"Surely, Major," put in Kirk, "there'll be empties heading for Knoxville. There are three other officers with me, and we're just as anxious to get back north as the Stockdales are."

Ian Stockdale ruffled out his always neatly trimmed beard. "Thunderation. A railway that runs in only one direction. Never heard of such a thing. You could at least tell us why."

With something like relief, Millard met the male challenge. "I could. But I'm not going to."

"You're going to give us the reason for that?" Lynn's voice was soft, but her eyes held the rebellious glint that Kirk knew so well.

Millard's beard jutted and he twisted in his seat to face the father. "You want to go to your friends in Richmond. They aren't *our* friends. As a matter of military common sense, I'm not telling more than I think wise. It's less than sixty miles to Chattanooga and there I'll turn you over, to someone who wears heavier stuff than gold leaves on his shoulders. You and your daughter can have this part of the car and I'll move ahead. If you've got any gear outside, better get it together. There's a captain on the platform. I'll tell him to detail some men to give you a hand. This is only a routine halt. Please wait here, Stedman."

As Millard and the Stockdales passed beyond the partition, Kirk heard Lynn ask pleasantly, "And what regiment is this, Major?"

Millard replied acidly, "A battalion of the Coldstream Guards!"

"The Coldstreams!" Lynn's voice was even sweeter.

"How interesting! *Very* raw recruits, of course. Won't you have to count on a great many being rejected as unfit for service when they reach their base?"

Kirk was still grinning when Millard returned, the lines about his eyes still deeper. The Major dropped onto a board bench, shaking his head as though a little dazed. "Well! You must have had a delightful trip through the mountains!"

Kirk answered sharply, "Let me tell you that she took the worst going, mountain streams, cliffs, snowstorms, wet camps, bad rations, like a veteran. And her father kept up with the best of us."

Millard looked quizzically at him. "You don't need to tell me one damn thing—though I can see you'd like to. I've got eyes and ears. Keep her the hell out of my sight or I'll end by giving her everything I know and a lot that I don't. However, I didn't ask you to wait just to hear the story of your holiday in the hills. You're a combat man and naturally you'll want to know what's been going on. Well, sir, you've hopped into the state of Tennessee, which isn't news to you. Also, you've taken a dive right into a hell of a kettle of boiling water." He ran his hook through his beard. "Trouble is, *we* didn't light the fire under the kettle. It was done for us. Here's what's been happening. I hope you like it."

He sank back on the bench, eyes half closed, as he sketched out recent happenings in the Southern theater for Kirk. On November 14, General Sherman had suddenly abandoned Atlanta, off in Georgia, and headed on *east,* objectives and destination unknown to most of the military world. Sherman's Confederate opponent, General John Hood, instead of following on Sherman's heels, had just as unexpectedly and mysteriously moved *west* into Alabama, had gathered his forces and now was suddenly driving *north* up into Tennessee toward Nashville. There was not, Millard thought, very much to oppose him. General George Thomas, the Virginia Unionist, was trying desperately to scrape up every

275

available man in the Nashville area. Two small Union corps under General John Schofield were massing against Hood's advance at a place called Pulaski, close to the Tennessee-Alabama border. Schofield was outnumbered by two or even three to one.

Millard broke off, tamped down his pipe with his hook. "You don't seem to like my story, Stedman," he observed dryly.

Kirk shook his head. "Not for a damn. If Hood can rip up through Nashville, there's nothing to stop him from going clear north to the Ohio River and across it. Or he could swing east and join Lee at Petersburg."

"Sure. It could turn the war upside down, and don't think that Hood doesn't know it," said Millard sourly. "His whole command knows it, too. They're hell-roaring and hellbending. Most troops love a fighter and that's what Hood is, for all his smashed arm and wooden leg. We've had plenty of reports from our scouts. Hood's men are actually *singing!*" He rapped his hook on the table to stress the word. "Here, in 1864, men are going into action, singing! Some parody on 'The Yellow Rose of Texas.' "

"And we've got just the two corps, IV and XXIII, to stop all that?" asked Kirk, moistening his lips.

"For the present, yes. Thomas has whistled for troops from other theaters, but it'll take a hell of a time to get them to Nashville. In the meanwhile, we're scraping up every man we can find, men discharged from hospitals, men back from furlough, clerks, orderlies, bummers, coffee boilers, Jonahs, beats, skedaddlers. That's what's aboard this train. First Provisional Battalion, they call 'em whipped up somewhere around Knoxville and herded onto the cars. There are other outfits like this one. But there won't be anywhere near enough. What's got to be done, of course, is to buy time, to delay Hood just long enough until Thomas's reinforcements reach him. If Schofield can hold Hood a bit or punish him badly, Pap Thomas *might* get those men. But I wouldn't give odds on it." Someone rapped on the door and he called, "Come in!"

A spent-looking sergeant entered, handed Millard a sheet of paper. The Major unfolded it, read it impassively, then stuffed it into his pocket. "Well, Captain, guess I can't give you a train ride after all. Telegram. Bridge over the Hiwassee's down. Supply wagons coming to meet us from Loudon. We'll hit for Pulaski over the road, smack across the Walden Ridge. H'm! You don't seem surprised."

Kirk gave a tight smile. "Maybe the Stockdales believed in your 'routine halt.' I didn't. You were waiting for something. Got a private courier system down to the Hiwassee?"

"Well, well. Maybe some of you Potomac boys have got brains after all. Yep. I had a telegraph boy tie into the wire south to Chattanooga. The train's to be held here. We get out. And there's another thing. I'll have to find room in some wagon for Papa and Sweet Alice. You know the song? 'Who wept with delight when you gave her a smile and trembled with fear at your frown.' Gah! If any 'Ben Bolt' had ever tried frowning at this Sweet Alice, she'd have taken his scalp and lined a pair of bedroom slippers with it!"

"What do you expect from a girl who'd been kidnaped and dragged across three or four mountain ranges? A nosegay of mignonette? Now how about me and the other officers?"

"Do what you like. Trail along with us. After we get to Pulaski there'll be plenty of Nashville-bound wagons. Hop on the nearest one. That's what I'll advise Sweet Alice and Papa to do. The road's still open, so far as I know, and trains are running north out of Nashville." He turned to the waiting sergeant. "Pass the word. All company commanders report here. Stedman, you better scatter and collect your bandits. This car'll be HQ till we start the column west. Look me up if you want anything."

Outside the car Kirk stepped into a scene so familiar that he felt a tug at his heart, a poignant realization of the months he had been away from the Army. He had witnessed that identical setting so often in the past—waiting troops reveling in the passage of minutes that made no demands on them. Some slept. Others scuffled, sparred, wrestled. One ingenious soul had detached a lamp from a car, and under its waning light dice pattered softly over a spread blanket. He might, he felt, have been anywhere in Virginia or Maryland and in any year since 1861.

Then off beyond the tracks another sound caught his ear, a softer, furry sound of voices, soothing, anxious to please. Words came to him. "Don't worry about your kit, miss. Five men's guarding it." . . . "Sure you're fixed right comfortable on that rock, lady? Cobby, fold another blanket for her, a hospital one that ain't got creepers to it." . . . "Found a mighty fine spring, miss, and here's my mess cup, all scrup with sand." Kirk made his way forward and found Lynn perched demurely on a boulder that was padded with a mound of blankets. A slouch-hatted corporal was handing her a cup whose newly scoured sides reflected the dim light from the coaches. Behind her, her rolls and bundles, along with her father's, lay on the ground, surrounded by five men who leaned on bayoneted rifles and snarled at anyone who came near. Kirk called, "Miss Stockdale!"

There was a resentful stir about Lynn and he felt himself definitely an intruder She was sipping from the tin cup, which she held in both hands like a child, and the corporal was beaming paternally on her. Handing the cup back, she smiled. "Thanks ever so much. That must be a wonderful spring. Why, Captain Stedman, you didn't need to bother about me. I'm being beautifully looked after."

The men turned defensively toward Kirk, one of them muttering, "Calls himself a captain, does he? Don't see no bars to his shoulders."

Kirk laughed. "Bothering about you is kind of a habit, I guess. The major wants me to get our party together."

Lynn moved gracefully as another blanket was slipped under her. "Well, *I'm* right here, so you can stop fussing about me. I don't know where Captain Furber and Left'n'nt Kell are. Father and Captain Pitler went up to the engine. Oh, and Mr. Cotesworth's gone. Said he wasn't one for squirrel-chattering, but wished us well." She suddenly slid down from the rock, eyes a-dance in the faint light. "Look! He gave me this, his own deerskin pouch. It's a real beauty, with porcupine quills worked into it and beads and things. I was so touched I could hardly thank him. He said I was real mountain stock and I was to keep it to remember him and the mountain people by."

"Good for the pilot," said Kirk. "That's the nearest he could come to a medal and you've certainly earned it."

Lynn's eyes dropped for an instant and she turned the pouch over and over in her hands. "Why, Captain Stedman! You never say things like that." Then her head went back and she sniffed suspiciously. "Have you been drinking with the Major? No, I guess not, and anyway I'm just saying thank you by being nasty again. That Major—he reminds me of Captain Cuttle in *Dombey and Son,* though that's mostly the hook. Really, he's much more like Mr. Dombey. I don't care whom he's like. He's going to give us a nice ride on his train and I'm going to sit back and listen to every click of the wheels and think, 'There's one more step I don't have to take.'" Her hands flew to her ears. "Heavens! What is that dreadful racket?"

Kirk turned quickly. Except for the group that had gathered about Lynn, the troops were on their feet, banging their rifle butts against the ground, yelling and howling in bitter disgust. He hoped, though not too optimistically, that Lynn was missing some of the language. Obviously word had spread that the command was to leave the train and hit west on foot. Lynn stepped closer to Kirk. He bent and whispered, "They've just learned. I'm sorry, but you're not going to get a train ride. The bridge over the Hiwassee is out. You'll have a seat on a wagon, though. I'm afraid the young men aren't too pleased. Now the news is spreading."

A man near by spluttered and choked as he forced back a paroxysm of cursing. "Hike, is it?" he finally managed to shout. "Not for me, that hasn't marched ten miles in the last two months! Let 'em fix the bridge. I c'n wait." He sat down heavily. Other voices joined in. "Where's them engineers that's always braggin' they carry spare bridges and tunnels with 'em? I'm plantin' my butt right here till that train moves south!"

Lynn's hand closed about Kirk's wrist in an unconscious gesture. "Is it—is it a mutiny?"

"Doubt it," replied Kirk, keenly aware of the small fingers tight about his wrist. "Looks bad, though. Scratch lot of men. They don't know their officers and their officers don't know them. It may be hard to handle."

The corporal who had brought Lynn the cup of spring water pushed toward her. "Look, miss, is that fair? Here's me, all ready to go home on furlough and I volunteer for this. They tell me, by train to Chattanooga and by train to Nashville. And now what's happened?"

From around the rock, from the track, men crowded up, moving under a cloud of ominous mutterings that deepened, swelled. Someone shouted, "Maybe she'll take word to the Major we ain't movin' till the train does!"

Lynn still clung to Kirk's wrist and he knew that she was trembling a little. Suddenly he whispered to her, "I've got an idea. It may make you pretty conspicuous, but we've got to do *something*. Will you get up on that rock with me?"

He could feel her shoulders straighten as the crowd

280

pressed closer. Her chin went up as she said quickly, "Yes. If you think best."

"I do. Come along." He shouldered his way forward, with Lynn close behind him, helped her onto the rock and sprang up beside her. The men began to shout: "She'll speak for us, she's a right one, she is!"

Kirk held up his hand and the tumult ebbed. He raised his voice. "Some of you here have looked after this young lady as though she were your sister, and I tell you, she won't forget it. She's a friend of every man of you."

Lynn stood very straight beside him, eyes fixed on the lighted car windows as a great "Yeeeay!" went up.

Kirk continued. "Let me tell you something about her. She hiked clear from the other side of the Great Smokies, day in and day out. Never missed a mile, never missed a step. Plenty of rivers and no bridges. Plenty of snow and no shelter and she was always the first up at reveille and the last in at taps. She hit those roads as if she'd been born and bred in the Army of the Cumberland. And she's waiting for no bridge to be fixed for her. She knows where she wants to go and she's going there." Kirk made a deprecatory gesture. "Of course, what's ahead won't be anything like the Smokies. Just the Walden Ridge. And she'll cross the Tennessee and the Sequatchie on regular bridges. She won't have to wade across in ice water the way she did back there. As I say, she's your friend, and if you want her to put in a word with Major Millard, I'll be mighty surprised if she says no."

Someone whooped, "That'll do it. Just tell him we ain't—" The voice died away uncertainly.

Unprompted, Lynn threw back her bright hair and cried in a clear, carrying tone, "Of course I'll speak to him, if it will help you at all. Captain Stedman's right. I *am* going on. I'd hoped that you'd be coming with me."

There was a dead hush by the tracks. Then a harsh

281

voice snapped, "Come on, you badgers! Fall in! She's not hitting west alone!"

To Kirk's surprise, there was no cheering, no waving of hats. The crowd about the rock melted away, formed in double line by the cars and stood waiting, each man leaning on his rifle and muttering to himself as though ashamed of the impulse that had run so strongly only a few seconds before.

Kirk helped Lynn down from the rock, chest swelling in exultation. "You did it. That last bit turned them your way!"

To his astonishment, Lynn turned quickly on him. "You shouldn't have made me do such a thing!"

"You were superb! Every man there must have felt that you were talking right at him. Now they'll march clear to the Mississippi if they have to."

Lynn's little fists shook at her sides. "And *why* are they marching? To kill off Southern troops, troops that all my friends are depending on! How *could* I have done it!"

Ian Stockdale's tall form emerged out of the darkness. "That you, Lynn, my dear? Here's a real treat for you. Captain Pitler took me up to the engine and we used the fire to make real coffee with sugar in it and here's hot buttered toast. Confoundedly ingenious fellow, the Captain."

Lynn's voice was suddenly calm and pleasant. "Oh, that was sweet of you, Dad. But really I couldn't touch a thing. Some of the men gave me rations."

"You're sure? How about you, Stedman? Better tuck into it. I hear we're for some more marching, but it's just the last stage of our trip. And do you know, I'm almost regretting it. Of course, I'm still going to make my report. Matter of sheer duty, you understand. But I must say that you fellows have been real sportsmen. Tired, Lynn, dear? Better sit down on this rock, and do try to take some coffee. It's really capital."

Kirk saw Jake's stocky form bobbing along toward

him against a lighted car and excused himself, leaving the father and daughter alone. Jake came running up. "Where've you been, Kirk? Did you get some of the rations that Stockdale was lugging? Wow, that was hot work at the firebox. I cooked my right hand so thoroughly that I took a bite out of it in the dark, thinking it was toast, and never knew the difference till I came to a fingernail. That true about the bridge being out?"

"Yes. There'll be wagons along in a few minutes and we better get together. Where are the others?"

"Mark's in the first coach. A hospital steward put a new bandage on his knee and says he can walk all right. Jabish is around somewhere."

A man appeared on the platform of the last car. "Captain Stedman! Major Millard wants Captain Stedman on the double!"

"You're popular around here all of a sudden." Jake grinned.

"It's about seats on the wagons, I guess. Will you ask Miss Stockdale to get her things together?"

"Ask her? Hell, there she is, right over there."

Kirk smoothed his black mustache. "That's a place where I'm *not* popular all of a sudden, especially right now. Go and see her, will you?" He raised his voice. "All right! Tell Major Millard I'm on the way!"

16

Cavalry Command

Hours and days and miles were ground away under the
steady flow of hoof and wheel and boot. The Tennessee
was crossed, the broad Walden Ridge, the Sequatchie,
and the column pushed on, heads down against a sudden onset of sleet over the Cumberland Plateau. Walking behind the last of the three supply wagons, Kirk felt
the surface of the road grow crisp and crackly, then slippery as a glaze formed on the trampled dirt.

His mind weighed the various hazards that the icy
coating might bring. Then he remembered that such
matters were no concern of his and the lost feeling that
had come over him when he first joined Millard's command deepened. Back in the mountains the solution of
every problem had lain in his hands: Should the last of
the corn meal be used up, on the chance that the next
few hours would bring more? Should fires be allowed at
night? Should a short cut be taken? Relief from such responsibility would ordinarily have been welcome, but

now it brought a sense of frustration. The problems that cropped up were not his. He was just an individual, loosely attached to the Provisionals, marching where he pleased, but feeling useless, almost a burden. And then there was Lynn.

When he had been in command of the little party, he had forced himself to look on her as just one more member of the group, someone for whose safety and progress he was responsible, as he was for that of the others. It may have been pure pretense on his part, but one that he had maintained with at least some success up to the time when they had come upon Millard's train. Now the role of impersonal leader had been taken from him and he was increasingly aware of the strong attraction that she exerted over him.

He had recognized something of that attraction at their earliest encounters, but those had been isolated incidents, without continuity and not likely to be repeated. During the mountain days and nights that attraction had grown without his daring to acknowledge it, despite her cool bantering, her rebelliousness, her outspoken defiance of him and her endless hostility to his cause.

At times, recently, he had found himself wondering how matters might have stood between them had they met under different circumstances, say, in peaceful times. He could conjure up mental pictures of escorting her to an undergraduate hop at Dartmouth, with Lynn always in a sweeping gown of the same canary yellow that lined her gray cloak and followed by the envious eyes of his classmates and their drabber partners. Or she might be waiting, deep blue eyes asparkle, on a Toronto wharf while his steamer edged close to the pilings. But their actual meetings led along no such sunny roads. And, in any event, would she have appealed to him so strongly had she been just one of a dozen or a score of pretty girls?

Plodding on through the sleet, Kirk told himself that

all such speculation was futile. There was no changing of circumstances, nor of the relation between the two. In fact, she seemed to have been avoiding him since the column first formed by the tracks four nights ago. She nodded pleasantly enough whenever he ranged up and down the road. But when he joined her and Jake the day that they crossed the Sequatchie, she had dropped back, saying that she had walked far enough. At each overnight camp, Millard had detailed men to build shelters for her and her father, well away from the troops, and had posted a guard within call of them. Probably it was all just as well. Lynn would remain distant, the journey would be over and that would be the end.

The camp site was beautifully chosen, a level field just under low, sharp cliffs that broke the force of the wind-borne sleet and formed a dry strip fifty feet out from their base. Kirk walked toward the wagons, whistling softly to himself. He had been inspecting, quite needlessly, the Major's horse, whose groom seemed to know his business very well. Just the same, being consulted about a rough patch of hair that might turn into a saddle sore made him feel less lost, more a part of the column. "Hope Millard's made sure that the Stockdales are drying out properly," he thought. "Can't expect civilians to look after themselves like—"

He stopped short. Lynn was standing with her back toward him near the end of the cliffs. Her gray cape was slung loosely about her shoulders and her arms lifted in a graceful gesture as she shook out a deep blue woolen scarf, acquired somehow on the march, and knotted it loosely about her hair. She tilted her head this way and that as she fluffed out the material in a bonnetlike shape. Then, satisfied, she slipped her hands into the pockets of her deerskin jacket under her cloak and strolled slowly toward the road, head back as though she were breathing deeply and enjoying every breath. At the road she turned, resumed her slow walk, taking care to put one foot just ahead of the other as though walking a tightrope. Suddenly she looked up and smiled. "You must be relieved to have us off your hands, Captain Stedman."

Kirk took off his battered hat. "Only because you're in better ones."

"That 'only' is really quite nice. How do you know they're better? You haven't been near us once since we left the railroad. You might at least have taken the trouble to find out how we were."

"Major Millard's a very good man. And you could have sent for me if there was anything I could have done."

Head a little on one side, she studied him. "It's done you good, being rid of us. You don't glower the way you used to."

"I never glowered at you, just over things that went wrong."

"Indeed you did glower at me."

"Well, only when you wanted to do something that would have slowed us."

"As if I wasn't just as eager to get on as you! Look, do you really think we'll reach the railroad tomorrow?"

"Millard's sure of it." Kirk nudged a stone with his boot to keep from looking too long at the vivid red of her lips, the soft curve of the lashes about the deep blue of her eyes.

She sighed. "I wonder what sort of people we'll meet in Nashville. Are they apt to be disagreeable to us?"

"No one's going to be disagreeable to you," said Kirk, looking at her.

"But we'll be among strangers."

"Your father's better than a whole mounted escort. And the four of us will probably be within call right through to Washington."

"But—but don't you have to stay here?"

"Army routine will send us back to the Army of the Potomac."

Lynn's eyes flashed. "Oh, I'm glad, so glad that you—that all of you are going north. It's going to be terrible for your people down here in Tennessee. They say General Hood's got more than fifty thousand men and Nathan Bedford Forrest's leading his cavalry. You've only got about twenty-five thousand. Oh, I've been listening! There'll be a big Confederate victory that'll change everything and—oh, I didn't mean it to sound that way—but you've known all along how I've felt—it's just that you, you four can't *do* anything to stop what's bound to happen—we're going to win. You must see that. But I don't want—" She turned suddenly, ran off along the base of the cliffs, her gray cloak flaring out behind her and showing flicks of canary lining.

Kirk stared after her. "Now what the devil's upset her all of a sudden? It's almost as if she *wanted* us to stay with her—and her father." He smoothed his black mustache, frowning. "Of course she does. She knows us. It'll be more convenient for her in a dozen ways, shuttled North among strangers, if we're within call. Guess it's the idea of starting off alone that scares her, though I certainly made it clear enough that we'd be along. Wonder if any of Millard's crowd know Nashville and Louisville well. Might be a good idea to get the names of the best shops. She'll want to refit there. And so will her father, of course."

The train trip southwest from McMinnville, begun so smoothly in clear November weather, came to an inglorious halt a few miles above the junction at Manchester. There was a man with a red flag in the middle of the track and a group of mounted officers waiting at a dirt road that ran west into rolling country. Kirk left the flatcar, where he had been perched on a wagon seat with Lynn and Jake, and ran forward where Millard was talking with a red-faced colonel. In a few minutes, he was back, swinging himself over the side. Lynn called, "What's wrong?"

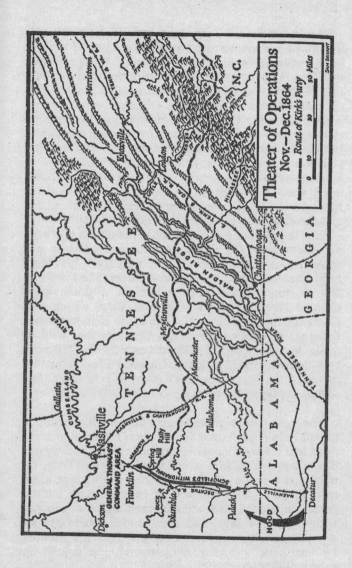

Theater of Operations
Nov.–Dec. 1864

━━━ Route of Kirk's Party

0   10   50 Miles

SAM BRYANT

N.C.

GEORGIA

TENNESSEE

ALABAMA

Chattanooga

WALDEN RIDGE

Knoxville

London

Murfreesboro

Manchester

Tullahoma

McMinnville

Nashville

NASHVILLE & CHATTANOOGA

Gallatin

CUMBERLAND RIVER

GENERAL THOMAS'S
COMMAND AREA

Franklin

Spring Hill

Rally Hill

Columbia

DECATUR R.R.

Pulaski

SCHOFIELD'S WITHDRAWAL

HOOD

NASHVILLE

Decatur

TENNESSEE RIVER

Dickson

"Plenty. The ride's over. Jake and I'll help you get your stuff together. We're taking the road again."

Lynn clasped her hands to her head. "And just when my things were getting a good sunning. Do go back and warn Father. It'll only take me a few minutes to pack. Are we going to walk again?"

"*You* aren't. The wagons come with us. But we'll all walk."

"Where to? Just to the main line north?" asked Lynn.

"That's closed. Troop movements."

Jake surveyed his worn boots mournfully. "Feet," he said, "you've been brought up handsome. Now do your duty. What did the boy with the eagles say, Kirk?"

"The whole map's out of kilter. Schofield's fallen back to Columbia on Duck River, about thirty miles north of Pulaski. Hood's after him, all right. Hurry call for all Union troops in transit to push west to Columbia." Then he saw Lynn's troubled eyes and puckered forehead. "Don't worry. You'll make Nashville all right. Northbound pikes are open and you'll roll through on this wagon or another one. It's just the Tennessee and Alabama Railroad that's closed. Guess they're figuring on moving troops up from Chattanooga."

Her eyes were still clouded. "But how about you and the others?"

Jake laughed. "We'll hook on to a wagon along with you. Or if there isn't room, we'll run under the rear axle like coach dogs. You can toss bones to us at the halts."

Lynn turned to Kirk. "Does he really mean that?"

"Didn't I tell you we'd *all* have to go north? Come on. The battalion's falling in and they'll start unchocking the wagon wheels in a minute."

Through the afternoon of November 29, three days away from its detraining point, the battalion and its wagons labored over a dirt road that ran west toward low, rolling hills. The air was warm and hazy and the dust churned up by boot and wheel hung low, barely rising above the wagon hubs. Kirk strode up the column, checking the state of the harness and calling to the drivers to have their mules' nostrils sponged out. As he overtook the lead wagon, a Cavalry sergeant on a lathered horse burst out of a side road, halted, then swung down toward the column. "Commanding officer! Where's the commanding officer?" croaked the rider.

"Two wagons down," shouted Kirk. "What do you want him for?" But the sergeant only lashed at his mount and whirled on past him. Kirk looked after him. "Now where the devil did *he* come from and what's he after? Must be getting close to *something*, anyway," Kirk thought. Then he turned and ran down the road.

He found Millard, bridle loose on his horse's neck, frowning at a sheet of paper as he rode on. The sergeant had dismounted and was sitting by the bank, panting. Kirk called, "Anything up, Major? Or isn't it any of my business?"

Millard motioned him to close in by the nigh stirrup and read on in silence. Then he folded the sheet, stuffed it into his blouse. "Guess this is everyone's business. They must have couriers covering every cart path in south Tennessee." He tapped his blouse. "Addressed to all commanders of troops on the march. Just like that. Damn it, Stedman, this doesn't look good, not for a hoot. We're not going to Columbia. Hood's flanked Schofield out of his position there. Schofield's falling back north again and it looks like the town of Franklin on the Harpeth River's going to be his next address—as long as Hood lets it be."

"Franklin!" exclaimed Kirk. "But that's only a hop below Nashville."

"Call it a half hop. Well, anyway, here's what happens to us. We keep on to a place called Rally Hill and we'll run into our own Cavalry there and report to the Cavalry commander, a man named Wilson, Major General, it says here."

"Anything else?" asked Kirk.

"Plenty, and it's lucky I know this slice of the world. There are two main pikes leading north to Franklin, a few miles apart and kind of parallel. My wagons branch at Rally Hill onto the nearer pike, the Lewisburg–Franklin. The troops push on to the farther one, the Columbia–Franklin pike. They're supposed to find Schofield on it, marching north. Maybe they will. But all this sounds like they're more apt to run into Hood or Forrest. Well, nothing to worry about—so far. At Rally Hill we'll see Wilson, get fresh news and maybe fresh orders. I'll lope through the column and drop a word to Pitler and the others." He turned his horse and rode off.

Kirk watched him, eyes narrow as he sifted out the news. It seemed to him that Millard was a little overoptimistic, perhaps intentionally so. With a further withdrawal north by Schofield, there was a very good chance that Confederate troops might be found between Millard's little command and the main Union body. In that case—He broke into a trot. When he reached the leading wagon, he caught at the handrail and swung himself up, balancing on the footrest. "You're driving like a veteran, Miss Stockdale!" he called.

Lynn, alone on the box, smiled down at him. "It's really no trick. I've had the reins for the last five miles." The wagon struck deeper ruts, swaying sharply from side to side. Lynn put out a hand and steadied herself on Kirk's shoulder. "Do you mind? Really, it is pitching badly now."

"Don't mind at all," said Kirk, foot braced against the iron step as he clung to the side of the wagon. "Just wanted to tell you. New orders. And they could mean that Hood's slipped past Schofield."

"Then he'd be between us and your people?" Her hand suddenly tightened on his shoulder. "You could be taken prisoner again. Please, please don't go roaming off by yourself!"

He looked up quickly. Her chin was set and her eyes were on the far horizon, lids flickering rapidly. He covered her fingers with his. "What I meant was," he began. "Well, if Hood gets very close, maybe I could talk Millard into sending you and your father into their lines under a flag of truce."

Her hand slid from under Kirk's, her eyes still on the horizon. "Oh. Under a flag of truce," she said faintly.

"Only if it's quite safe, of course. Now, really, I've got to go down and see what Jake is up to. I'll be back soon as I can." He dropped to the ground and worked his way past the 2nd Provisional Company. As he cleared its head, he looked back. Lynn was still sitting there, staring ahead. "Funny," Kirk thought. "I'd have said she'd jump at the chance of getting to the Rebs under a flag. Still, I guess it is a scary idea, being sent off through the dark with guns banging all around. I've seen her take greater chances, though, and think nothing of them. Oh, hell! Of course she's right. She could be shot a dozen times in the dark before she'd gone fifty yards from our lines. She's got a head on her. She sees the difference between taking ordinary chances and sheer recklessness. She's going to stay right where she is."

Dusk was falling as Kirk and Jake tramped along in advance of the point that Millard had thrown out well ahead of the column. Free of the choking cloud of reddish dust kicked up by boots and hoofs, Kirk looked up at the first scattered stars that glowed low in the sky. "Damn it, Jake, the good weather's going to hold. A day or two of rain might slow Hood up enough to let our whole crowd get clear of Franklin."

"Could slow us down, as well as Hood. Never was partial to getting my feet wet. What I say is—" Jake's voice suddenly rose in a high screech. "Hey, look-at-'em-look-at-'em-look-at-'em! Honest to Jesus horse soldiers! Starboard, on that side road! Oh, my God! I've got to get over there and touch one of 'em to make sure he's real!"

Kirk was staring with Jake at a file of Union troopers riding toward the main road. "Cavalry Sabers and carbines! Jake, we're home!"

"Let's give 'em a hail and—"

Hoofs clattered up from the rear and Major Millard overtook the pair. "So you saw them, too, did you? Means we're close to Rally Hill. I'm going on to report to General Wilson."

With a sudden impulse, Kirk swung himself up behind the Major. "We'll guide you right to him," he cried.

"Sure!" yelled Jake, catching at the nigh stirrup leather.

"Damn it!" shouted Millard. "When I want aides I'll detail them myself."

"You'll need us as interpreters," panted Jake. "Maybe the General doesn't speak infantry."

Millard burst out laughing. "All right, you insubordinate coffee boilers. Come on." He set his horse at an easy trot along the road, Jake bounding along beside him in tremendous leaps.

From his perch behind the Major, Kirk saw more and more troopers through the fading light—troopers watering their mounts, troopers grooming horses, troopers slinging coffee pots over little fires. Over the pat-pat of hoofs, Jake shouted, "Kirk! They got Spencer carbines!"

"Yes, Spencers!" called Kirk. "See the way the sabers are slung? Must have some new kind of hook. Ay-yay! Smell that. Field forge. Red-hot shoe going onto a hoof! There they are! New kind of field-forge limber!"

Millard bawled, "Oh, my God! Will you two maniacs quit chattering horse talk? I just want to report and get out—get back to the foot boys where there's some sanity!"

"Here's your chance!" Jake's words were jolted out of him as he pounded along, towed by the stirrup leather. "Must be Rally Hill dead ahead. Big, long bastard. Guards. Hi! A two-star flag by that little cabin off to the left."

Millard swung toward it, dismounted by the shaky porch and strode in, Kirk and Jake at his heels. A smart lieutenant stood by an inner door while a short, slight man in a beautiful white shirt, trooper's breeches and long boots frowned at a map on a long table. He had a thin, boyish face, marked by a neat mustache and imperial. Millard called genially, "Hello, sonny. Where's the General?"

"Here," said the other tersely.

"I know. We could make out the two stars even in this light. But get him, get him."

The slight man straightened and Kirk felt his own shoulders stiffening as very keen eyes, old for that young face, played over Millard. "James Wilson, Major General, Chief of Cavalry, Military Division of the Mississippi. You wanted to see me?"

Millard flushed brick red under his beard. "Sorry, General. Major George Millard, commanding 1st Provisional Battalion from Knoxville, under orders to report to General Schofield."

Wilson smiled and his eyes seemed more suited to his face. "Quite all right, Major. These men your guides?"

"Passengers, sir. Captain Kirk Stedman, D.C.I.T., fairly fresh out of Libby, Captain Jacob Pitler, D Troop, 1st Maine Cavalry, ditto. I've got two more escaped horse officers with my column. I suppose they'll be sent right back to the original units now."

"That's regulation," said Wilson, eyes playing over Kirk and Jake. "Did a change in orders reach you on the road, Major?"

"Right, sir. Wagons break off here north up the Lewisburg–Franklin pike. Troops go west to the Columbia–Franklin pike. That is, unless you've fresh orders for me, sir."

"None at the moment. Better get your command onto the hill and then report back to me."

"Very good, sir. But there's one other thing you ought to know. Stedman, tell the General about your Canadians."

When Kirk had finished his account, Wilson tugged at

296

his goatee. "I may have heard of more irregular things in my life, but I can't think of any just now. There's nothing I can do about them, but I don't want any non-benevolent neutrals messing around back of my lines. You go with the wagon train, Major, and make sure that that pair stay put. We'll see what Schofield wants to do with them at Franklin. That's all, Major, for the present. But I want a word with these two captains."

Millard left and Wilson turned to Kirk and Jake. "Well, gentlemen, Regulations say you're to get back to your outfits as quick as you can. However, if you've the least notion that I'm going to let even one seasoned cavalryman slip out of my grasp, you better get rid of it. I've been sent cavalry drafts every bit as mixed up as Millard's lot—expired furloughs, convalescents, stragglers, men who've served out sentences. I've formed them up somehow in the last few days, but I'm short of officers. Or, rather, I was. Understand?"

Kirk could only stare at him, but Jake burst out, "Oh, my God! Damn right we understand—sir!"

Wilson smiled boyishly. "All right. Stedman, you'll take Provisional Troop A, and Pitler, B. Lieutenant Hedges here will show you where they are and he'll rig you out with some sort of uniform and equipment. You'll find your men a scratchy lot. You're to have them in combat condition by tomorrow morning. You'll take your commands along with Millard's up the Columbia pike. By the time you get to Franklin, you ought to have a fair idea of how to handle your men. Then report with them at my headquarters. I'll be somewhere out the Triune road, east of Franklin and on the north bank of the Harpeth, and I'll expect you both to show me two manageable cavalry troops. Anything to add, gentlemen?"

Kirk stifled an impulse to throw his hat across the room, to shout, "A cavalry command of my own again." But he managed to come to attention. "We'll be proud to serve under you, sir. Where do we find our men?"

An hour later, Kirk walked down the lower slopes of Rally Hill. He was in his true element once more. And, within reasons, he was suitably clothed and equipped as a Union officer. He wore a kepi with a dead man's name inked on the sweatband. Tarnished captain's bars clung to the shoulders of a cavalry jacket that fitted quite well. His breeches were new with a wide yellow stripe down the outer seams and his dragoon boots with their jointed knee pieces might have been made for him. Hedges had been apologetic about the saber, one of the heavy, straight-bladed Prussian type, but Kirk, unlike most cavalrymen, had always preferred it to the newer issue with its lighter, curved blade. And his pouch held plenty of rounds for the Colt that the Cherokee had spirited away from a Confederate posse long weeks ago.

To offset all this, there was the feeling of apprehension about the future. Hood was on the loose and driving hard while Schofield fought and maneuvered for the essential days and hours in which an adequate force might be gathered somehow about all-important Nashville. Probably at that very moment, loaded transports were working south up the Cumberland to that city, but the reinforcements they carried were doomed if they had to disembark at the Nashville jetties under the fire of Hood's artillery.

He was even more doubtful of any role that he himself could play in the coming action. He had just returned from his meeting with Provisional Troop A and it was clear that to describe them as a "scratchy lot" had been an understatement. The first sergeant was a sullen ex-Regular who despised his new unit and took no pains to hide that fact. The other noncoms were unsure of themselves and of their authority over their men. The ranks contained a good leavening of competent, seasoned troopers, but they were from a dozen different units, strangers to each other and to their noncoms.

Their equipment was nothing to raise morale. Most had sabers and Colts, but instead of carbines they had been issued long, clumsy, single-shot infantry Spring-fields. Horse furniture was adequate in quantity, but some of the saddles were covered with rawhide which was sure to dry out and split, causing crippling saddle sores. The horses were a stable sergeant's nightmare. There were commandeered carriage horses, troop horses with barely healed wounds, wagon horses not used to a saddle and a good half dozen taken from the horsecars of the Nashville Street Railway Company. And Kirk was sure that he had caught the sharp, sour reek of mange, though he had not been able to track down its source.

Now the men were grumpily resiting the picket line onto ground that not only gave the horses better stand-ing but was also much nearer a good watering place on Flat Creek. This order had brought a growling protest from First Sergeant Ganey. "Hell, we got orders to move out in a couple or three hours, Cap'n." Kirk had re-plied, "Ever hear of orders being changed? And even if it's only for a half hour, the horses'll be better off on that solid ground and we can water quicker. Get 'em go-ing." Ganey had still grumbled, but there had been no more argument and the shift was proceeding smoothly.

Kirk walked on. "I can draw more coffee from Wil-son's wagons. That ten dollars Wilson's aide advanced me. Can buy enough cigars from the sutler to give every man a couple. Men get edgy without tobacco. Wonder how Jake's getting on with his crowd."

When the light cart had rattled off to his new com-mand with the coffee and cigars, Kirk took a short cut back along the outskirts of the camp. The night brought him an orchestration of sound that linked the remem-bered past vividly with the present—the uneasy stir of troops trying to rest in the face of the knowledge that drum and bugle would rouse them soon; the distant rustle of shifting hoofs and, nearer, the chump-chump-chump of muzzles deep in feed bags; the whine of a wick being drawn through a rifle barrel; the thud of un-willing feet on some detail; the quick hiss and crackle as

299

twigs were thrown onto a fire; the whack-whack of a pistol butt sinking a tent peg; the joyous light patter telling that a mule had slipped its halter shank and was trotting loose through the wagon park. A deep voice was working its way through "Die Beiden Grenadieren," overdoing the pathos of the lines:

*"So nimm' meine Leiche nach Frankreich mit,
Begrab' mich in Frankreichs Erde."*

To sing so glibly of shipping bodies to France, to Michigan or Indiana or New Hampshire was hitting too near home on the eve of probable action. He kept on up a steep path between two low shoulders of Rally Hill that should bring him very soon to his relocated lines. A single light burned twenty yards ahead, perhaps some farmer looking for strayed stock. Then he saw that it was a lantern on a low branch.

He came abreast of it as though wading into a soft, golden pool. There was a stir beyond and out of the darkness came a voice that drove all other thoughts from his mind. "Who's that? You, Father?" An instant's pause, then, "What on earth are you doing in those clothes?"

Kirk suppressed a gasp. "Lynn! This is no place for you. You're way out beyond the guards."

She came nearer. "You're in uniform. You've got a sword, too. Boots and spurs!" Her voice dropped. "Where are you going?"

His heart beat faster, mostly from relief—he thought—that she had ridden over his use of her first name. "Oh—all this stuff? Why, General Wilson seems to have drafted me." He furtively tucked back the cuffs that had worked down past his wrists.

Lynn stayed at the far edge of the pool of light. "What for?"

Surprised by the lack of assurance in her tone, he answered, "He gave me command of some cavalry. I've got

300

to go and see about them now. Are you sure you're all right here? Where's your father?"

There was something mechanical in her reply. "We're quite all right, thanks. There's supposed to be a guard down the path and Father's gone to see Major Millard."

"Well, that's fine. I'll try to see you before we start. I'm pretty busy, though."

"Before we start?" There was an odd note in her voice as though his statement disturbed her. She went on, perhaps trying to reassure herself. "But you'll be coming with us. I know that much. All the cavalry's going up the Lewisburg pike with the wagons." She stepped out into the full glow of the lantern and he felt a sudden shock. It had been easy enough to speak offhandedly about getting back to his command while she stood, almost impersonal, just beyond the yellow rays. But now he looked down on her crown of corn-colored hair, into the deep blue of her eyes, that were puzzled, even a little hurt, and at her lips, parted as though to ask another question. And he remembered, looking down at her, that he would not be going along the Lewisburg pike, walking or riding near her.

He cleared his throat. "Oh—about the pike—you see—" he began.

Her hands crossed and crept slowly inside the opposite cuffs of her deerskin jacket. "You're hiding something," she said.

He looked away, forcing a casual laugh. "Oh, no. That is—the General wants me and Jake to go up the Columbia pike." He pointed off in the dark. "It's just over there. Just a hop and a step. About the same as being on the Lewisburg pike, almost."

An expression that he could not interpret came over her face. Then she said, "You're leaving—us."

"Oh, not really. I told you that the Columbia pike—"

"I've seen the maps." Her lips set in a tight line and he expected a familiar outburst. She stood silent for a moment, and her glossy leather sleeves stirred as though

301

her fingers were digging into her elbows. She said in a flat voice, "You said you were busy. I mustn't keep you." She turned away, hugging her elbows to her.

To his amazement he caught a glint of something bright gliding down her cheek. He took a quick step forward, caught her in his arms. "Lynn!" She struggled, trying to break his grasp and straining to free her hands from her sleeves. Her shoulders were shaking and her head twisted sharply away from him. He said gently, "Lynn!"

In a strange, broken tone she said, "Leave me alone!" Then, with a ghost of her old manner, "You've always bullied me. Back there at Frederick's Hall you mauled me about just because—" Her voice broke again and her slim body shivered in his arms.

"Look at me, Lynn! We're marching out pretty soon, but you're going to hear this, because there may not be another chance to say it. I kept my thoughts about you to myself all through our trip. For one thing, I had to, if we were all to get through. For another—well, there's been your feeling about the times we live in."

She finally freed her hands and pushed hard against his chest. "Don't go on!"

"*Please* listen, Lynn! You must have seen that I admired you way back at Frederick's Hall, and still more when you came to Libby. On this march I've seen you day in and day out." He caught her wrists, turned her toward him while she strained away, bright head thrown back, eyes half closed. "I know what you are and I'm telling you, not as a Yankee to a foreign friend of the Rebs, but as man to woman, that you're superb. As man to woman I'm telling you that we've shared so much that, no matter what happens, you'll always be part of me, and whether you like it or not, I'll always be part of you." She lowered her head quickly and he saw in that brief moment that her cheeks glinted in the light. "Have you nothing to say to that?" he asked softly. She struggled against sobs and stood silent while he caught

302

both her wrists in one hand and slipped the other about her quivering shoulders. "Nothing to say?" he repeated.

She shook her head and her hair brushed against his face. Then she whispered huskily, "Only what I've said before and over and over."

He bent lower, face buried in her bright hair. "Sure, Lynn?"

"Yes, yes!" Her tone was almost harsh. "Yes!" All at once she gave a long, uneven sigh. Her hands slipped from his grasp, met below his shoulders. "Kirk, Kirk, I've tried so hard to hate you and now you've spoiled it all!" Her head pressed forward against his chest. "You've always made it so difficult for me. I was furious with you at Frederick's Hall, but I knew all along no one could have been more thoughtful and gentle. When I saw you at Libby, you looked so thin and drawn and tired that I wanted to rock you in my arms instead of gloating over you. And on our march you looked after me every second and I said bity, clawy, nasty things to you in return." She gave a little sniff against the blue of his coat. "I *did* try hard, and it was no use. And I was cross when that little crippled girl turned to you instead of me when she was hurt."

She stopped and Kirk was keenly aware of the swift rise and fall of her bosom against him, of her fingers running softly over his back. He whispered, "Am I right, Lynn, that we're part of each other, in spite of everything?"

Her head turned slowly. "Kirk, dear, don't you think you've made me say a great deal already? Must I go over every thought I've ever had about you? Here you are, bullying me again, and I rather like it, now." A fastening at the top of her jacket had given way and Kirk had a glimpse of white throat as her face lifted toward his and her breath went out in a long, tremulous sigh. At last she freed herself gently. "Kirk, your men."

He laughed against the curve of her neck. "I could say that I was just thinking of them, and I'd be lying.

Just of you, Lynn. Anyway, we meet in Franklin in the morning."

Her hands caught at him. "Franklin! Oh, it's so hard to say, even to think about, but do be careful!"

"Nothing to be careful about. Scouts say that everything's rolling smoothly up the pike."

"And there's something else. I do feel differently about you. But about the war I don't. I can't."

"Your beliefs are your own and honest, Lynn darling. Keep them. But we've got a lot more to talk about, about things that wars and national borders don't touch. Things about us, my dearest. In the meantime—"

For an instant they clung to each other. Then she dropped her arms. He raised his hand to his kepi and went rapidly along the path, carrying a full heart to the lines of Provisional Troop A.

17

To the Harpeth

Kirk pulled up at the side of the road and watched his troop ride past through the dark. Glowing red dots spotted the columns of fours, and from time to time a trooper, recognizing him, called out, "Thanks for the seegars, Cap'n," or "Had me two pots coffee, all to myself, sir. Was elegant." Kirk raised his hand in acknowledgment of each hail. The troop looked a little better to him with every mile that was passed. If they'd only keep closed up more. Ranging up and down the road to enforce this would only wear out the converted carriage horse that he rode. When the end of the column came abreast, Kirk called, "Sergeant Ganey!"

The first sergeant detached himself. "Sir?" he said grumpily.

"The men have got to keep closed up. I haven't seen you doing a thing about it."

Ganey shoved back his kepi. "Ain't no use tryin' to do anything with this lot of gowks, sir."

305

"Seems to me you don't like this assignment much, Sergeant."

"Damn right I don't. I always served with good outfits, not with militia broom-drillers like these."

"You haven't done one damn thing to help. A troop's as good as its top soldier, no better. You better start acting like one. Do the kind of job that I know you can do, from your record, and I'll back you to the limit. Soldier on me and I'll bust you before daylight. Now button up your jacket and get busy."

Ganey stared at him, fastened his jacket slowly, then gave a passable salute and trotted off up the column. Kirk could hear his rasping voice: "Close up, you dumb-heads."

Kirk watched the troop tighten up as the men brought their mounts into better alignment. Then he cocked his head toward the east. Over the pat-pat of hoofs and the sound of boots that followed he caught a distant rumbling and clanking. He sighed, half relieved, half regretful. Lynn and the wagons were on their way north on the Lewisburg pike. Lynn! Once again the realization of her swept over his whole being. Lynn turning away with a bright drop on her cheek. Lynn struggling in his arms and denying that tear and later ones. Then the sudden melting and her arms about him and her body pressed to his and her face lifting to him.

With a shake of his head he partially freed himself from those memories and closed up with his troop. There were level fields to the right and he swung his sets of fours into them, went through a few simple evolutions. It was hard to tell in the dark just how well such movements were carried out, but at least the lines did not become clubbed, and when the troop re-formed on the road, every man answered to the quick roll call. Sergeant Ganey co-operated, though sullenly.

A steep-banked stream gave a chance to try a fording under assumed fire, and as he watched, Kirk sensed that unmistakable feeling of a group of men growing solid and manageable under his hand. The seasoned troopers were beginning to recognize a skilled touch, were meshing themselves with the shadowy forms to right and left, to act in almost unconscious accord.

Off by a dark mass of trees, bushes crackled, hoofs thumped on the ground and a familiar voice yelled, "Hey! What kep' you?"

Provisional Troop B rode in a ragged line across the field toward the ford, whooping, yelling, waving sabers behind a stocky man a few yards in front. Jake bawled some highly unconventional order and the line jerked to a halt. Kirk rode out to meet him, shook his shoulder and received a smart thump on the back in return. "What's happening, Jake?" Kirk asked. "I was told you'd be falling in behind Millard's lot back there."

Jake settled his jacket. "That's how we started. Been a change in march orders since. Some eagle boy had the brains to see we were too good to trail along behind infantry. We're to close in on you." He scratched his head. "Close in on you. Jesus. Seems like old times, doesn't it? Only that's not the D.C.I.T. you've got there."

"Sure isn't. And you're not riding in front of D Troop, 1st Maine."

"What the hell's the matter with them? They're a swell outfit."

Kirk watched the men behind Jake. He was sure that his troop could come to a halt more smoothly than Jake's had. But he caught a feeling of camaraderie among these men. They were talking in muffled voices, laughing, scuffling. A few more hours and they would answer Jake's slightest gesture as a schooner obeys the skilled touch at its tiller. He was not surprised. He knew of no troop commander in the Army of the Potomac who could take over a new, possibly hostile outfit as Jake could. With a joke or two, a few seemingly casual orders, a dash of blistering reprimand that somehow left laughter and not resentment in its wake, he always brought it under his hand.

307

"There's not a damn thing wrong with them," Kirk answered. "Now better pull right in behind me and drop off a couple of connecting files to link up with Millard. Ride along with me. You left the hill after I did. Did Lynn and her father get off all right?"

"Ever know that gal to miss out? Wilson gave her blankets and made sure she was with the best driver. Oh, and she told me to tell you that she was a complete failure, whatever that meant."

A quick glow crept over Kirk. "Funny thing to say, wasn't it?" He smiled to himself. "She'll probably explain it when I see her again."

"Yeh. Probably, Another thing: I don't remember her calling you 'Kirk' before, except that time when she ducked her neat little self in that river. Must have been kind of excited about being on the last lap of her trip. All she can hear is someone yelling, 'All aboard for Bowling Green, Louisville and the Ohio.' "

"Seems likely. Are Mark and Jabish staying behind Millard?"

"Mark is, but Jabish, well, he's joined that company his Michigan cousin belongs to. They only had one officer and he got doubled up with a flux at Rally Hill."

They wound on through the night, Kirk and Jake riding in the gap between the two troops. By a sagging sawmill where water creamed over a damn, Ganey cantered up. "The point you put out, sir. Reported sound of traffic ahead. Proceeded myself to investigate. Crossroad half mile ahead. Heavy columns of infantry, marching north. Returned to report to you, sir."

"Good stuff, Sergeant, and thank you," said Kirk, cheered by this evidence of a new Ganey. "Take the rear of the troop and keep in touch with Captain Pitler. Jake, I'm going ahead." He trotted past his own troop, cleared the four-man point thrown out in advance. There was no doubting Ganey's report. The air was thick with the heavy crunch of infantry on the move. Soon he could see dimly the formless flow of weary foot

308

soldiers coming on endlessly. There was something eerie about their passage. No one talked or laughed, no pipes or cigars glowed in the ranks. He watched the lurching slouch of the spent men, the different regiments marked by cased colors borne on sagging shoulders. When he made out a sufficient gap between the rear of one unit and the head of the next, he brought his troop onto the pike, knowing that Jake and the others would be close behind.

As soon as his troop was firmly settled in the column, Kirk pushed on north along the dark road, reining in to question officers who dozed uneasily in their saddles, then working along still farther in hope of verifying the information that he had picked up. At the end of a mile or more of riding, he turned back toward his command, weighing and sorting out what he had heard.

Militarily, the picture was clear enough, assuming the bulk of his data to be correct. From the Union point of view it was disturbing. Hood and his Confederates were following along, well spread out, somewhere to the south, but just where no one seemed to know. The problem faced by the Union General John Schofield depended entirely on just how closely, just how fast, Hood was able to drive his eager men.

First of all, the Union wagon trains and artillery must reach the town of Franklin, a few miles ahead, and cross to the north bank of the Harpeth River, and onto the Nashville pike. Most men with whom Kirk talked were sure that the Harpeth bridges were all down, and that meant a slow passage of the stream by the fords.

After every last mule and every last wheel had cleared the north bank, the rest of Schofield's command would follow, falling back north, like the wagon trains, to the shelter of Nashville and whatever troops General George Thomas had been able to scrape up.

But if Hood did press hard and fast on Schofield's

heels, and Kirk knew nothing about Hood's character to suggest that he would lose as much as a second, then a stand would have to be made on the high ground about Franklin to cover the passage of the precious guns and wagons. Cold shivers ran along Kirk's spine as he thought of that prospect—a Union force, outnumbered more than two to one, turning to face the Confederate onslaught with a bridgeless river at its back.

Still, that was the infantry's problem. No one could tell him anything about James Wilson's cavalry and wagons, off on the Lewisburg pike to the east. Several officers were sure, however, that the Confederate Cavalry under Nathan Bedford Forrest had managed to work over between Schofield's main body and Wilson. Kirk's breath went in when he thought of Lynn, off there on the dark pike with the wagons, exposed to those violent eruptions on supply trains and convoys for which Forrest and his men were famous. Still, that other pike was not so very far away and he had heard no trace of the sudden, vicious spattering of shots which would accompany a Forrest coup.

He pulled his mind abruptly back to the military phases of the situation. Perhaps Forrest, with larger game in sight, would not bother with the trains, but would concentrate on driving Wilson across the Harpeth, well east of Franklin. Then he could curve around west to crash into the rear of the Union force covering the river crossings for Schofield's trains. And Kirk and Jake and Mark were to report to Wilson there on the north bank, to join him in blocking Forrest. And Forrest was not a man to let himself be blocked easily.

When he regained his troop, he had a few words with Sergeant Ganey, whose earlier sullen hostility had turned into a sort of terse respect, and then rode on to find Jake and Mark, who would surely have picked up information against which his own could be verified or disproved.

The terrain was brightening and Kirk, from the flank of his troop, could look ahead down a long, gentle hill with an endless column, already showing faintly blue in the growing light, trailing on north down the Columbia pike. A red-eyed major of Ohio Infantry, toiling on beside Kirk on a sprung-kneed horse, gestured ahead. "Fought over this country before," he said in hoarse, jerky sentences. "This is Winstead Hill. Rise beyond us is Carter's Knoll. Nice little plantation on it. Franklin's just behind the knoll. See a steeple or two in a minute. Town's just on the edge of the Harpeth and I wish to hell I had my boys right over on the north bank now. Still, that knoll and the land around it is not a bad infantry position if we have to make a stand."

"Maybe Hood won't come on as fast as we think he will," said Kirk, his mind on the lands that lay to the east, the "cavalry country" where he would have to find Wilson.

The major grunted. "Huh! Guess you don't know Hood. Oh, hell! I've got to rest this beast before he crumples under me." The major pulled off by the side of the pike and dismounted.

Kirk heard a din in the rear and Mark and Jake came clattering up, frowning as though pondering some immeasurably weighty problem. Mark called, "Kirk, we've been thinking—"

"About Franklin!" Jake chanted. "May be a hell of a mess there! Wagons in the streets! Guns! Caissons! Horses being led out to water!"

"Streets jammed," chimed in Mark. "Might get held up for hours!"

"Stragglers!" cried Jake. "Under foot everywhere!"

Kirk eyed them suspiciously. "I've seen an army on the march before."

Jake went on. "Been figuring. Might save time if you went ahead, nosing out a route for us. Then we'd all go through, slick as stripping a skin off an eel." Kirk managed to catch Jake's eyes and Jake's look of profound

311

military thought vanished in a grin. "Hell! We know who's there and we've seen you looking at her and her looking at you, even when she acted mad, for a long spell of weeks. Go on. Ganey'll look after your troop for a couple of miles."

Sunlight was glowing stronger from the east, riding on the soft breeze of an Indian-summer dawn, as Kirk trotted on. Elms and locust trees trailed long shadows over the hazy grass and the bulk of the ginhouse threw out a black rectangle. By a stretch of neat rail fence, Kirk reined in and looked back. There was a fine grove of locusts just off to the west and over its tops a stone wall showed in a gray, shimmery bar across the slope of Winstead Hill. East of the pike a long hedge of Osage orange stirred its spiky branches in the wind.

He looked farther down the pike. His own troop, with Jake's and Mark's, was pulling well over to the right of the highway, as though making room for some oncoming body that he could not see, and the narrow gap between the two prominent knobs was empty. Then it was filled by the bulk of a whitetop, another, still another looming behind it, coming on endlessly. Over a cart path that paralleled the pike a four-gun battery of artillery jolted along and distant flecks of scarlet guidons told of others following.

Kirk's fingers drummed on his pommel. He had taken it for granted that most of the wagons and guns, which must cross the Harpeth ahead of anything else, were well beyond the main body, probably in Franklin itself. Yet the wagons still came on and more batteries emerged from pools of shadow out in the fields, clanked on north. This could only mean that infantry units were still on the pike, clear back to Spring Hill, eight or ten miles away from Carter's Knoll.

He started his horse again. Here was the Carter place on his left, a few outbuildings of brick or wood, a trim story-and-a-half brick house set well back from the pike.

Its woodwork was white and a fine fanlight brought sharp memories of other houses along the Merrimac or the Piscataqua. The front door was open and an elderly man, two women close behind him, was watching a few blue-jacketed orderlies picketing horses beyond the smooth lawn. A brass-spiked pole sunk deep in the turf bent as the breeze fluttered out a red and white flag bearing the single star of a brigadier.

Beyond the house Kirk straightened up as the whole pattern of the terrain took shape before him. There was the village of Franklin just below him with white steeples soaring from a mass of roofs and trees while the Harpeth wound about it in a great twisted horseshoe of living water. The Union position could be anchored with each flank touching the river like a straight line across the open end of a warped U. Off to the east a deep railway cutting ended at a shattered bridge that ran onto the steep north bank. A battery of artillery was emerging from a ford near the bridge and climbing a twisting road that led to a high, round hill scarred with earthworks, probably the Fort Granger of which he had heard earlier. The guns were rifled Parrotts and from the fort they could command the cutting, the fields beyond it, perhaps even the slope on which the ginhouse and the Carter buildings looked down. Carter's Knoll was a fine defensive position—if only there were a few thousand more troops to man it.

Suddenly the reason for his ride, overlaid as it had been by professional thoughts, sprang back into his mind. As he followed the sharp turn where the Columbia pike bent eastward into the village, the long east-west main street lay before him as on a map. It was thick with the blue files of Wood's division, hurrying on to the fords, but nowhere, not even in the broad square, could he see a single wagon.

He touched his spurs to his horse and trotted up the left flank of a column of Indiana infantry that stumbled along like sleepwalkers, staring up at him from reddened eyes. Then at the first crossway, marked West Margin Street, he pulled in. Whoever was in charge of traffic certainly knew his business, for bulky whitetops stood waiting along the north–south streets, leaving those that led east to the fords unobstructed. He hailed the nearest driver, whose wagon bore IV Corps markings. "Where are the Cavalry Corps wagons?" he called.

The driver turned a stupid face toward him. "We're IV."

"I know. I'm looking for the Cavalry wagons."

"Dunno. We're IV."

Kirk rode on impatiently past the looming whitetops. Bridge Street on his right, leading to the river, was empty. Then West Margin ended and he swung into North Margin and passed other streets, Indigo, Cross Main, all packed like the others with IV Corps vehicles and still no driver or harassed officer could or would tell him anything of Wilson's wagons.

Cameron Street, and more IV Corps and a battery of artillery. Then at the corner Kirk saw a tall man with a glossy new Union overcoat slung about his shoulders talking with a group of civilians. The man turned his head, showing a rather weather-worn face and neatly trimmed, square, iron-gray beard. Kirk vaulted from his horse. "Mr. Stockdale! Is Lynn all right?"

Ian Stockdale faced him. "Ah, good morning, Captain Stedman. My daughter"—he gave the slightest emphasis to the word—"is quite well. I've just been telling these gentlemen something of our adventures. Perfectly extraordinary. They are natives of Tennessee and yet they've never seen their own mountains!"

"But Lynn—"

Stockdale inclined his head to the civilians. "If you'll excuse me for a moment, gentlemen. Captain Stedman was with us in your mountains." He stepped close to a battered wagonside. "Yes. My daughter told me, naturally enough, of your talk together. You can't blame me for being surprised, though you mustn't take that as

314

any reflection on you personally. I have great confidence in Lynn's judgment and level head and she assures me that you two have come to no definite understanding."

"I have, so far as I'm concerned, sir. I only hope that Lynn—"

"Exactly. But you won't want to hurry her decision. Our wagon leaves quite shortly from the next street and General Schofield, who received me most courteously, has given us a pass on the first train north from Nashville. We shall have a long journey ahead of us and she will have ample time to make up her mind." He smoothed out his beard. "I was disappointed, though, that the General did not feel that he should receive that report which I've prepared on our abduction by you. He says that it should go to General Thomas at Nashville. Confoundedly odd, the trouble I've had in delivering it. First Major Millard, then General Wilson and now—"

"Excuse me, sir. I've left my command to come here and find out—"

Stockdale smiled unexpectedly and laid a hand on Kirk's shoulder. "To find out where Lynn is. It would have been fairer if I'd told you right at the start. She's in that house, there, back of the lilac hedge. The owner, Mrs. Iverson, took her in so she could rest."

"There?" cried Kirk. "Will you tell her that I'm here?"

Stockdale smiled again. "The front walk is only a dozen feet away. I imagine she'll recognize you when she sees you." He nodded, turned back to the untraveled civilians.

The lilac hedge was a fine, thick growth, tough enough, Kirk thought automatically, to hold up a rush of infantry, and as he ran up the walk, the hedge's high stems shut out the crowded side street as though a curtain had been dropped. There was a well-polished double door set in mellow brick, and before he could reach for the bright brass knocker, both sections flew open and Lynn stood there, eyes wide in unbelief and then lighting up in a flood of warmth. "Lynn! Last night—" his words tumbled out—"I couldn't go to you—was it bad?"

Her arms went toward him, then checked. She caught at his hand and drew him into the yard. "Not in the house. Your uniform! They've sons with General Hood." All at once she was in his arms, clinging close. "Yes, it was awful—without you, not knowing about you. Nothing much happened, really. People kept coming out of the dark and firing at the wagons, but it was always a long way behind us, oh, a very long way. And we had to leave the Lewisburg Pike and go over dreadful roads. It's been worse this morning, not knowing where to look for you and wondering if anything had happened!"

He pressed his cheek close to hers, stroking her hair, holding her, so soft in the familiar brown homespun. "No need to talk, darling, so long as we're both thinking what we thought on the path to the camp last night."

"Every word of it, and, Kirk, you'll cross right away, won't you? We'll be getting an army train out of Nashville just as soon as we get there and you simply must be with us."

He repressed a start, then stroked her shoulder. "As quick as I can. We'll follow just as soon as the guns and wagons are over the fords."

Her hands tightened on his sleeves. "But you and the others have got to be sent back to the Army of the Potomac. Everyone says so."

"Yes, just as soon as General Wilson releases us."

"You can't be more definite than that?" Her eyes dropped. "Kirk! The men were saying that there's going to be fighting right here, that General Hood's coming on with all his force. Mrs. Iverson's getting out Confederate flags to welcome him."

He tried to smile. "Remember all that talk about battles when we were with Major Millard? Every day they said we were walking into one and nothing ever happened. All we have to do is wait until our wagons and guns are across the Harpeth and then we follow. Hood is miles away."

She was silent for a moment, then raised her head with a rather tremulous smile. "So I needn't have worried, need I? Now please take me to our wagon. My things are there and I've said good-by to the Iversons."

He caught her hand as they went down the walk. "If I should miss you at Nashville, dearest, there'll be plenty of trains rolling north. I'll be on the next one to yours or the one after that."

He could barely hear her words. "Do try to be with me. I feel pulled apart so much. I—I want General Hood to win." Her nails dug into his palm. "But you—darling, I can't want that when I think of you."

They joined Ian Stockdale and followed him down North Margin Street, Kirk leading his horse. Lynn pointed. "There are our wagons, by the river. They said we could wait by the ford and get on there. It's just beyond that burned wagon bridge."

A driver waved from the nearest whitetop, marked with crossed sabers. Kirk stopped. "Is that yours?"

"That one in the field," said Stockdale. "The driver's an extraordinarily competent chap. Civil, too."

Lynn cried, "There go some wagons into the ford. IV Corps. We follow them."

Kirk watched the heavy whitetops lurch into the Harpeth. The passage was going to take an appallingly long time. What a ghastly pity that the wagon bridge had been burned beyond repair, along with the railroad bridge farther east.

Stockdale exclaimed, "That looks like part of our escort coming down to the river from the next street. Thought they stayed—"

"It's not our escort!" Lynn cried. "It's—yes—Captain Pitler's leading them." She began waving.

Jake whooped, clattered over with Mark Furber behind him. "Just the people I was looking for! Save seats for us on the first train out of Nashville, will you?"

Lynn's face lit up. "I knew you'd all be coming with us. Kirk keeps talking about 'as soon as General Wilson releases us.' "

"Oh, Kirk's so pessimistic that he'd lower lifeboats in a dead calm. Say, Kirk, they wouldn't let us go through Cross Main the way you said, so I brought my troop and the rest down here to water. But our way'll be clear in about ten minutes." He touched Lynn's arm. "Watch out for these engineer boys. Guess they're going to scrape the ford banks." He stepped aside as a column of earth-stained men, laden with rifles, picks and shovels, clumped down toward the river.

Mark hopped up on a low mound to watch them. Then he cried, "Why doesn't someone do something about that bridge? The pilings are sound. You could saw down to clear wood, level off the tops, then put on new stringers and planks. It'd hold infantry, maybe even wagons."

A gruff voice behind snapped, "Who said that?"

They all turned and Kirk, Jake and Mark came to attention. A thickset man with major general's stars had ridden up and was glaring at Mark while one hand pulled at the beard that forked out from each side of his clean-shaven chin. He had a small-featured face that looked puffily irritable, Kirk thought. Then he noticed the steady eyes and mouth and changed his estimate.

"I said it, sir," answered Mark.

"I'm General Schofield and I'd like to inquire just why a Cavalry captain takes it upon himself to criticize the Corps of Engineers."

"I was just wondering, sir. I've built bridges in civil life, railroad bridges."

Schofield leaned forward, crossed his arms on his pommel, eyes darting from Mark to the bridge. Then he said, "How many men, what tools and supplies would be needed?"

"As an estimate, sir, about a hundred men, twenty saws, twenty kegs of spikes and—"

318

"How about lumber?"

"Knock down those sheds, sir. The wood's heavy and sound."

Four weary-eyed aides clattered up behind Schofield. Without looking around, the General rasped, "Here at last, are you? Get this officer's name and unit. Send an order to his commanding officer relieving him of all other duties. See that he gets the men and the stuff that he needs. He's detailed here till the job's done. Let Captain Twining of the Engineers know." He straightened, stared at Lynn and her father as though seeing them for the first time. Then he smiled, took off his hat. "Sorry we didn't know about this young man earlier or you might be on your way to Nashville now." He bowed, set his horse at the ford, three of his aides splashing after him.

Jake looked reverently at Mark. "Say, one of the rings on my canteen strap's busted. Suppose—suppose maybe you could fix it for me?"

Mark laughed. "When I get this bridge job done." He turned to Lynn, kepi in hand. "Be sure and save those seats for us. Maybe we'll be along quicker than we thought. All right, Lieutenant, show me where the men and the tools are." He mounted, rode off with a farewell wave.

Lynn squeezed Kirk's hand. "Now everything's beginning to go right!" Then the light in her eyes faded. "Our wagon! Oh, not yet, not yet!"

Kirk's hands closed over hers. "Sweetheart, you've been detailed to go to Nashville to arrange for transportation and—" He tried to go on lightly, then, regardless of onlookers, bent, felt her arms straining about him. Abruptly she turned, sprang onto the seat where her father held out a hand to her. The mules plunged forward, the wheels hissed into the blue waters of the Harpeth. As the wagon rocked across, Kirk, jaw tight and hands clenched, stared after it. Lynn was hidden by

319

the tall hood, but he caught a last flutter of gray, a flick of bright canary.

Bridle over his arm, he walked off to the troopers at the watering place, and Jake clattered up to him. "Now, here's what I figure, Kirk. We'll bust Mark's troop two ways, thirty-five men apiece."

"Guess so," muttered Kirk.

"See, with those noncoms of his and a lot of his boys serving together before, we can really show Wilson something on the Triune road."

"They'll fit in somehow."

"Sure. Line 'em up, one four of yours, one of Mark's, one of yours and so on. Same for my men."

Kirk roused himself a little. "What'll I do with Ganey? I can't make him step down for one of Mark's men. He's done a good job so far."

"But Mark didn't have a top sergeant, so Ganey's all right."

"H'm. Divide the troop in two. Ganey'll take half and Mark's senior sergeant the other. We'll have close to a hundred men apiece, but they'll shake down on the road."

"Yep. You've got the senior troop, so you do the sorting out."

Kirk mounted and rode ahead, shouting, "Noncommissioned officers, Provisional Troop C, report here at once."

Jake smiling to himself, swung into his saddle and followed Kirk.

18

"Their Leaders Fallen
Their Standards Lost"

Two miles out on the Triune road, Kirk drew off to one side and watched the troopers ride past. It was the first time that he had seen them by daylight. The march to and up the Columbia pike had been at night, and on the short stretch over from Franklin, he and Jake had been too busy with reorganization to have a good look at them. As the fours went past him, his mind, through long habit and training, began to cast up an estimate.

Although the men swayed in their saddles from lack of sleep, many of the squads kept a very fair dress and there was no straggling. His attention darted to the all-important horses. Here and there he noted a limp or an uneven gait that told of a saddle galling back or shoulders. A bad case or two of mange. Clinking sounds meant that several mounts would have to go to the blacksmiths at Wilson's field forges.

His eyes went to the troopers again. Their equipment was well tended and every canteen was soaked, showing that the men had filled them. The uniforms were more than odd. The men wore broad-brimmed hats, kepis, even a few of the ghastly, feathered "Fra Diabolos" under which the Regular cavalry had ridden sheepishly before the war. There were short, neat cavalry jackets, dizzily frogged and braided bandsmen's coats, civilian frock coats. Some unfortunates had been issued voluminous, fuchsia-colored zouave pantaloons.

A deep, self-important voice behind him intoned, "A fine body of men, Captain."

He turned, swore in disgust as Jake grinned at him from the back of a strawberry roan. "Hell, I thought you were a field marshal at least! Let's go on and report to Wilson. His flag's up ahead there."

"You go. I'm scared of generals since Schofield press-ganged Mark. I'm dreaming of someone with two stars grabbing me and making me chop wood or balance a ledger or do embroidery." He raised his voice. "Column—ha-a-a-lt! Troopers dismount! Loosen cinches! Smooth out your saddle blankets and sponge out the nostrils."

Kirk waved to Jake and rode on toward the flag that fluttered in the warm haze of the morning. Horses were picketed in the fields and troopers were sleeping near them, heedless of the sun that beat in their faces. He saw the markings of the 8th Iowa, 4th Kentucky, 2nd Michigan, 1st Tennessee, then a single-starred flag with a heavily mustached brigadier snoring under it. As Kirk made for the two-starred flag, Lieutenant Hedges, commander of Wilson's cavalry escort, called to him from under a sere-leafed apple tree. "Good morning, Captain. You made good time getting here and the General won't mind it one bit."

Kirk dismounted. "Glad of that. Where is he?"

Hedges laughed. "Off on the south bank, inspecting the fords and pushing out vedettes."

"No sign of Forrest?"

"Not since early morning. Funny, he usually moves

faster than this. You and Pitler and the rest better get some sleep till the General yells for you. You'll find water and good cover in that draw off to the south there. Now tell me what you need and I'll see that you get it." He flipped open a notebook to a fresh page, jotting down the date, November 30, 1864.

It was well past noon when Kirk struggled up out of deep slumber, roused by Sergeant Ganey's hand on his shoulder. Ganey jerked a thumb at the south crest of the draw. "The General, sir. Thought the Captain would like to know."

Kirk got to his feet, rubbing his eyes. Wilson's slim, boyish figure was sharp against the hazy warmth of the sky, erect, a pair of binoculars raised. "Thanks, Sergeant. Better get Captain Pitler up, too. Oh, there he is, on his feet. Come on, Jake! Let's find out what we're supposed to be doing."

Kirk started up the slope, Jake scrambling on behind him. Wilson still stood motionless, his glasses steady. But something about their angle puzzled Kirk. The Cavalry general should have been scanning the lands to the south over which Forrest's tough troopers would sooner or later come pouring. Instead, the lenses seemed to be focused on Carter's Knoll off to the west, that same rise with its brick house over which Kirk had passed earlier.

The General turned abruptly as he heard the clank of sabers behind him. "Good morning, gentlemen," he said with a tight smile. "You did a fine job getting over here. I had reports from Hedges and others." His glasses lifted again, swung toward Carter's knoll, clearly visible in the west. "Yes. Very good work." Then he let the binoculars swing from their strap and Kirk caught a glint of hard, professional satisfaction in the young eyes. "I've been south out there. My patrols have made contact with Forrest." Wilson's mouth tightened. "I can handle Forrest. He'll never get across those fords. I can handle him with what I've got right here." He swung suddenly toward

Kirk. "But I'm scared stiff about Carter's Knoll off there. General Cox is in command and he's thin, too damn thin. Take your commands and report to him, dismounted, to be used as he sees fit."

Kirk's heart sank. "We're not to act as cavalry, sir?"

"You'll act as Union soldiers where you're needed most. Get your men moving right away." He seemed to forget about Kirk and Jake, raised his glasses and swung them south. With a tight smile he said, "I've got him, by God, I've got Forrest."

Kirk started back, bitterly disappointed. A crucial action was pending in which his arm of the service was to be pitted against one of the greatest cavalry leaders. There would be sharp, grueling work along the fords and he could not catch the infection of Wilson's hard confidence. While the struggle was going on, his men and Jake's would be jammed into the works going up along Carter's Knoll, chained to an infantry action in which painfully acquired skills and experience would count for little.

Jake's hand fell on his shoulder. "Never mind, this is just for today, and I'm betting that later we'll have all the chances we'll ever want to go out and play with Mrs. Forrest's boy. Anyway, if someone with two stars says you're wading through snow now, he's damn well right and you're mutinous if you don't agree with him. Let's get the boys moving."

Stripped of its horses, the nondescript column of about two hundred men tramped south through Main Street, trouser bottoms still soggy from the ford at the end of Cross Main Street. Kirk walked with Jake on the left flank. A few wagons still rolled in from the south, but the side streets, so jammed before, were empty and there were wide gaps between the rear of one whitetop and the noses of the mules that followed it. Most of the homes, neat cottages and larger brick houses alike, were shuttered and the doors were tightly closed. Union

324

colors fluttered hopefully or prudently from a few windows and there were some Confederate flags, brightly defiant. As they came onto the Columbia pike, Jake cried, "Hear what that driver was yelling? They're running wagons, big ones, over Mark's bridge. Hey! What's this—muster day? Look at all the soldiers!"

The reverse slope of Carter's Knoll was thick with troops, settling down on both sides of the pike after a wearying march. Men were taking off their shoes and slapping their feet or rubbing their shoulders where packs had chafed. Here and there bright silk was swallowed in oilcloth as color sergeants drew waterproof casings down over furled flags. Officers knelt in little groups, talking in low tones or scribbling in tattered field notebooks. Kirk's men shouted, "Hey, what outfit?" Tired voices answered, "Opdycke's brigade, Wagner's division," or "24th Wisconsin," or, "125th Ohio."

"Thats the roof of the Carter house over those trees," said Kirk. "We can have Ganey fall out the men while we report to General Cox."

"You do the reporting. You salute better than I do."

"All right. Be back as soon as I can." Kirk went on up the gentle slope that was thick with blue uniforms. Staff officers were mounting and dismounting. Long columns of infantry moved off to the right at the double, haversacks flapping and rifles jarring against shoulders. Some fifty feet south of the house, shirt-sleeved men were whacking away with picks and shovels, scooping out a trench line that ran west through the fields past the farm office and the brick smokehouse. Less than a hundred yards still farther south, men were clustering along the first line of works. Sweating gunners rolled a four-gun battery into position just at the left of the pike. Off by the ginhouse, limbers were dropping two more pieces.

The front door of the Carter house was open and the same old man whom Kirk had seen that morning was looking anxiously out, one hand holding back a fretful little boy while a pinafored girl peered past his elbow. Under a locust tree in the front yard a bearded brigadier with a lined, weatherbeaten face frowned over some papers. Kirk swung toward him, saluting. "General Cox, sir? I'm from General Wilson."

The brigadier turned weary but pleasant eyes on Kirk. "From General Wilson, eh? What can I do for you?" Kirk made his report and the tired eyes brightened. "That's damn fine of Wilson. Yes, I certainly can use you, every man I can scrape up. Where's your command?"

"At the right of the pike, sir, this side of Colonel Opdycke's brigade."

Cox stuffed the papers in his pocket. "Put yourself under Opdycke's orders. If Hood doesn't attack, fall back with Opdycke to the north bank of the Harpeth."

Kirk's eyes widened. "But Hood's sure to attack, isn't he? General Wilson was in touch with Forrest's advance when we left."

Cox pursed his lips. "Hood's main force is over the other side of Winstead Hill, about three miles south of us. But it's after three o'clock now and the sun sets at five. Time's running away from Hood. Well, late as it is, he still may attack, and if he does, he'll come hellbending with his men steamed up like locomotives. Last summer at Atlanta they came on yowling and throwing rocks and hunks of wood at us. So better take a good look at the ground ahead here and then report to Opdycke. I'm going over to the far left, back of Stiles's position, and see if I can make out anything." He called for his horse and rode off.

Kirk surveyed the terrain and found that its main features had stamped themselves on his mind that morning. Beyond the first line of Union works the Columbia–Franklin pike ran on south, dipping down the slope of the knoll, flowing smoothly over a level stretch, then rising to climb the shouldering bulk of Winstead Hill. Far

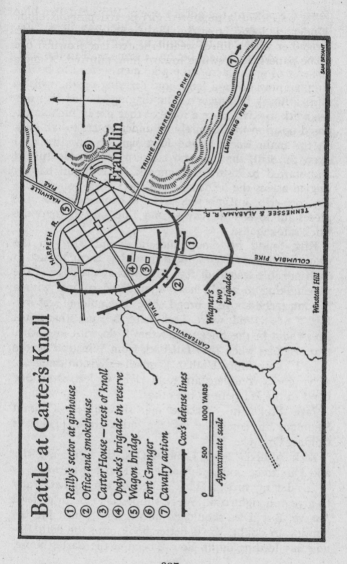

Battle at Carter's Knoll

1. Reilly's sector at ginhouse
2. Office and smokehouse
3. Carter House — crest of knoll
4. Opdycke's brigade in reserve
5. Wagon bridge
6. Fort Granger
7. Cavalry action

▬▬ Cox's defense lines

Franklin

NASHVILLE PIKE

HARPETH R.

TRIUNE — MURFREESBORO PIKE

LEWISBURG PIKE

TENNESSEE & ALABAMA R. R.

COLUMBIA PIKE

CARTERSVILLE PIKE

Wagner's two brigades

Winstead Hill

SAM BRYANT

Approximate scale
0   500   1000 YARDS

down the pike, up the north slope of Winstead, two blue brigades lay east and west of the highway in a wide, shallow V that pointed south up the hill. There was cover for many of them behind a stone wall to the west, but east of it and across the pike men seemed to be digging, ripping down a fence and carrying off the rails to form a flimsy breastwork. The digging seemed like useless work to Kirk, since a force of that size in such an exposed position would surely be under orders to fall back on the main works at the least sign of any attack in strength. Still, that was no concern of his. He turned and started back to his command. A four-gun battery jingled across the fields between the Carter house and a big corn-crib, unlimbered, and the cannoneers ran the pieces up to the sketchy second line, just beyond the brick smokehouse.

Kirk found his troop and Jake's sprawled on the ground, their veteran's instinct telling them to snatch each possible second of rest. Jake was at the edge of the pike talking to a tall, heavy-shouldered colonel with a big mustache above a broad chin. The colonel was saying, " . . . and we're back here because there just isn't room in the lines. What they'll do with our other two brigades when they fall back from Winstead's more than I know. Since Nathan Kimball's division came up, we've got a complete arc from right to left, from one bend in the Harpeth to the other."

Jake broke in, "Excuse me, sir, this is Captain Stedman, in command of the other troop. This is Colonel Opdycke, Kirk."

Kirk saluted. "From General Cox, sir. Captain Pitler and I are to be under your orders till further notice."

"Under my orders? That's fine, though I haven't any to give you right now. We're supposed to be in general reserve. But if we should go into action, which I'm beginning to doubt, you'd better hook onto the 88th Illinois, my leading outfit. You've been at the Carter house, haven't you? Could you see anything of our other brigades, Conrad's and Lane's, way out on the pike?"

"In plain sight, sir. They're entrenching out from the stone wall."

Opdycke frowned. *"Entrenching?* What the hell for? They're to come plowing back here if Hood shows the least strength against them. Well, come on over to the 88th Illinois and meet Colonel Smith."

A few minutes later Kirk and Jake lay on the grass at the crest of the knoll. Men were still working frantically at the second defense line and a team of horses was dragging up a fallen locust tree, sluing it around to form a natural entanglement. Kirk shook his head. "Hate to see trees go. That grove was lovely this morning and now it's a mess of stumps."

"Sure, but that line'll look lovely with all those branches sticking out to trip up Rebs. Look, another general over by the oak. Must be General Wagner. Wish he'd whistle his boys in from Winstead, so we could all go home." He sat up, listening, then cupped his hands about his mouth. "Oompah, oompah, oompah! Who's giving us the pretty music?"

"I don't hear anything. Yes—got it now, but it's not from our lines." Kirk sprang to his feet. "It's more than just bands, Jake."

There was no mistaking the sound. From the hidden south, drums were beating, a soft, fuzzy rapping that slowly grew, a score of drums, forty, fifty, a hundred. The band music died, but the staccato beat rolled on. *Br-r-r-rm! Br-r-r-rrmm!* The beat was clearer now. *Br-r-r-r-rrrmmm!*

Kirk looked back. A few yards down the slope the men of Troops A and B were struggling to their knees, faces toward the south and eyes questioning. A ripple passed over Opdycke's six regiments and hands went instinctively to cartridge pouches. Opdycke, standing in the middle of the road with his colonels, caught Kirk's glance and nodded to show that he too had caught the sounds.

"God!" shouted Jake, leaping up. Kirk faced about.

The bare sky line of Winstead was broken, tattered, and a long, long wave of dark figures flowed north over the crest while drums beat on, insistent, menacing. *Br-r-r-rrm!* From far right to far left the dark lines came on in open order, unhurriedly, surely. The crest was empty, filled again, and line after solid line of companies rolled north behind their skirmishers. *Brrr-rrr-mm!* Red and blue battle flags of the Confederacy flowered like quick-opening tropical blooms against the dun of the hillside, while drummers on every company flank rapped out the ominous beat. *Br-r-r-r-rrrmm! Br-r-r-r-rrrmmmm!* On they came with a flash of bright bayonets and the streaming red and blue high overhead.

"Coming on in brigade columns!" muttered Kirk. "Look! Batteries trotting up in the intervals!"

Jake cleared his throat uncertainly. "Yeh, we got callers! And where the hell is General Cox? Isn't his post up here by the house?"

But Kirk was staring at the shallow blue arrow that lay across the pike on the hillside, pointing south toward the steady advance. "Wagner's men! God Almighty! Are they going to sit on their butts all day?"

Jake was yellin, "Get out, get out, get out. It'll be too late if—"

A few yards away, General Wagner, frock coat open over a sweat-streaked shirt, was waving a cane and roaring, "We're going to stand there and fight! Stand right there!" An aide was shouting, "But, sir, but, sir! Orders! Don't you remember, sir? To fall back before any show of strength?"

Wagner's stick waved higher. "Damn the orders. That little Dutch Conrad of mine'll rip the hell out of 'em! He's got *my* orders to, and Lane!"

Jake's eyes were blank as a sleepwalker's. "Kirk! Wagner said, 'Rip the hell out of 'em!' Two little brigades against—" Jake licked his dry lips and was silent.

Close by Kirk, a scholarly-looking major observed dispassionately, "Ah, yes, Wagner's making the same mistake that General Pennefather did at Inkerman in the Crimea in '54. Trying to meet a main attack with outposts. Interesting." The major suddenly turned away and was violently sick.

The fringes of the dark lines were crowding closer to the shallow V on Winstead Hill. *Br-r-r-r-rrrrmm! Br-r-r-r-r-rrrrmmmm!* Little gouts of smoke spurted out from the stone wall, from the pitifully shallow shelters to the east, were answered from the dark clouds of skirmishers. For a moment the advance wavered, checked, and a prolonged burst of rifle fire lashed out from the V. The dark knots and the dark lines gathered, poised. The drums beat on. Then the storm broke.

Kirk had heard the Rebel yell often enough, but never had it come to him in such a high burst of frenzied intensity, soaring, piercing, spanning the three quarters of a mile between him and the nearest waves. It seemed to strike full on him and him alone. It was direct, personal, marking him down, beyond any help from the thousands of his fellows on Carter's Knoll.

And there was visible fury in the onset. Men in the gray ranks waved their arms, seemed to be reaching out with clutching hands at the blue V. Mounted officers, colonels and generals, rode between the surging lines, standing in their stirrups, turning in their saddles to whip their men on with sweeping flashes of sword blades. And high above all the battle flags sailed like flights of bright-winged birds, screaming and triumphant.

Now Kirk could see that the great unbroken line was gray, not merely dark, and the drumheads were booming white disks on the company flanks. The pattern changed as he watched. The Rebel lines were a V, free-flowing on the wings but bent back in the center by the shallow blue arrow where Conrad and Lane stood their ground like a blue rock in a swift-flowing tide of gray, magnificent in their very helplessness. Then the blue rock was gone, the Rebel yell keened higher and higher and down the center of the hill rolled a confused mass of blue and gray, rolling toward the very heart of the Carter's Knoll defenses.

And where was General Cox? Kirk had last seen him riding off to the far left of the line. His horse might have fallen with him, a stray bullet might have found him, any number of commonplace combat accidents might have kept him from his post at the moment that he was most needed, when a controlling hand at the Union core might have staved off disaster. Whatever the cause, he was not on the knoll and aides and officers were shouting urgently, desperately for him.

Suddenly Kirk was yelling, waving his kepi above his head. All along the first defense line, answering brightness billowed out in the soft, smoky air. The Union colors marked the center of each regiment and beside them sailed the flags of a dozen states—Illinois and Iowa, Ohio and Indiana, Pennsylvania, Kentucky, Missouri, Kansas, Tennessee—then smoke began to dim the bright hues as rifle fire plunged south from the first entrenchments. Left and right, by the ginhouse, the pike, off beyond the brick farm office, bronze Napoleons let go their coughing thuds. Far to the rear a series of sharp cracks stabbed the air and there were quick devil screeches high overhead, eruptions of red-flecked smoke over the attackers as the long-range Parrotts from Fort Granger on the north bank broke their silence. But the high-pitched yell soared on and the assault quickened.

By the gap where the pike entered the works, an officer was shouting, "Hold your fire! Hold your fire! General Strickland's orders. God damn it, you're shooting down your own men!" A horse danced past Kirk and General Wagner raged in the saddle, swinging his cane, yelling, "The bastards, the cowardly bastards. They ran!

332

My men ran!" Kirk took one more look at the pike and the fields that edged it. Without the least trace of order, the mixed torrent of blue and gray poured on toward the works. From the Union right and left, regular, controlled volleys blasted out, but in the center the defenders stood helpless, rifles useless in their hands. And the battle cry of the Confederacy keened higher and higher. Then he heard himself say in a quiet tone that surprised him, "We better get the boys on their feet, Jake. Opdycke'll be wanting us."

Jake's eyes were no longer blank. "You damn fool, you gave them stand-to a good three minutes ago!" He grinned. "Come on. The Rebs are acting quarrelsome."

Opdycke was a few yards away on the pike, talking with the colonel of the 125th Ohio. "Orders were positive. Move only on orders from General Cox, and nothing's come from him. You all right, Stedman and Pitler? Good. Just keep aligned with A Company of the 88th and—"

Kirk shouted, "Colonel Opdycke! Wagner's division has been smashed. Our center'll cave in, sure as hell!"

Opdycke's broad chin jutted and he whipped out his Colt. "Damn orders!" His voice slammed like a field piece. "The command is 'Forward, double time!' "

Kirk slipped in at the left flank of his troop between a cavalryman and a slouch-hatted Illinoisan of the 88th, shouting, "Ganey! Keep our right closed with Captain Pitler's left." Then he was swept on with the whole line. He had a weird feeling that his feet were not touching the ground, that he was being carried along by a heavy torrent. There were deep-throated roars all about him and from the rear he heard the pound of hundreds of boots as the rest of the brigade followed, echeloned out to the right and left. A few yards in front, Colonel Opdycke drove on, big shoulders lowered and head drawn in like a boxer's, closing with an opponent.

They were at the crest of the knoll with the Carter house looming through smoke at the right front. A wave

333

of fugitives in blue, hatless, weaponless, raced toward them, eyes pale in flushed faces. Kirk shouted, "Open up and let 'em through. They're Wagner's men. Let 'em through and close up!" A horse reared among the flying men and General Wagner slashed down right and left with his cane, yelling, "Stand and fight, God damn you!" Then the General was borne out of sight in the rout.

The two tides met, mingled, but Opdycke's brigade drove on. The fugitives were thicker now. Some had kept their arms, were looking about as though seeking a rallying point. Kirk cried, "Close with us. You, Corporal, get your men into our line."

Then from the uproar that raged ahead a single voice rang out, triumphant and unmistakably Southern. "Follow 'em in! Right into their works with 'em! We got 'em, we got 'em!" Confederate colors tossed and flapped in the smoke where the pike entered Cox's lines and swarms of bewildered men in blue poured north, sweeping around Opdycke's flanks, butting through his lines. Opdycke bellowed, "Forward! Forward! They've got into our works!" A bloody-faced sergeant rammed a flagstaff into the ground and stood knee-deep in dust and swirling smoke, yelling, "Rally on me!" Kirk recognized the flag of the 44th Missouri and read disaster in it. The 44th had been in the first line at the right of the pike and must have given way along with Wagner's flying men. Then he saw more disordered clusters of blue east and west of the Carter house. The whole center must have been smashed.

All at once there was gray before him and a confused mass of Confederate infantry swirled on toward Opdycke's front. The screeching yells were higher, sharper. Kirk shouted, "Hold your fire. In with the bayonet," and braced himself for the shock. Ahead, Opdycke's Colt was slamming away, was emptied. A gray man with a contorted face flung himself on the Colonel. The colt swung in a tight arc and the gray man slipped down, knees buckling. Then Kirk was in the midst of the melee himself.

Never before had he seen such fighting. Men threw down loaded rifles, sprang at each other with bare hands, fists smashing and knees driving up. He tripped over a snarling tangle of blue and gray that rolled with savage clawings and hoarse, animal cries. As he recovered, he had a glimpse of Opdycke jamming his smashed revolver into an oncoming face.

The gray mass was denser, pressing harder, and Kirk drove on, head lowered. A man rose in front of him, rifle butt poised. Kirk squeezed his Colt, felt the hammer click on an empty chamber, saw a bayonet dart out from under his own right arm, stab into the gray body that was so close. He hurled the empty weapon into an oncoming mass, stumbled over a rounded stone, snatched it up and sent it smashing after his Colt.

His feet went from under him and arms snapped about his chest, his knees. He rolled on the ground, trying to free himself, knew that a third man was dancing about him with a bayonet, waiting a chance to lunge. The bayonet was gone and the arms about him slackened. He struggled to his feet, saw three bodies on the turf and men in blue tramping past them. A bareheaded man thrust the bayoneted rifle into his hands. "The Captain better have this, sir," croaked a voice.

Kirk clutched the barrel, panting, "Thanks, Ganey!" took a step backward and brought up against a brick wall. "Carter house. How'd I get here?" he thought dizzily. His head cleared and off to the right he saw Jake, dropping to one knee and firing carefully into the smoke and dust ahead. Someone was yelling, "We're driving 'em, driving the God-damn Rebs!"

The second defense line, with the wooden office and the brick smokehouse looming over the improvised works, was just ahead and gray figures were lunging toward it from the first line. Kirk shouted, "The guns! They'll get the guns!" The four Napoleons stood off to the right, a few dead gunners lying about them. Kirk waved to his men. "Troop A! Follow me!" and began to sprint, leaping over bodies, over huddled, writhing wounded. Smoke thickened about the guns, eddied away and gray knots were pushing hard toward the silent pieces. The trail of the nearest gun was ten yards away, five—Kirk dove forward, snatched at the trailing lanyard as he hit the ground. A howling redhead in torn gray flung a rifle at him and he felt the butt smash against his shoulder. The lanyard was in his hand and the redhead had seized a length of fence rail and was jamming it down the muzzle of the Napoleon, probably with some wild idea of disabling the gun. Kirk tugged at the lanyard, praying that the piece had been left loaded. There was a shattering roar, and the piece shot back in recoil as he rolled clear. He staggered to his feet in time to see the long rail go whirling end over end into a mass of charging Confederates. He felt deathly sick as the rail struck like a vast, whirling knife. A head rolled clear onto the grass, men lay clutching ripped bellies, dragged themselves off, trailing mangled arms and legs. Clean, honest killing was one thing, but this—

Strong hands caught him by the shoulders, shook him, and Jake, white-faced, panted, "When you hit 'em, you sure hit 'em." Kirk stifled his retching. "The damn fool, jamming that rail into the gun. What harm did he think it'd do?"

"Huh! Plenty of harm, but not the way he figured." Jake rubbed an unsteady palm across his face.

For the moment, Kirk forgot the involuntary butchery that he had caused out in the field and studied his friend. "Had a bad time?"

"Seen easier. Haven't had a chance to think about it yet. Anyway, we got a second to breathe now." He pointed south where a gray swarm was running back to the old first line, vaulting and scrambling to the ditch on the far side. Away off to the right and left the

336

struggle clanged on as fiercely as ever, but there was an odd hush over the immediate front.

"May not last as long as a second. Let's get the line straightened out. Hey, good enough." His troop was manning the inner side of the second line anchoring on the brick smokehouse, edging and spacing themselves right and left without command.

Jake spoke a little more briskly. "One thing about a bunch of old-timers like ours: Don't have to tell 'em what to do. Mine are tying on to your right. Damn, but this has been a close thing!"

Kirk wiped his forehead. "I didn't even know we were driving them till I brought up against the Carter house. What happened?"

"Opdycke," said Jake tersely.

"Lucky something did or we'd be wading the Harpeth now. Here come some gunners down past the big corncrib. Must be the crews that were chased away from these guns." He shouted, "Hi, Johnny Red-legs! Better take charge of your guns."

"Got other visitors, too," said Jake, sinking onto the trail of the nearest piece.

Colonel Opdycke, bare-headed and with a large, purpling bruise on his forehead, was coming toward them with General Cox. The General was saying, " . . . I'd have been here long ago, but my horse went crazy down by Stiles's left. Held me up quite a while. Anyhow, you did just what I'd have ordered if I'd been here. Now how about this position?"

"I can hold it. I've linked up with General Reilly on the left of the pike, so the Rebs have got just a loop of our old first line."

Cox pulled at his beard. "Pretty long loop, though. We'll want to chase them out of it. Why hasn't your 30th Illinois gone in?"

"Because we advanced in echelon, sir. They got squeezed out."

"I understand. Well, if you want them, why not pull

337

out Stedman's and Pitler's men and move the 30th down from behind the house? Colonel Strickland can give you room to your right if you need it. That suit you? Fine. And isn't that Stedman and Pitler right there by that piece?" He stepped nearer. "Good evening, gentlemen. The Colonel tells me you both did fine work and I won't forget it. Now the 30th Illinois will take over the line you're holding."

Kirk thought, "In reserve. Put us in reserve. Just thirty minutes to pull ourselves together."

As though reading the unspoken hope, Cox went on. "I can't put you in reserve, because we haven't got one. Also, General Reilly's pretty thin over by the ginhouse across the pike. So please get your commands ready and report to him."

The two troops marched in parallel columns, cutting a wide arc in behind the Carter house to avoid the stray shots that whined over from the south, and then heading east across rolling fields that hid the lines from them. The long-range guns back in Fort Granger were sending shells screeching away across the smoke-filled sky. Rifle and field-gun fire crashed louder and louder from the Union left. A weird, yellowish light covered the terrain, livid, opaque, like winter sunshine trying to cut through a fog. Jake shook his head. "Sun's mighty low. You see the same thing off Isle au Haut in thick weather about sundown."

"Maybe an hour of daylight left," said Kirk. "That slamming's getting heavier off there."

They pushed on east. Details of sweating men labored stubbornly across the fields, lugging heavy ammunition boxes, their feet slipping maddeningly on the slick brown grass. A steady trickle of wounded drifted north, eyes on the ground and hands clutching at hastily bandaged arms or thighs. The eerie light formed ghastly halos about them from head to foot as they loomed through the haze, monstrous, distorted.

Jake said, "I kind of liked it better back there by the

smokehouse. Wonder if Opdycke can really get on without us."

"Why worry about that?"

"Worries," said Jake, "are always waiting to happen to me."

"We'll have some fresh ones for you in a minute. We'll have to leave this dead space and slant up the slope to the right. That'll bring us to the ginhouse field. We better swing from column into line. It'll be handier if Reilly wants to use us in a hurry."

The roaring tumult swelled with each step that Kirk climbed. Then he topped the low crest and fifty yards away the gable end of the high-shouldered ginhouse seemed to float on the low-hanging clouds of smoke and dust, gold-tinted by the sun. Through the ground shimmer the front line showed vaguely, a low breastwork against which half-seen figures in blue were crowding, while others raced up to join them. Jake yelled across the advancing lines, "Something's going to bust off there."

"I know. Double time, Troop A." He raced for the near end of the ginhouse, calling, "General Reilly! Where's General Reilly? Reporting from General Cox!"

A smoke-stained man in a grimy shirt and broad hat marked with a star turned quickly. "I'm General Reilly. What do you want?"

"Just orders, sir, for myself and Captain Pitler."

Reilly waved a long arm. "Anywhere! Forward! Just jam in where you can. The Rebs are coming on again. Get in and hit!"

Kirk shouted over his shoulder, "You heard what the General said! Crowd in and get to work."

The earthen parapet was no more than four feet high, topped with heavy logs from under which dirt had been scooped to form crude loopholes. The inner side was ditched and Kirk had to crouch only a little to keep his head covered as he sprang onto the firing step, wedging himself in between two men at a loophole. He looked out and gave a sudden shout.

They were coming on, not a hundred yards away, rank after rank of gray men, bayonets aslant, yelling mouths open under broad hats and the warflags tossing and straining. They came diagonally down from the Columbia pike and across the fields, wave after wave. From the east, fresh masses were storming up, crowding against those directly in front. More and more came over a low rise, emerging against the strange misty gold of the sky line to sweep on after their fellows.

Someone yelled, "Fire at will!" and smoke ripped out from the parapet. A dozen yards to Kirk's left, two Napoleons slammed out through log embrasures. The gray waves spilled out little clots that rolled to the ground, lay there as boots pounded over them. The man at Kirk's right shrieked, "That's General Cleburne, Pat Cleburne. We're going to catch it now." Through the loophole Kirk saw a striking man magnificently mounted on a bay horse, tall and erect in the saddle, galloping diagonally across the advance, waving a gray hat and shouting. The bay leaped in the air, pitched to the ground, tried to struggle to its feet, collapsed. The gray rider lay pinned under him, motionless.

A man was punching Kirk's arm. "God-damn fool, what you come here without a gun for? Them Rebs ain't come to play!" A smoke-grimed hand thrust a rifle and cartridge pouch at him. Buckling on the pouch with sweating fingers, Kirk tried vaguely to remember where his Colt was, what had happened to the rifle that Ganey had given him. Why hadn't he realized that he was unarmed, why hadn't Jake noticed it? "Guess we were all pretty tired," he muttered between his teeth as he thrust the rifle under the head log. His finger froze on the trigger. The gray lines, ripped and torn but always closing up, were less than twenty yards away, the front rank firing as it came. There was no point in aiming. Fire into the gray of them, reload, and don't for

God's sake drop cartridge or rammer. Fire again, reload with fingers so hard to control.

There was gray in the ditch on the outer side of the works. A head, a torn gray coat swarmed up the earthen wall just in front of him and he jabbed with his bayonet, felt it meet tough flesh, then suddenly slide into something soft and yielding. The gray coat was gone, nearly tearing the rifle from his grasp as the wearer fell back into the ditch. His loophole was blanketed with more gray that struggled up and up. Fire blasted across his cheek and he flung himself to one side, looked up to see a man on the parapet, five men, a dozen, firing down into the inner ditch. He gripped his rifle by the barrel, swung hard at the backs of two gray knees, and a Confederate crashed, yelling, into the works, where blue arms seized him. Now the whole top was lined with gray and a white-faced officer was driving a flagstaff into the dirt and the starred St. Andrew's Cross of the South fluttered out.

There was blue on the parapet and men fought hand to hand as they had fought by the Carter house so long ago, over an hour ago. Something whacked against Kirk's neck and he snatched at it. His hand closed about the worn, smooth flagstaff and the Southern colors trailed along the fire step. He pushed the pole away, sighted on a man above him, but before he could pull the trigger, the man was gone. The whole parapet was clear of attackers.

He pressed back to his loophole, ears ringing with the crack and slam of rifle and fieldpiece. The gray waves were falling back, thinned and battered, over ground that was littered with dead and wounded. The fine bay horse still lay out on the grass and its rider was still pinned under it, motionless, one gray arm stretched out as though reaching for the hat with the wreathed general's insignia on it. So Irish Patrick Cleburne, the only foreign-born officer to reach major general's rank in the armies of the Confederacy, had led his last charge.

341

A man, sandy head bare and a rifle in his hand, jostled up beside Kirk, shoved him roughly away from the loophole. "Where the hell did you come from, Jake?" panted Kirk.

"I damn near came from the Angel Gabriel. Look!" He edged closer to the loophole, snatched suddenly into it, gave a hard tug and slowly drew a rifle through from the outer side. Someone beyond the works yelled in profane wrath. "See what I mean, Kirk? The Rebs got chased out, sure. But a hell of a lot of 'em are still in the outer ditch. They can't come over here. And if they try to go back, our boys'd plug 'em before they'd gone ten feet. Some of them are huddled down in the ditch, same as I'd be if I was a Reb. But a lot of 'em are still mad at us and keep shoving rifles under the head log and firing." He examined his trophy. "Guess I'll keep it. It's better than my old Springfield. Damn it, our pouches are getting empty, though."

Someone in the rear bawled, "Yeeeeay! The ammunition details! Hurry up, you men. Dump the cases anywhere."

"Saved!" muttered Jake, watching the long string of puffing men staggering on past the ginhouse with ammunition cases. Then another voice yelled, high and shrill, "Sweet Jesus! Watch the front. They're forming again!" Kirk dropped from the fire step, ran along the line. It was not hard to pick out his men. That feathered hat, this braided bandsman's jacket, the frock coat that had once been an officer's, those Zouave pantaloons. He tugged at the arm of each alternate man. "Fall out. Go to the rear. Draw ammunition for two men. That's it, Sergeant Ganey. Get 'em moving!" Back of the line someone was yelling, "Can't get the Goddamn things open!" And outside the Rebel yell ripped again and the drums took up their *Brr-r-r-rrrrmmm!* . . . *Brrr-r-r-rrrmm!* Kirk darted to the nearer casemated Napoleon, caught up an issue ax, calling to the outraged crew, "I'll bring it right back!"

342

The bluish boxes lay scattered just back of the line and men were clawing at the wooden covers, hammering them with stones. Kirk shouted, "Give me room!" and swung his ax to split the first case open. Blackened hands shot past him, clutched at the wrapped cartridges, and he moved to the next one. Outside the drums beat louder and the yells keened higher. A tentative ripple of fire shot out from the Union lines and one of the Napoleons slammed. Kirk swung on as the cases were dumped at his feet. When the last cover was split, he ran, ax in one hand, rifle in the other, back to the gun pit. As he reached it, the Number One snapped, "Stand clear!" and tugged at the lanyard. The piece roared out, bowled back a few feet and was manhandled into position again.

Kirk dropped the ax and stood staring through the broad embrasure. It was like a repetition of an earlier scene—the same packed ranks, the soaring colors, the thudding drums and the mad, screeching yell. Then the gray ranks poured forward in a mad torrent. Smoke billowed and eddied, the Napoleon roared again, but still the waves came on, formless and frenzied. Kirk fired through the embrasure, dropped his butt to reload. The embrasure was blotted out. He had an impression of bare, sweaty heads, wild eyes, and gaping mouths fringed with yellow teeth. He swung his rifle butt into a gray belly, felt his hands and arms tingle as something smashed the weapon from his grasp. He caught up the ax, lashed at a matted black head, saw it suddenly crested with bloody froth. A rammer staff jabbed past him from behind. A Colt slammed and slammed. A man yelled, "By Jesus, I'll take a few of these God-damn Rebs with me when I go!"

The gun pit was clear of living foes. Kirk picked up a Rebel rifle and darted out. Back of the parapet he stumbled over a body with a smashed head and gaudy Zouave pantaloons that were stained deeply purple about the waist. "One of my men," he muttered. Then

343

he saw blue figures scrambling to the top of the works, firing downward. He shouted, "Troop A! To the parapet," and swung himself up. In the rear, Reilly's voice clanged, "You Kentuckians with the repeaters! Up with you!" Slouch-hatted men with repeating Spencers were swarming onto the works and their intense volume of fire drilled into Kirk's ears. Down below a gray mass was reeling, swaying, stumbling, falling. From the ditch a man wailed, "Jesus, Yanks! Quit it. We had enough. We're surrendering!" Through smoke-filled dusk Kirk saw gray men throwing down their rifles, heaving their hands high. He called, "Let 'em through if they're unarmed. Pass 'em to the rear. See? Where that officer's waving? All right, Ganey! Get the troop together. Up the line and see what's happening there."

Kirk dropped to the inner ditch, ran by men who were still firing through loopholes. He shouted, "What's your target? Oh, that you, Jake? Thought you were farther up."

Jake waved a burned-cork hand. "Get farther along, where the line bends. The Rebs are still driving there."

Kirk slapped Jake's shoulder as he went on, heard the rest of his troop pounding after him. He plunged to the nearest vacant loophole. The line bent back even more sharply than he thought and he looked out directly onto the flank of a charging gray company, not thirty yards off. He shouted, "Fire at will!" but his voice was drowned in a raving fury of quick rifle fire as the broad-hatted Kentuckians, running along the parapet, turned their Spencers loose in a ripping, unbroken blast. Kirk fired once, reloaded, then dropped his butt. The whole attack had been swept away, cut down from the side as though a scythe had sliced along it. Men lay motionless in the outer ditch, writhed helplessly, tried to drag themselves away. A few yards beyond Kirk a huge black horse, whose housing bore the insignia of a Confederate brigadier, lay across the works, head and forelegs dangling toward the inner ditch, haunches slumping

344

outside. A Confederate flag lay near the hind hoofs. Another quivered on the parapet itself. Inside the works, a man in blue walked calmly along, four other poles with tattered silk rustling under his arm.

Kirk stepped back and leaned panting on his rifle. Over the pounding of his pulses, a half-remembered tag of poetry teased at him. Was it Lord Bryon?

> . . . *a shattered host,*
> *Their leaders fallen, their standards lost.*

But only part of this host was shattered and there were other leaders and other standards. Probably at that very instant, a fresh attack was forming. He raised his head. That firing, strong and steady. It must be close to the Carter house and it was underscored by Union cheering. The shouts grew stronger and stronger. Then the firing ebbed, died, but the cheering went on. "Opdycke," muttered Kirk. "He's retaken the old front line up there. Better go and tell Jake. He'll want to know. My God! Hadn't noticed before. It's just about dark."

Uneasily, yet with an odd feeling of exhilaration, Kirk moved with his troop through the night, probing cautiously south over the course of the attacks that had shattered themselves against Cox's works. He was on the left end of a blunt V whose point was two platoons of Spencer-armed Kentuckians and whose right arm was Jake's command. The soft, unseasonable air hung heavy over the rolling country and the few stars that showed, veiled in a misty film, gave out little radiance. Kirk glanced back over his shoulder. The works from which he and the others had sortied so cautiously half an hour ago were no longer visible, masked by night and the battle smoke that still hung low, heavy and sluggish.

He felt rising ground under his feet and judged that the V was mounting the same gentle slope down which

345

Hood's gray masses had poured earlier. A quarter of a mile more ought to be enough and then the Kentucky major would order a return to—

Out of the dead dark, rifles flashed and bullets whined overhead. Then the blunt point of the V slashed out in rapid fire as the Spencer magazines fed their charges into the chambers. In quick flares Kirk saw a crest twenty yards beyond, had a glimpse of running men. A high voice cried, "It's Yanks. Whole God-damn corps. I'm gittin' out!"

The firing died and there were no more shots from the crest. A whistle blew from the center and the whole command halted, rested on grounded arms. There were shots far to the right, a burst of scattered fire from the left. Once a prolonged roll of rifle blasts echoed west of the Columbia pike, faded. There was a moment of utter silence, so intense that it almost hurt. Kirk strained his ears, heard a vague shifting and movement far to the south, but there was no ominous rasping rumble to tell of another major assault on the way.

The minutes crept by. Then the whistle sounded again, two long blasts, one short. Kirk faced his command about, saw a dim mass in the center start north, waited until the V had been re-formed and closed in on its right flank, still hardly able to believe what his senses told him. General John Hood, with his missing leg and shattered arm, would not attack again that night. General John Schofield, directing the battle from the north bank of the Harpeth, and General Jacob Cox, fighting it from Carter's Knoll, had saved the Army and perhaps Nashville—at least for the time being.

And how would December 1, 1864, dawn? Kirk shook his head. Hood still had greatly superior numbers and Schofield's command was mortally weary and thindrawn. Of course, perhaps at that very moment, fresh Union columns were pushing south from Nashville to bolster the lines. They might even come in such strength that Hood could be swept away, rolled back to the far

Tennessee River. "That'd be all right," he muttered. "And if they don't come, it'll still be all right. We'll hold on here. Even if we have to be propped up on the firing step, we'll hold."

The works were in sight and the men about Kirk suddenly began a high-pitched chatter as though a truth had dawned on them. "Hey! Chris'sake! We piled up that God-damn Hood as bad as we done along Peach Tree Creek at Atlanta!" . . . "As bad? We ripped him a hell of a sight worse today!" . . . "Don't start struttin' too soon. Maybe he'll come a-smashing again, soon's he gets his breath!" . . . "What if he does? Hasn't he thrown everything he's got at us a dozen times today? And didn't we always kick his face in?" . . . "Sure did! Hey, I'm bettin' we'll take off after him, come dawn, bust up whatever he's got left." . . . "Yeh, by God, and we could do it—only, sufferin' Moses, I'm wored out!"

Killing fatigue slowly ebbed from Kirk and he stepped along more briskly. Only now did he realize that Schofield and Cox and their little force had battered out a staggering victory, there on the slopes of Carter's Knoll.

19

March Orders

Kirk woke in pitch darkness, hands shaking and throat tight with an impulse to shout in alarm. Then he heard a low voice at his ear. "Major Hale from General Reilly. Get your command together. No talking, no lights. Hurry it up. We're moving out."

Kirk rolled to his feet, automatically clutching his rifle. "*What!* We're not going to give up these works, are we?"

"Orders. You and Pitler fall in behind the 104th Ohio. A guide will show you where."

Kirk knelt, gently pressed the neck of the man beside him. "No talking. Wake the man on your right, have him pass the word along. We're pulling out." One by one the men of Troop A staggered to their feet, silently formed double ranks on the ground where they had been sleeping, twenty feet behind the works. A gaunt figure stood stiffly to attention before Kirk, whispering, "Sir, will the Captain receive the morning report?" Kirk bent to catch the words. "Seven killed, eight badly wounded, ten lightly, nine missing, sir."

"Thank you, Sergeant." Thirty-four out of ninety-two, not excessive for such hot action. It was a pity about the badly wounded, but most of them were old soldiers and would realize that in a night evacuation they would have to be left behind. A few surgeons would stay with them and in the morning Hood's troops would occupy the position and prisoner casualties would be treated promptly.

There was movement along the works and Kirk saw men climbing out over the parapet past those who still manned the fire step. Everything was proceeding according to sound practice. A skirmish line would lie well out in the fields until the last possible moment, to guard against any surprise attack. With a muffled bumping, cannoneers were rolling the two Napoleons out of the embrasure, some holding up the trails while others tugged at the wheels. It would be a long, killing job, manhandling the guns back to the waiting limbers that must be at least five hundred yards to the rear. Anger, born of intense fatigue, swept over Kirk. *Why* yield up this ground that had been defended so long and so successfully?

He felt a hand on his arm and turned to see Jake beside him. "Just saw the guide, Kirk. The 104th's about fifty yards north of us."

"But what the hell are we getting out for?"

Jake slapped his shoulder. "Because we got our lessons all done and teacher says we can go out and play now. There's the Major beckoning to you. Lead out and I'll hook on to your rear."

Kirk touched the nearest man, saw hands move as the signal was passed along. The troop flowed from line into column and there was no need to urge silence. No palms slapped against rifle butts as right-shoulder shift was carried out; no feet tramped heavily as the squad pivots marked time. The command moved north over the fields, the files walking delicately, holding their bayonet sheaths close to their sides to hide any clank and jingle. A tall figure came close to the column, spoke in a low tone. "A good withdrawal, Captain. And your troop did fine work today."

Kirk swung his arm up in salute. "Thank you, General Reilly." His men kept silent, but he could sense a gratified stir passing down the ranks.

There was nothing more for Kirk to do. His troop would keep on the heels of the 104th, fearful of being left behind. There were no commands to give, no worry about keeping closed up or men straggling. The stimulus of responsibility died away in his mind and he knew only deep, racking fatigue. Unsuspected cuts and bruises nagged at him. A powderburn on his cheek smarted hotly. The soles of his boots slipped on the smooth turf, brought on spasmodic leg cramps.

There was a different sound, a harder beat, in the air. He was no longer slipping and the firm surface of the Columbia pike was under his feet. His stomach gripped in alarm as he saw lights off to the left. Then he relaxed. Of course there were lights. Unbroken blackness on the crest of the knoll would have drawn instant attention from Hood's watchers on Winstead Hill. But glowing windows in the Carter house blostered the assumption that General Jacob Cox and his command had not stirred.

The house was just as he had seen it by day. Not quite as he had seen it, though. Windows were shattered and red-armed surgeons moved across the bright oblongs, bending over Carter tables where wailing men waited the knife. A broad golden shaft fell across the lawn, lighting up a smashed wagon, a huddle of bodies, a dead horse. The front door was open and the same old man stood peering out as though he were a permanent fixture like the ginhouse or the wooden farm office in the second line.

Kirk's head swayed as he walked, sagged forward,

351

jerked back just in time to keep him from falling. An arm from the ranks slid under his, steadied him. He caught muffled words: "Cap's asleep on his feet." . . . "Wonder he ain't dead. Jesus, when I first seen him, I thought he was just a paper-collar dude from the Army of the Potomac." . . . "Maybe you been wronger in your life, but I doubt it like hell. Figger he'll get to stay with us?"

A half-seen officer under a tree was calling mechanically, "Follow left down Indigo Street, follow left down Indigo Street." Kirk roused himself, suddenly aware that the column had entered Franklin. Indigo Street, that had been so crowded with wagons. Lynn! With luck she might be in Louisville by now, looking out onto the broad Ohio while her father hunted up transportation to Washington. But he couldn't let himself think of Lynn just now. He would soon be looking on the Harpeth, not the Ohio. It was highly probable that Schofield had prepared positions on its high north bank, protected by the river. In that case, fresh duties would fall on Troop A and he would need a clear mind to meet them.

North Margin Street and the river at its foot and a long, high shed burning fiercely, the Harpeth aglow with reflected flame and Mark's bridge a solid black bar across to the far side. Someone yelped, "My God, the Rebs'll see that fire! Get in and kill it!" A mounted officer shouted, "Keep in ranks! We got all the help we need." From the water's edge a long line of men passed slopping buckets up to the shed while Engineer details ripped at the walls with hooked poles.

The horses of the two Provisional troops stood quietly in a field well out of reach of the blaze, and the men from Carter's Knoll began calling to the horse guards who had been left behind out of action. "Hey, Rube, get Cap's horse saddled up!" . . . "Jerry, where the hell are my saddlebags? I left 'em with you." In a few moments, both commands were mounted and clattering across the echoing bridge.

A few lights burned up on the north bank as Kirk rode at the head of his men from Mark's bridge, but he could detect no stir, no milling troops or waving lanterns to suggest a concentration point. He looked from far right to far left, increasingly convinced that he was coming into the fringe of an army, not its heart. Could Schofield be massing farther back from the river, hoping to hit Hood as the latter came up from the fords? That was not like the careful Schofield.

A lantern flashed by the side of the pike, lit up a group of officers who shouted, "Keep on going. Keep right on going!"

Wearily Kirk asked, "Keep on going how far?"

"How far the hell do you think? Till you're told to halt!"

It was hard to understand that order to push on north, though the intent might be to clear the roads of mounted troops while infantry commands were shifted along the heights. He let the troop overtake him, called, "Keep right on ahead, boys." He lowered his voice. "I'll call a halt at the first good place to pull out." Some of the men grunted, others swore apathetically. Like him, they had been counting on a rest as soon as the north bank was scaled. At least the horses were fresh and fed, could go on for a long time while the men dozed in their saddles.

Suddenly the night was alive about him. He and his men overtook a long column of infantry. The dark fields on either hand were astir and uncounted boots rustled over the grass. At a side road a battery waited its chance to swing out onto the pike. Kirk could see the first piece, a Parrott, and surely one of the group which had blasted Hood's waves at long range from Fort Granger. But why shift them from that position that covered the fords and the approaches of the Harpeth? There was more infantry ahead, then a battery, three batteries of

353

Napoleons with their jingle, bump and clank and the cannoneers stumbling on behind the carriages, letting themselves be towed by bits of trailing rope clutched in blackened hands.

A chill seized Kirk. Schofield was rolling his whole command back and there would be no stand on the north bank. How far was Nashville, key to all Tennessee? Eight miles, possibly ten? Fatigue built terrifying ideas in his mind. Perhaps Hood had not been so badly damaged at Franklin after all. He might have received fresh divisions, might at that very moment be straining up Carter's Knoll and down to the fords. General George Thomas, holding vital Nashville, might not have received hoped-for reinforcements, might be waiting for Schofield's command to join him before giving up the city and all it meant and falling back and back into Kentucky, to the Ohio River.

In that case, the struggle at Franklin, all the dogged tenacity against overwhelming odds, all the blazing counterattacks, like Opdycke's, had been in vain. In that case—well, Kirk's own particular job was to see that Provisional Troop A would be ready to meet whatever lay ahead.

Night was slowly dying and the fields and hills were turning from black to gray. Kirk saw men running toward the pike, laden with dripping canteens. Trees, level ground, running water. He called, "Pull off the pike to the left. Half-hour halt. Loosen cinches, slip your bits. Light all the fires you want and get your coffee boiling!"

The sun was above the horizon and the blue columns were pushing north across a plateau with sharp hills to right and left. From his saddle Kirk looked out on an interminable flow of infantry, broken here and there by swaying gun barrels and the bob and lift of horses' heads and the dull twinkle of turning spokes. A mile to the right, a mile to the left were other highways, the Nolensville and the Granny White pikes, alive with marching men and rolling artillery. The Franklin pike dipped off the plateau and the north horizon was blocked by more hills, ragged at the sides but with curiously flattened tops. "Forts!" muttered Kirk. "Can we be giving them up?" He moved on with his troop over flat farmlands. The northern hills, carved and shaped by engineers, that sheltered Nashville were a bare mile ahead. The sky brightened and dark patches on the slopes stood revealed as gun embrasures with blue figures moving about them. Were the forts being dismantled and the guns dragged away?

All at once there was bold color on the crest. It was repeated right and left as the new sun picked out unfurling Union standards. Kirk's horse shied as wild cheering ripped out on both sides of the pike. He was bringing his troop through a solid hedge of blue infantrymen that lined the road as far as he could see, fresh, rested troops who had not known Franklin, who wore numbers and insignia that were strange to him. Broad-brimmed hats waved frantically, sailed in the air, were lifted high on bayonet points. "Franklin! Franklin!" The name battered up through the air, echoed, was repeated. "Yeeeeeay! XXIII Corps! The Franklin boys that gave 'em hell!" . . . "Franklin! God-damn ol' IV Corps, fightin' bastards!" . . . "Yeeeeeay! The Franklin boys!"

There was a light, open carriage beyond the last of the cheering men from Nashville and in it stood a frail little old man whose long white hair straggled from under a visored flat-topped cap of Mexican War days. A frogged blue cloak, scarlet-trimmed, smothered his bent shoulders as he tried valiantly to hold himself erect, balancing one thin-fingered hand on the arm of a tall young girl who stood with him. The other hand met the visor in a shaky salute, thumb and forefinger gripping the cracked leather to still their trembling. The wrinkled old face was wet in the sunlight and the shrunken lips struggled to hold firm.

Kirk clutched at his saber, swung it up in salute, shouting, "Eyes left!" to his troop. The command was unnecessary. Spontaneously the men had come to attention and each four, as it came abreast of the carriage, turned eyes and head smartly to the left, held them there until the carriage was passed. Kirk looked back as he sheathed his saber. The little old man was standing valiantly erect, unaided, and his hand was steady on his visor. Then the carriage was beyond Kirk's vision.

Slowly the impact of the cheering troops, of the old Unionist of another era faded and Kirk's earlier fears gnawed at him. Hoofs clattered from behind and Jake pulled in beside him. "Kirk, I'm worried worse'n I've been since we got out of Libby. What the hell's going to happen?"

As though arguing against his own dark thoughts, Kirk replied, "Those boys cheering back there didn't seem exactly scared."

Jake shook his head. "You know troops. They'll holler at anything from an issue of beans to a colonel getting kicked by a mule. And then that old veteran in the carriage. He kept calling, 'Stay with us, boys, stay with us!'"

"He could have meant, 'Stand by, whatever happens,' something like that."

"Maybe. But the few new troops we've seen aren't anywhere near enough to make a difference and we can't go on fighting Hood at odds of two or three to one forever. Here's something else: One officer hollered to another, 'See you on the other side of the Cumberland,' and the other said, 'Maybe—if we're lucky.' And neither of them looked too damn happy about things."

A major, riding down the pike, reined in suddenly to stare at Kirk and Jake. Then he shouted, "Cavalry! What the devil are you doing on this road? Well, never mind that. Pull out past these footboys ahead and follow the road right in between Fort Negley and Fort Morton. Keep right on into Nashville. Make for the State House. It's on a hill with a tall, thin tower stuck on its roof. Ask for Colonel Caswell. He'll give you orders!"

"Right, sir," said Kirk hesitantly. "Ah—what do we do then?"

"Ask him!" The major trotted on.

Kirk and Jake rode silently on up the slope that led over a shoulder between two forts with their terraced outworks sloping down to the plain. Jake burst out, "God damn it, he didn't tell us anything!"

Kirk stopped his horse suddenly. Then he said huskily, "No, but this does!" He swept his arm in a wide arc. High above on the right the heavy casemates of Fort Negley scowled down and Fort Morton loomed to the left. And left of Morton, curving in a vast semicircle, were more and more hills, all scarred with trenches and redoubts. From their vantage point, the two were looking at the inner side of Thomas's main line of defense. And from an inner line ahead of them, curving like the first, columns of infantry were pouring, making for the outer barrier. Batteries of artillery rolled along, climbed hacked-out roads to the crests. Here and there gun crews were emplacing pieces that had just arrived.

"God," muttered Jake, awed. "Just count the regimental flags! Double and more the number we had at Franklin. And, hey! Off to the right—more and Goddamn more going past Fort Negley!" He took off his kepi and rubbed his sleeve across his forehead.

Kirk's eyes went from the endless columns, the batteries, to the great outer arc of works, to the inner. It was obvious that General Thomas had anchored his lines right and left on a bend of the Cumberland as Cox had sited his on the Harpeth at Franklin. The future unrolled sharp and clear before him. Hood would have to come on against Nashville, or let his battered command fall back south into a military vacuum. Knowing Hood, there was no doubt of the choice that would be

357

made. His frantic gray columns would be hurled against works ten times as strong as Franklin, held by a force now more than double his and commanded by the coolest, steadiest defensive fighter in either Army—the Virginian, George Thomas. And Thomas could lash out, too, surely and powerfully. Kirk cleared his throat. "Jake, it's all over, done, finished!" he said huskily. "This'll be the end of Hood's army. There'll be nothing left of the Confederacy except Lee, away off there at Petersburg."

Jake's jaw worked as though he found speaking difficult. Then he gave a bounce in the saddle. "You go ahead and figure out the 'wills.' I've got a lot of 'is's' riding me. Now remember, the first one to sight a colonel who looks as if his name ought to be Caswell lets out a roar."

Kirk started his horse. "Sure. Then I want to find the provost."

"You've done something bad and want to ask him to arrest you?"

"He's damn sure to know about any foreigners coming into the city and what train they got out."

"I must have chucked my brains away with the worn-out saddle blanket last night and just not noticed," said Jake.

They were through the main works, past the east flank of the second line and riding among scattered houses along a tree-lined street. Dispirited men in civilian clothes were coming out of front yards and slouching on into town or sitting slackly in ill-kept carriages that turned quickly down side streets at the sound of cavalry hoofs. A few women stood on shallow verandas, looking out with dull eyes until a glimpse of blue uniforms hardened their expressions and sent them inside behind slamming doors.

"These homefolk tell me a lot more than all that cheering back there," observed Jake. "The spark's out of 'em. Not a glare left for us. They've had bad news that

358

told 'em they might as well tuck their bonnie blue flags away in the garret and rip up their WELCOME, GALLANT HOOD signs. Christ, I'm not gloating, just reading things. Nashville's been back under the Union flag since '62 and a lot of these Secesshers must have got their hopes mighty high when they heard Hood was coming north to them, knowing how little we had to throw against him. But they all look like they're figuring same as you today."

"There's plenty for them to see." Kirk pointed to the Nashville and Chattanooga tracks cutting through the city. A train was halted by some vacant lots and blue infantry poured from the cars. From the east another locomotive whistled. A pretty woman by a garden gate started at the sound, cried, "More of them coming, more!" and, covering her face with her hands, ran into her house. Then Kirk sighted the Capitol tower, rising clean and sharp from a high hill ahead. There were halts at cross streets to let infantry plod on toward the lines, to give way to rumbling batteries outward bound. And when the street was clear, there were sharp grades to climb, so steep that even the soaring tower was hidden.

Then the spreading stone building was before them, perched on a scarred round hill, and the steps that climbed in a massive sweep to meet the square columns of the facade were planked and sand-bagged and the muzzles of fieldpieces gaped among graceful lampposts, bronze-capped. The open space in front of the Capitol was thick with men in uniform, with civilians, while army wagons and farm wagons jolted along at the foot of the hill. Here and there carriages worked on and it was obvious from the faces of some of the occupants that the news from Franklin was not unwelcome.

In a muddy lot that looked up toward a collection of untidy shacks, close to the Capitol, the troopers dismounted with grateful and blistering oaths and began looking over their cinches and blankets. Kirk turned

359

command over to Ganey, then called, "Come on, Jake. There seem to be two or three assembly points on the steps. Caswell may be there."

Jake ducked away. "I got one of my bashful streaks. You report for us and tell him what a fine chap I am, polite to old ladies, kind to animals, little children just love me. *I'm* going to the provost's office."

He darted off and Kirk started for the Capitol steps. There was a flurry on the crowded sidewalk in front of him. Men and women shifted, sidled, and Kirk stepped out into the street. From between a lumbering fat man and a very tall woman, a small hand reached out, caught at his sleeve, and a muffled voice called, *"Kirk!"*

He cried out in amazement, covered the clinging hand with his. Then he wedged into the crowd, scabbard and holster bumping into people, weaving forward a half step at a time while the little hand held tightly to his. He jammed past the fat man, found himself face to face with Lynn, who had her free arm tight about a lamppost. Her cheeks were aglow and her blue eyes very bright and her white teeth showed between slightly parted lips. Bracing himself, he forced the crowd to flow past him. "Lynn, you darling! Whatever are you still in Nashville for?"

Pressed close to him by the surge of the crowd, she said hurriedly, "You're safe, you're safe, Kirk! Such awful stories leaked out of Headquarters and we just didn't know—"

"But you shouldn't be here. I thought—" An elbow jarred against him. "Won't this crowd ever thin out?"

Her hands closed on the front of his jacket. "They're all going to the public market. It's only open once a day for a few hours. Here's our chance." She glided through a momentary gap in the press, into a boarded-up doorway, drawing him with her. "What were you saying?"

"That you and your father ought to be at least in Louisville by now."

"Kirk, dearest, is that a nice welcome?"

360

"No, but Nashville isn't a nice place just now. What happened? The provost couldn't have made trouble, not with that letter Schofield gave you."

"The provost and everyone were very courteous."

"There must have been trains going north. Lord, I thought all the time that you were safe. Were the trains too crowded?"

She looked up at him, standing very close in the narrow doorway. The ghost of a smile stirred the soft corners of her lips. "I couldn't get on."

Her nearness, the melting softness of her eyes tugged at his heart and his arms went out to her, then checked as a jostling shoulder reminded him of the crowd. "I wish I could have been here, darling. I'd have gotten you a seat somehow."

Still smiling and eyes half closed, she murmured, "Perhaps if you'd been on the train you could have found room for us." Her expression clouded. "Kirk, Kirk, you do look so thin and drawn. Was it terrible at Franklin?"

"I've seen easier places. But the trains north—"

Her smile came back and she stroked his arm gently. "Whenever did you find time to shave? And your uniform's brushed. I've always liked that about you. Even in the mountains you managed to keep trim."

With a finger he tilted her soft chin a little upward. "Lynn, look at me. There were trains and you had your letter."

She met his eyes. "I—I just couldn't get on, that's all."

He smiled, aware of the swift racing of his heart. "Tell me why?"

Color mounted under her smooth skin, tinted the white lift of her throat. "Do I have to?"

"No, darling, but I'd like to hear you say it."

Her forehead wrinkled and the corners of her eyes puckered. "Do you think for one instant that I could have borne going north, not knowing about you? Sweetheart, you said at that cavalry camp that I was

361

part of you and you were part of me and we always would be like that. So I just couldn't leave part of me in Tennessee. I couldn't go. I told fearful fibs, did stupid things and managed to miss about four trains yesterday. The provost thought I was an awful ninny, until I confessed, and then he was very nice to me. And this morning I heard that the men from Franklin were coming into town and that near the Capitol would be the best place for news."

"You're a rather wonderful girl, Lynn, and I'm very much in love with you and I wish we were somewhere else."

She colored again, but her eyes stayed steady on his. She looped a finger through a buttonhole of his jacket, smiling up at him. "We'll all be going north together."

The light and joy of the moment left Kirk as though a lamp had been turned out. "Colonel Caswell," he said thickly.

Hand to her throat, Lynn asked quickly, "What about him?"

"I've got to report to him for further orders."

It seemed to him that not even her eyelids moved as she said, "Of course. Find him and then come back and tell me."

"But I can't leave you in this shabby doorway and in the crowd."

"That's just where you're going to leave me. I'll be all right. General Thomas's provost guards keep this town as safe as Bay Street in Toronto. Please hurry. You see, I'm rather interested in what happens to part of me."

Fifteen minutes later Kirk came down the Capitol steps and across the street. Lynn, waiting with hands folded in the doorway, closed her eyes for an instant, then raised her head. "All right, darling," she said. "I know what orders mean. Oh, don't look so despondent, Kirk. Just tell me how long it is before I have to watch you ride off again."

362

"Not till afternoon, Lynn honey. We've got reports that Hood's just starting north across the Harpeth. Allowing him time to reform and so on, it'll be—let's see, today's December first—he won't be near Nashville in any strength till tomorrow."

Someone called, "Why, there you are, Lynn. Where did you vanish to?" Ian Stockdale was making his way toward them through the thinning crowd.

Lynn waved. "You were so long with that exchange broker that I thought I'd go on and see the markets and then I met—"

"Bless my soul! Glad to see that you're safe, Captain Stedman." His face grew serious behind the iron-gray beard. "Really incredible, that fight at Franklin. I don't see how General Hood can possibly engage again. I have reliable information that he lost more men than your Burnside did at Fredericksburg. It's been a tragic thing for us and our friends."

"Naturally, I can't think of it the way you two do," said Kirk. "Well, that fight's over, and Hood's men were fighting for what they believed in every bit as much as we were."

Lynn laid a hand on his cuff. "You've never said one word to try to change the way we think and feel. I promise you I'll always respect your beliefs as you have ours."

Ian Stockdale nodded. "Wherever we are, Captain, we'll always remember that you followed your convictions. It was a little hard to grasp when we first met you that Yankees could have convictions. We'd seen the war only from the other side and we had our old memories." He reached into his pocket, "And by the way, do you happen to know the name of the general commanding the Department of the Ohio?"

"I'm afraid I don't, sir. That command changes hands pretty often."

"Pity. Well, someone will know. I had an interview with General Thomas, a most courteous man, but he felt that he was not qualified to receive the report I'd written about your seizure of us and suggested that we apply in Cincinnati. And that reminds me, Lynn, that we have an appointment with the provost at ten o'clock."

"Father," said Lynn, "I've made up my mind that—"

Ian Stockdale broke in, "Well, this does seem like old times. Here comes Captain Pitler. Happy to see that you're safe, too, sir."

Jake, grinning, came trotting up, saber banging against his boots. "Got wonderful news for you two, sir. There'll be five trains in between noon and sunset. The first'll start back about four, so there you are."

"But Captain Pitler—" Lynn began.

Kirk cut in. "I found Caswell. We report to Wilson at a place called Una out on the Murfreesboro pike at three-thirty. I've found where to draw fodder, rations and ammunition."

Jake's grin widened. "There's the real, deep-sea cavalryman for you! Always thinking about his horses and his men. Look, the provost gave me this." He handed Kirk a paper.

Kirk unfolded it perfunctorily. Then his eyes narrowed. It was a pencil copy of a telegram, stamped OFFICIAL. He read in silence, handed it to Lynn. He closed his eyes as she took it and the words still seemed to flow back of his lids:

THE ESCAPED PRISONERS, CAPTAIN KIRK STEDMAN, D.C.I.T., CAPTAIN JACOB PITLER, 1ST MAINE, CAPTAIN MARK FURBER, 1ST MASS., FIRST LIEUTENANT JABISH KELL, 5TH UNITED STATES, WILL REPORT AT ONCE BY THE MOST EXPEDITIOUS MEANS TO HEADQUARTERS CAVALRY CORPS ARMY OF THE POTOMAC FOR IMMEDIATE ASSIGNMENT AT THE URGENT REQUEST OF PHILIP SHERIDAN, MAJ. GEN.

H. W. HALLECK, MAJ. GEN.

Lynn crumpled the paper in her hands. Her eyes were incredulous, then sparkled, then grew suddenly misty.

Her lips quivered a little as she said in a low voice, "'Most expeditious means.' And a lot of trains coming in today. We'll go north together. Dad, don't you understand?"

Ian Stockdale looked stern, then began to smile. "Yes, everything. There'll be no trains missed today."

"Let's hurry. I'll get my things together. Kirk, darling, do whatever you two have to and then come to our boarding house, Church Street, just off Eighth Avenue. Come along, Dad." Kirk held out his arms, and regardless of her father, Jake and passers-by, Lynn flew into them, clung close for a moment, then broke away and hurried off with her father.

Jake looked after them. "The luck of some people! *I* step out onto a dock at Libby and what happens? *You* row off with the finest girl I ever sighted, barring one, State-a-Maine. Well, the provost's found Jabish and Mark, so we're all safe in port."

"Wonder how Washington knew we were here."

"Millard telegraphed to Knoxville and they relayed to Washington. And now Sheridan's asking for us! Seems he runs cavalry the way we figured it ought to be run. Just the same, I'd kind of like to see the end of this Hood business."

"You saw the end of Hood at Franklin. This will just be an epilogue. His army's done and the South's got nothing left but Lee's."

A troop of cavalry clattered by and Jake eyed it wistfully. "Don't you think maybe, just for a few days, we could pretend we hadn't seen that telegram?"

Kirk linked arms with him. "Come on. We've got to see to the boys and then rush for Church Street."

He looked east. Far down the sidewalk over bobbing heads he saw Lynn's bright hair, a blue scarf thrown back from it, as she hurried on beside her father. Soon he and Lynn would be together, Potomac bound, would stay together until orders sent him into the field again. Then he would ride south with the Cavalry Corps under

Phil Sheridan, south toward Richmond. But this time the goal would not be the freeing of a few thousand men from Belle Isle, but a vaster liberation, the liberation of the whole country, North and South, from the grip of war, and then the restoration of the Union. In his heart he knew that his time there could and would be no failure.

Another tumultuous romantic novel
by Patricia Matthews,
author of the multi-million
copy national bestseller,
LOVE'S AVENGING HEART

Love's Wildest Promise

P40-047 $1.95

Sarah Moody was a lady's maid in a wealthy London home. But suddenly her quiet sheltered world was turned upside down when she was abducted and smuggled aboard a ship bound for the colonies. Its cargo—whores to satisfy the appetites of King George's soldiers in New York. Was Sarah destined to become one of these women? Or would she find the man she was searching for, the man who would help her to fulfill Love's Wildest Promise.

If you can't find this book at your local bookstore, simply send the cover price, plus 25¢ for postage and handling to:

 Pinnacle Books
275 Madison Avenue, New York, New York 10016

The epic novel of the Old South,
ablaze with the unbridled passions
of men and women seeking
new heights for their love

Windhaven Plantation

Marie de Jourlet

P40-022 $1.95

Here is the proud and passionate story of one man—
Lucien Bouchard. The second son of a French nobleman,
a man of vision and of courage, Lucien dares to seek a new
way of life in the New World that suits his own high
ideals. Yet his true romantic nature is at war with his
lusty, carnal desires. The four women in his life reflect
this raging conflict: Edmée, the high-born, amoral
French sophisticate who scorns his love, choosing his
elder brother, heir to the family title; Dimarte, the in-
genuous, earthy, and sensual Indian princess; Amelia,
the fiery free-spoken beauty who is trapped in a life of
servitude for crimes she didn't commit; and Priscilla,
whose proper manner hid the unbridled passion of her
true desires.

"... will satisfy avid fans of the plantation genre."
—*Bestsellers* magazine

If you can't find this book at your local bookstore, simply
send the cover price plus 25¢ for postage and handling to:

 Pinnacle Books
275 Madison Avenue, New York, New York 10016

In the tumultuous, romantic tradition of
Rosemary Rogers, Jennifer Wilde, and
Kathleen Woodiwiss

Love's Avenging Heart

Patricia Matthews

P987 $1.95

The stormy saga of Hannah McCambridge, whose fiery
red hair, voluptuous body, and beautiful face made her
irresistible to men...Silas Quint, her brutal stepfather,
sold her as an indentured servant...Amos Stritch, the
lascivious tavernkeeper, bought her and forced her to
submit to his lecherous desires...Malcolm Verner, the
wealthy master of Malvern Plantation, rescued her from
a life of poverty and shame. But for Hannah, her new
life at Malvern was just the beginning. She still had to
find the man of her dreams—the man who could un-
leash the smouldering passions burning inside her and
free her questing heart.

You've read other historical romances, now <u>live</u> one!